STAGING JAPANESE THEATRE: NOH & KABUKI

IKKAKU SENNIN
(The Holy Hermit Unicorn)

and

NARUKAMI
(The Thunder God)

by

John D. Mitchell & Miyoko Watanabe

Foreword
by
M. Leigh Smith

Cover illustration by Nancy del Aguila
Art work by Michael Cooper

Published by
Institute for Advanced Studies in the Theatre Arts Press
in association with Florida Keys Educational Foundation, Inc.
Florida Keys Community College

First Edition

Library of Congress Catalog Card Number: 94-072814

ISBN 1-882763-06-8

Printed in the United States of America

Video tapes of Aspects of the Japanese Noh, and Kabuki are available for purchase or rental. Contact Gilbert Forman (212) 581-3133 or John D. Mitchell (305) 296-8926. A video tape (from a film made in Japan) of Baiko and Danjiro, as *Taema* and *Narukami*, including cast, is also available from the Institute for Advanced Studies in the Theatre Arts. The fee for this video is $50. and requires a $100. deposit refunded upon the return of the video.

Additional orders for *Staging Japanese Theatre: Noh & Kabuki* may be obtained by writing to Fordham University Press, University Box L, Bronx, New York, 10458, Attention: Margaret Noonan.

DEDICATION

In memory of Earle Ernst, who was among the foremost scholars, writers and professional theatre directors to write on Kabuki. He was a cherished friend of the authors of this work.

and

Jane Fujita, of Tokyo Japan, who was most helpful on the occasion of the second IASTA production of Kabuki's classic *KANJINCHO* under the direction of Koshiro VIII and Matagoro II. A special friend and resource person in Japan, Jane has been helpful with *STAGING JAPANESE THEATRE.*

TABLE OF CONTENTS

ACKNOWLEDGEMENTS

It would overburden this book to acknowledge all the many who made possible the Institute for Advanced Studies in the Theatre Arts pioneer productions of Noh and Kabuki. However, the text, the introductions, and the logs cite these many people and the admirable role they played in enabling professional American actors in New York, Denver, and Nantucket to have these unique experiences.

The Northwood Press of Northwood University publication of ACTORS TALK: ABOUT STYLES OF ACTING reveals how eloquent are these actors who saw these two forms of Japanese theatre contributing to their acting experience.

The audiences in each of the cities noted where the plays were performed carried away insight as to a culture which may have seemed remote to them. One instance may be cited. For the Denver International Festival revival of the Noh play *IKKAKU SENNIN* the actors learned that some spectators came to each successive performance that week!

I wish to acknowledge certain friends, family and colleagues who have contributed to this book and were invaluable in making the IASTA productions of *IKKAKU SANNIN* and *NARUKAMI* a reality. Among them are the late C. George Willard; Robert Epstein; Dr. Mary W. John; Douglas Overton, the Japan Society; Kunizo Matsuo; Alan Smith; William Dietz; Russell and Mimi Porter of Denver University; Dr. William A. Seeker, President and M. Leigh Smith, Executive Director, of the Florida Keys Community College.

I wish to acknowledge my family, wife Mimi, sons John, Daniel and Lorenzo, and daughter Barbarina, as well as their spouses.

Much praise to Gilbert Forman, Executive Vice President of IASTA for steadfastly seeing this book through publication. Paula Downey and Kathi Gray were the typists who got the manuscript in a computer. Thanks also to Zach Reit, who was there when needed.

A special acknowledgement of long-time friend and colleague George Drew, one of the original founders of the Institute. He returned to IASTA as Noh consultant and designer. His original 'fluid' arrangement of levels for a flexible stage enabled him to relocate the acting area- with a *hashigakari* bridge- and audiences seated on three sides of the platform stage.

The traditional pine tree background by Michael Allen Hampshire, a non-Japanese, drew high praise from the Sadayo Kita and assistant director Akiyo Tomoeda.

For the outdoor Denver International Theatre Festival production, a special Noh stage of redwood was constructed. Here, collaboration with the University of Denver school of music made it possible to have on stage - seated in formal Japanese style - a male chorus. Their chanting of the chorus in English was cued with tapes of the music performed by the Kita Noh School of musicians of Tokyo.

Each evening on another part of the University of Denver campus, an IASTA production of Sophocles' ELECTRA was performed. The audience moved from one acting area to the other performing area. The two short plays enable spectators to experience the function of the chorus in an Asian play and a classical Greek Tragedy.

An acknowledgement of gratitude and thanks goes to Andrew Field, whose command of both Japanese and Chinese made him an invaluable asset of this publication. Coupled with his linguistic skills, he is adept at typing Japanese characters in a computer with special fonts. An important fact is that Andrew was able to type the Japanese in the American format of horizontal, as opposed to vertical lines (as the Japanese do). All of Andrew's expertise made possible and a reality this bi-lingual book *STAGING JAPANESE THEATRE: NOH & KABUKI.*

Thanks to Jane Fujita of Tokyo for her tireless efforts to locate scripts essential to this book.

Cast of *Ikkaku Sennin* — Denver

Peter Blaxill; Jack Eddleman; Tom Keo; Roger Stuart Newman; Russell Falen; William Martin; Armand Coullet; Bruce Spears; Barry Yourgrau; Tuggie Yourgrau; Carl Mowrey; Ben James; Verne Olsen; John Hansen;; Jerry Finley; Homer Smith.

Cast of *Ikkaku Sennin* — New York

Glen Lincoln; Maya Warwick; Peter Blaxill; Rober Newman; Takeo Miji; Reid Shelton; Courtney Campbell; E. Reid Gilbert; Patricia Hall; Marge Randolph; Maggie Newman; Lavina Nielsen; Marvin Reedy; Tom Keo; Delos V. Smith, Jr.

Cast of *Narukami* — Denver

Stephen Daley; George Gitto; Miyoko Watanabe; Eric Tavares; Jack Eddleman; Jane Alexander; Margaret Blohm; William Burdick; Bill Henning; Gene Scrimpsher; Chris Williams; Ron Weiss; James Johnson; Alexandra Czarnecki; Molly Hoover; Gil Oden; Ken Campbell; Jacqueline Hand.

Cast of *Narukami* — New York

Bert Berger; Stephen A. Daley; George Gitto; George Drew; Joy Dillingham; Annette Hunt; John Wynne-Evans; Marvin Peisner; Robert Stattel; Crystal Field; Elaine Winters; Gene Gregory; Carl Jacobs; Albert Ottenheimer; Rosalyn Newport; Erle Hall; Dina Paisner; Alan Rossett; David Lunney; Steve Press.

Cast of *Narukami* — Nantucket

Stephen Daley; George Drew; Miyoko Watanabe; Robert Stattel; Edward Zang; Sheri Bickley; Patricia Bucar; Pamela Captain, Richard Cary; Gardner Garretson; Dale Parry; Miller Lide; Elaine Winters; CeCe Drew.

Ikkaku Sennin and *Narukami* were performed for the 121st annual meeting of the American Psychiatric Association in 1965.

FOREWORD

The appeal of Asian theatre in America today confirms that the Theatre of the Far East is a remarkable and catalytic experience for a Western audience. Surely, there are few art forms which can match the incredible discipline required and the timeless use of kinetic energy in its purest form.

Twenty-some years ago I had the opportunity to live in Japan for a couple of years. My immersion into the Japanese culture quickly taught me that there existed a spiritual-like reverence for Kabuki and the actors who performed in it. The intensity of the performances instantly commanded respect and rapt appreciation the is shared in the faces of the audience. Even from my perspective as a visitor, it was easy to appreciate the fullness of meaning beyond the spoken word.

Today's burgeoning movement of products, capital, technology, information, and ideas around the world is growing at an ever-increasing rate. The globalization of tastes and ideas creates a hunger for the stimulation of broadening our art forms mediums, and impressions.

The futurists are telling us that the sovereign power of individual nations continue to decline because of the increasing globalization of markets communications and finance. As this trend continues, it becomes increasingly more important for us to preserve the rough-hewn art forms which long ago shaped the theatre of today.

It is, therefore with a great deal of pride that the Florida Keys Educational Foundation and Florida Keys Community College collaborate with the Institute for Advanced Studies in the Theatre Arts in supporting the production of this book. While some might consider it an unusual collaboration, given our location in the Florida Keys, it only serves to emphasize the universal appeal of the Kabuki Theatre and Noh plays.

M. Leigh Smith
Executive Director
Florida Keys Educational Foundation
FLORIDA KEYS COMMUNITY COLLEGE

Pictured from left to right are Tomoeda Akiyo, Jerome Robbins, and Kita Sadayo

INTRODUCTION TO NOH THEATRE
by
John D. Mitchell

The Institute for Advanced Studies in the Theatre Arts (IASTA) performed *The One Horned Hermit* (Ikkaku Sennin) in English. This tale from the repertoire of the Noh Theatre was acted and danced and successfully moved audiences. Its appeal was immediate. It proved a revelation to many of the Japanese who were among the spectators, because in English it was accessible to them. In all respects there was no compromise: it was pure Noh. The one difference was that the text was in English.

Formidable as was the challenge for American professional actors to recreate a Noh play, it succeeded. The approach by IASTA arose from a realization that a Japanese actor trained in the style and method of this early form of theatre was essential to an American production.

Even though actor members of a school of Noh do not think of themselves as directors in the Western sense, Kita Minoru — as head of a Noh troupe — was sanguine that a 16th-generation Noh actor could do the job. His son Kita Sadayo agreed to come to IASTA accompanied by Tomoeda Akiyo, another member of the troupe.

Noh actors learn the craft at an early age — even perform at an early age — and then, as mature actors, they teach. It is possible to see why being a stage director did not daunt Kita Sadayo.

The performing of Noh is seamless; no one element stands out apart from the whole. The American actors who performed the Noh play had had experience of musical theatre, and they brought to rehearsals training in dance and singing as well as acting.

From Jerome Robbins' observations of rehearsals, it was apparent that these actors entered into the experience with zest and patience. It was not easy for them — the weight of the costumes, the feeling of claustrophobia induced by the masks. Moreover, the demands made on the muscles seldom used in realistic acting were taxing.

At the time, these were his impressions from the rehearsals of <u>Ikkaku Sennin</u>: "It was like turning on a light that illuminates another terrain of the theater. Through extreme disciplines and limitations of space, costume, voice, action, expression, gestures, music and pitch; through the distillations of the essence of drama; and through an awesome, tender and religious love of the theatre, its props, costumes and the very surface of the stage itself, a final poetic release of beauty is achieved.

How the Production of Noh at IASTA Evolved
Log 1954

July 4th, 1954. Morning. Members of a traveling seminar in the theatre arts — of which the author was leader — studied the stage of the Kanze School of the Noh.

Afternoon. A distinguished Noh actor of the Kita troupe demonstrated the basic elements of song, dance and recitation for the acting of a Noh play.

July 16th, 1954. Upon return to Kyoto, the author and members of the seminar attended a rehearsal and instruction of a student in acting on the Noh stage of the Kongo School.

Friday, April 17th, 1959. In the evening, all went to a Noh program, arranged to introduce aspects of Noh, a traditional theatre of Japan's to the foreigner. This was the tenth performance of Noh drama sponsored by the International Noh Drama Club.

The club's choice proved provocative and rewarding. First: music of the Noh theatre. Surprisingly, since Noh troupes are all male, it was a lady who performed the music. (However, we have since learned that very often aristocratic families will send their children, both boys and girls, to a Noh troupe for training in Noh songs and the more simple Noh dances. For a young girl, this is an accepted means for learning refinement to perform a Noh dance and, is considered a social asset in the traditional Japanese family)

Next on the program was *Kyogen*, comic dances and pantomimes; these are presented as part of a Noh program as comic relief and for contrast.

The major Noh play of the evening was entitled: *Funabenkei*, which is made up of several episodes from the tale of the legendary Japanese hero, Benkei. We were to come upon this character impersonated on the Kabuki stage, as part of the evening bill.

July: Benkei is the central character in *Kanjincho* (The Subscription List), derived from the Noh play.

House lights are not dimmed during a Noh performance, making it easy to read the program, and for Japanese to follow the text with parallel Japanese. The complexity, due in part to recondite Japanese, of Noh has been somewhat exaggerated; the symbolism with a small amount of preliminary orientation and program notes is grasped. The Noh play is basically the acting out of a story. A performance is not as difficult as some have come to believe.

Certain elements are characteristic for this form of Japanese theater. The acting of a story has been formalized. But there is no loss of audience identification with the characters' and Noh provides entertainment. Movements of the actors conform to the physical structure of the Noh stage. The choreography: formalized patterns of movement have been refined and are mastered by each generation of Noh performers.

An important measure of the pleasure derived from seeing a program of Noh performances is through appreciation of the excellence with which a pattern of movement is executed by the performers. Music is an integral part of the Noh performance: the singing of the musicians and the chorus and the cadences of the drums support and accompany the actor. (This integrated use of music and choral speaking suggests parallels with the ancient Greek drama.) The Noh chorus had also been an influence on the style and format of Kabuki plays.

The chorus serves many functions: it can be the supplementary or secondary character; it may be used for relaying information to the audience or for communicating feeling experienced by the central character or characters of the play. It may describe weather conditions or the locale of the play (of some importance, since the story is being acted out on an almost bare stage). Use of the chorus frees the actor from much dialogue so that at moments he may concentrate on pure gesture and dance.

There may be conflict creating tension and the tale of the Noh is likely to be far away in time and in an era remote for that of the viewer.

The Noh Theatre utilizes effectively a bridge to the acting area; the runway is at the audience's left and at an acute angle to the square stage of the Noh theatre. The plays exploit the high dramatic impact of major entrances and exits down this bridge — the *hashigagari* to the stage. A sudden lifting of the multi-striped curtain at the far end of the bridge is exciting; when *a* supernatural character, wearing wig and mask enters, it is very pleasing aesthetically and thrilling.

A formalized and bare platform stage evolved for the Noh. There is magnificence and grandeur in costuming. Not all characters in the Noh plays wear the mask. When it is used by a character, it is exploited fully for its theatricality. Theatricality is achieved through the sparing use of stage properties,and these properties are abstracted, stripped to bare essentials. For example, in *Funabenkei,* the boat used is scarcely more than a few ribs of what would be a boat. What may have been motivated by need and aesthetics has gained another element, the theatrical.

The conventions, the simplicity, of the Noh theatre prove an audience easily accepts the rules of the game.

It is a form of theatre which has evolved and has been refined over a long period of time. Expert performing of Noh requires a growing into performance, beginning at an early age, perhaps four years, and then continuing throughout a lifetime. It is a theatre of which the whole is larger than the sum of the parts. The Noh theatre, derives from acting families; members of the troupe live and work most closely together.

To translate the Noh play and to effect a transition worth doing to another theatre is not likely to prove easy. But it is a challenge worth meeting and it may prove catalytic for a style of Western theatre.

Log: 1959

Friday, April 24.

On this morning, the leader and seminar group went with Miss Watanabe to the Kita school of the Noh, near the Meguro station of the underground.

The Noh theatre was behind a very large gymnasium. It had its own traditional Noh stage. In a room which opened on to the auditorium, we sat and talked with Mr. Kita, the grandson. He was the actor we were to see rehearse that morning. The Noh play which was to be rehearsed was *Ataka*, which episode is the basis for the Kabuki play, *Kanjincho*.

The Kita school is considered the most recent of the Noh. It began about three hundred years ago! The Kita family has now reached the sixteenth generation, represented by the grandson. The father and the grandfather are celebrated actors and are still active in Noh.

During the visit with Miyoko Watanabe to the Kita School of the Noh, Kita Minoru and his son, Nagayo, took us on a tour of the stage, explaining the aspects of the stage. We were also shown many Noh costumes. They seemed to like to tell us how much the costumes were worth. (It seemed very American; for Americans are often curious as to how much something costs.)

The stages of garbing the Noh actor — before he puts on the mask — was demonstrated. The actor was dressed in one richly embroidered in gold and silver thread, with colorful decorations, then one robe after another. As they did so, the value of each robe was told. Only a band of the underlying costume would show. A member of the seminar commented, saying, "But only a border of this very richly embroidered and costly robe is seen by the audience. Why? " The response was, "The actor knows."

Kita was asked to describe what the actor might do before performance. He said, "This will differ with different actors. Some spend their time backstage in contemplation and meditation before going on to perform."

He added, that during April, when he had been preparing and rehearsing the *Ataka*, "I have been *living* the character of Benkei. But one day while riding on a streetcar, my thoughts were diverted from Benkei by a pretty girl; forcibly I brought myself back to *living* the character of Benkei." He concluded, "Most important in performance is re-creation of the spirit of the character." He quoted a Japanese proverb, "One must put the spirit of Buddha into the image of the Buddha.

"We have already had five rehearsals of this Noh play, which on Sunday will be presented to the public. However," he said, "this is not many rehearsals, but then this production did not require many rehearsals. As recently as three years ago, we had performed *Ataka*."

The grandson, Kita Nagayo (now head of the troupe), told us he had been learning roles since he was a child of four. He expressed it as, "our theatre is an integral part of our living," and he added, "We know all the lines of all the music and the dance steps of the *Ataka* from early years. Therefore, the rehearsal is not so much for movement or for the refreshening or relearning of the lines, music or dance steps, it is for the re-creating of the spirit of the character." He returned to his earlier statement, "The totality of the performance is a part of our living, and there is no marked departure between what we do during performance in the theatre and in the street; all must be close to the main goal in our life: performing.

During rehearsal, the grandfather, a man in his seventies or eighties, was watching the performance. He was wearing traditional Japanese dress: hakama, kimono, tabi. All the while smoking a cigar, which seemed very large for this diminutive man, he moved about restlessly, viewing the rehearsal from different parts of the seating area. It gave to rehearsals a 'show-business' atmosphere, in marked contrast to the solemn, mystical attitude toward rehearsal, performance, and reincarnation of character, as expressed by the grandson.

For a balanced view of theatre practice, it is essential to see theatre in action, as well as talking about theatre with its practitioners.

There was a certain casualness about the rehearsal: two actors playing retainers to Yoshitsume were in Western-style business suits. The other actors, musicians and chorus wore rehearsal kimonos.

One actor was absent from rehearsal so the grandfather tossed in lines from time to time, as needed; at other moments one of the chorus did likewise. Although there was intense concentration upon the role, the grandson Kita, playing Benkei, would at times with his hands indicate to an actor playing a scene with him to come closer or not to come close.

During the rehearsal, one of the musicians, with a closed fan beat out the rhythm on a block of wood for the musicians and for the performance.

Following the uninterrupted rehearsal, the grandfather made suggestions, rehearsed his grandson — as Benkei for certain bits and pieces for corrections — movement or phrases. He gave advice to the musicians, and he rehearsed a few phrases of the singing.

Following the rehearsal, a traditional stage ritual took place (which was explained by Miyoko Watanabe). Mr. Kita, as a younger actor, bowed to this grandfather, who had been observing and giving helpful comments during the performance. Also, he bowed to the senior musicians.

The Noh play *Ataka* takes longer to perform and seems more drawn-out than in Kabuki. Kabuki had evolved as popular theatre for the merchant class. Noh was a court theatre, popular with the samurai and the aristocracy, who had leisure time and had cultivated a taste for plays of long duration.

Log 1964

In Tokyo, Japan, the author meets with the Kitas of the Kita Theatre and the School for directing of American professional actors at the Institute for Advanced Studies in the Theatre Arts, New York, in the Noh play, *Ikkaku Sennin.*

Friday, May 29th
<u>Arrival in Tokyo Japan</u>

Saturday, May 30th

The weather was warm, for a meeting at the American Embassy with Mr. Tenny respecting the IASTA's Noh project.

Monday, June 1st

8:30 am: Telephoning the American Embassy to arrange for a meeting with Dr. Fahs. Arrangements were made with Mr. Tenny and Ms. Lipper.

3:30 pm: A meeting with Mr. Fahs at the Embassy Annex, No. 1 [a South Manchurian railroad building: Room 610].

Tuesday, June 2nd

9:00 am: The day was cloudy. A meeting with Mr. Barnett of the Fulbright Commission.

Wednesday, June 3rd

Morning: A first meeting with Kita Minoru and Kita Sadayo. Discussion of the need to tape the musicians and the Noh chorus for performances. The Institute for Advanced Studies in the Theatre Arts's tape recordings of music and choral chanting would replace the live musicians and chorus.

4:30 pm: A meeting with Mr. Yonezawa at the Kokusai Bunka Shinkokai [a Japanese Government Cultural Affairs organization].

Thursday, June 4th

10:30 am: A meeting with Kita Minoru at the Imperial Hotel; he explained that there was a problem recording the music and chorus. The nature of the problem was that the musicians and the chorus take their cues from the *actors*. The question was: how to tape them without the voices of the actors — speaking the Japanese text — being on the tape?

As instructed by the American Embassy, Fred Hoff (an American scholar in Japan with a knowledge of the Noh texts) was telephoned. The objective of this conversation would be to invite him to translate the Japanese text of the Noh play, <u>*Ikkaku Sennin*</u>.

Friday, 5th

9:30 am: Meeting with Frank Hoff. an agreement was reached as to his translating the play *Ikkaku Sennin* and having it ready before my departure for the

United States.

Wednesday, June 10th

The weather was clear. A meeting with Frank Hoff and a discussion respecting the translation.

Thursday, June 11th

10:00 am: A meeting with the International Noh Club. Hosts were Martin Cohen, an American in Japan, and Manso Nomura, a specialist for kyogen.

2:00 pm: A meeting at the Imperial Hotel with the Kitas and with Frank Hoff.

A solution had been found for the taping of the music and their chorus. In the words of Mr. Kita Minoru, taping is to be made of the performance. Following that, in a studio, their musicians would with earphones listen to the taped performance.

Thus they would get their cues from the actors for the IASTA performance. The microphone would then only record chorus, musicians (music and the choral singing).

There was great rejoicing on all sides.

Friday, June 12th

Departure for New York.

Log, 1964, of Rehearsals and Performances of *Ikkaku Sennin*

Tuesday, September 15th

Kita Sadayo and Akiyo Tomoeda arrived.

12:00 noon: A meeting with John Barnett.

That evening, Robert Epstein, Executive Vice President of IASTA, and the President of IASTA took Mr. Kita and Mr. Tomoeda to dinner. Miyoko Watanabe was present as interpreter for the Japanese directors.

During the meal, Mr. Kita said that the play would have to be performed in Japanese! This came as a shock, for it had been discussed and had been agreed upon in Tokyo, Japan, that the play was to be performed by American actors *in English*, using Frank Hoff's translation.

Understanding of the Japanese temperament — that it was not advisable to argue with them head-on, we began to discuss with them the length of time it would take — and the challenge to get American actors to learn Japanese — to perform in Japanese.

Once it had been established that the Institute was prepared to go ahead with what was now proposed by the Kitas, the real problem surfaced. The translation of Frank Hoff was accurate, but it did not match the rhythm of movements and of the music. If that were solved, according to the Kitas, then it could be performed in English. That *was* the only way it could be performed in English.

The American poet, William Packard, had provided the Institute with assistance on earlier productions. He was sought out to see if he could adapt, poetically, the Frank Hoff translation — so it would conform to the movements and the music. Although William Packard did not know Japanese, he was not deterred from attempting it.

Wednesday, September 16th

The morning and afternoon were devoted to production meetings of the IASTA staff for the Noh production.

Dinner was arranged at the Nippon Club, of which the IASTA President was a member, for officers and staff of the Institute, Kita Sadayo, Tomoeda Akiyo and Miyoko Watanabe.

Monday, September 21st

11:00 am: Casting begins under the supervision of the Kitas for the Noh play.

Tuesday, September 22nd through
Saturday, October 3rd
Rehearsals

The two Noh performers were to work with Institute actors who wished to be cast in the play. Casting was to be later.

There was an initial introduction to the style of a Noh play and the Noh theatre. Rehearsals were to be from 11 o'clock in the morning until lunch; afternoon rehearsals from 3 to 5 pm.

Wednesday, September 29th

The first showing of the film *Ikkaku Sennin* — as performed by the Kita troupe.

Thursday, October 1st

A second showing of *Ikkaku Sennin* film — followed by a costume parade, [the costumes for the production had been made in Japan — larger to accommodate American actors].

Monday, October 5th through
Wednesday, October 7th

On Wednesday, at 7:30, the Japanese directors and officers of the Institute went to Sarah Lawrence College where Kita Sadayo and Tomoeda Akiyo performed. A reception followed.

Tuesday, October 6th

A meeting with the Director of the Japan Society, Doug Overton, in his office at the Japanese Society. He welcomed the Kitas to the United States, speaking to them in Japanese.

Wednesday, October 7th

4:30 pm: There was a program of projection of the slides of the production as performed by the Kita troupe which the Kitas had brought with them from Japan.

Thursday, October 8th through
Friday, October 9th
Rehearsals

Friday, the Kitas were driven to the country home of the Mitchells for a break from rehearsal.

Monday, October 12th through
Saturday, October 17th
Rehearsals

Sunday, October 18th

Officers of the Institute and the Kitas were taken to a dinner party at the Player's Club, Grammercy Park. This was possible since the President of the Institute was a member of the Player's Club.

Monday, October 19th through
Saturday, October 24th

Rehearsals and training sessions continued as preparation for performances of the Noh play.

Monday, October 26th through
Saturday, October 31st

Training sessions and rehearsal.

Thursday, the Kitas performed at the Institute for members of the Japan Society; Friday, the Kitas performed at the Institute for members enrolled in the Institute.

Monday, November 2nd through
Saturday, November 7th

A series of dress rehearsals.

Monday, November 9th through
Thursday, November 12th

Dress rehearsals continue.

Friday, November 13th

The Noh play was performed at a matinee.

Saturday, November 14th

A matinee of the Noh play.

Sunday, November 15th

Two performances of the Noh play, 5:30 and 7:30, followed by a Japan Society reception.

Monday, November 16th

Two performances of the Noh play, 5:30 and 7:30.

Thursday, November 17th

Two performances of the Noh play.

Friday, November 18th

An evening performance of the Noh play.

Saturday, November 19th

An evening performance of the Noh play.
3:00 pm: A seminar was held for discussion of Noh Theatre.

Tuesday, November 24th

2:45 pm: A performance of the Noh play.

Tuesday, December 8th

Officers of the Institute drove to Washington with Kita Sadayo and Tomoeda Akiyo.

Wednesday, December 9th

Kita Sadayo performs at the State Department and a meeting with members of the audience followed. No performances on Wednesday since some actors were in performance elsewhere.

Thursday, December 10th

The officers of the Institute and the Kitas returned to New York from Washington.

Monday, December 14th

2:30 pm: A discussion between the Kitas and the actors of the Institute. The actors who had performed in the Noh production said farewell to the Kitas who departed for Japan.

ASPECTS OF NOH
by
Kita Sadayo

I came from Japan, far, far away, to direct you in a Noh play. I hope that I will have happy and fruitful work with you.

Since the time of the creation of Noh, five different plays have been presented within one day — to make one whole day's production. Today only three or four are played. But still, five programs a day is the orthodox way to perform Noh. So three times a year we perform five programs a day.

Noh must be acted under extreme rigid rules. First the actor has to learn the basic elements of a Noh play. The most important is form. Second, the singing is very important. The most difficult aspect is how to walk on the Noh stage; just to stand is extremely difficult. If the actor masters the form: how to walk and how to stand the actor then has practically arrived at all of Noh.

The reason why Noh exists today as a pure artistic form is that the *Tokugawa Shogunate* ruled that Noh was to maintain its style. That is why today we can now still see Noh in such a pure form. There has been change since the time when Noh was created by Kannami and Zeami. In the late 16th century a Noh performer — a politician and soldier as well — performed twelve numbers in a day. If a Noh troupe were to perform twelve numbers in a day, now, it would take 24 hours. For example, the Noh play *Pine Winds* takes about two hours to perform. But 400 years ago — when performed — it must have taken 25 minutes.

We assume that the Noh actors performed with incredible speed in earlier times. To perform it with that pace now, the performance would be chaotic. So the present form of Noh must have been shaped later than the *Tokugawa* era.

To explain why Noh has been slowed down must be due to Noh's having been placed on a higher plane. Were Noh to be performed at a faster speed than it is performed now, it would lose all its dignity.

We often discuss whether Noh be considered a drama or an opera. I have come to think that Noh is to be considered a synthetic theatre form — including all the characteristics of all the performing arts including opera and poetic plays.

One element separates Noh from all other theatrical forms. It is *Yugen*. *Yugen* has to exist in any Noh play — no matter which category. In *Ikkaku Sennin* — which you are to perform — *Yugen* is to be found. *Yugen* exist — even in a Noh play like *Ikkaku Sennin.* This you will understand through performing. *Ikkaku Sennin* is more dramatic than most Noh plays.

Four or five hundred years ago the concept, the aesthetic, of Noh was performed just as an entertainment. *Yugen* didn't exist. Within the past three and four hundred years *Yugen* gained in importance and depth. To my mind, *Yugen* should be visible instead of just imagined by the audience. Without *Yugen,* Noh might have taken the same road as Kabuki — becoming a popular theatre.

When I was very young I used to watch excellent performers perform Noh.

A Noh actor may hypnotize an audience when he comes out through the curtain at the end of the *hashigari* — the bridge. Such a performer appears not to be breathing at all. The audience seems in a trance. Only a performer who has thoroughly mastered the very basic technique of Noh can have achieved such an effect.

In the past it was believed that you master all the basic forms before you reach twenty-five; otherwise you might as well give up performing Noh. One's muscles get tighter and stiff. No matter how one may strive afterwards, one can never achieve Noh acting.

Japanese Noh
by
James R. Brandon

Between the tenth and the thirteenth centuries, performers of a number of Japanese theatre forms vied for audience attention and for the patronage of Buddhist temples and the court in and around the important cities of Nara and Kyoto. Jugglers and acrobats, singers of epic romances, and players of various kinds of short plays and dances especially those known as dengaku, literally field music, and *sarugaku*, monkey music — were part of the theatre scene. Both *dengaku* and *sarugaku* troupes performed sketches, songs, and dances, but as independent pieces. Around the middle of the fourteenth century, the *sarugaku* troupe leader Kannami Kiyotsugu (1333-1384) introduced into his performances a sung dance section, the *kusemai* or *kuse*, thus for the first time giving the dance a genuine dramatic function. In the *kuse* section of a play, a crucial tale of the past is narrated as the protagonist dances out the story. Kannami's new way of performing was called *sarugaku*-noh, and in time this was shortened to Noh.

Kannami's son, the famous Zeami Motokiyo (1363-1444), was twelve years old when he was seen performing Noh by Yoshimitsu, the shogun, or military ruler of Japan. Yoshimitsu was captivated by the boy's beauty and grace, and he brought Zeami to the palace in Kyoto to be his catamite. Zeami spent most of his adult life at the court, even after his patron died. In the sophisticated atmosphere of the shogun's court, he raised Noh from a plebeian, almost rustic, theatrical form to an exceptionally subtle art. Zeami was not only the chief performer of his troupe (inheriting this position from his father) but also the writer of more than one hundred plays. And in a series of treatises on the practice of his art, he established the aesthetic basis of Noh. For four hundred years following Zeami's death, Noh troupes were supported by feudal lords in Kyoto and in the outlying provinces, thus preserving down to the present the texts of Noh and the style of performance[1] as well. About two hundred and forty plays make up the Noh repertory that is performed today. Another two thousand or so plays have been written, but are not performed. Plays are divided into five groups according to subject matter and style: god (*kami*) plays, congratulatory pieces praising the gods; warrior (*shura*) plays, in which the protagonist is usually a slain warrior who appears as a ghost and relives his sufferings; woman (*katsura*) plays, in which the protagonist is a woman; miscellaneous plays — one type concerns a woman driven mad by grief for a lost child or lover, another a character who is obsessed, and a third, known as living person plays, an unmasked male protagonist; and demon (*kiri)* plays, in which the protagonist is a demon, devil, or supernatural figure.

1

There are five schools of Noh troupes — Kanze, Hosho, Kongo, Komparu, and Kita. Some plays are performed by all five schools, others are the property of one, or several, of the schools.

A day's performance in Zeami's time was made up of one play from each group, staged in order, and interspersed with comedies called *kyogen*. A program of five plays was viewed as an artistic entity. Atmosphere, tempo, and tension changed perceptibly from one play to the next. The god play was quiet and dignified, the warrior play active and strong, and the woman play radiated elegant beauty. Increased tempo marked the fourth play, and in the demon play, a furious battle between demon and hero was resolved with the demon being killed or subdued — thus bringing the performance back to a congratulatory mood similar to that of the first play. Zeami wrote that the five-play series should be organized according to the principle of *jo*, or introduction (first play); *ha*, or development (second, third, and fourth plays); and *kyu*, or scattering (fifth play). According to Zeami, also, each play was to be organized into *jo, ha, kyu* — beginning, middle, end — with the same principle of artistic progression in mind. Significantly, the *jo-ha-kyu* concept is derived from *gagaku* court music, and not for literature.

Noh plays are deeply impregnated with the doctrine of Amida Buddhism, according to which human salvation is achieved through prayer and penance. The profoundly pessimistic Buddhist theme of the impermanence of life is common to a number of plays (not, however, to *Ikkaku Sennin*). A noble warrior is slain before achieving his dream of conquest; a beautiful young woman eagerly sought after in her youth wanders alone in her withered old age. In Buddhist thought, the soul that clings to earthly attachments after death dwells in a purgatory of ceaseless torment. Plays of the second and third type concern these tortured souls.

Only a small number of characters appears in most Noh plays. In a text they are designated by their role-type and not by their character's name. The *shite*, or doer, is the central figure, and is usually an aristocrat, a court lady, or a powerful spirit. The *shite* completely dominates a performance; other actors are mere by-players. It is the *shite* who always performs the *kuse* dance and other important dances. Normally the shite is masked. The shite may have attendant courtiers, retainers, or maids (*tsure*). In the play there may be a noble child role (*kokata*) or roles for other minor characters (*tomo*), all of which are acted by lesser performers associated with the shite actor's school. The *waki*, or supporting role, is most often that of a priest who initiates the action or the play. Only rarely is the *waki* an antagonist to the shite. The waki may have attendants (*wakizure*), acted by performers associated with the *waki*'s school. *Kyogen* actors play roles of villagers or other commoners (kyogen actors also perform the kyogen farces between two Noh plays).

Plays are presented on a raised stage, about eighteen feet square, with a highly polished Cyprus floor. Scenery is not used, but constructed props and hand props commonly are. A bridgeway (*hashigakari*) about thirty feet long, leading from stage right to the dressing rooms, is used for exits and entrances. The tempo of song and dance is regulated by accompanying music, played by musicians who sit in view of the audience at the rear of the stage. One flute, two hand drums (one large and one small), and in some plays a stick drum compose the small Noh ensemble. A chorus of six to ten actors from the *shite* group sits on the left side of the stage. Several other actors, disciples of the *shite* and sometimes of the *waki*, assist their teachers on the stage. They give and take away hand properties, adjust costumes, and move larger set properties. All performers in Noh are male.

The most important influence on the aesthetics of Noh theatrical art is Zen Buddhism. From austere Zen came the principle that suggestion is preferable to flat statement, that subtlety is preferable to clearness, that the small gesture is preferable to the large, that, in short, the secret of beauty lies in restraint.Beauty in Noh is refined and it is everywhere: in the chaste planes of the masks, in the simplicity of the stage, in the rigor of the line of musicians or chorus on the stage, in the quavering tone of the actor's chanting voice, in the elegant movements of the performers. Zeami described the unique beauty which Noh strives toward in two terms: mysterious and sublime. Mysterious beauty, or *yugen*, is the ephemeral beauty that lies in impermanence. The cherry blossom, delicate and fragile, is touched by the wind and in an instant is scattered and gone. Elegance is tinged with the sadness of passing. The sublime would appear to be Zeami's more mature view. In sections of Noh that suggest the sublime, melancholy over the impermanence of life gives way to serenity and acceptance. The beauty of the sublime is the beauty of old age, restful, at peace with the world. It is silent, austere. That such a theory of beauty was developed for a theatrical art must impress us deeply. Indeed, there is no other form of theatre in the world in which the externals have been more thoroughly abandoned in favor of elliptical, concentrated, austere expression.

Noh is not a storyteller's art; it does not (in most cases) present the unfolding of a human action. Rather, through recollections of the past, it evokes a mood an emotion, a religious state. Human characters appear on the stage, but they are not three-dimensional figures living the usual round of daily routine. At the most extreme they are quite literally momentary manifestations of the spirit world; at the very least, they exhibit an unworldly degree of composure and restraint. Through the gradual increase in tension created by the steady musical accompaniment, the chanting of the chorus, and the formal movements of the characters, content is subsumed to form, until the knowledgeable spectator perceives the occurrences before him, not as emotionally bound human actions but as elegantly formed patterns of sound and color that impinge on his emotions peripherally if at all. Noh is the purest of the art forms of theatre and consequently makes the most demands on its audience.

[The following is from James R. Brandon's *Traditional Asian Plays,* Hill & Wang, New York, 1972, (p.173-182). We express our appreciation to Mr. Brandon and his publisher for their permission to excerpt from the book.]

The play *Ikkaku Sennin*, or *The Holy Hermit Unicorn*, was written by Komparu Zenpõ Motoyasu in the last half of the fifteenth century, one generation after Zeami's time. It may be performed as a play of the fourth group (because the hero is a living person) or the fifth (because the hero is a wizard with supernatural powers). It is in the repertory of the Kanze, Komparu, and Kita schools.

The action in *Ikkaku Sennin* supposedly takes place in an Indian kingdom, though there is nothing specifically Indian in the play except the single line stating that India is the place of action. The play dramatizes an ancient legend from India and China. A hermit priest, through his powers of meditation, traps the dragon gods of rain in a mountain cave. Then after a time drought threatens the land. In order to free the gods so they can make rain, the emperor orders one of his most beautiful court ladies, the Lady Senda Bunin, to visit the hermit and seduce him. The play begins as she (the *shitesure*) arrives at the hermit's mountain retreat with a court official (the *waki*). They enter to the usual opening music (*shidai*) and the *waki* stands at the conventional name-saying place, upstage right. He announces who he is and the purpose of their journey (nanori). This is followed by a travel song (*michiyuki*), which accompanies the crossing of the *waki*'s group onto the main stage, a movement conventionally indicating arrival at their destination. With the *waki*'s group now in position, the shite — the hermit — appears within a hut, already placed on stage, and chants his opening lines (*sashi*).

In this, and in the play's subsequent development, *Ikkaku Sennin* follows the usual Noh structure. The *waki* is a minor character who simply guides Lady Senda on her journey. The overriding importance of the *shite* is clear: the hermit absolutely dominates the performance, though in plot terms, he is acted upon and is not.an initiator of action. The play's climax typically occurs in a dance section, in this case not a *kuse* (there is no event out of the past which requires explanation), but a violent *hataraki* dance, when the hermit battles the dragon gods and attempts to prevent their escape.

The play illustrates how conflicts are often attenuated in Noh. There is a direct and strong opposition between the hermit and the court lady when he is first disturbed. In the following scene, she gets him drunk and seduces him. These scenes could be dramatized very effcctively, as they are in thc Kabuki version of this story, *Narukami*. However, in the Noh the incipient conflict between the hermit and Lady Senda is almost immediately resolved when he allows wine to be served. His seduction is only suggested in graceful dance patterns by Lady Senda, and the indirection of this scene is further emphasized by the lyric verse of the chorus, "dance to the music of flutes." The words are not strong narrative, as they might be if the conflict were of greater concern. Lady Senda's formal role is minor; she is only a *tsure*, or secondary player, and is given but one line to speak in the play. Yet she dances several important sequences and is, within the overall theatrical pattern, of considerably greater importance than the *waki* figure.

Ikkaku Sennin balances several qualities of Noh in fairly equal proportions. There is some conflict, but not much. There is beautiful dancing, but it does not have the central importance that dance would have in plays of the third group. The play is rooted in religious concerns, yet there is nothing truly spiritual about its story. There is a touch of the erotic that is not explicitly developed. It is perhaps in the especially active finale that the play's individuality is best seen. The dragon gods and the hermit energetically whirl the long manes that surround their fearsome, glaring masks. Movements and music rise to a furious climax, then dissolve into stillness.

A translation of *Ikkaku Sennin* by Frank Hoff was adapted for production at the Institute for Advanced Sudies in the Theatre Arts by William Packard. Like all Noh texts, about half of the Japanese script for *Ikkaku Sennin* was composed in verse of alternating phrases of seven and five syllables. Usually two phrases are sung or chanted within the strict eight-beat Noh musical measure. Several metric patterns are possible. In the *hira nori* pattern, for example, the seven-syllable phrase fits into the first four beats of a measure and the five-syllable phrase into the second four beats. These rhythms create a constantly flowing sound pattern that is almost hypnotic in its effect upon the audience. In order to recreate this vocal effect in English, Packard followed the Japanese syllable count exactly in his adaptation.

The performance traditions of Noh have been maintained — with some minor changes of course — from Kannami's time down to the present, so each detail of blocking, gesture, dance, music, vocal style, costuming, and emotional interpretation for *Ikkaku Sennin* is rigidly set. For this production at IASTA a replica of a Noh stage was built, somewhat larger in area than a stage would be in Japan, but incorporating a bridgeway, pillars, and a smooth dancing area. Authentic cosumes, properties, and masks for Lady Senda, the hermit, and the rain gods were brought from Japan. Actors and actresses (a departure from Noh's all-male tradition) were trained daily in basic movement by the Noh actor Kita Sadayo. Vocal intonations were patterned after the original Japanese and timed to taped music. The most significant change made in the text was the elimination of the chorus lines at the.end of the play. They describe the battle between the hermit and the rain gods. The danced action was felt to be sufficiently clear without the lyrics.

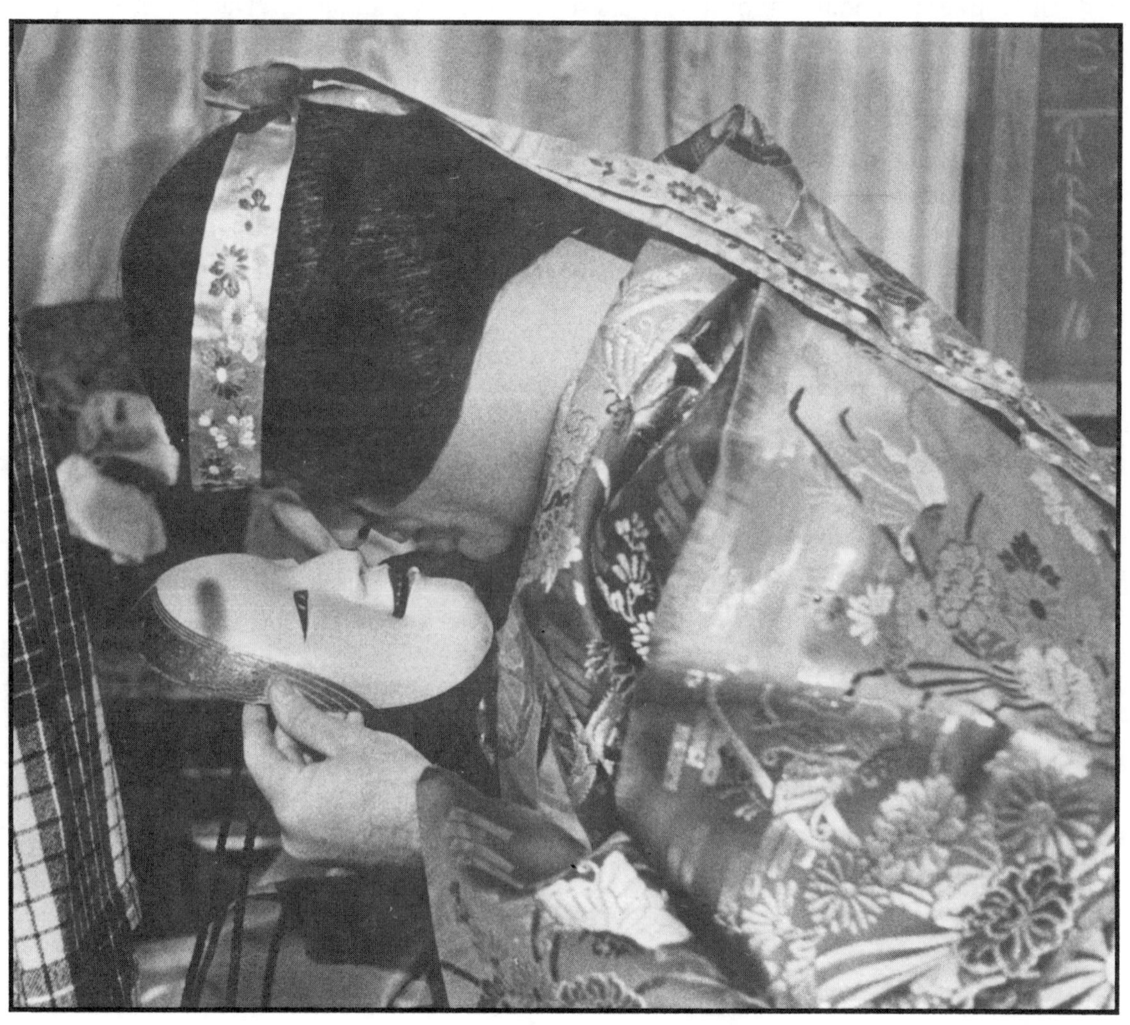

Jack Eddleman

IKKAKU SENNIN
(The Holy Hermit Unicorn)

A Japanese Noh Play

by

KOMPARU ZENPŌ MOTOYASU

English translation by Frank Hoff
English verse adaptation by William Packard

Performance script by Aida Alvarez. English verse adaptation by William Packard, commissioned by the Institute for Advanced Studies in the Theatre Arts (IASTA) for use in the production directed by Sadayo Kita, of the Kita Noh School.

Kita Troupe

ABOUT THIS ADAPTATION

Ikkaku Sennin was written hy Komparu Zenpõ Motoyasu (1453-l532), although its origins are certainly much earlier, in the Japanese legend of Ekshringa, or "one-horn." *Ikkaku Sennin* is a holy hermit unicorn who has captured the dragon gods and kept them from causing rain to fall; eventually this hermit is seduced and loses all his magic power, through an encounter with the beautiful Lady Senda Bunin. It is interesting that there is also a Kabuki play, *NARUKAMI*, which deals with this legend, and is derived from the older Noh play.

The Institute for Advanced Studies in the Theatre Arts (IASTA), in New York, had already produced *NARUKAMI*; it was directed by Onoe Baiko VII, of the Kabuki theatre in Japan. Consequently, when the Institute came to consider the choice of a Noh play, it was natural that *Ikkaku Sennin* should come up for discussion. Kita Sadayo, of the Kita school of the Noh in Tokyo, was IASTA's visiting director in the fall of 1964, and he agreed that *Ikkaku Sennin* would be a good introduction to the Noh theatre for American audiences.

So Kita Sadayo and his assistant, Tomoeda Akiyo, began rehearsals of *Ikkaku Sennin*, with American professional actors, at the Institute's theatre in New York. Incidentally, this was the first time in history that Japanese Noh actors have taught thc techniques of their ancient theatre, to non-Japanese, for a production outside of Japan.

But there was a serious problem with the text. Frank Hoff, an American poet presently living in Tokyo, had made a fine literal translation of Ikkaku Sennin. However, Mr. Kita and Mr. Tomoeda were afraid that it would compromise the spirit of the Noh theatre, to depart too far from the traditional voice patterns and inflections of the phonetic Japanese text. So it was necessary to make the English adaptation correspond syllable for syllable with the Japanese text; also, certain conspicuous vowel sounds in the Japanese had to have an exact equivalent in English; and finally, the very pronounced rhythms of the Noh theatre required a great many abrupt, distinct monosyllables in English.

In my adaptation, I tried to achieve as much o£ this as possible. I suppose this is the only English version of a Japanese Noh play, which has been especially adapted to the traditional rhythms and inflections of the Noh. And yet, I do not think the fact that this text has met most of the technical requirements, and is still highly poetic, is all my own doing. The autumn imagery of *Ikkaku Sennin* is so subtle and poignant, that it has somehow survived all the various stages of translation and adaptation and rehearsal and performance. It is still there, and perhaps it is almost as haunting as it is in the original.

—William Packard

The IASTA *IKKAKU SENNIN* production, New York

Ikkaku Sennin

CHARACTERS

Ikkaku Sennin, *a wizard*

Shinda, *a court official*

Lady Senda, *a beautiful young girl*

Two Dragon Gods

Chorus

Lady Senda's Attendants

Stage assistants

Symbols on Diagrams

1K = Ikkaku Sennin
LS = Lady Senda
W = Waki
K_1 K_2 = Kuroko — Stage assistants
S_1 S_2 = Palanquin carriers

The Institute for Advanced Studies in the Theatre Arts' (IASTA) performance of the *Ikkaku Sennin* was scored in Laban Notation — at their request. It was the decision of the authors to utilize solely their *mise-en-scene* diagrams for all movement — as well as for Lady Senda's dance and the Dragon Gods dance. The dances were phrased with the music, but precise phrasing was not taught nor were counts given.

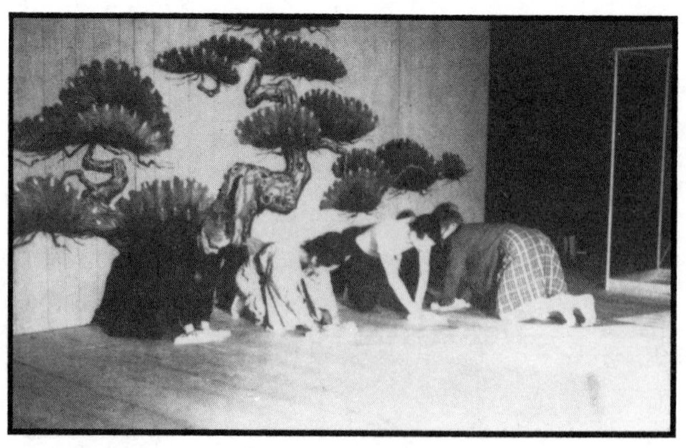

American actors polishing the stage with soy bean curd

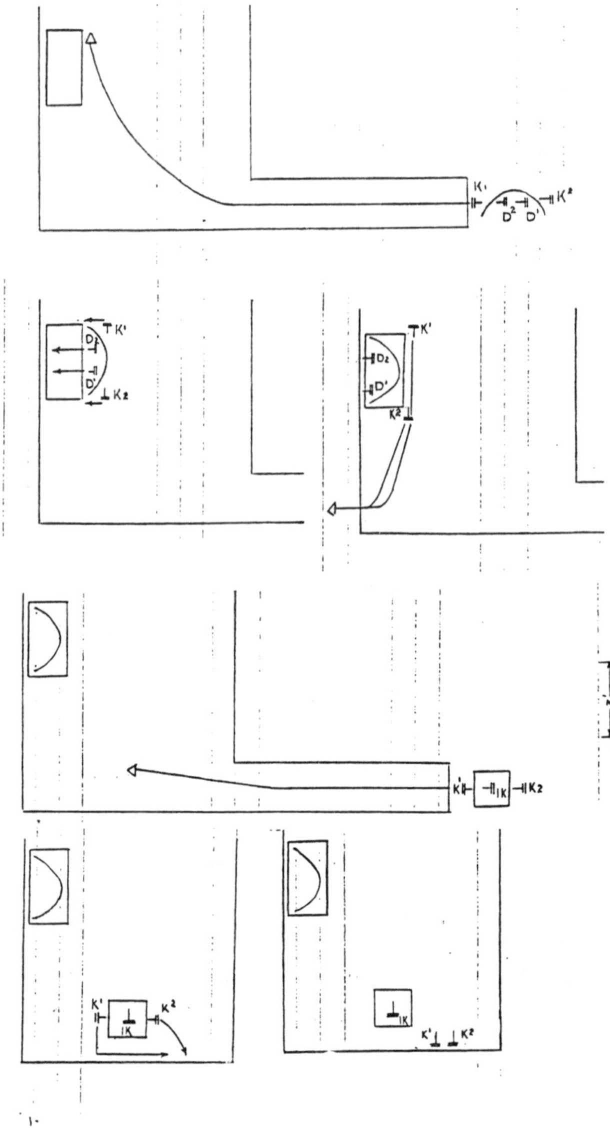

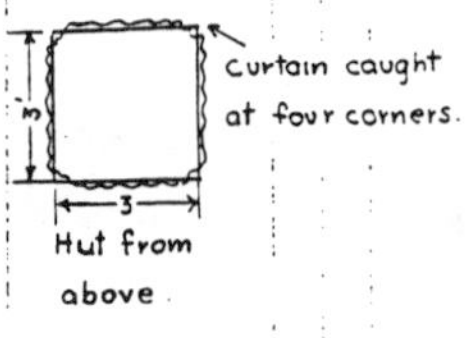
Curtain caught at four corners.
3'
3'
Hut from above

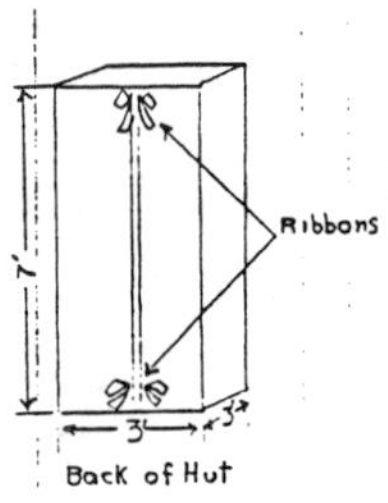
Ribbons
7'
3'
3'
Back of Hut

The Staging of Ikkaku Sennin

As do the young the young untried actors, *deshi*, American actors polish the wooden surface of the Noh stage with soy been curd. '*To achieve respect for the stage on which they are to perform.*' Upstage is a large wooden panel on which is traditionally painted a twisted pine — the only scenery of the Noh stage.

Kuroko: *Stage Assistants* bring out the props; they are placed on stage before any characters appear. Placing them is handled as part of the performance proper.

The *agemaku* curtain at the end of the *hashigakari* bridge — stage right — is lifted and a platform is brought to the stage proper and is placed stage left. The Kuroko return with a basic woven prop shaped in a semi-circle. It is covered in rich fabric. This is the symbolic rock cave within which the Dragon Gods are trapped. They place it on the platform.

The One-Horned Hermit's hut, covered in a jet-blue drape, conceals the hermit who is within the construct. He is not seen by the audience. This prop is brought down the bridge and is placed up stage center.

By means of the 'hurry-up-door' — left upstage — the Dragon Gods slip onto the platform and are concealed by the symbolic rock cave. The Kuroko place themselves upstage right of the hut and sit Japanese-sytle.

Three people are needed as well as an hours time to dress Lady Senda for a forty-five minute performance. All items of the costume have to be rolled three times — exactly. Left over right and right over left. All under-garments are to be put on with ritual. A wooden 'Y' is placed against the base of the actor's spine. To this is attached the *obis.* On this hangs the heavy costume. The outer robe, which the audience sees, is the most beautiful. The dressing of the actor is part of Noh tradition.

Then follows the ritual of the mask. The actor does not place it on his face. He bows to it; he turns it over, holding it always at two small holes where the strings are located. It is then the actor lowers his face into the mask. Once he has tied it on, he may sit up. Next he dons the wig and the headdress.

Fully clothed in the costume, the actor sits in front of a mirror for fifteen minutes so that he and the mask become one. It is a quiet time, a spiritual time.

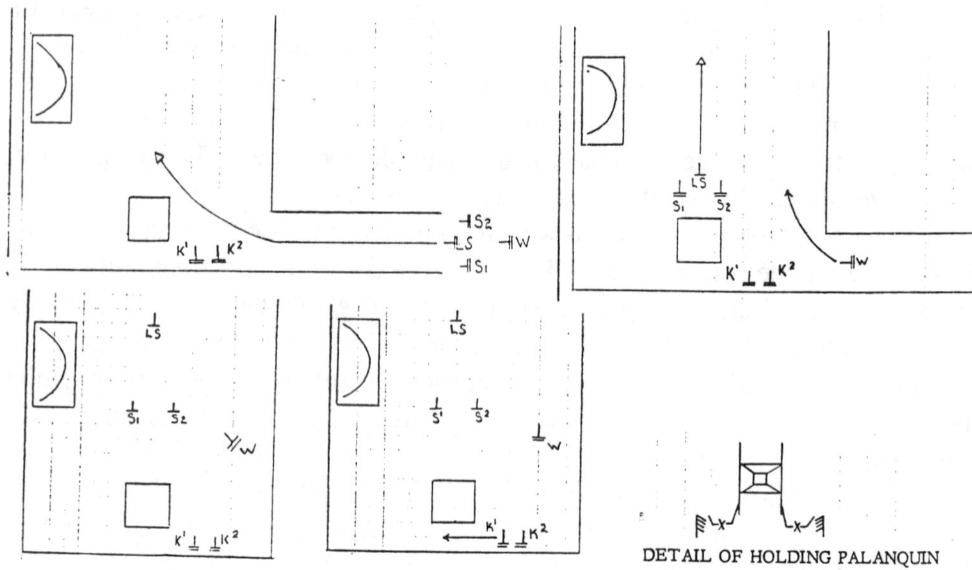

DETAIL OF HOLDING PALANQUIN

The Action of the Play Begins

To the sound of the flute, the *agemaku* curtain is lifted slowly. Lady Senda Bunin enters on the bridge followed by two *waki tusre* who are carriers of the palanquin — symbolic of a carriage in which Lady Senda Bunin rides. She is elaborately robed and wears a mask. She is followed by the court official, the *waki* ; Shinka. He is richly garbed but is without mask. All move slowly down the *hashigakari*, sliding their tabi-cladded feet in the formalized walk of Noh.

Lady Senda stops left and kneels. The *waki* takes a position upstage left.

The Hermit, Ikkaku Sennin, is within a cage, covered with a drape. Once the play has begun, the drape is drawn to reveal him.

ワキ官人詞

（サラリ）これは天竺波羅那国の帝王に仕へ奉る臣下なり。さてもこの国の傍に。一人の仙人あり。鹿の胎内に宿り出生せし故により。額に角一つ生ひ出でたり。これによってその名を一角仙人と名つく。さる子細あつて龍神と威を争ひ。仙人神通を以て諸龍を悉く岩屋の内に封じ籠むる間。数月雨下らずわ。帝この事を歎き給ひ。色々のぼ方便を廻らし給ひわ。

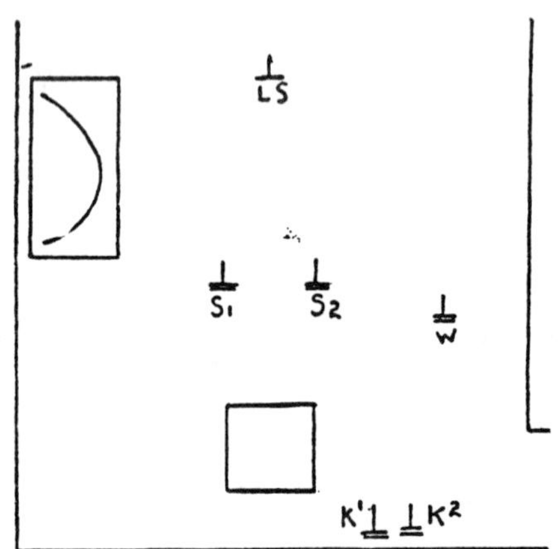

SHINDA (*WAKI*)

The prince I serve is a great prince, he is the
emperor of Barana
who rules a kingdom of India, with many
lands along the Ganges.
Now in the country of this prince there lives
a hermit
and he is a wizard. He was born from the womb
of a deer, and
he has a horn,
one single long horn,
a horn that sprouts out of his forehead,
sprouts out of his forehead,
and therefore we have named this wizard
Ikkaku Sennin, holy hermit unicorn.
Once Ikkaku Sennin and the great dragon
gods had an affair of honor,
and the wizard won out, the holy hermit
unicorn used his magic
to undo the dragon gods,
he drove them into a cave and made them
stay inside.
Away in that cave, for many years they
could not cause rain to fall.
Since then, my prince has come to grieve,
he sees that his whole countryside is dry,
and so now he knows
he has to free those dragon gods.

The narrator, who does the long introduction to the plot, eventually sits down, upstage; he does nothing for the next 45 minutes. But, he must remain focused. The two kuroko have to concentrate fully at all times. The head has to be kept poised at the end of the spine — very strongly held up and the neck never loose. The head, as well as the body, is never relaxed. There is tension in the neck that is constricting but it is converted into energy. The intense concentration — so characteristic of the Noh actor — seems to mesmerize the audience.

When the performer stands on the stage without any movement, he looks as if rooted to the stage. When he starts to move, he has to maintain that image — firm and solid on the stage. When Kita-sensei was in training as a very young actor, each night his teacher examined the soles of his tabi to see if the entire sole had been evenly soiled.

Characterization of the One-Horned Hermit, Ikkaku Sennin, *developed out of response to the plot line, the language, the imagery. The type of mask worn by this character stimulated the imagination of the actor. Being in the mask and wearing the wig — being laced in by the very restrictive costume contributed to characterization. The Hermit had to be communicated with the actor's voice and movements.*

ここに旋陀夫人とてならびなき美人のぼ座わを。踏み迷ひたる旅人の如くにして。仙境に分け入り給は。夫人に心を移し。神通を失う事もあるべきとのぼ方便により。夫人を具し奉り。唯今かの山路に分け入りわ。

一セイ立衆上

（ツヨク）山遠うしては雲行客の跡を埋み。松寒うしては風旅人の夢をも破る。かり寝かや。

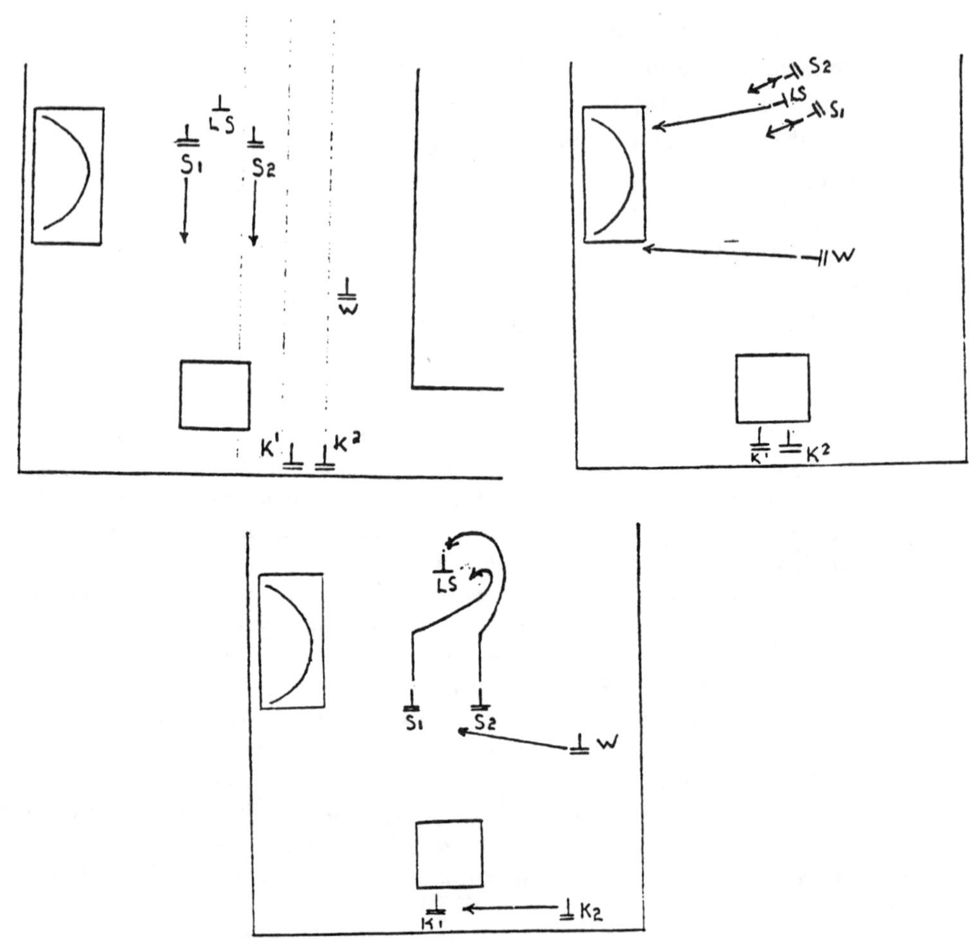

SHINDA (*WAKI*) —Continuing—

(SHINDA pivots left slightly to face LADY SENDA.)

Listen, this is the prince's plan, this is
the beautiful young girl
who is going to go up into the mountains,
there where the wizard lives, the holy hermit
unicorn, and he may make a mistake and
think she's lost her way.
Then he may fall in love,
he may say this young girl is so beautiful,
he has lost his heart and art
and all the magic that he used to use.
It may work out that way, that's what the
prince is hoping for,
and so we're going to carry her up to the
unicorn.

ATTENDANTS

(Still standing and holding the canopy frame over LADY SENDA*, they sing the following travel song.)*

Mountains and mountains and mountains,
mists that cover over all the weary travelers,
cold winds that blow through the open
woods, as we keep going,
no sleep on the mountain side,
no sweet dreams for us.

There is to be little expression of emotion in characterization. Much is left up to the actor to develop his characterization. This comes about as he becomes increasingly emotionally involved in the character and is following the plot line.

Movement is controlled as if moving against resistance and as if a heavily weighted atmosphere was pressing against the actor. On the stage, moves are made with the body, arms, and hands tensed. The hand holding a fan is gripped in front of the actor in a designated position. Any move is made slowly; at an increase in tempo, movement and action are performed as if the actor is moving with resistance — thus is achieved a great deal of tension.

（上歌、スラリ）露時雨もる山陰の下紅葉もる山陰の下紅葉。色そふ秋の風までも身にしみまさる旅衣。霧間を凌ぎ雲を分け。たつきも知らね山中におぼつかなくも踏み迷ふ。道の行方は如何ならん道の行方は如何ならん。

ワキ詞

（寛タリ）日を重ねて急ぎわ程に。いつくとも知らぬ山路に分け入りてわぞや。そに怪しき巌の陰より。

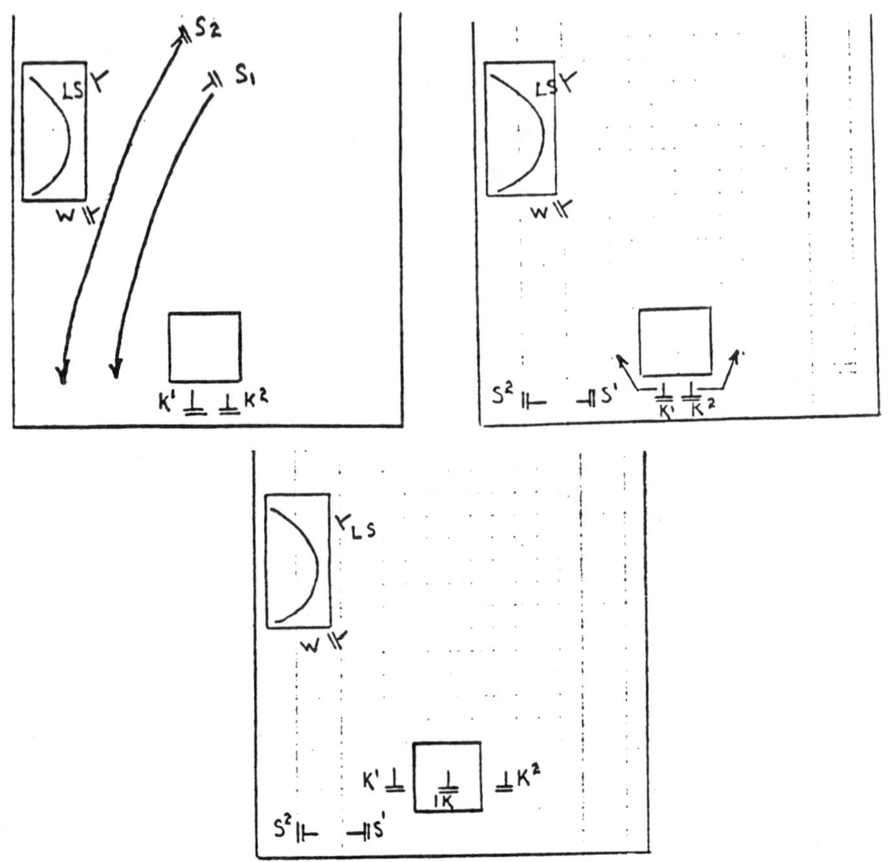

ATTENDANTS —Continuing—
Dew that drops like rain,
dew that drops like rain, like rain
on the deep ravine
so that even the lowest leaves receive water,
change to strange autumn colors.
We are kept so cold
as we keep climbing, climbing, climbing on
our way.
The road goes through so much mist,
through clouds on high hills.
How do we know where we are?
Up in the mountains
we do not know where we are,
we wander around
wondering where does this road go, this road
we're on,
does anyone know anything about this road?

SHINDA (*WAKI*)
(*Pivots front and speaks.*)
Day after day, we've hurried on our way,
traveling on this old road that no one knows
about,
now we are lost, we are all worn out.
Look, there are many rocks, they are lying
on the ground and piled up in a mound, I
wonder why?

Kita-sensei *declaimed the lines of the text in Japanese — along with gestures. The American actors were invited to try to equate vocally what the directors were doing with their voices. In trying to imitate a Japanese sound, the actors found it creative and a lot of fun. The lines of the text eventually —which had to be spoken in English —did not come very close to the way in which the Noh actor spoke the lines in Japanese. The actors ultimately came up with an intoning of the text that was evocative of the Noh style of delivery.*

*That style of delivery is a tense, gutteral sound (*a closed sound*); all of which is difficult to imitate. The American actors imitated the sound largely by drawing out the vowels of the words, striving to make some words sound gutteral. All this was achieved with no lose of projection of communication.*

Each movement phrase should have a definite shape: a beginning, building to a climax, followed by a resolution of being poised for the start of the next phrase. Movements — like the glide —involved an increase in tension and then a diminution of tension.

吹き来る風のかうばしく。松けいの枝を引き結びたる庵あり。若しかの仙境にてもやわらん。暫くこのあたりに徘徊し。事の由を窺はばやと思ひわ。

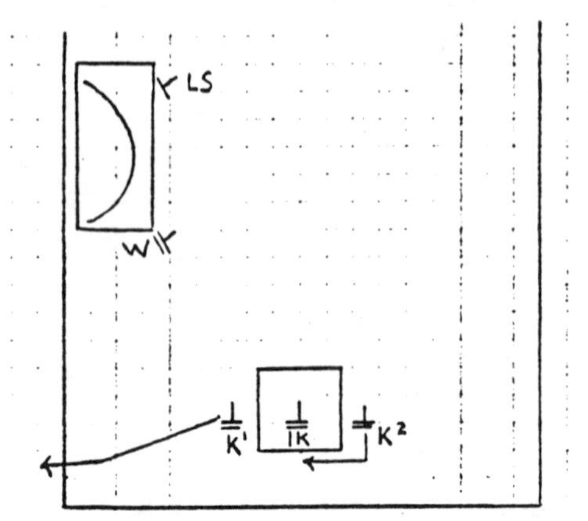

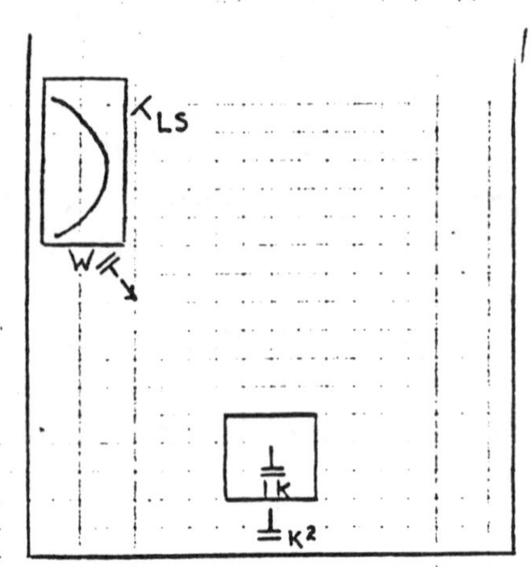

SHINDA *(WAKI)* —Continuing—
—how sweet the breezes as they blow over the rock pile, I can tell the smell of pine. Perhaps this is where the wizard lives, the holy hermit unicorn, perhaps this is the place. We could keep quiet and get close to it, slowly, slowly, get close so we can see if the wizard is hiding inside.

(During his speech the STAGE ASSISTANTS *cross to the back of the hut unobtrusively and untie the curtain. They hold the curtain and wait for the proper moment to lower it.* SHINDA *turns again to* LADY SENDA *and asks her permission to stay.)*

Gracious lady, if your patience will permit it, we would like to stay right here.

*(*LADY SENDA *shows no sign that she agrees. She moves slowly to the downstage corner of the dragon cave and sits.* SHINDA *moves to the upstage corner and sits. The* ATTENDANTS *lower the canopy frame, place it against the back wall of the stage, and kneel facing each other. The* STAGE ASSISTANTS *lower the hut's curtain slowly to reveal* IKKAKU SENNIN *sitting with right knee up and holding a fan in his right hand, which rests on his knee. He is an extraordinary sight as seen through the bamboo poles of the hut. His ornate brown-and-blue kimono is covered by a light overgarment of sheer black material. A leaf-shaped apron is tied at his waist. A huge black wig stands out around his face in great wisps. A single horn, fixed into the wig, protrudes from his forehead. He wears a mask with a face very old and gnarled but at the same time tender. His nonfolding Chinese fan is blue, gold, and orange. He is not frightening; rather, he gives the impression of wisdom. The* ASSISTANT *right passes the curtain of the hut to the* ASSISTANT *left, who exits with it through the small door left. The remaining* ASSISTANT *unobtrusively nudges* IKKAKU SENNIN *through the cagelike bars of the hut to cue him. In a deep, rumbling voice, which seems to come almost from thc ground,* IKKAKU SENNIN *tells* SHINDA *they should leave him to his solitary life.)*

Levels of sitting and kneeling indicate the rank of the character. Kneeling with the toes uncurled indicates a very low rank.

シテ仙人サシ上

（確カリ）瓶に谷漣一滴の水を納め。鼎には青山数片の雲を煎ず。曲終へて人見えず。紅上数峯青かりし。梢も今は。紅の秋の景色は面白や。

ワキ詞

（寛タリ）いかにこの庵の内へ申すべき事のわ。

シテ

（重ンモリ）不思議やここは高山重畳として。人倫通はぬ所なり。そも御身は如何なる者ぞ。

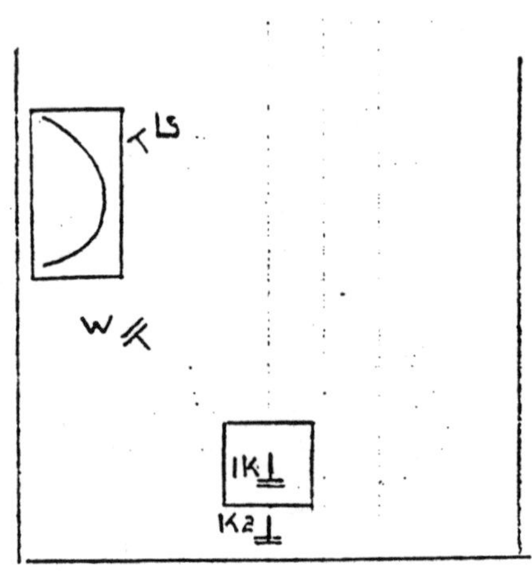

IKKAKU SENNIN (*SHITE*)
I scoop water from deep streams with my magic gourd, I call forth all my art,
I lift up clouds that have folded over forests,
and I make them boil swiftly,
then I play music.
But I play alone.
The mountains rise up high above river banks.
Green leaves suddenly become the color of blood.
I play music and I play alone in autumn.

(On the last two lines of IKKAKU SENNIN*'s speech* LADY SENDA *and* SHINDA *rise from their portion, kneeling on one knee, pivot slowly toward the hut, and move forward one step.)*

SHINDA (*WAKI*)
Listen to me, listen, this is a traveler, we have lost our way and we want to speak to you.

IKKAKU SENNIN (*SHITE*)
Who's there?—I thought I would be free in these mountains,
I thought I would be able to escape from the human race,
and now someone comes—
O please leave, please leave, as fast as you can.

Directors Kita and Tomoeda never mentioned characterization. When an actor asked questions about how they should feel about their character — or an action, or what were the acting aspects of the plot, one or the other would simply answer, 'That is a Western question.' The response always got a chuckle from the actors, but they found it frustrating. The actors did what American actors know. They incorporated into their style of acting internal monologues for the characters.

Kita-sensei referred often to yugen. *When questioned he told his actors that the word yugen was untranslatable, that there were no Western words for it. One actor interpreted it as 'spirit', 'depth', 'soul'. It could also mean 'grandeur' or 'beauty'.*

ワキ

（サラリ）これはただ山路に踏み迷ひたる旅人なるが。日もやうやう暮れかかり前後を忘じてわ。一夜の宿を御貸しわへ。

シテ

（重ンモリ）さればこそ人間の交はりあるべき所ならず。とくとく帰り給へとよ。

ワキ

（サラリ）そも人間の交はりなきとは。さては天仙の住家やらん。まずまず姿を見せ給へ。

シテ

（閑カメ）この上は恥かかながらわが姿。旅人にまみえ申さんと。

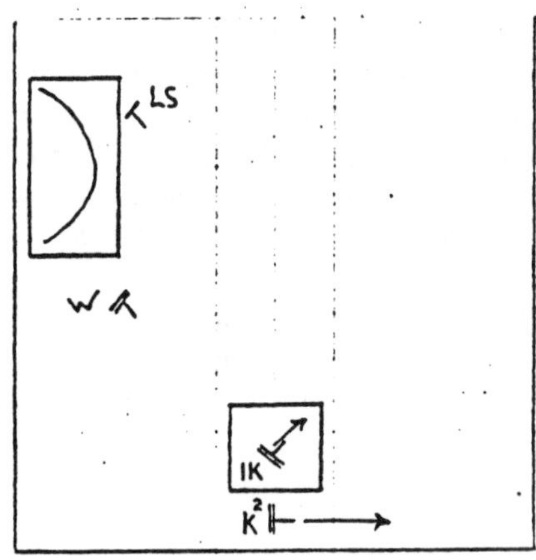

SHINDA (*WAKI*)
(Pleads to be allowed to stay.)
No, listen to me, listen, we are travelers and we are lost,
and the sun is setting,
and the road is dark,
so won't you let us spend the night right here?

IKKAKU SENNIN (*SHITE*)
No no, I told you to go, this is no place for you to stay, so go, I say you should go far from here.

SHINDA (*WAKI*)
(*Adamant.*)
You say this is no place for us to stay, and is that because the holy hermit unicorn lives here?
Come out, I say, so we can see your face!

IKKAKU SENNIN (*SHITE*)
(As yet motionless.)
I am getting up, I am coming out of here,
I am going to show myself to all these travelers!

The mask worn by the Hermit *has only a small hole centered in each eye. Due to the weight of the wig and the single horn, the eyes of the mask tended to be lower than the actors eyes. The actor is able to see, but only with no peripheral vision. This lose of peripheral vision aids in making deliberate head movements, because the head may not be jerked around losing awareness of where one is. The actor can only see by moving the head and body at the same time. The* 'eye-fixing pillar' *helps the actor orient himself onstage.*

The foot of the actor is never to be lifted to step — even after a short pause or after standing still for a long time. Stamping the foot or stepping over a door sill did require lifting the foot; to do so the heel had to be higher than the toes and the sole of the foot was never to be seen. The actor's are never straight — as in Western dancing. Knees should suggest an elastic quality. What guides movement is the power that prevails around the hips and stomach.

In rare Noh plays — when a gentlemen pays a visit to a lady at night and suddenly it starts raining and it is pitch dark, the Noh performer does not lift the toes. Thus, he shows he's searching the way and travelling fast. All other times the actor has to lift the toes.

上歌同

（ウケテ閑カメ）柴の枢を推し開き。柴の枢を推し開き。立ち出ずるその姿。緑の髪も生ひのぼる牡鹿の角の。束の間も仙人を。今見る事ぞ不思議なる。

ワキ詞

（カツテサラリ）唯今思ひ出だしてわ。さては承り及びたる一角仙人にてぼ座わか

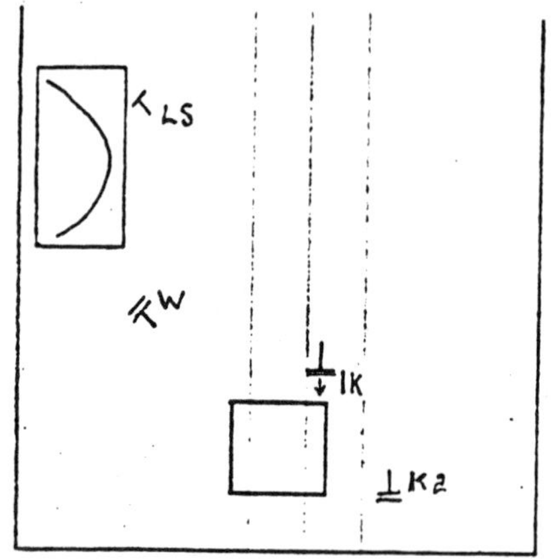

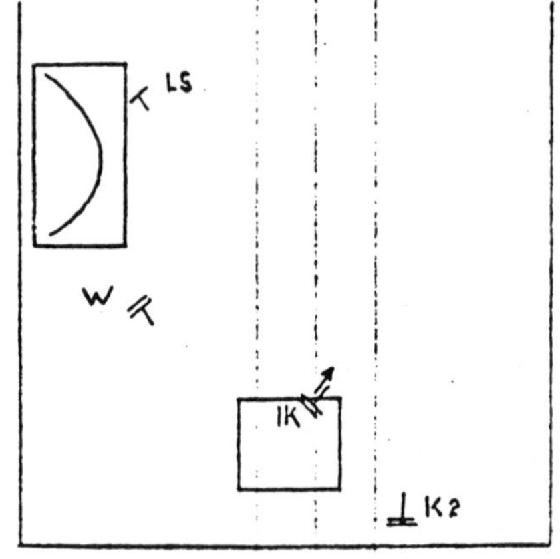

(Slow music of flute and drums. As the CHORUS *begins to sing with an almost sinister feeling,* IKKAKU SENNIN *slowly rises and opens the bamboo gate to the hut. He steps out, and his robe is adjusted as he does so.)*

CHORUS

(Offstage.)

He takes the great grass gate and swings it
to one side,

(MUSICIANS *inject cries of "Iya," and we hear drums whack.)*

he takes the great grass gate and swings it
to one side,
now he is aroused—
look, look at his face!
Black hair snarled on his proud brow,
a single long horn sprouting out of his
forehead.
See how he stands here — if he disappeared
we would still see him stand here,
strange and wonderful!

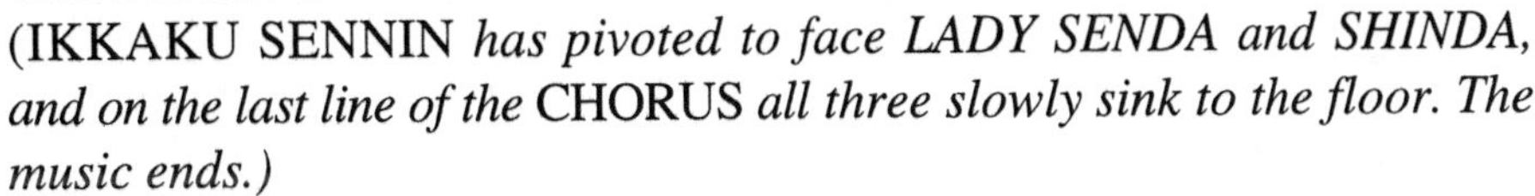

(IKKAKU SENNIN *has pivoted to face LADY SENDA and SHINDA, and on the last line of the* CHORUS *all three slowly sink to the floor. The music ends.)*

SHINDA *(WAKI)*

Are you the hermit we have heard about,
which they call the holy hermit unicorn?

The actors weren't able to count the music — Western style. To the American actors the Japanese seemed to have been born with a feel for the music — or Noh actors had learned it through years of training.

The American performers had to master it by listening to it — forgetting about counting it. The actors found it worked pretty well by listening to the music over and over at rehearsals. They gradually learned to move to the music and where the drum beats increased in tempo. For them the drum beats were sign posts along the way — that is for the actor to be in a certain position on the stage executing a particular gesture. Through repetition it was possible for them to be on target.

シテ

（閑カニ）さんわこれこそ一角と申す仙人にてわ。さてさて面面を見申せば。世の常の旅人にあらず。さも美しき宮女の貌。桂の黛羅綾の衣。更にただ人とは見え給はずわ。これは如何なる人にてましますぞ。

ワキ

（サラリ）さきに申す如く。踏み迷ひたる旅人にてわ。旅の疲れの慰みに。酒を待ちてわ。一つきこし召されわへ。

シテ

（確カニ）いや仙境には松の葉を好き。苔を身に着て桂の露を甜め。

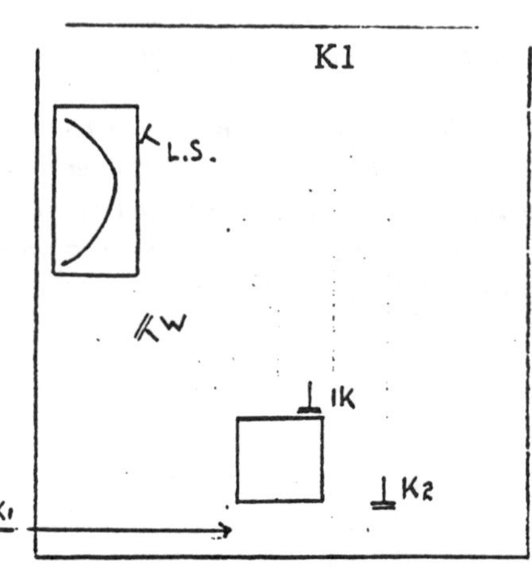

IKKAKU SENNIN (*SHITE*)

I am ashamed to say it
but I am he, Ikkaku Sennin.
Tell me, who is this beautiful young girl, and
tell me, why is one so fair on this rough
road?
She should be found at court, some sort of
princess—O the grace
that gazes from his smiling eyes,
she is like the silent sky,
or like the sweet peace of the deep sea,
she is not like the people of this world.
Travelers, you must tell me, who are you and
why have you come here?

SHINDA(*WAKI*)

O now, we are no one you would ever notice,
we are only strangers who got lost.
Here is some sake which we brought along
with us, to cheer us up on our long journey.
My lady kindly offers it to you, so
do take a cup of this fine wine!

IKKAKU SENNIN (*SHITE*)

We hermits prefer to eat the needles of pine
trees, the clothes we wear are made of moss,
and we do not drink anything but dew.

The legs are bent — in most of the movements. Buttocks are stuck out, creating a small dip--a little 'U' in the actor's back. The stomach — laced in by the sashes of the costume makes the actor appear to be overweight, for the stomach protrudes.

When movements are executed correctly, the illusion is that the shoulders are moving smoothly on an even keel. Shoulders are never to bob up and down. This coupled with the gliding steps of the actor creates a wonderful and fascinating effect since the toe comes slightly upward as the feet slide along. Even if the steps are taken very rapidly, the toe has to lift.

Kita-sensei *talked mostly about gesture and movement — their quality. He had little to say about the reading of lines.*

幾年経れども不老不死のこの身なり。酒を用ゆる事あるまじ。

ワキ

（サラリ）尤も仰せはさる御事なれども。ただ志を受け給へと。（スラリ）夫人は酌に立ち給ひ。仙人に酒を勧むれば。

シテ詞

（ウケテ閑カメ）げに志をしらざらんは。鬼畜にはなほ劣るべしと。

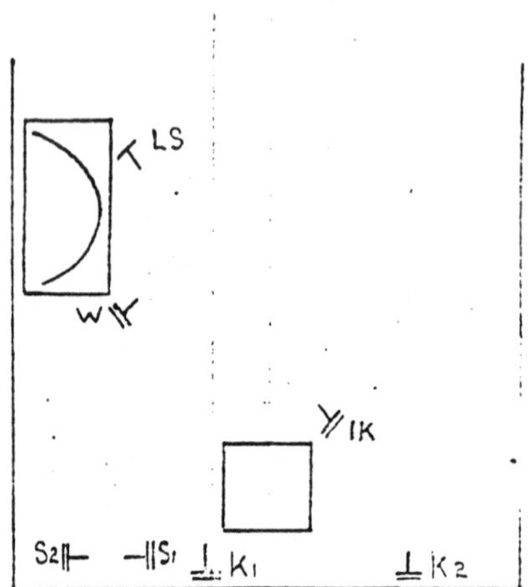

If my lady asked it as a special favor.

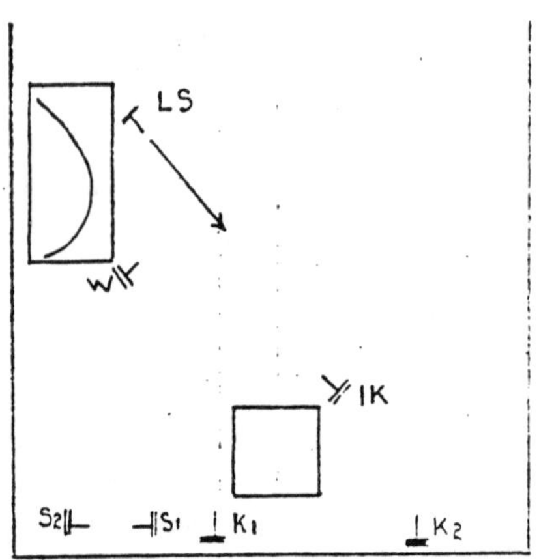

The beautiful girl rises...

IKKAKU SENNIN (*SHITE*) —Continuing—
Year after year, we do not age, we do not
change, we do not even die.
And that is why I say I do not want your
sake.

SHINDA (*WAKI*)
(Appealing to the HERMIT*'s innate courtesy.)*
You say you do not want our sake, but then
(He pivots on his knee to indicate LADY SENDA.*)*
would you take just a little if my lady asks
it as a special favor?

LADY SENDA (*TSURE*)
*(*LADY SENDA *opens her fan, holds it horizontally in front of her to represent the sake, rises, and takes a few steps toward* IKKAKU SENNIN. *In a clear, light voice she speaks her only line in the play.)*
The young girl rises, rises to pour out some
wine,

(*TSURE*)
she urges the hermit to try some sake.

IKKAKU SENNIN (*SHITE*)
(Unable to resist her beauty and charm.)
When travelers ask a favor, how can anyone
refuse?
—impossible, only the devil would say no.

The actor portraying Lady Senda *does use his own masculine voice. He does not strive to pitch it higher or make it seem feminine; he seeks to find gradations of pitch comparable to those that the Noh actor uses (such cannot be notated).*

In rehearsal the Lady Senda *imitated Tomoeda's delivery. The actor spoke of it as slipping and sliding along the pitch. This, on the only line:* 'The young girl rises to pour out some wine,' *—urging the* Hermit *to drink the sake.* Lady Senda *uses a fan to mime pouring the sake (in Noh, the fan can be an all-purpose prop, symbolizing a lot of things.*

In a small turn the heels are always on the floor. The heel never leaves the deck of the stage. To advance the heels do not come together.

Movements are based upon a long sliding walk. There are variations of gestures as hands are gripped in front of the body — arms and fists up or down. The Noh vocabulary of gesture is limited. But within that the actor can portray a lot.

同上

（引立テ、朗カニ）夕べの月の盃を。夕べの月の盃を。受けるその身も山人の折る袖匂ふ菊の露。うち口ふにも。千代は経ぬべき契りはけふぞ初めなる。

ツレ女

（サラリ）面白や盃の。

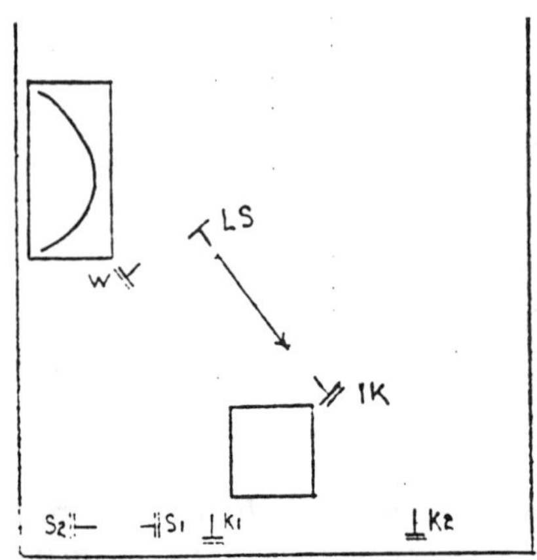

The hermit reaches out....

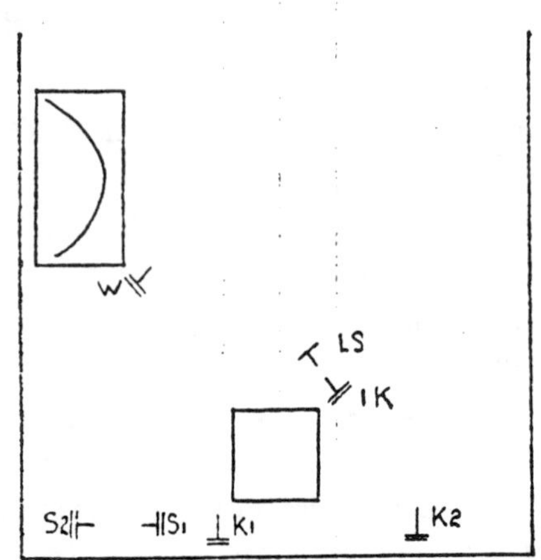

(Sake pouring)

(Music begins. As the CHORUS *sings its song of wine to the haunting melody of the flute,* LADY SENDA *crosses to* IKKAKU SENNIN. *She kneels beside him, pantomimes—with her fan—pouring him some wine, then opens the fan and sweeps it up and out to the side in a wide, graceful arc.)*

CHORUS

A cup of wine is like the moon in the night sky,
a cup of wine is like the moon in the night sky.
The hermit reaches out and takes the cup of wine,
just as a hermit once plucked a chrysanthemum,
the dew dropped down to the ground.
O that was so long ago, so long ago,
but I will love you for that long.

(As there are no realistic movements in Noh, only a slight nod of the HERMIT*'s head indicates he has drunk the wine after raising his body from the low stool on which he has been resting and which the* STAGE ASSISTANT *now quickly removes. A moment later the* HERMIT *drops his left knee to the floor abruptly, and we realize he is now intoxicated.)*

IKKAKU SENNIN (*SHITE*)

(Singing.)

O blessed ecstasy, the cup of wine!

The actor is to strive for the right heel to be in front of the left toe. He is to turn in the left toe by twisting it in twenty-five to thirty degrees.

Each character has his own way of getting there — in his own rhythm. Each has his own 'voice'.

Kita-sensei *gave to the actors a splendid acting image:* 'Put your thought out in space and draw your body to the thought.' *(The actors found it a wonderful idea for a way of acting.)*

The pillar at the corners of the stage enables the actor to gauge in space where he is on stage. He will find it easy to go right off the edge of the stage executing some of the moves. He cannot see the edge of the stage. Lady Senda *had many steps where she had to rush forward and stop suddenly. As* Lady Senda, *the actor oriented himself by keeping aware of the waki pillar — downstage actors left. It was well over on stage where for much of the play Lady Senda had sat. The acting of the role is summed up as mental concentration, physical tension, and footwork.*

同

（サラリ）面白や盃の。廻る光も照りそふや。紅葉襲の袂を共に翻し翻す。（ツヨク）舞楽の曲ぞ。面白き。（スラリ）糸竹の調めとりどりに。糸竹の調めとりどりに。

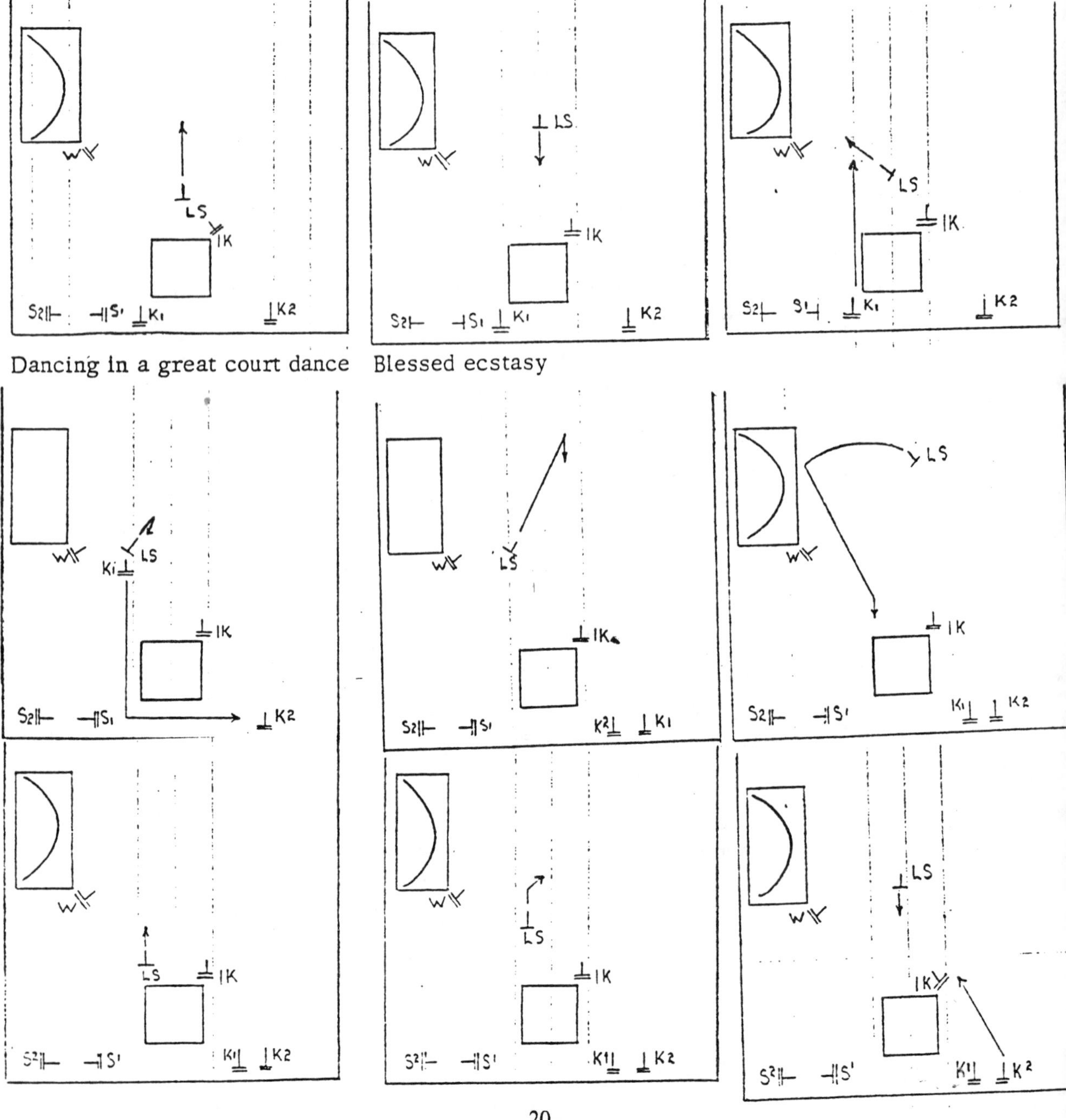

Dancing in a great court dance

Blessed ecstasy

CHORUS

(Continues the song of praise.)

O blessed ecstasy, the cup of wine!
—it is like the moon that circles in the night
sky,
Red leaves on the autumn hills,
see the silk sleeves.
Two leaves move,
like two sleeves that are dancing together,
dancing in a great court dance,
blessed ecstasy.

(Music begins and accompanies LADY SENDA*'s danced seduction of the* HERMIT. LADY SENDA *slowly rises from her kneeling position and crosses down center. There she bows ceremoniously, bringing both arms overhead. The music of the flute begins as she slides her feet smoothly on the mirrorlike floor. Her arms flow in beautiful movements, manipulating her fan. She dances alone until the* CHORUS *again is heard, accompanied by the dynamic sounds of the big drum. The* HERMIT *watches her seductive dance, and when she begins a second variation of steps, he rises to join her, always slightly behind in tempo. They dance together, sometimes in unison, sometimes in opposition.)*

Dance to the music of flutes, dance to the
flute music.
Dance to the music of flutes, dance to the
flute music.

In Lady Senda*'s dance of seduction there were differing kinds of foot stomps: soft, loud, louder; there were gradual increases in speed, followed by decreases in speed — all with sliding movement. It was found that any number of steps — slides — may be taken to arrive at a certain point at correct timing. This was the only* 'ad libing' *allowed.*

Lady Senda's *Dance*

さす盃も。度度廻れば夫人の情に心を移し。仙人は次牙に足

弱車の廻るもただよふ舞の袂を片敷き臥せば。夫人は喜

び官人を引き連れ遥遥なりし山路を凌ぎ。帝都に帰らせ。

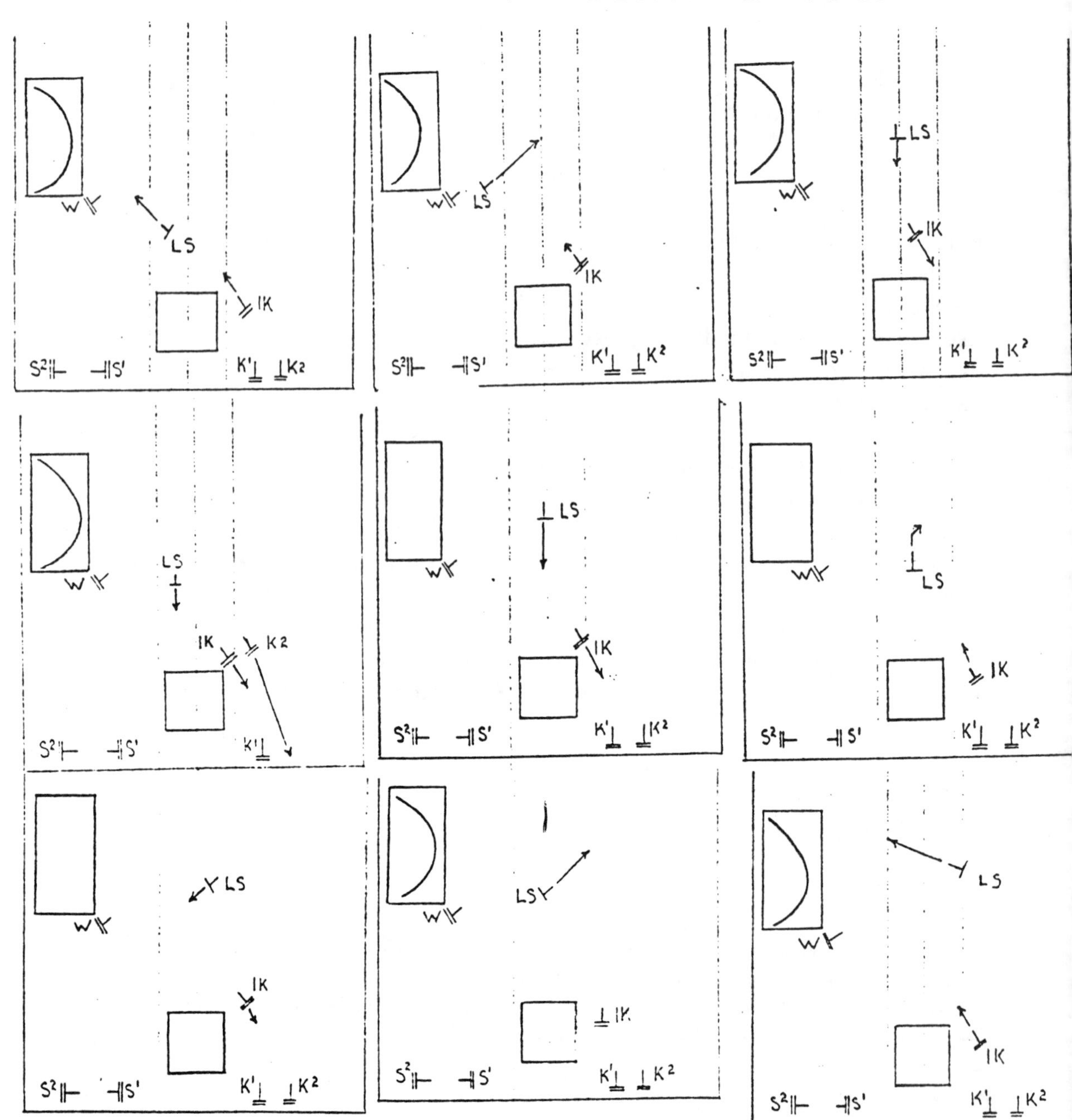

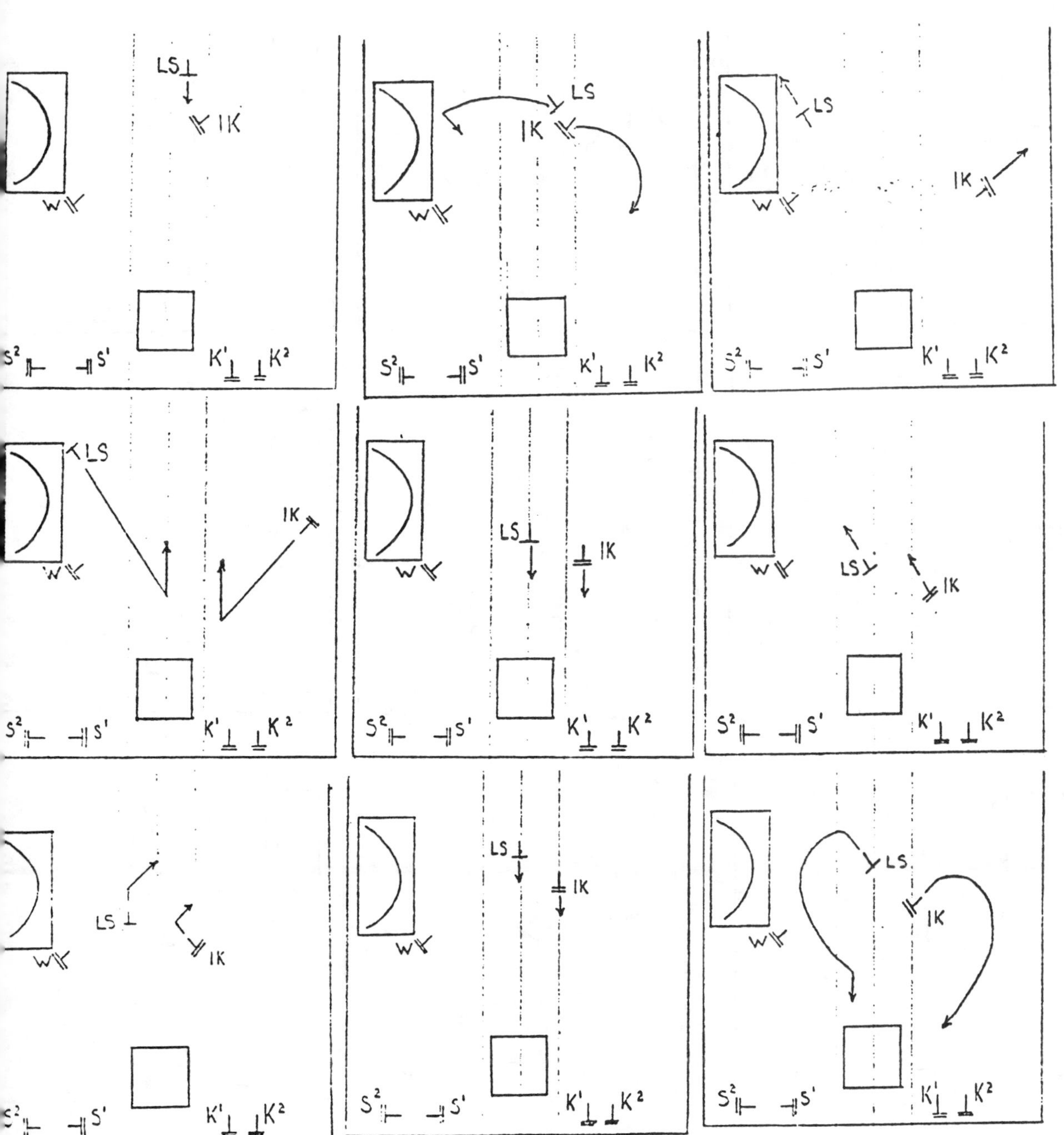

LS
IK
W
S²
S'
K'
K²

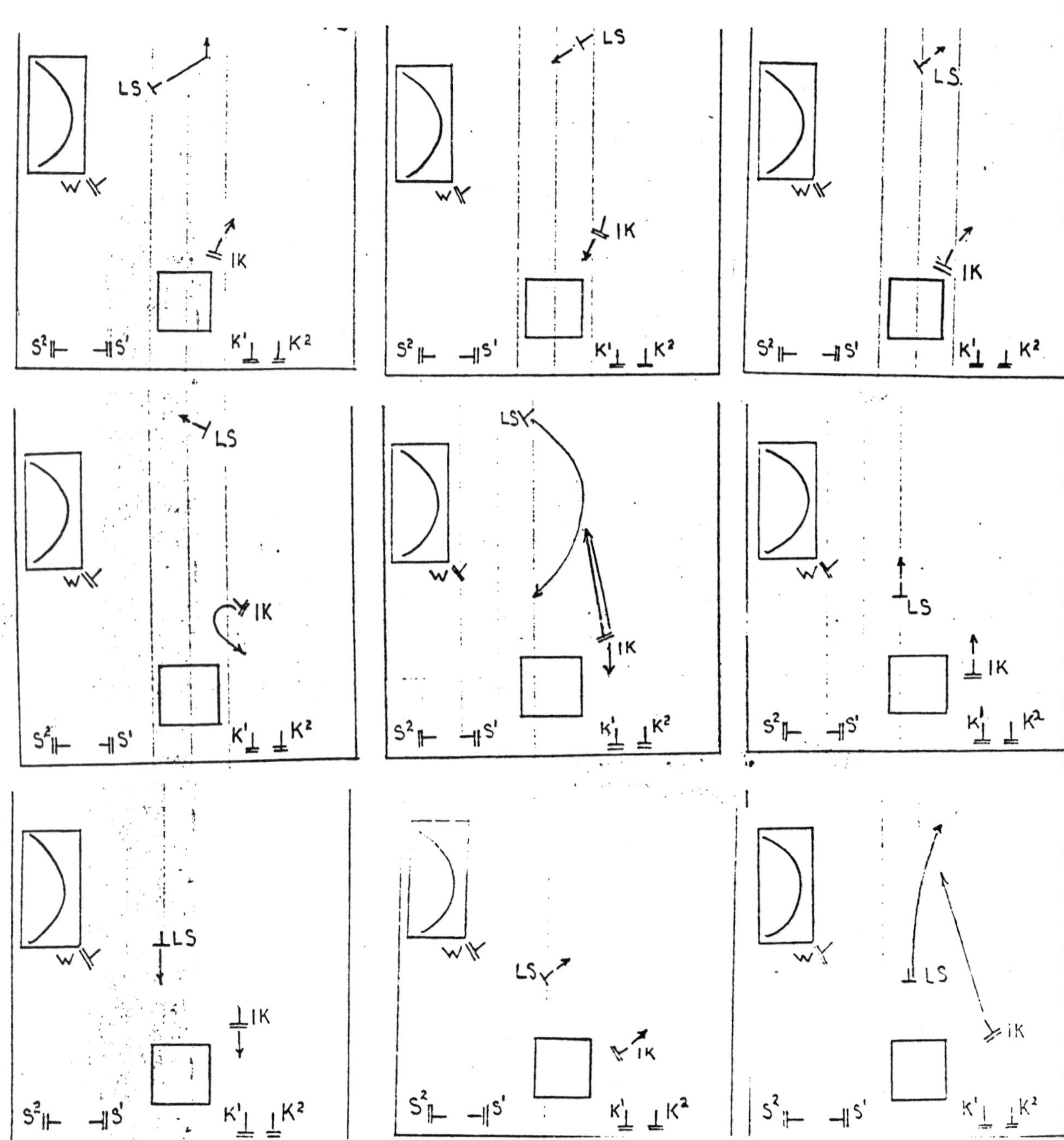
LS
W
IK
S²
S¹
K¹
K²

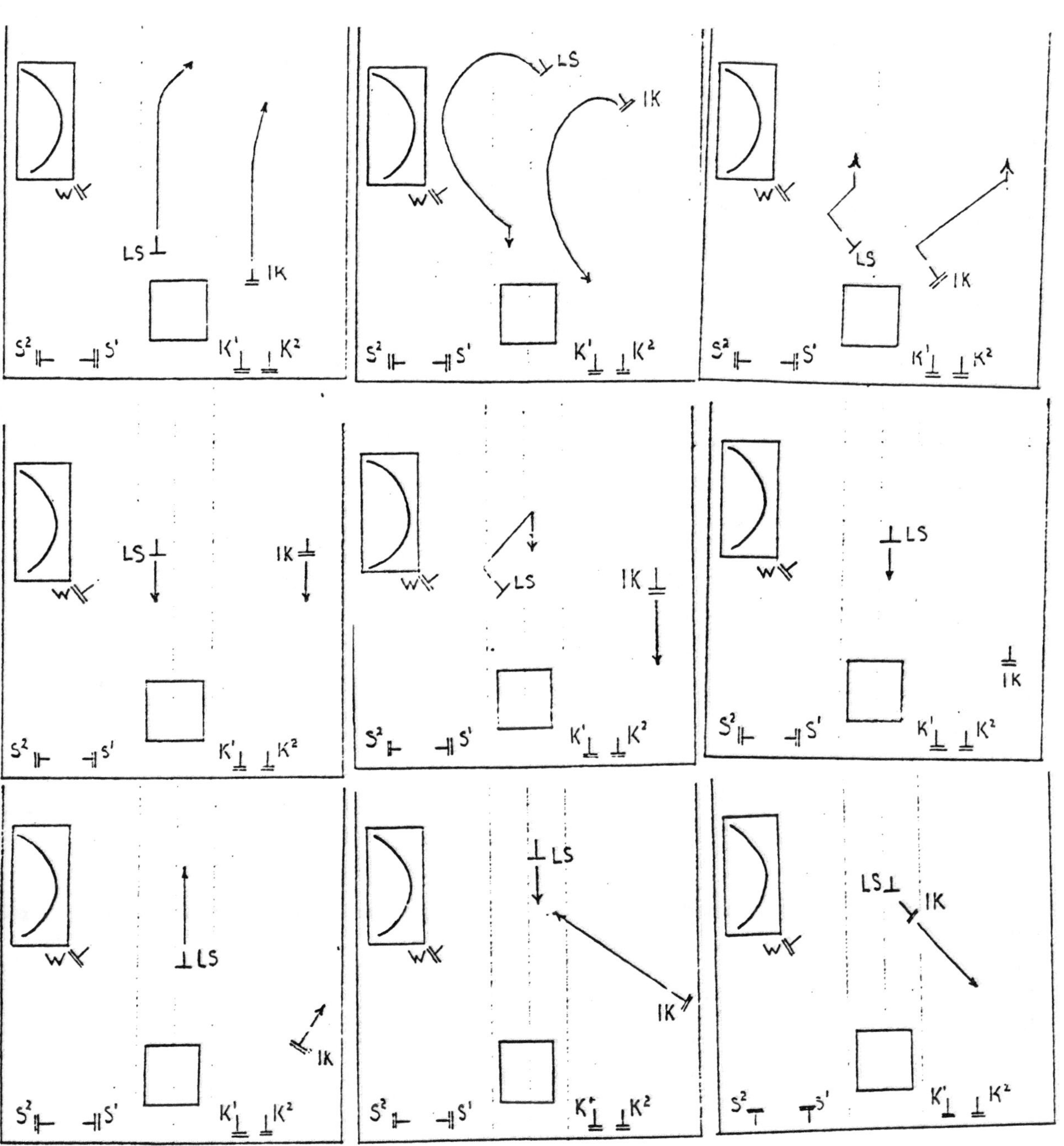
W
LS
IK
S²
S¹
K¹
K²

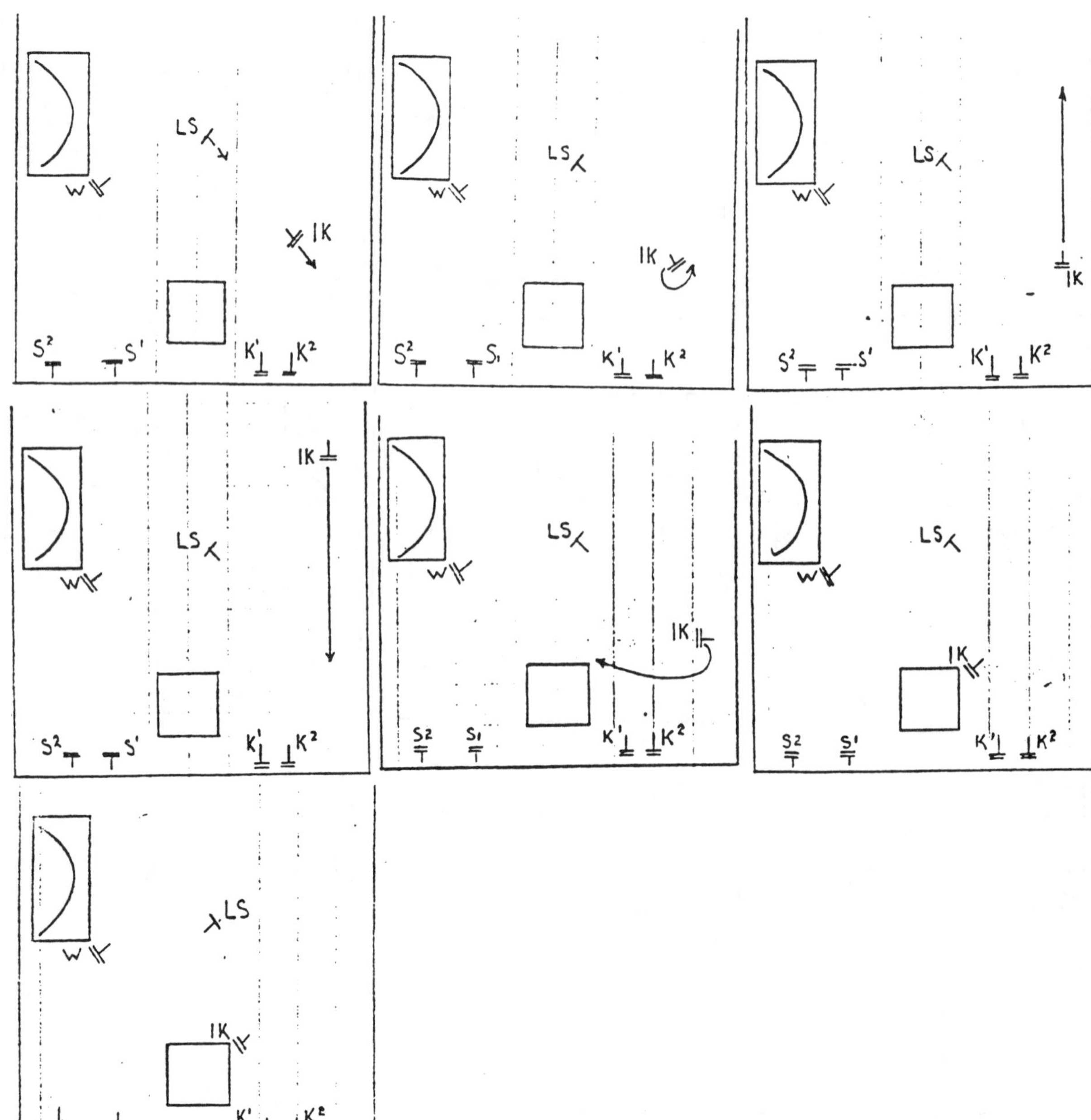
LS
W
IK
S2
S1
K1
K2

CHORUS —Continuing—
Pass the cup around, around, pass the cup
around, around.

(At the critical encounter of the dance the WIZARD *places his left hand across the breast of* LADY SENDA*; she repulses him by stiffly lifting her right arm. The* WIZARD *staggers backward, then forward again; then he goes into a spin, takes two turns, and sinks to his knees. He raises his right arm so that the* kimono *sleeve covers his face, symbolizing that overcome by love and* sake, *he has fallen into a stupor.)*

The hermit has fallen in love, he has fallen
in love.
See, his feet have grown weak, and see
how the hermit is beginning to falter and fall,
he keeps turning in circles,
now he wraps his sleeve around him
and he sleeps.
The beautiful young girl is pleased,
she tells eversone to come away
and they all go down the mountian, they go
down the rough mountain road,
until they are already at the court of the
prince.

When the Hermit *crossed to* Lady Senda *and put his hand on her shoulder the actor had been directed to execute a small movement forward with the arms. The actors inner monologue (*which he had devised*) was* 'Watch it!', 'Here I come to get you.' *When the actors executed stomps, as directed, his inner monologue was:* 'Take that!' *These acting thoughts enabled the actor to keep it alive.*

During rehearsals of Ikkaku Sennin *for the revival in Denver,* Kita-sensei *said to the same actor who had played* Lady Senda, 'I am pleased. I am to give you a present. Now when the *Hermit* comes to *Lady Senda* — rather than just touching the shoulder — he is to come and put a hand clear over to what would be *Lady Senda*'s left breast.' *For Noh, this was highly sensual.*

The Hermit *has a fan: when he's lost his magical powers due to his imbibing the* sake, *instigated by* Lady Senda, *his dropping of the fan symbolizes his loss of control over the* Rain Dragons. *His austerities had given him this power.*

In Noh the fan is used as an extension of the hand. Whereever the fan went, the actor followed. The tip of the fan is aligned with the center of the body when the arm is in a forward position.

給ひけり。（手強クサラリ）かかりければ岩屋の内頻りに鳴
動して。（大キク）天地も響く。ばかりなり。

シテ上

（手強クサラリ）あら不思議や思はずも。人の情の盃に。酔
ひ臥したりしその隙に。龍神を封じこめ置きし。岩屋の
俄に鳴動するは。何の故にてあるやらん。

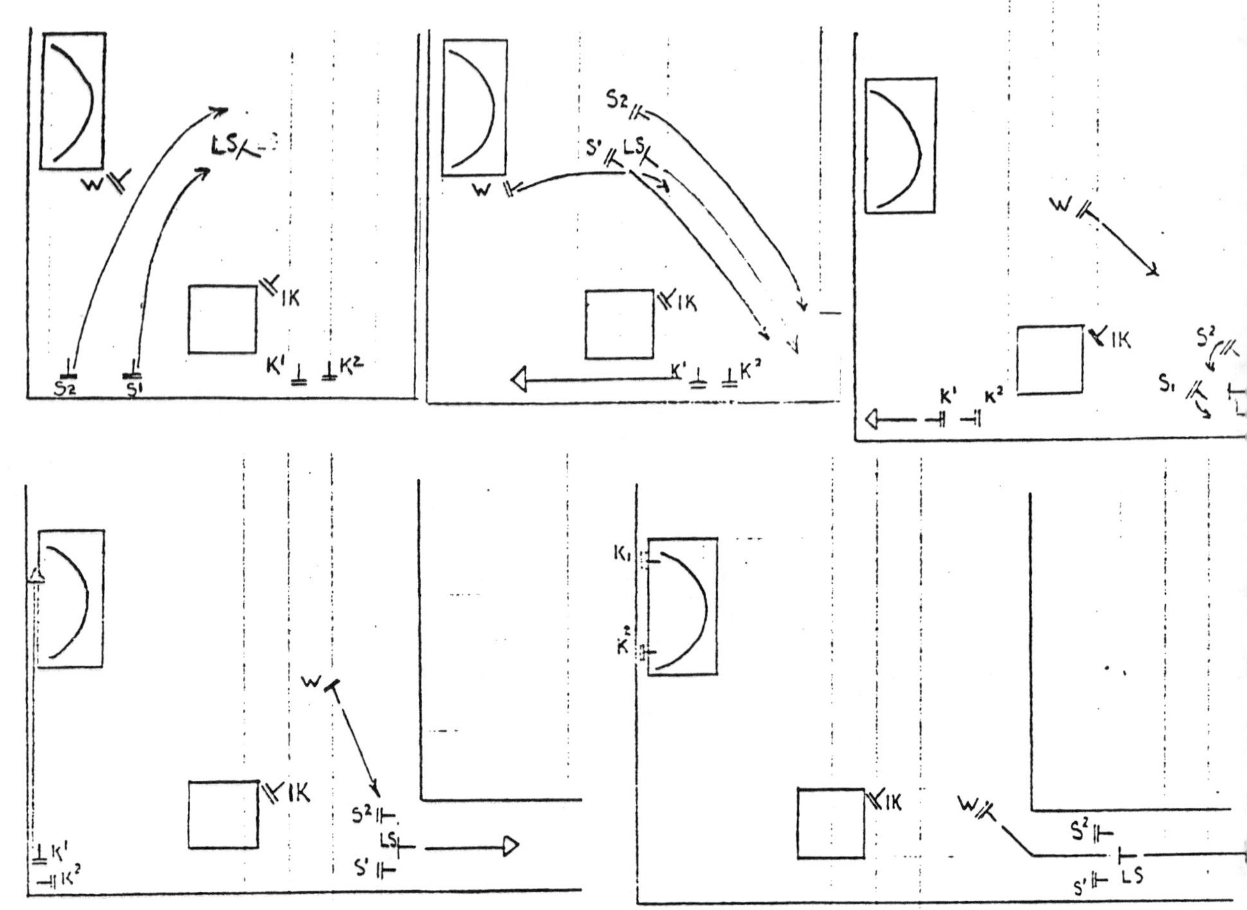

(Quickly LADY SENDA *closes her fan and turns upstage to* SHINDA. *The* ATTENDANTS, *having risen when the* WIZARD *began to falter, cross down to her and raise the canopy frame over her head. They all turn and move onto the passageway. There they pause momentarily, then cross swiftly off as the passageway curtain is lifted for their exit. The music ends. Suddenly there is a loud "thwack" of the drum, and the* WIZARD *awakens. The* STAGE ASSISTANTS, *who moved behind the rock cave when the procession went off, quickly untie the tapes that hold the two pieces of rock together and stand ready to push them apart.)*

CHORUS

Rumble rumble rumble, where is it coming from?
Rumbles thunder from deep inside the cave,
rumbles cause earthquakes and make all creation shake.

IKKAKU SENNIN (*SHITE*)

(Kneeling, turns toward the cave and reproaches himself for his weakness.)

Why have I been sleeping, sleeping all this while?
—it was the wine, it was the beautiful young girl,
it was the need for some sleep.
Rumble rumble rumble, something's wrong,
there's thunder coming from inside the cave,
there where the dragon gods are kept captive.
Rumble rumble rumble, something's wrong,
what is it?

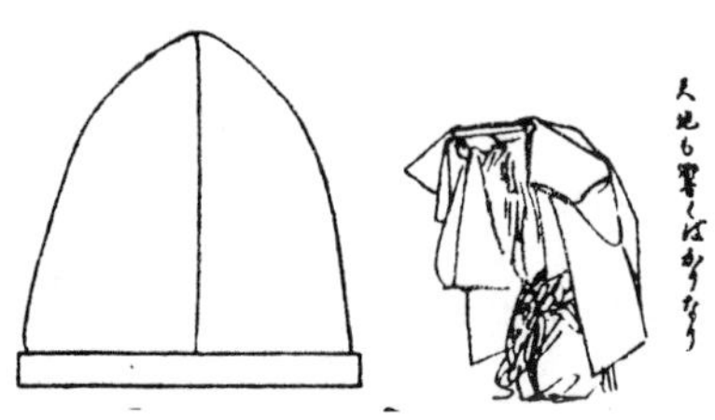

Kita-sensei wanted the tabi-clad feet to look like white fish floating freely in a pond. At the same time the performers were asked, while moving, to create heat between the foot and the deck of the stage through pushing fiercely into the flooring. This would not negate their appearing to be white fish floating freely. This also created an illusion for the audience that the feet had never been lifted off the stage. The only time the foot was lifted from the deck of the stage was at the time of a stomp.

子方龍神天上

（サラリ）いかにやいかに一角仙人。人間に交はり心を迷はし。無明の酒に酔ひ臥して。通力を失ふ天罰の。報いの程を思ひ知れ。

同上

（確カニ）山風荒く吹き落ちて。山風荒く吹き落ちて。空かき曇り。岩屋も俄かに揺ぐと見えしが磐石四方に破れ砕けて。諸龍の姿は。現れたり。

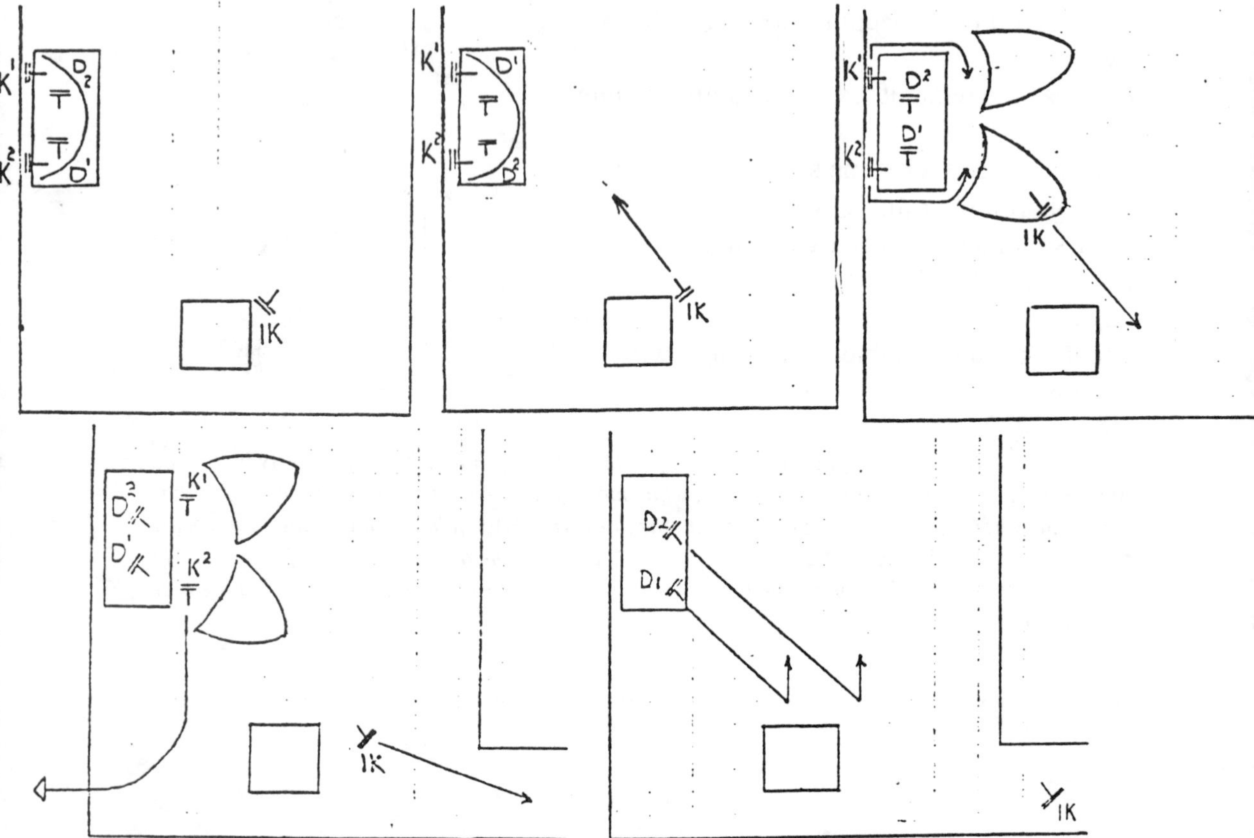

DRAGON GODS

(*Unseen within the cave.*)

Holy hermit unicorn,
you were dancing with humans,
and you let yourself get lost in lust,
and you confused your mind with wine.
No wonder now you do not know you are undone,
no wonder now you have no power.
Unicorn, you are about to lose the magic
that you used to use.

(They vigorously announce that the WIZARD, *having succumbed to human temptation, has lost his power over them. Ending their chant with his name, they almost sing in elongated syllables. Music for their dance begins.)*

(IKKAKU SENNIN *rises, advancing to the center of the stage, a sight cue for the* STAGE ASSISTANTS *to push apart the two pieces of the rock cave in what seems to be an explosion.* IKKAKU SENNIN *retreats up right to the edge of the passageway as the rock falls to the floor and is swept up and carried off through the small door left by the two* STAGE ASSISTANTS. *Two* DRAGON GODS *jump off the platform and move upstage center. They are an impressive sight with their flowing red wings topped with dragon headpieces. They wear dragon masks and carry wands. Jackets of blue and gold and wide, split trousers of orange and gold are worn over their* kimonos *— one of green, orange, and white and the other of orange, blue, and white. They begin an exciting and militant dance of strong, sweeping movements. Symbolizing heaven and earth, they raise their wands majestically, then turn, swoop down on one knee, and point their wands to the floor. They circle the stage in unison, always retaining three feet of space between them. In a final diagonal cross they move from up right to the platform and leap onto it, then turn to face the* WIZARD. IKKAKU SENNIN *speaks the final words of the play, intoning his self-doubt, stamping once for emphasis.)*

The Noh actor who wears a mask never stands with his head held straight, the chin up. The chin always has to be down a little — making a slight double-chin. He never looks straight out. There is always a suggestion that he is looking down; thus, the mask is seen fully by the audience.

The actor in Noh never does free open movement. He is always pushing against air as if the air were heavy. This makes the relatively short Noh performance very exhausting.

シテ

（手強クサラリ）その時仙人驚き騒ぎ。

同

（ウケテサラリ）その時仙人驚き騒ぎ。利剣をおつとり立ち向へば。龍王は黄金の甲冑を帯し。玉具の剣の刃先を揃へ。一時が程は。闘っひけるが。仙人神通の力も尽きて。次牙に弱り。倒れ伏せば。

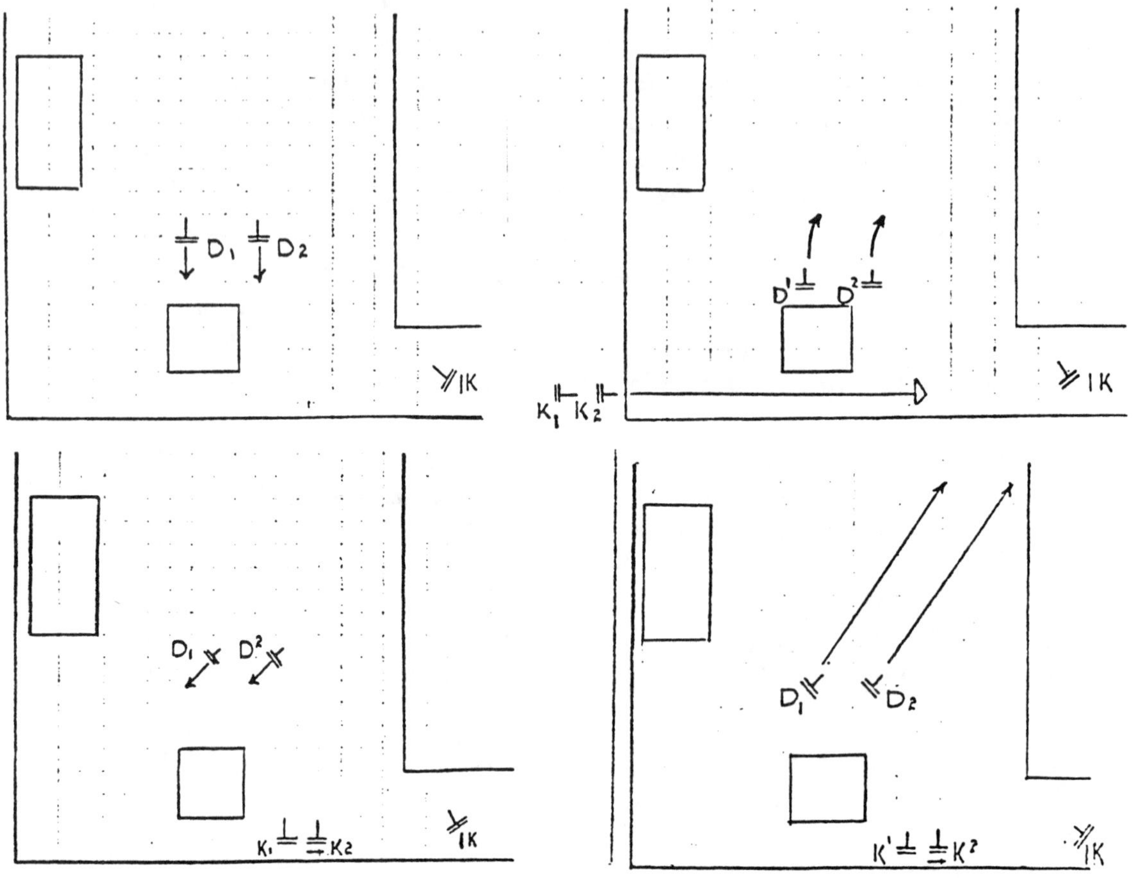

(Symbolizing heaven and earth, they raise their wands majestically, then turn, swoop down on one knee, and point their wands to the floor. They circle the stage in unison, always retaining three feet of space between them. In a final diagonal cross they move from up right to the platform and leap onto it, then turn to face the WIZARD. IKKAKU SENNIN *speaks the final words of the play, intoning his self-doubt, stamping once for emphasis.)*

CHORUS

Listen, listen to the wind, to the wind
whistle.
Listen, listen to the wind, to the wind
whistle.
See the darkness of the sky.
Earthquake breaks the cave, breaks the cave,
boulder stones thrown down to the ground.
Rocks that block the great cave are all cast
aside in a landslide.
Behold O holy hermit, here are the great
dragon gods!

IKKAKU SENNIN (*SHITE*)

Now, holy hermit unicorn,
I do not know what to do.

CHORUS

Now holy hermit unicorn, he does not know
what to do.
He takes a sword and he goes toward the
great dragon gods.
The dragon gods are in the armor of their
own real rage.
They create a few naked blades to use on
the unicorn.Now they hit and hit and hit, and now it is
all over.
Holy hermit has now lost his heart and art
and all his magic.
He goes round and round 'til he drops down
on the ground.

Each gesture is done with physical tension. Movements with the hands — raised — are done slowly. The raising of the right hand is a very simple gesture, but again it has to be done with tension as if the hand were pushing air.

龍王喜び雲を穿ち。雷鳴稲妻天地に満ちて。大雨を降らし。洪水を出だして立つ白波に。飛び移り。立つ白波に。飛び移つて。また龍官にぞ。帰りける。

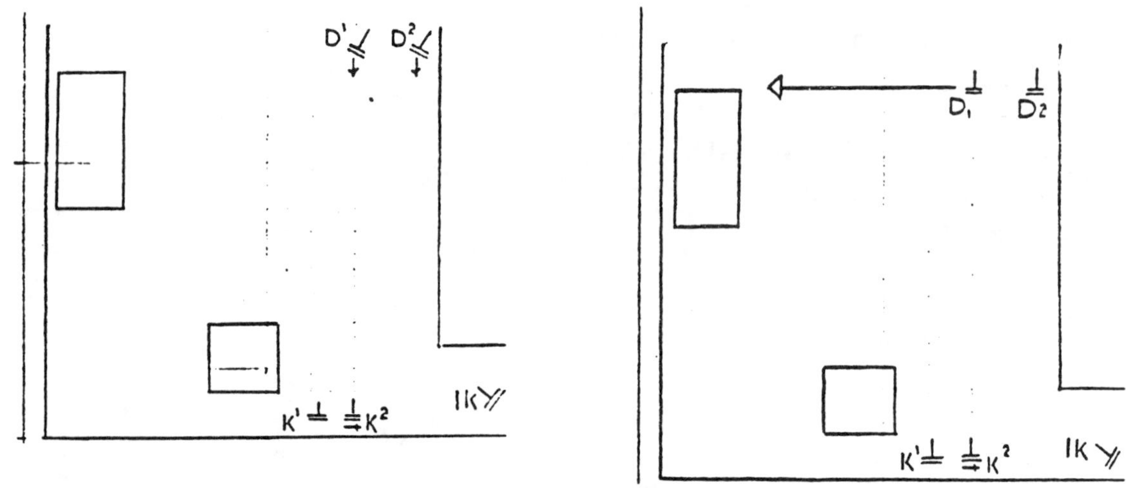

CHORUS —Continuing—
Now the great dragon gods call together all the rain clouds.
Now there is rumbling thunder, now there is brightness of lightning,
and it rains and rains and rains,
the great dragon gods make it rain.
Then they tly through the sky and over the ocean,
then they fly through the sky and over the ocean.
The great dragon gods return to their great dragon home.

(The HERMIT *accepts the challenge of the* DRAGON GODS. *The music becomes faster.* IKKAKU SENNIN *pivots by the passageway, receives a short wooden sword from a* STAGE ASSISTANT *at the same time that he passes the* ASSISTANT *his fan, and without breaking the flow of his movement, moves toward center stage. The* DRAGON GODS *leap from the platform to the stage; they cross the* HERMIT*'s sword with their wands.* IKKAKU SENNIN *fights courageously, but he cannot defeat them. To rapid beating of the drum, in a "big rhythm," he backs falteringly upstage. He drops to one knee and lets the sword fall from his hand. In an instant a* STAGE ASSISTANT *moves in to pick it up and carry it off left. The* WIZARD *crosses to the passageway, defeated. On the passageway, and considered to be invisible, he moves swiftly off as the curtain is lifted for his exit.)*

The costumes aid this type of movement characteristic of Noh, for the embroidered robes are weighty; the actors are bound with sashes into the costumes. Two dressers are ever on hand to assist the actor into his costume. Several layers of kimono-like robes are held in place with obi sashes. The audience never sees the robing of the actor which is done precisely according to time-honored ritual. The elaborate under-garments, put on in layers are highly embroidered and expensive, but the audience sees only an inch of each. The Noh actor would not be able to dress himself.

The most difficult thing in Noh is how to move with resistance and to avoid the appearance of chopping. Kita-*sensei advised that the Hermit sustain at all times tension and feel in the space in which he moves is from here to here. By moving with all his might the actor feels as if his heels are burning. This too is very difficult to do without making choppy movements.*

Triumphant, the Dragon Gods *dance to bring the rain that will end the drought.*

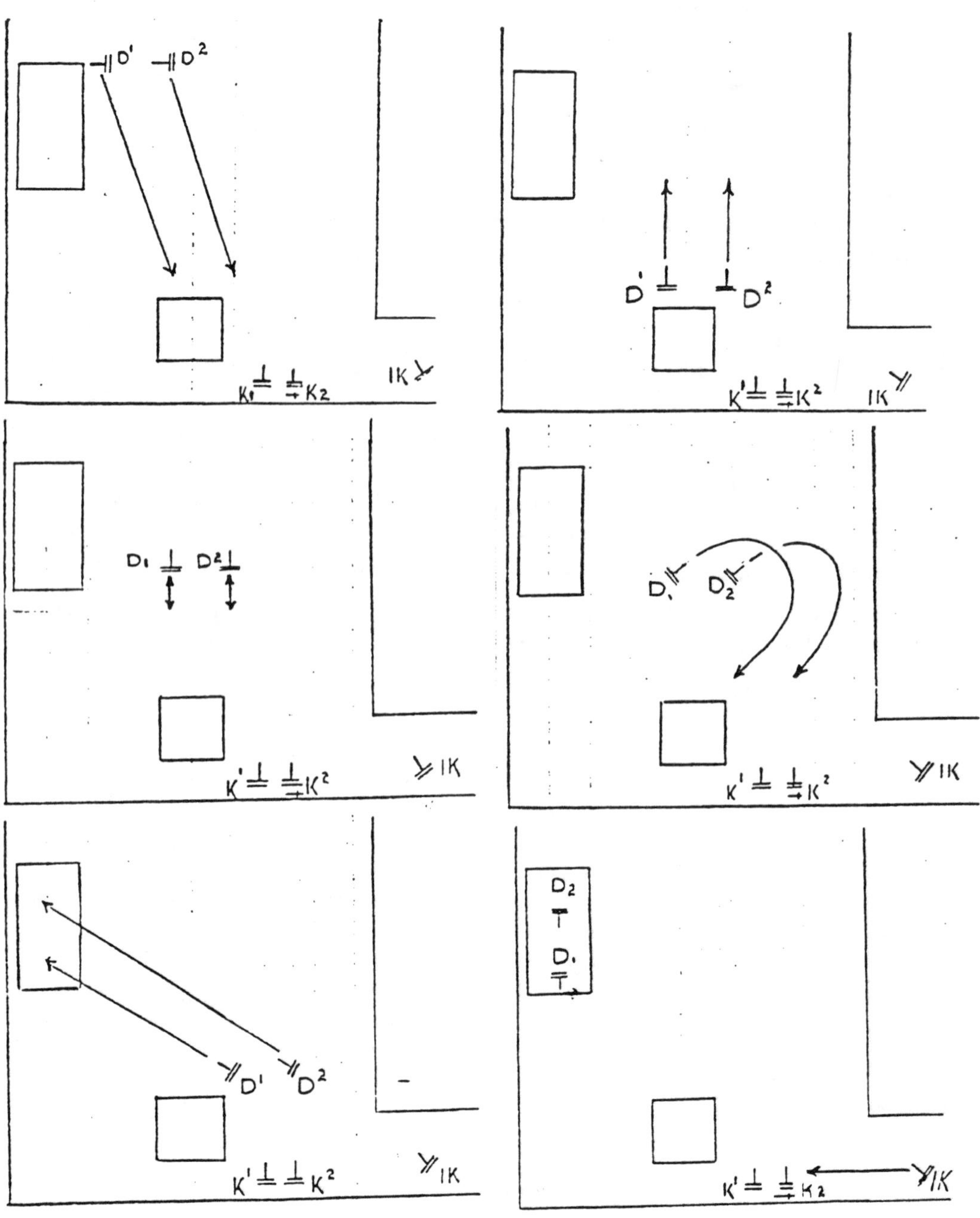

The Dragon Gods *swoop across the stage.*

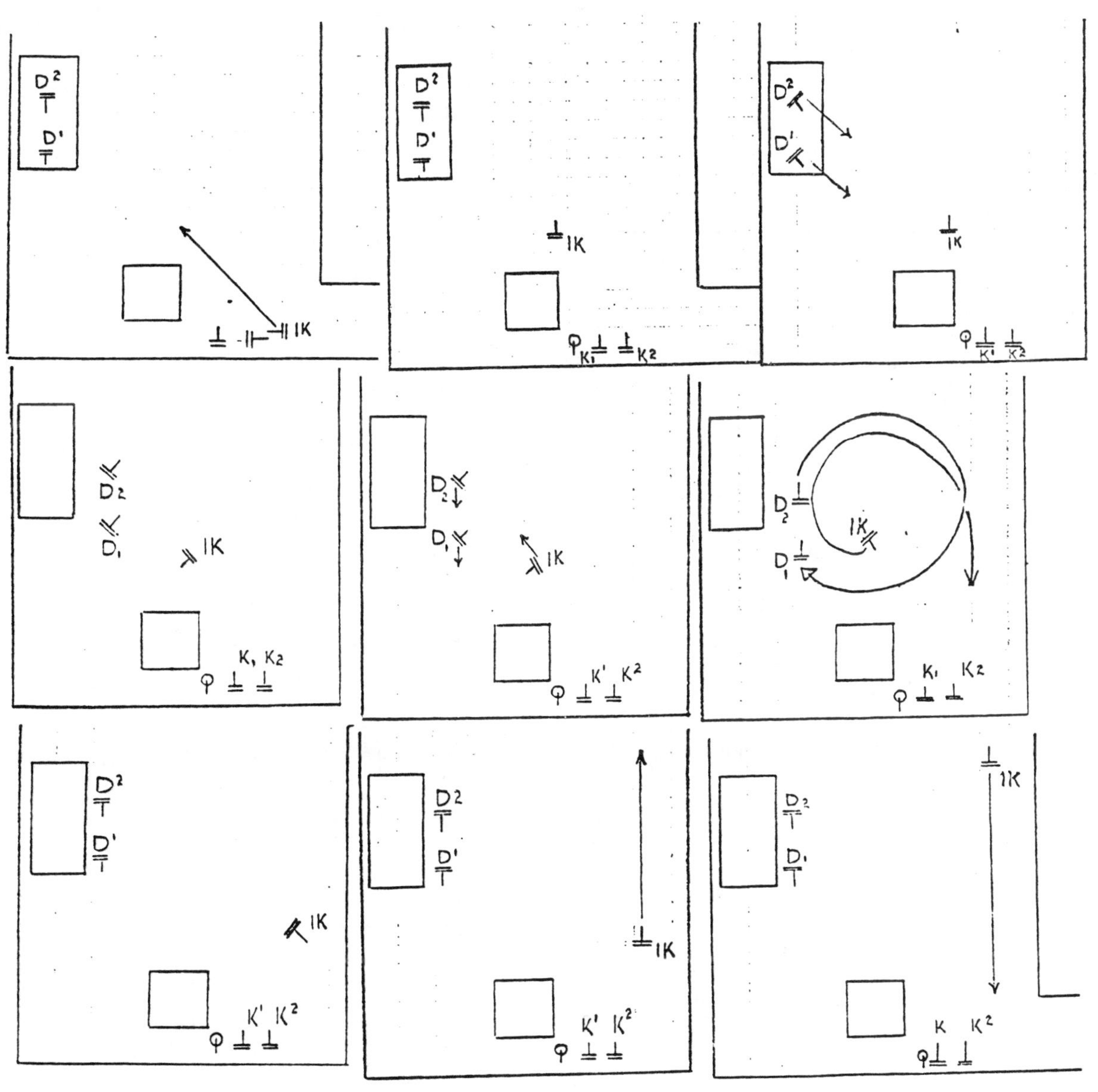

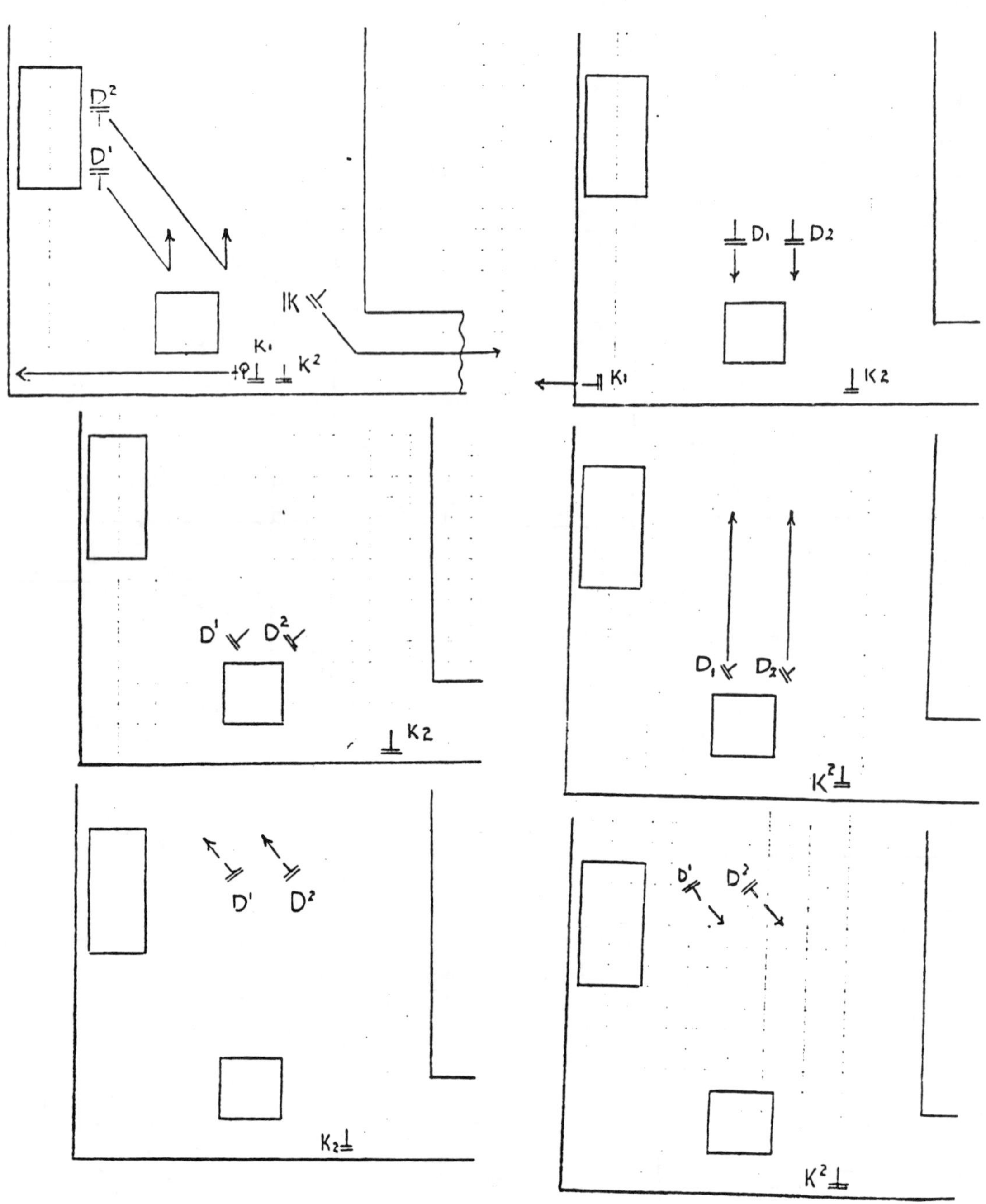
D²
D'
K
K₁
K²
D₁
D₂
K₁
K2
D' D²
K2
D₁ D₂
K²
D' D²
K₂
D' D²
K²

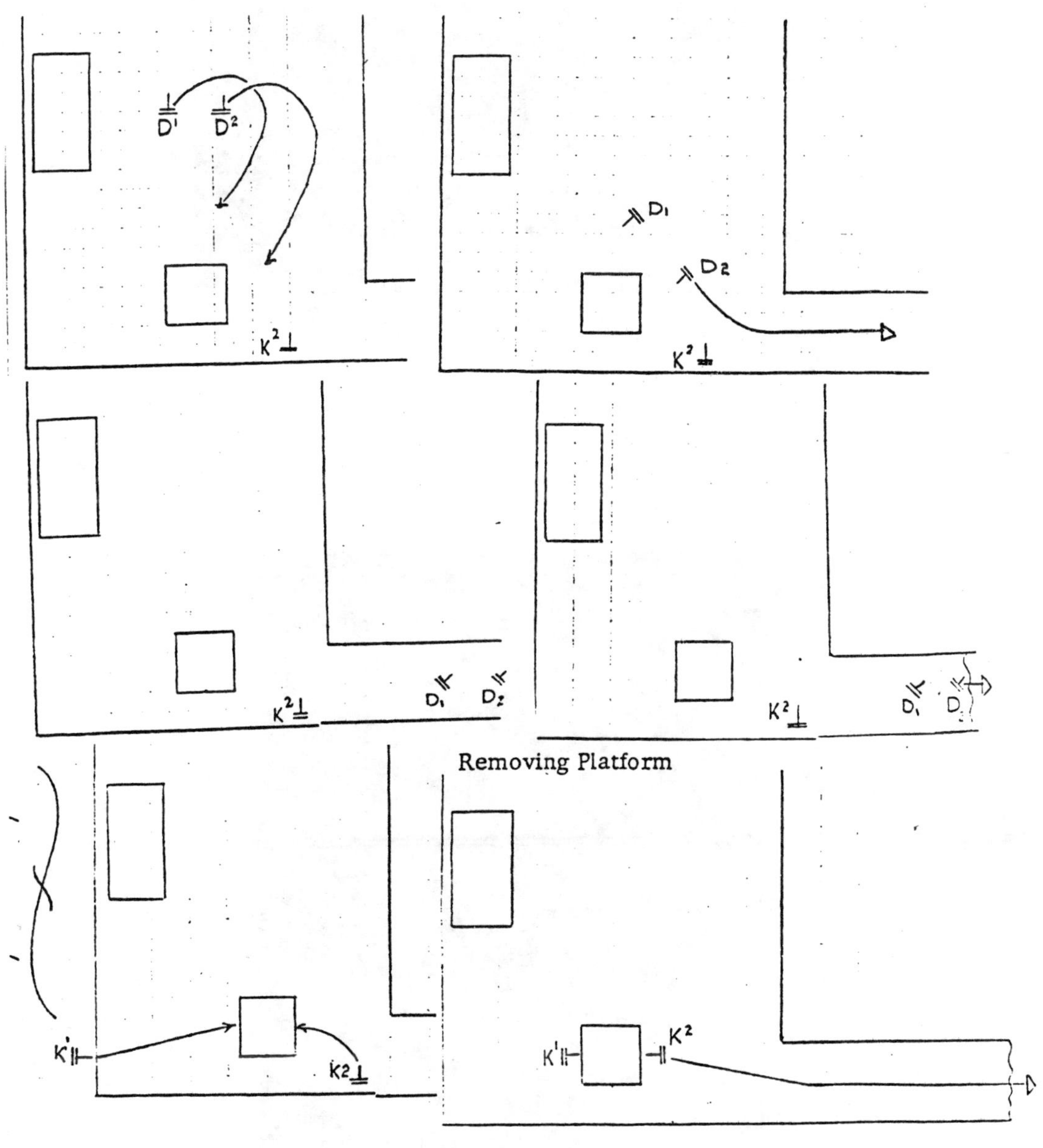
D¹
D²
K²
D₁
D₂
K²
K²
D₁
D₂
K²
D₁
D₂
Removing Platform
K'
K2
K'
K²

Finally the Dragon Gods *cross to the passageway as if flying through the skies. They stop at the third small pine tree. They stamp, signifying the end of the dance. Then they jump, turning in the air, as if leaping into the sea and returning to their dragon home. They raise their left arms and flip the sleeves up and over to hide their faces, in a movement which symbolizes their invisibility. The music ends with a flourish of the flute and the final cries of the* MUSICIANS, *"Iya-o-o,iya-o-o!" The* DRAGON GODS *turn, and as the passageway curtain is raised for them, exit in silence.*

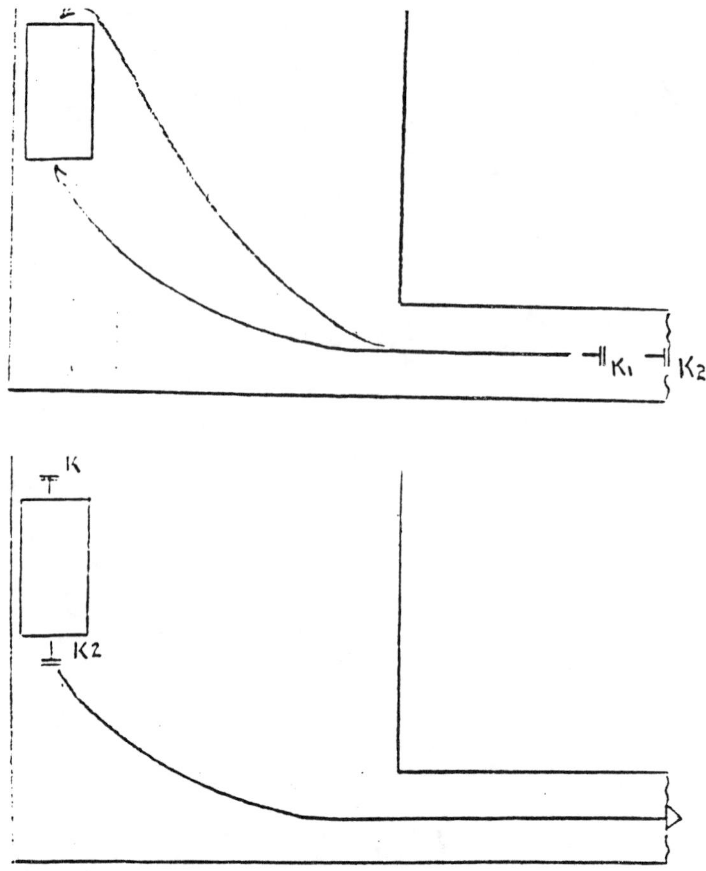
K1
K2
K
K2

The props are now removed in view of the audience and with no music. The STAGE ASSISTANT *who had exited with the* HERMIT*'s sword re-enters, and together the two* ASSISTANTS *lift the hut and carry it off down the passageway. They re-enter and remove the platform the same way. The play is finished. There are no curtain calls.*

In Japan the Dragon Gods *are likely to be performed by child actors without masks. Adult actors, as the* Dragon Gods, *wear masks. They need to make sure — on the return movements — to know where the platform is, for the masks make it difficult to locate where it is.*

For the Dragon Gods *to make the leaps, they must jump like a cat. If they lunge, they appear too heavy.*

Frank Hoff Version	Japanese in Roman Alphabet
I serve a great prince of India who rules lands along the Ganges.	kore wa Tenjiku Barana Koku no teiõ ni tsukaetatematsuru shinka nari.
In our princes country lives a hermit. He is a wizard.	Sate mo kono kuni no katawara ni Sennin ari
He was born from the womb of a deer and has a single horn, one long single horn sprouting up out of his forehead.	shika no tainai ni yadori shyusshõ shitaru yue ni yori, hitai ni tsuno hitotsu oiidetari.
This single horn gives him his name. They call him *Ikkaku Sennin*, "the herrnit with the single horn."	kore ni yotte sono na o Ikkaku Sennin to nazuku.
An affair of honor came up between the wizard and the dragon gods.	saru koto arite Ryujin to i o arasoi
The wizard got the upper hand. He had magic powers on his side.	Sennin, no jinzũ o motte
He drove the dragon gods into a cave and locked them up tight.	shoryu o iwaya ni fũjikome okitarishi ue ni
But the dragon gods bring the rains, so with them locked up tight like that inside, there has been no rain for a number of years now.	sũnen ame kudarazu sõrõ.
The prince is grieved to have his land languish in drought.	Mikado kono koto o nageki tamai
So he's been trying everything he can to free the dragon gods.	iroiro hõben o megurashi sõrõ
Now he's come up with this scheme.	Koko ni Sendabunin tote narabinaki
The girl riding here is a beauty without peer. That you can see.	bijin no goza sõrõ o
He wants her to be taken for a traveler who's lost her way.	fumi mayoitaru ryojin no gotoku
That's the impression he wants her to give the wizard once she has made her way, along with the three of us, up into the mountains where he lives.	senkyõ ni wake iri tamawaba

The idea is that he'll fall in love, lose his heart and with it his magic powers.

kano bunin ni kokoro o utsushi, jinzũ o ushinoubeki to no go hõben ni yori,

That's the prince's plan and why we're accompanying her now up into the haunt of the mountain hermit.

tadaima Sendabunin no ontomo
mõshi
senkyo ni wakeiri sõrõ

kano
(*sashi*)

(The *waki-zure* join the *waki* in this travel song.)

Mountain upon mountain
Mists that swallow up travelers
cold winds that roar down over pine forests
No sweet dreams for us on the mountain side.
An uneasy rest is all we get on our way.

yama tõkushite wa
kumo kõkaku no ato o uzumi
matsu samũshite wa kaze ryojin no
yume o mo yaburu

karine kana
(*michiyuki*)

Mists and autumn rains
Pierce the deepest ravines
Drench the lowest leaves
Bring on autumn colors.
An autumn wind chills
Travelers on their way.
Our road lies through patches of mist.
Our road cuts across cloud banks that cling to the hillsides

tsuyu shigure
moru yamakage no
shita momiji
moru yama kage no shita momiji
iro sou aki no
kaze made mo
mi ni shimi masaru tabigoromo
kirima o shinogi
kumo o wake,

No sign of which way's right.
Deep in the mountains
Helplessly
We wander lost.
Where does it lead
Where does it lead, this road we travel?
(*waki*) Day after day we've hurried on our way.
But the truth is we only get more and more lost, traveling a mountain road that leads ... who knows where?

tatsugi mo shiranu
yama naka ni
obotsukanakumo
Fumimayou
michi no yukue wa ikanaran
michi no yukue wa ikanaran
isogi sõrõ hodo ni
izuku to mo shiranu sanchu ni
wake iri sõraeba

What a strange looking mound of rocks.
How sweet a smell the wind carries away from it. What an odd hut made of pine and *katsura* branches.

fuku kaze kõbashiku shõkei eda
o musubitaru iori no sõrõ

Could this be the place where the hermit lives?
Let's look around.
Let's inspect it from up close.

moshi kano senkyõ nite mo ya
sõrõran.
shibaraku haikai shi
koto no yoshi o ukagabaya to
zonji sõrõ

(The *shite*, the wizard, speaks from within his hut.)

I scoop up water from deep valley streams in a gourd.
I boil clouds folded over pine forest hillsides in a caldron.
Sometimes I play from my own entertainment.
But when the music's over, still no one has come to call.
Mountains soar up beside the river banks.
When I look up . . . Lo!
Branches green just yesterday are suddenly crimson.
What a lovely autumn hillside.
(The following dialogue is between the *waki*, speaking as if into the hut, and the *shite*.)
(*waki*) Hello. Hello in there.
I want to speak to you.
(*shite*) Strange! Mountains piled up high on all sides. You would think this would be one place no human could get to. Go away, won't you. Go away.
(*waki*) We are travelers who have lost our way. The sun is setting. Already we can't make out one ridge from the next. Won't you let us spend the night here?
(*shite*) There you are. Just what you would expect. This is no place for men to come to. Off with you. Off as fast as you can.
(*waki*) You say this is no place for men to come to. This could be just the place, then, where the hermit lives. Reveal yourself. Come, show us your face.
(The *shite* takes the next two lines which describe his own getting up and coming out. His speech is then taken over by the chorus as he comes out of the hut. The device is a remnant of the narrative origins of the Nō.)
(*shite*)
Getting up, coming out of the hut I'll show myself to the travelers.
(*chorus*)
The grass gate
He swings it to one side
Rising, striding out . . .
Look his face!
Green hair tangled on the brow
In the midst sprouts up an antler.
He stands there

byō ni wa kokuren itteki no mizu
o osame
kanae ni wa shōzan suhen no kumo
o senzu
kyoku oete
hito miezu
kōshyō subō ao karishi
kozue mo ima wa kurenai no
aki no keshiki wa omoshiro ya
ika ni kono iori no uchi e
mōsubeki koto no sōrō
fushigi ya na koko wa kōzan jōjō
to shite, jinrin kayowanu tokoro
nari.
haya haya kaeri tamae
kore wa fumi mayoitaru ryojin
naru ga, hi mo yōyō kurekakari,
zengo o bōjite sōrō.
ichiya no yado o onkashi sōrae
sareba koso ningen no majiwari
arubeki tokoro narazu
toku toku kaeritamae to yo
somo ningen no kayowanu tokoro
to wa, sate wa senkyō ni ya
iritsuran.
mazumazu sugata o mamie tamae
ideide saraba tachiidete
ryojin ni sugata o mamien to
shiba no toboso o oshihiraki
shiba no toboso o oshihiraki
tachi izuru
sono sugata
midori no kami ni
oinoboru o shika no tsuno no
tsuka no ma mo sennin o

An instant only. But seeing him Oh wondrous sight!	ima miru koto zo fushigi naru
(*waki*) Are you the hermit we have heard about, the one with the single horn?	kore wa uketamawari oyobitaru Ikkaku Sennin nite watari sōrō ka
(*shite*) My shame, but true. I am "one horn."	hazukashi nagara ikkaku nite sōrō
That girl there. She is not the usual run of traveler you meet on the road. She's more like a lady you might find at court, some beautiful princess or other.	sate are ni mashimasu wa yo no tsune no ryojin ni arazu. samo utsukushiki kyujo no katachi,
Eyebrows like a crescent moon. All gossamer and brocades. No ordinary mortal. Who are you, travelers?	katsura no mayuzumi raryō no koromo sara ni tadabito to wa mietamawazu sōrō. ika naru hito nite watari sōrō zo.
(*waki*) No one special, just travelers who have lost their way. We have brought along some *sake* with us to ease the wear and tear of the road. Why don't you have some too. Here, drink up!	iya kore wa fumi mayoitaru ryojin nite sōrō tabi no tsukare no nagusame ni shu o mochite sōrō hitatsu kikoshimesare sōrae
(*shite*) No. Hermits prefer pine leaves. That's what we eat. Moss is what we use for dress. The dew that collects on the katsura tree is our drink. Year after year may pass, but we are always the same. No change. No getting old. No dying. We have no need for *sake*.	iya senkyō ni wa matsu no ha o suki koke o mi ni ki katsura no tsuyu o namete, toshi wa furedomo furō fushi no kono mi nari sake o mochiyuru koto arumaji
(*waki*) If you insist, there's no disputing. Still . . . if we ask it of you as a special favor, you can't refuse then, can you?	geni geni ōsewasaru koto naredomo tada kokorozashi o uketamae to
(The following line describing her own action is the only one taken by the *tsure*.)	
The woman rises to pour out wine. She urges the wizard to drink. She presses it upon him.	bunin wa shaku ni tachi tamai sennin ni shu o susumureba
(*shite*) not to give way when travelers ask a favor, I would be ungrateful beyond the devil himself.	geni kokorozashi o shirazaran wa kichiku ni wa nao otorubeshi to
(The chorus takes the following long passage except for a single line taken by the *shite* midway through it.)	
That was what he said.	
The moon in the evening sky is like a wine cup.	yūbe no tsuki no sakazuki o
The moon in the evening sky is like a wine cup.	yūbe no tsuki no sakazuki o
The hermit takes the cup.	ukuru sono mi wa yamabito no

Wasn't it a hermit in the poem once	
Who plucked the chrysanthemum?	oru sode niou kiku no tsuyu
And a sleeve all sweet with its scent.	
Brush away the dew nestled in the flower:	uchiharou ni mo
A single instant in their world	chiyo wa henubeshi chigiri wa
But a thousand generations pass in ours.	
I'll love you that long.	
Let my pledge begin from this moment.	kyo zo hajimenaru
(During the above song the *tsure* rises, goes over to the *shite* and mimes pouring out *sake* for him.)	
(*shite*) Ah pleasure.	omoshiro ya sakazuki no
Pleasure . . . wine . . . cup (*shite* rises)	
(chrous) What ecstasy.	
The wine cup passes round.	omoshiro ya sakazuki no,
Like it the moon goes round the night sky,	meguru hikari mo teri sō ya,
Its beams all shimmering.	
Crimson leaves on the autumn hills	momijigasane no
Glimmer under the moon.	
Ply upon ply of matched sleeves.	tamoto o
Red and deeper red.	
Two dancing together	tomo ni
Fluttering sleeves	hirugaeshi hirugaesu
A court dance	bugaku no kyoku zo
What ecstacy.	omoshiroki
(The *tsure* dances. Somewhere along the way the *shite* is carried off by the beauty of it all and joins the dance.)	
(chorus) The music of strings and of flutes accompanies their dance.	shichiku no shirame kazukazu ni
The music of strings and flutes accompanies their dance.	shichiku no shirame kazukazu ni
Piece after piece is played.	
Cups are passed round again and again.	sasu sakazuki no tabi tabi megureba
His heart is fixed in her utterly.	bunin no nasake ni kokoro utsuri
Gradually the hermit's dancing feet begin to tremble and falter	sennin wa shidai ni ashi yowaguruma no meguru mo
like a wagon with a loose wheel.	
Still he dances on	tadayou mai no
Until at last wrapping his still fluttering sleeve about him	tamoto o katashiki
He pillows himself down to sleep.	fuseba
The woman is pleased with what she has done.	bunin wa yorokobi
She calls the attendants off with her.	kannin o hikitsure
Passing together over the mountain road that	harubaru narishi yamaji o shinogi

seemed so endless in their coming	
Already they are back in the capitol.	teito ni kaerase tamai keri
(The *waki*, *tsure* and the attendants leave the stage. The *shite* is asleep on the floor.)	
(chorus) All the while rumblings could be heard coming one after another	kakarikereba iwaya no uchi shikiri ni meidō shite
deep from within the cave. Heaven and earth reverberate to the rumblings.	tenchi mo hibiku bakari nari
(*shite*) Strange! I became drunk with human passion and then, drowsy with wine, lay down to sleep for a while.	ara fushigi ya omowazaru hito no nasake no sakazuki ni, eifushitarishi
Now there is a rumbling and a thundering deep from within the cave where I locked up the dragon gods.	sono hima ni ryujin o fūjikometarishi, iwaya no niwakani meidō suru wa
What can it mean?	nani no ue nite aru yaran
(Two child-actors who soon appear from the "rock pile" dressed as dragon gods call out from within to the *shite*.)	
Oh, Ikkaku, Ikkaku the wizard.	ika ni ya ika ni Ikkaku Sennin
You consorted with men.	ningen ni majiwari
You abandoned yourself to lust.	kokoro o nayamashi
You let yourself become drunk with wine that confounds the will.	mumyo no sake ni eifushite
And you slept.	
You have lost your magic powers.	tsūriki o ushinou
Now, learn the punishment which heaven sends for your offense.	tenbatsu no mukui no hodo o omoishire
(chorus)	
Winds come whistling down the mountain in their fury.	yamakaze araku fukiochite yamakaze araku fukiochite
The sky is overcast.	sora kaki kumori
The cave is wrenched with a violent undulation.	iwaya mo niwaka ni yurugu to mieshi ga
Crags on all four sides are rent apart.	banjyaku shiō ni yaburekudakete
Out rush the dragon gods.	shoryo no sugata wa awaretari
(The "rock pile" breaks into two and they appear.)	
(*shite*) The wizard is aghast and trembles	sono toki sennin odoro sawagi ki
(During the following taken by the chorus there is very rapid dance or mime.)	
The wizard is aghast and trembles.	sono toki sennin odoroki sawagi
He snatches up a fine-edged sword to meet them.	riken o ottori tachi mukaeba
The dragon gods wear the armor of divine wrath.	ryoo wa shinni no katchu o taishi
They muster a row of naked blades,	jaken no tsurugi no hasaki o sōrō
swords to strike down the unbeliever.	
The fight lasts no time at all.	ichiji ga hodo wa tatakaikeru ga

The hermit has already exhausted his magic powers.	sennin jinzū no chikara mo tsukite
Little by little he flags until at last he drops to the ground.	shidai ni yowari taore fuseba
In their joy the dragon gods call together all the clouds in the sky.	ryoo yorokobi kumo o okoshi
In their joy the dragon gods fill all heaven and earth with the noise of thunder and the glimmering of lightning.	raiden inazuma tenchi ni michite
The heavens open and there is rain.	taiu o furashi
They pour out a deluge.	kōzui o idashite
Over the white caps of the sea they skip	tatsu shiranami ni tobi utsuri
Over the white caps of the sea they leap	tatsu shiranami ni tobi utsutte
And return to their dragon home at last.	mata ryugu ni zo kaerikeru

An attempt at Western notation

- 2 -
We would still see him stand there
Strange and
won - der ful......
SECOND CHORUS
Slow
A cu-p o----f wine is like the moon in the night
sk------y
A cup o----f wine is like the moon
in the night sky
The her-mit reaches out and takes the cup of

SECOND CHORUS (cont)
-3-
wi--ne Just as a her-mit--mit once plucked chry-san- the-mum
The dew drop-ped down to the grou---nd Oh that was so long a
go-----o So long a go, but I will love you for that lo--ong---.
Shite:
Chorus:
O bles-sed ecsta-sy the cup of------ wi----ne O bles-sed
ecs-ta-sy the cup of...... wi-------ne It is like.....
the mo-on that cir-cles in the night sky. Red leaves on the

au--------tumn--- hills
See the silk sleeves
two leaves move li--ke
tw---o sleeves that are
dancing to--ge--ther
(off key....
dancing in a great
court dance
Bless---ed ecs----- ta----sy ------------
THIRD CHORUS
Dance to the
mu--sic-- of
flu---tes dan--ce
to the
flute mu
.... sic................
Dance to the
mu--sic of

Third Chorus (cont)

bea--ti--ful young
girl is pleased she....tells ev'ry one....to
come a -way and
they all go down the
mountaintain they
go--
down.. the rough moun-tain road, un
til they are al---
rea------dy--- at
the....... court of
the prince.

The set for Narukami

Woodblock prints of Taema and Narukami

Kabuki

Theatre as Beauty of Form

A Note About This Adaptation

This English version of *Narukami* is an adaptation with minor changes and some freedoms in making the translation. Wisely, Miyoko Watanabe kept in mind that the text is for American audiences for whom the American actors were interpreting the Kabuki play. Rather than retain at times topical references, meaningful to a Japanese audience — Kabuki buffs — she chose an image or reference that was in the spirit of the original and lucid for Americans, actors and audience.

Onoe Baiko, as director and interpretor of the play was fully cognizant of these slight changes and approved heartily of them. He is a practical theatre professional.

A first and critical challenge was to make the Japanese lines of dialogue horizontal to match the English text on facing pages. There are diverse versions of *Narukami* — over the centuries different Kabuki actors contributed change based on their performances.

Getting the Japanese lines horizontal was possible thanks to Andrew Field, a wizard with a computer, and two Asian languages (credited in the Acknowledgments); he had a computer available with many different Japanese fonts.

My American actors told me there was always a great feeling of tradition in rehearsals; they did not question my direction. They felt, they said, the need and desire to become part of a tradition. Trained in Kabuki, I took a sharp interest in details, and as I had been trained from childhood, I asked them to copy my form. I learned that aside from dance training, this was an unusual procedure for American actors, but I was convinced it was necessary and was enjoyable for the actors. I knew exactly what I wanted in space, and I molded the actors into the patterns of the play. There is no room for improvisation in this style. I worked for visual perfection and a filling out of the emotions, but in my staging of NARUKAMI, *I left the creative process up to the actor — outside rehearsal. I wanted and demanded great precision of movement.* —Baiko

Onoe Baiko VII at rehearsal with his American actors.

INTRODUCTION TO KABUKI THEATRE

by

John D. Mitchell

Americans who had visited Japan before World War II, as well as those who participated in the occupation and administration of Japan after World War II, had become aware of a unique theatrical form known as Kabuki. In the late 1940s my awareness of Kabuki was through having been encouraged, by Dr. Carty of the Speech and Drama Department of Manhattan College where I taught, to see the *Azuma Kabuki Dancers* performing in New York City.

Some have disparaged that troupe of dancers with the designation Kabuki as being misleading; however, their performing, their costumes, makeup, and music made a deep and lasting impression on me. The *Azuma* troupe served as a valuable introduction for many Americans to a traditional Japanese theatre.

The memory lingered on, and I began to read whatever I could find that expatiated on this early multi-media theatre. The first book I wolfed down was by Faubion Bowers. It ranks high among the many books on the subject which I have read since. I single out the one book that is the very best on Kabuki: one by Earle Ernst.

Having co-produced with A. C. Scott, I cite as well his excellent books on Japanese theatre: they are three in number. They rank with his splendid books on Chinese theatre, specifically, Peking Opera.

My good fortune was to pursue western theatre. Each year through travel to Europe, I laid up experiences of seeing plays of Moliere, Shakespeare, Goldini, and Schiller; yet tucked away was a hankering to get to Asia and, most importantly, to Japan. I had read of Noh, had talked to the colleague whose master's thesis had been on that earlier form of Japanese theatre. It eluded me; it continued to be an enigma.

Not until 1954 was I able to set foot for the first time in Japan. A World Study tour — of theatre around the world — for which I was a leader, had been organized for comparative research and study of theatre of Asia and Europe. It was unique that nine weeks was devoted to circumnavigation of the globe and seeing theatre. The group had short stays in San Francisco and Hawaii, short visits to enable the group to adjust and prepare for intensive travel.

Varied and rich experiences, beyond expectation, were entrancing encounters with music, art, culture, as well as theatre. All were observed in hospitable ambience. In Japan happenings ranged from hearing composer Miyagi performing on the koto, delighting in the performances of the *takarazuka* all-girl theatre of Osaka. Actors explained the recondite characteristics of Noh. All were inspiring and insightful.

The headiest experience for me was the performances of Utaemon at the Kabuki-za, Tokyo. Also we were fortunate to see the great and aged Kichiemon perform. I returned to the Kabuki-za to see provocative and inspiring acting.

Theatrical and grandiose as its sweeping style is, its actors are masters of realistic acting. On this occasion I was witness to vignettes of naturalistic, charismatic acting by Nakamura Utaemon VI. His performing was the equal in realism to the Moscow Art Theatre.

It was my good fortune, both in 1954 and 1959, to meet a fellow American, a *nisei* from California, Miyoko Watanabe. My fortuitous coming to know her redounded to the benefit of the Institute for Advanced Studies in Theatre Arts (IASTA), for she was to become one of the most important resource people for IASTA over a period of more than three decades. Under her tutelage I saw performances, made visits backstage, and gained admission to the dressing rooms of stars.

There had developed within the Japanese community in California an amateur Kabuki troupe which toured as far as Hawaii. Miyoko Watanabe had been a member of that troupe. Shortly after we'd met in 1954, I asked her how she happened to be in Japan. "I had been assisting Mr. Otani, president of Shochiku, Ltd., on his visits to the United States." was her response. "He had said to me, 'I'm impressed with your being bilingual and your intimate knowledge of Kabuki.' It led to his inviting me to come to Japan to study and to learn the styles of Kabuki. He was eager that someone take back traditional theatrical Japanese art to the U.S.A."

Miyoko's devotion to her life work had been such that during more than eight years that she had been in Japan, she had not returned to the United States to visit her parents in California. Once one has been accepted as a student, a *deshi*, by a master for instruction in acting, dance, music, it is a commitment. The distance is great between Japan and California; both time and money were lacking for a flight across the pacific. Miyoko spent as much time as possible backstage at the Kabuki-za getting to know the actors, the musicians, the stagehands; for knowledge in depth of Kabuki, she sought out the people in charge. Assiduously, she made thorough study of the texts of the plays which supplemented her observation of rehearsals and performances. Academic courses on Japanese theatre, Kabuki, and Noh at Waseda University gave depth to the mastery of the form.

Among her mentors were the Kabuki actor Ichikawa Ebizo (later to succeed to the august and imposing Kabuki name of Danjuro), the choreographer Fujima under whom Kabuki stars trained in the dance, and Professor Kawatake, curator of the Kabuki collection at the theatre museum of Waseda University. At the time we met she had already given dance programs in Tokyo, and among her performances was the Kabuki dance drama *Musumi Dojoji*.

In 1959 Miyoko Watanabe, at the request of Shochiku, Ltd., made a sound track on tape providing an introduction and comments, as well as a simultaneous translation into English of the dialogue of the popular Kabuki play *Kanjincho*. This innovation in Japan was later to prove invaluable on the occasion of the Kabuki's performing in Europe and in the United States as well as for the visit of the Osaka puppet troupe known as Bunraku.

In 1959 Japan was the last country visited and provided a climax to research and a scouting for master directors of the world for the Institute for Advanced Studies in the Theatre Arts' program.

Three of the founders of the Institute for Advanced Studies in the Theatre Arts had flown over the North Pole to arrive in Japan. The flight involved re-fueling in Anchorage, Alaska! Matuso Kunizo greeted us at the airport. As a entrepreneur he was to figure significantly later in achievement of our mission to produce Kabuki — in English — with professional American actors. I had kept up correspondence with Miyoko Watanabe, so it was a joyous occasion for us to see her. Our goal was — as it had been in Europe and the U.S.S.R. — to observe the training and rehearsal practices of traditional Japanese theatre. Paramount was our wish to extend an invitation to a Kabuki actor to come to the Institute to direct Kabuki in English.

Miyoko had found that several of the Kabuki actors were receptive to being invited. The moment had arrived for me as president of the Institute for Advanced Studies in the Theatre Arts to decide on whom to invite.

The Training of the Actor

At once we of the Institute sought to observe training sessions — assuming that senior actors of the troupe train younger actors. Miyoko Watanabe corrected that impression, "Instruction in acting rarely takes place in a formal way. There are few formal times when a master actor teaches his protegé or another actor of the troupe."

She went on to expiate as to the nature of instruction, "I had once seen a protegé of a distinguished Kabuki actor rehearse part of a scene. At moments it had seemed to me that the young actor was doing badly. I was shocked then at the older actor's not saying anything to the young actor to correct him, or to show him where he was wrong or where he was right.

"I spoke of this to my acting mentor, and he said, 'The young person growing up to become an actor must find his own way to the part. Given time and opportunity for observation he will correct his errors or deficiencies. (He paused). We are sincere in our desire not to tamper with or attempt to influence or to interfere with the individual expression of a developing Kabuki actor.'"

A young American, Takeo Migi, who had come to Japan on a Japanese government scholarship from the Hawaiian Islands to learn traditional Japanese dance and acting, had been overhearing our conversation with Miyoko. He added, "Sometimes my master will not say a word to me during a long lesson." One of us, then, raised the question with the two of them, "How else does it take place?"

The answer was, "Training does occur by having the young actors backstage full time, playing small parts in the productions and spending any free time observing the performance from the wings. These actors that you're seeing out onstage began their training and their testing of *themselves* in the roles they are now playing as early as the age of four. Even sometimes earlier.

"Mature actors continue to take lessons in music and dance under famous instructors. Promising children of the actors study dance under the same choreographers and teachers."

All that has been said is well summed up in the book on Kabuki by A. C. Scott: *"...it is under his father or the actor whose family he is attached to he acquires his knowledge and in the theatre itself. The day that he makes his first appearance on the stage in a play marks his theatrical christening; he assumes the name which is the junior title of the family he belongs to, after that he acquires his next name on the succession principle, marking his climb up the rungs of achievement."*

It was our good fortune that at the time we were learning of Kabuki under the tutelage of Miyoko Watanabe, the eldest son of one of the stars of the troupe was to assume a name which has the Japanese appellation of *kojo*. As we witnessed this event from the wings, we saw the representatives of the troupe were onstage, in the appropriate, traditional costume, wigs and makeup. A set had been especially made for the child's *kojo*. The father did the introducing before the audience. He sat *kamite* (actors' left stage) which is considered the superior portion of the stage. (In the staging of a drama always person of higher ranks; e.g. male characters, are placed stage-left of other characters.)

Kneeling beside the father was his son; remarks by the troupe were addressed directly to the audience. Some of them were witty and did get laughs from the spectators. The child, however, remained very quiet and very attentive to the stage ritual of his name giving. He did have his moment when he spoke a few lines in response to something his father had said. The audience seemed to enjoy this insertion into the morning's bill of plays very much.

The mastering of the technique of acting in Japan differs from what we had observed in the other parts of the world, Europe, East and West, and the United States.

In summation the actor develops into a mature actor over a period of years through observation, imitation, and identification. One may describe it, in other words, as being largely non-verbal and non-directed training. Since the Kabuki Theatre has an uninterrupted evolution of more than 300 years, this approach to the art of acting did — and still does — work.

Musicians

Music and sound effects are a significant part of every production. Miyoko explained, "That black grill angled upstage down near the proscenium conceals a room behind which are the musicians. This partition — which is little more than that — conceals the *shamisen* players. Their music is most often used. In addition to the string instruments there is the large drum, the hand drum and various instruments for providing sound effects."

Backstage Personnel

We asked as to the number of stagehands that was required to run the show. The answer given to us was, "A crew of 17 stagehands is required for each performance. Since each day five persons have a day off, it is possible to say, if we add those for the building of scenery and all activity that goes on behind the proscenium — including administrative personnel — the production requires a crew of 80 men."

Takeo Migi interjected, "On the second level above the musicians' room, actors' stage-right, are located the stage electricians."

Our guide to the backstage elaborated, "The theatre is equipped with a turntable, *mawari-butai*, as well as various elevator stages used for making exits and entrances onstage. As you know, a unique feature of a Kabuki theatre is the *hanamichi,* a runway extending from the stage to the rear of the auditorium. There at seven-tenths is a *suppon*, an elevator, for exits and entrances of ghosts or supernatural characters."

Scenery and Props

The day before dress rehearsal onstage we had seen scenery being painted on the floor backstage. Later, during dress rehearsal while performing was in progress, from the wings we saw the setting up of scenery for the second act of the play — behind the first act's set. All was taking place quietly.

As needed during the first act — at actors' right-stage — two minor actors were busily creating sound effects: in large, rectangular wicker baskets dried beans and peas were rolled back and forth to achieve the sound of rolling surf — poetic and at the same time a realistic sound.

The Kabuki-za has a great wing and gridiron space and equipment. It was possible speedily to fly cypress wood flooring — used for a Kabuki dance drama derived from the Noh. The depth of the stage is considerable enabling a stage crew, as has been pointed out, to set up a second act set: a complete multi-room Japanese inn of impressive size. As soon as it was needed, the inn was rolled onstage, replacing the scenery of the preceding act.

Capacious wing space enables the musicians to observe the action onstage.

"There are two prop departments: one department has to do with large set props; the other department has to do with hand props."

"There is a competitive feeling and rivalry, I am told," added Takeo Migi, "about which department has control over certain props."

"It is hard to say sometimes if it's a set prop or hand prop," said Miyoko Watanabe.

IASTA's research and scouting group arrived in Tokyo at the end of May, and there was a hiatus in performances at the Kabuki-za. The actors were not at liberty: they were utilizing the five days before the resumption of the next month's bill of plays rehearsing.

As Cicerone for the four of us founders of the Institute, Miyoko was unsparing of her commitment to us. Accompanied by her we observed rehearsals taking place on the fourth floor Shochiku Kaiken, the corporation's office building. At the time we had arrived there was a buzz of activity: people coming and going in rehearsal kimonos in each of four large rehearsal areas. There was a narrow corridor lined with glass windows from which one looked down on the roof tops of Tokyo. The raised acting areas of tatami mats could be closed off from each other — *and* from the corridor — by sliding panels of shoji. Each of the four areas was 40 feet long and 18 feet deep. When needed the four areas could be opened up into one large rehearsal area. At the time of our arrival in early afternoon two of the rehearsal rooms were in use. The end area had been set aside for relaxation: eating food sent in and for preparation and drinking of tea between 'being onstage.' The other far end area was abustle with a corps of actors rehearsing mob scenes, dances, fight scenes — designated as *tachimawari.*

We removed our shoes once we were invited to the center area where a rehearsal was in progress. Despite the fact that throughout the fourth floor there was bustle, hubbub — and noise — the actors seemed impervious and accustomed to the sounds of rehearsal from adjoining areas and conversations in the corridors.

For the rehearsal that was taking place — what would have been downstage — where there was a long table. Seated at it were two persons. One was known as the *kyogen sakusha* — this literally means playwright. On this occasion — as was explained — there was a prompter and stage manager as is common in the theatre everywhere. The prompter was 'feeding' lines to the actors as needed.

The actors were working from 'sides' — thus they had only their own lines; the prompter had the complete script. Miyoko informed us *sotto voce,* "It's most likely that the script from which the prompter works has notations regarding certain actors needing to be coached, or reminded of traditional stage business." During a rehearsal break, she added, "In olden days this function had been undertaken by the playwright. As playwright he was the authority they looked to. He had written the play, and it was being rehearsed for the very first time.

"Playwrights in the long history of Kabuki rarely achieved fame, and today many of the authors of celebrated, popular Kabuki plays are unknown. Down through the ages, in some cases, there was an unbroken lineage: the *kyogen sakusha*, a prompter, who would have been trained by someone who in turn had been trained by someone who at the commencement had been trained by someone who ultimately had been trained by the original playwright."

Seated next to the prompter at the long table was *the* master musician. He was being consulted, at times advised as to what the actors wanted for coordinating their dance and their poses, *mie's*, with a musical accompaniment.

"The young actors grouped up against the shojis are the actors' protegés. Among these may be a star actor's son. When the senior actors rehearse, the young are quiet and reverent, intent on observing what the actor to whom he is attached as — *deshi* — is doing. This is the way in which the emerging Kabuki actors learn roles and the *kata*, the traditional patterns of acting that have early on evolved with the role.

"Their observation serves the performance as well, for later he may be onstage in a minor role or serving as a *koken* — akin to Peking Opera's property man — a *koken*'s responsibility is to adjust quietly and as unobtrusively as possible the actor's costume, or to hand the actor needed props or to remove props.

"In this manner the actor learns through rehearsal, through observation of performances, the Kabuki style of acting. When a young actor is playing a supporting role, he is ever alert to observe. It is not uncommon for a young actor to do sound effects in the wings during a performance. Since sound is important and essential, this task is not demeaning."

During a second rehearsal break, Miyoko went on to say, "The apprentices of a master actor often live in his, the master's, home as a member of his family." She pointed at an actor, saying, "There is present at this rehearsal a protegé of the star Shoroku. The protegé is the son of a famous Osaka actor, but his father had him sent up to Tokyo to learn from Shoroku."

We had been told that these actors had only from three to five days for full rehearsal before each new bill. We were much impressed that these actors were able — in such a short space of time — to revive old and standard classics, were sanguine about committing to memory a new play. Even one by a contemporary author!

At the run-through, some actors knew their lines, but one or two still read from 'sides.' At one point Shoroku informed other actors that he was going to skip a part of the scene and go right on. One of the plays had been derived from Bunraku — the 18th-century doll theatre. Being rehearsal, much time was given to setting the timing with the *joruri*, the man who chants the dialogue, reciting some narration of the plot and action. Use of a *joruri* in Kabuki had been borrowed from the Bunraku Theatre, which still exists in Osaka.

At rehearsal Miyoko Watanabe introducted us to Onoe Baiko VII, one of the most famous *onnagatas*. During free moments, with Miss Watanabe acting as interpreter, he chatted with us. He was affable and most friendly.

I had noticed that from time to time during rehearsal he had his ear close to a radio. I was curious. "Baiko is keen on baseball," said Miyoko, "Actors say when you can't find Baiko rehearsing, you'll find him somewhere listening to a ball game." Onstage he portrays a female character, but without makeup or costume — rehearsing — he appears to be just another actor.

"I hope you'll be pleased," said Miyoko Watanabe, "Mr. Baiko has invited you to come and see him make up there in his dressing room in an *onnagata* role for one of his performances "

From this meeting was to come about the first production ever in English of a Kabuki play directed by a master actor/director.

"Each day, seven days a week for 25 days, there are two bills of plays being performed at the Kabuki-za. The morning bill commences at 11 a.m. The evening bill commences at 4:30 p.m. lasting until 10 o'clock at night."

Day of Performance

We were backstage, and curtain time was about to arrive for the morning bill of plays. There was an air of excitement, much coming and going. Passing us in the hallway was the celebrated actor Nakamura Utaemon VI. The role he was to play was a tragic one.

"Observe his walking backstage," said Miyoko quietly. "Intermarriage over many generations of leading Kabuki families has sometimes resulted in defects. You may have noticed Utaemon walks with a pronounced limp. Let us take up our position in the wings to observe his making an entrance. You will be in for a surprise."

Utaemon was keyed up, giving sharp commands to his attentive *deshi,* the supporting actors fluttering around him. One was carrying a makeup box, another fans and props, and a third carried a lacquered tea tray. They kept close to him as he made his way to the stage.

It was a marvel to witness. Once Utaemon had hit the curtain line he glided out on the stage where he performed as if he were light and agile as gossamer.

The appointed time came for us to meet and to be the guests of Onoe Baiko VII. Dressing rooms are in another wing of the backstage area. There before the dressing room — once we had removed our shoes — we were ushered into a larger room. The flooring was of tatami. Before a low bureau with a large oval mirror, sat Baiko, kneeling. Having pasted down his own eyebrows, he applied thoroughly a white base, then he drew on carefully bamboo leaf-shaped eyebrows. What followed was application of rouge to his cheeks and lips.

Once the *onnagata* makeup had been completed, an elaborate, richly embroidered costume was brought into the dressing room. Dressers assisted as he donned an elaborate kimono. Younger apprentice actors, already in costume, were at his side being helpful. These actors were his *deshi* for whom Baiko has responsibility. In some cases *deshi,* young actors of the troupe, may live in the actor's home. In this close relationship with the star actor, the *deshi* may be called upon by the star actor for 24 hours a day — so close is the relationship between the young actors and the leaders of the troupe.

The moment the elaborate costume had been brought into Baiko's dressing room, as an added ritual, other actors with whom he was to perform assembled in the small foyer adjoining his dressing room. In respectful silence, they knelt there, an act of homage to a great actor of the troupe. Once bewigged and costumed, Baiko knelt before the mirror, ignoring the hubbub of the conversation going on about him, and spent some moments concentrating on his made-up visage in the mirror.

"In the Japanese Noh Theatre, which uses masks, the actors devote time to sitting before a mirror wearing the mask and meditating on the reflection in the mirror," whispered Miyoko Watanabe, "thus they achieve an identification with the mask they are wearing in the drama. Contemplating the makeup, a Kabuki actor — in his way — seeks identification with the character he is to play. In Baiko's case, as an *onnagata*, he is becoming at one with the maiden *Fuji Musume*."

After we had left Baiko's dressing room, Miyoko Watanabe shared with us the following information, "At the rear of the auditorium just behind the *agemaku* curtain of the *hanamichi* runway there is a mirror. There before it is a small tatami mat. Here, as you have seen in the dressing room, the actor may prepare himself for an entrance down the *hanamichi*. The mirror is vital to the actor and his performance. Large rings are attached to the *agemaku* curtain held on a rod. As a stagehand pulls back the curtain, the rings passing over the metal rod make a loud, rattling noise alerting the audience — as does a spot light — that an actor is about to make an entrance down the *hanamichi,* headed toward the stage."

Rewarding had been hours spent at rehearsal sessions, performances, talking with Kabuki actors backstage and in the wings. George Drew, IASTA's designer, met with costume, wig and scene personnel. He found it fascinating that they were descendants of families who had served the theatre as scenic artists for generations.

A complex and subtle relationship exists between actors and the commercial company which controlls the Kabuki theatre. Actors — we learned — were not free agents as are actors elsewhere in the world. Before our departure from Japan, we realized that our goal to produce Kabuki plays in English in New York was being stonewalled, not by the actors, but by a wary management. Difficulty had originated from our having been misguided — with the best of intentions in the world — by the Japan Desk at the U.S. State Department. Before we had set out for our trip around the world, we had been advised that in Japan our approach to the Shochiku Ltd. was to be through the Japanese Foreign Offices, the *Gaimusho*. A latter-day thought is that Broadway theatrical managers might have got their backs up if a request from the Comédie Française had come to Broadway via a governmental agency of Washington, D.C. "Who are they to tell us?" might easily have been an American theatrical manager's reaction.

Kabuki management had said no to IASTA's offer of an invitation to a Kabuki actor. Daily letters of mine — adding up to 100 or more — were sent after our return to the United States from Japan. I wrote to persons of status and influence. "See to it that the Institute for the Advanced Studies in Theatre Arts be permitted to invite a Kabuki actor to come and direct American professional actors."

In the fall of 1959, in New York, my having spontaneously done a favor for Matsuo Kunizo, prompted him to say to me, "When do you want your Kabuki actor?" *Mirabile dictu*. Late summer Onoe Baiko VII arrived.

Onoe Baiko VII had acheived fame for his dance performances; he excells in **Wisteria Maiden** (*Fuji Musume*), and dance is one of the bases for training the Kabuki actor. In advance of his selection of a cast (three deep) for *Narukami* (Thunder God), several days were devoted to teaching a part of traditional Japanese dance to his American professional actors. As an *onnagata* actor, Baiko with

Miyoko Watanabe inducted the Institute's actors in this classical dance.

Miyoko from the start had become central to the production as associate director to Baiko. She had two professional honored names from the choreographers who taught the Kabuki stars. She translated the play *Narukami.*

For the American actors it was a unique experience — rehearsing a Kabuki play as if they were in Tokyo at the Kabuki-za. The two-year training program at the National Theatre, Tokyo, was not to be initiated for another decade. They relished the time-honored traditions. They felt deeply a respect for Baiko as director. Three casts performed. Many observed from day to day. This six-week period passed quickly in harmony, and there was mounting excitement as the day of the first performance approached. A first performance when American actors would perform in Kabuki makeup, wigs and elaborate costumes.

George Drew's fluid and flexible design of the IASTA stage made it possible to have that requisite feature of Kabuki performances, the *hanamichi.* There was the tri-colored curtain of persimmon, black and green — which is pulled from stage left to stage right.

There had been some trepidation as to what would be Onoe Baiko VII's reaction to the small 100-seat studio theatre of the Institute, for he had come from the Kabuki-za that has a proscenium opening of 90 feet.

Fears were immediately dispelled, for he said with an air of delight, "This is so like in size the theatre of my ancestors." The 17th and 18th century Kabuki theatres of Edo — the former name of Tokyo — were very small.

NARUKAMI

CHARACTERS

Priest Narukami (Thunder God)

Kumo No Taema (Rift of the Clouds), *an Imperial Court Lady*

Bonze Hakuumbo (White Cloud), *an Acolyte, pupil of Narukami*

Bonze Kokuumbo (Black Cloud), *an Acolyte, pupil of Narukami*

Acolytes

Chorus

2 Kokens (Stage Assistants)

Kyogen Sakusha (Playwright —originally— and gradually assumed innumberable duties including counting rhythm with hyoshigi —wood clappers— for the opening and closing of the curtain.)

The action takes place at a secluded mountain retreat by a waterfall.

STAGE DIRECTIONS

15 minutes before curtain:	Stage manager strikes K1 twice from backstage office.
5 minutes before curtain:	Stage manager goes to dressing rooms striking K1.
1 minute before curtain:	Stage manager strikes K1 three times (mawari). Stage is ready.
5 seconds before curtain:	Stage manager strikes K1 twice. Everything is ready. Actors are at their places.
As curtain opens:	Stage manager strikes K1 continuously until curtain opens. When it's fully open, K1 is resoundingly struck once.

The emphasis of a pose (mie) is made by tsuke.

Back black curtain is drawn.

Drum, cymbal from stage left.

The mie and final pose of the play are very important in establishing the status of the characters. Hands and arms of the actor lead the turning of his body; never does another part of the body lead. The actor, standing on one foot and holding his arm before him in a set position, turns his head abruptly, jerking it to a full stop. Crossing his eyes, it is a mie. Simultaneously, a stage assistant at the side of the stage strikes blocks of wood on the floor to punctuate the pose. The use of wood blocks, for percussive effect is an incredibly stimulating sound to an audience; it builds suspense and emotion.

鳴神

第二場　北山岩屋の場

トー東花道より早つつみにて、白雲坊、黒雲坊出る。

白雲　聞いたか、聞いたか。

黒雲　聞いたぞ、聞いたぞ。

ト本舞台へ来たり、

白雲　これ黒雲坊、何を聞いたぞ。

黒雲　お江戸ではじめての＜雷神不動北山桜＞の評判を聞いた。

白雲　たわけもの、そんな事ではない。師の坊鳴神上人の行法の訳を聞いたかと云う事じゃ。

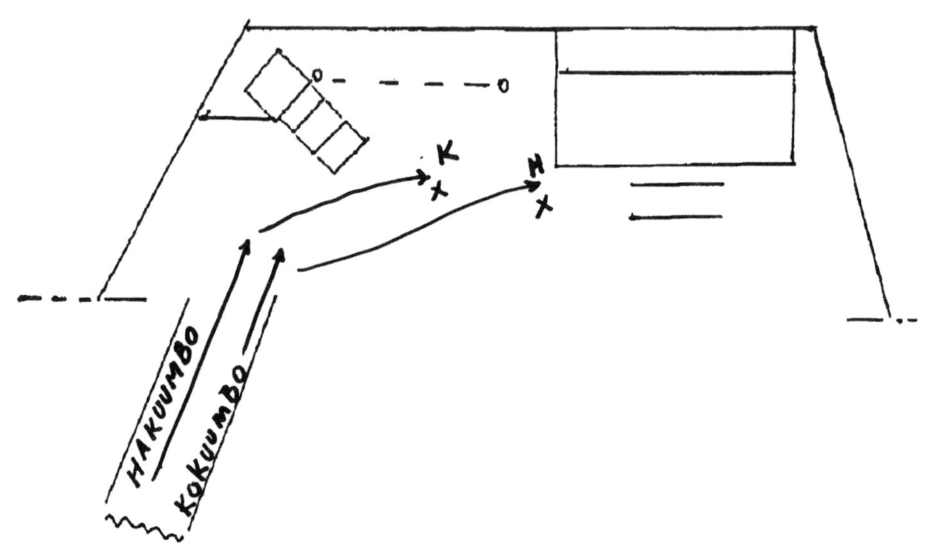

(Childhood days atmosphere. The first line of HAKUUN *and the first line of* KOKUUN *are said twice offstage behind the* agemaku *curtain.* HAKUUN *enters left with KOKUUN on his right, both coming down the* hanamichi *runway to stage center. The two of them alternately repeat their first line until they reach the stage from the* hanamichi. *By the time* KOKUUN *has said* "No, I haven't heard the reason,*" both have arrived at center stage. They face front.)*

HAKUUN

(With rosary in his hand, he leads.) Have you heard? Have you heard?

KOKUUN

(With rosary in his hand, he follows HAKUUN.*)* Yes, I heard! Yes, I heard!

HAKUUN

Here, here. From a while back you have been saying "I have heard, I have heard," but *(With emphasis.)* <u>what in the world</u> *(He pauses.)* <u>did you hear</u>?

KOKUUN

Behind the main temple... *(Pause.)*...I heard a nightingale.

HAKUUN

You fool, that's far fetched from the subject matter. I'm asking if you have heard the reasons for our Master Priest Narukami performing these esoteric religious austerities?

While directing NARUKAMI, *Baiko said to the actor upon* HAKUUN*'s phrase "...what in the world did you hear?", "More emphasis." Baiko wanted the two acolytes,* HAKUUN *and* KOKUUN *to be rather like two marionettes, simple fellows. He was insisting that neither individualize nor play to the audience for laughs. The goal of the production is to achieve ensemble acting throughout.*

黒雲　その訳は何にも知らぬ。

白雲　知らざあ、云って聞かそう。この度師の坊鳴神上人の行法というは、戒壇お許しの願いを立てられたところ、その願いがお許しに成らぬというて、三千世界の竜神を封じこんで、世界に雨を一滴も降らせまい、という行法じゃ。それで見い、まずこの三月余り、一滴の雨が降らぬは、何ときついものじゃないか。

黒雲　されば、このように雨が降らいでは、苗代時に向こうて、百姓のいかい難儀じゃ。

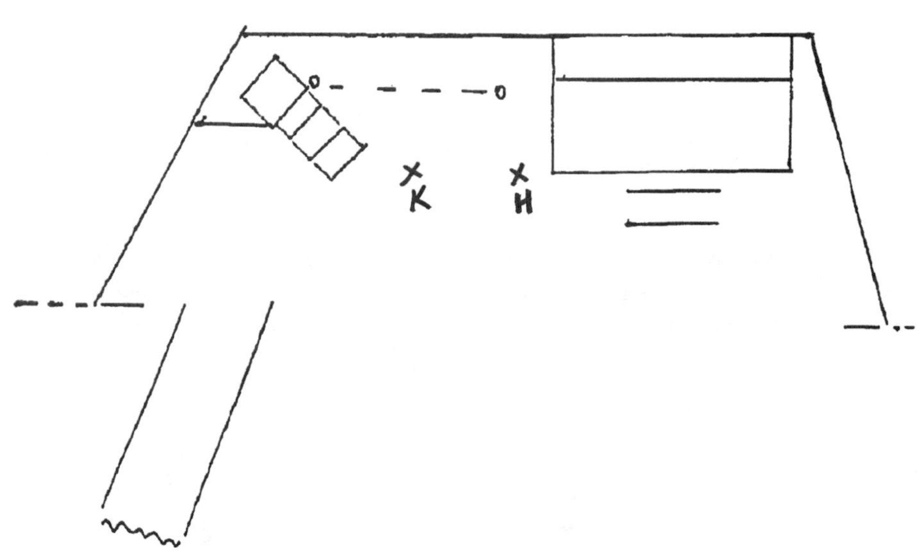

KOKUUN

(Loudly.) No, I haven't heard the reason.

HAKUUN

Fool, how can one be so ignorant of this matter? *(Pause.)* If you don't know, I shall humbly deign to tell you. *(Pause.)* Our Master Priest Narukami is performing . . . .

(Music begins and continues at a low level for the remainder of HAKUUN*'s speech.)*

these austerities because it seems *(Pause.)* that he made a request to the Imperial Household, *(Pause.)* but the Imperial sanction was not granted. Thus he has shut in the Dragon God who controls the rain, and is performing the religious austerities to prevent even *(Vocal inflection.)* a drop of rain from falling. As you can see, for these thirty days not even one drop of rain has fallen. That's really something, *(Pause.)* is it not?

KOKUUN

Well, this drought will be enjoyed by the children for flying kites, *(Pause.)* but with the coming rice-planting season the farmers will encounter great hardship.

Music is an integral part of the art of Kabuki. The percussive effect, the sounding of wooden clappers at the opening and closing of the play, are among Kabuki's most unique elements. With rhythmical, staccato measures, the wooden clappers underscore the actions during the course of the performance.

白雲　いや、難儀と云えば、今日はどうも気が滅入ってならぬわえ。

黒雲　さあ、その気うつがはっきりと成るような薬があるが、何と飲まそうか。

白雲　何じゃ、よい薬があるなら、どれ、チト飲もう。

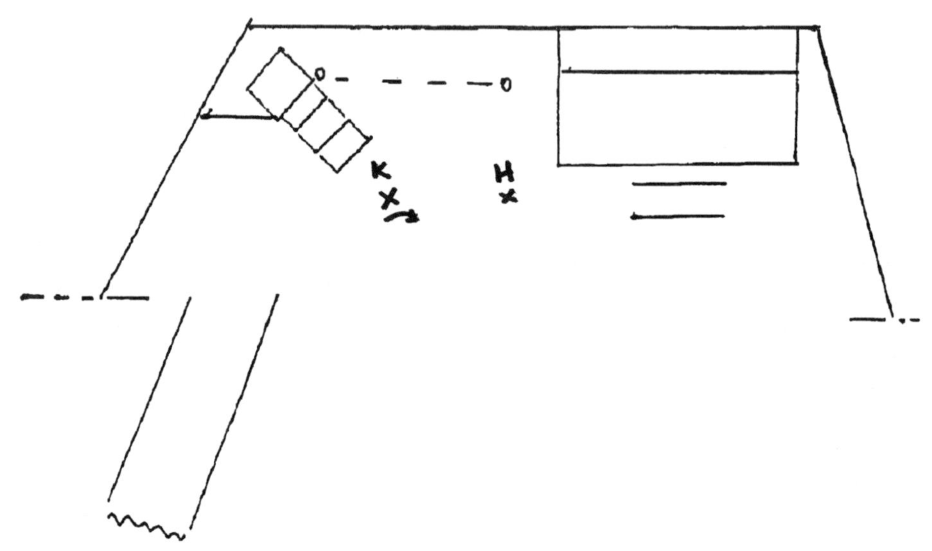

HAKUUN

(Slowly.) To bring misery upon the farmers is a means to plague the Emperor.

KOKUUN

Now *(Turns head left to* HAKUUN, *confident.)* I understand. So that his austerities will not be disturbed he has ordered you and me to act as guards here.

HAKUUN

So, *(Defeated inflection.)* just as you say. *(Defeated inflection.)* Ah, I feel melancholy; I feel dull.

KOKUUN

Well, *(Takes one step toward* HAKUUN.*)* I have some good medicine to cure your melancholy. Would you like to drink of it?

HAKUUN

What? You have medicine to cure melancholia? Then let me have a little.

Onoe Baiko VII, for a quarter of a century, has been one of Japan's "living treasures," *an officially certified master of the multiple arts of Kabuki and one of the best* (performer of women's roles) *in the all-male Kabuki. He states* "Kabuki is a very, very strict style. I still hone my skills by practicing body movements, nude, before a mirror. My father was a hyper-critical man. Even in the winter, we did rehearsals in the nude before a mirror. Only that way can you understand how your entire posture looks."

Baiko, now 78, began his stage career performing as Ushinosuke Onoe IV at the age of 6. He continues, "I found playing some of the comics not as restrictive for me as it was for actors playing the leads. I found once I had mastered the clown role of one of the acolytes I was able to make it my own: the movement, the way of walking, and the manner of speaking. Once I had been able to take on that, it became a style in which I could still feel creative. . . and not just a puppet." "You have to master the form but if that's all you achieve, it's empty. You, the actor, must fill it."

黒雲　飲まそう飲まそう、

（股倉より樽を取り出しながら）そうれ、この通り、股蔵じゃ。何とたしかな蔵へ入れて置いたであろうがな。しかも又、又蔵の発熱でよい呑加減じゃ。

白雲　エ、不届き坊主め、お師匠様に申し上げねばならぬ、と申すは余りに勿体ない。

いっぱい飲もうか。

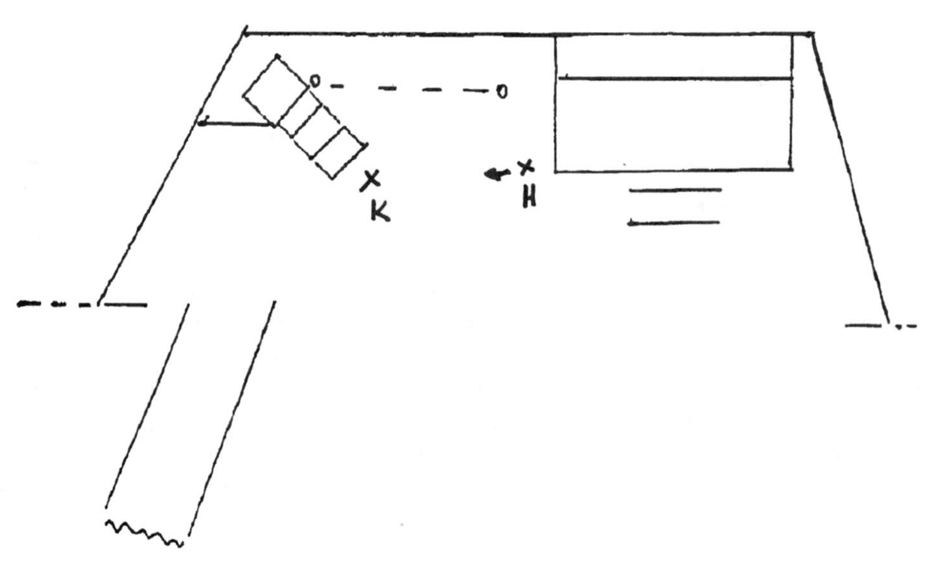

KOKUUN

You shall, you shall. It's a medicine called a "*cure-all.*" *(He reveals a hidden bottle from his left sleeve. Takes medicine from left sleeve with right hand. Shows it to* HAKUUN *with outstretched hand.)*

HAKUUN

Why you insolent fellow? You subversive priest!

KOKUUN

What do you mean, subversive priest?

HAKUUN

(Slowly.) Here from within you are breaking Master Priest's commandment of abstinence. You scoundrel! This matter cannot be ignored. I'm warning you; I'm going to report the matter to our Master . . . . *(Turns toward master, then back.)* but, if I did, that would make the sake go to shameful waste. All right. I'll have a drink, too.

A man's hands are held wide aprt to look larger and stronger. An actor needs trememdous coordination of body, suppleness, ability to adjust from one position to another, and he must have perfect balance.

The most distinguishing feature of Kabuki as a theatrical art is that all elements place primary emphasis upon the actor. At the heart of Kabuki acting is classical Japanese dance, so that 80% of the training is physical and 20% is vocal. Even in a realistic Kabuki play, the most trivial gestures are frequently more closely related to dance than to acting. Nearly every gesture is accompanied by music. There are scenes where symbolic actions have been carried to a level of abstraction, and the resulting formalized actions of the character are no longer relevant, but directly conflict with the rational interpretation of the role.

黒雲　飲んでもよいかや。

白雲　そこが臨機応変というものじゃ。

黒雲　というたところが骨がない。

白雲　あるともあるとも。兜頭巾という骨じゃ。（ト懐より干蛸出す。）

黒雲　あの、ここな生臭坊主め。師の坊へ云わねばならぬ。いや、聞かぬ、聞かぬ。

ト白雲留めるも黒雲聞き入れず,

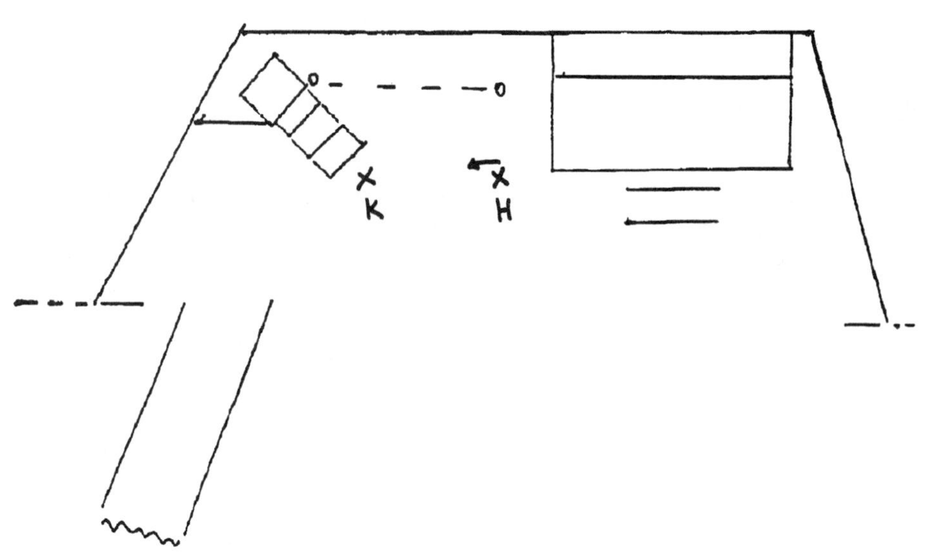

KOKUUN

Is it all right to drink?

HAKUUN

Sure, one must learn to adapt oneself to circumstances. *(*KOKUUN *takes a cup out of* kimono.*)*

KOKUUN

But there is no appetizer to be had with the sake. Oh, I should have brought some tangerines or chestnuts.

HAKUUN

Don't worry! Don't worry! *(Pause.)* I have something here. Something called a "*helmet-hood.*" *(He reveals an octopus from left sleeve.)*

KOKUUN

(Rapidly and ferociously.) You pulpiteer! What do you mean by eating a forbidden octopus. I'll report this to our Master Priest.

(Music stops.)

HAKUUN

Here, here. I can't have you blabbing this.

黒雲　モーシ、お師匠様、白雲坊が蛸をくらいおる。

白雲　黒雲坊が酒をくらいまする。

黒雲　おのれ、くらわすぞよ。　（トなぐる）

白雲　あいた。

トー丁析、岩幕ふり落とす。

白雲　幕が開いた。

本舞台一面険岨なる岩山。正面上手寄りにかき上げ土手。三方に〆縄を張り不動尊像を祭りし庵。伊予簾をおろす。下手大滝前両側の青竹に〆縄を張り渡す。その下手大岩、蔦かずら登り口あり。上下のかこいは岩組。両僧、庵の両側に控える。

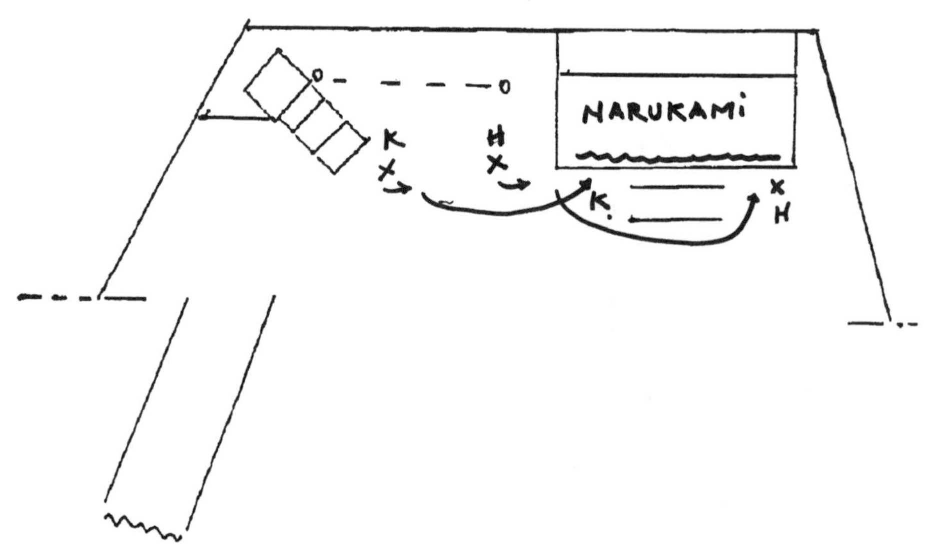

KOKUUN

No, I won't listen. I won't listen. *(Turns away.)*

HAKUUN

If you won't listen to me, I won't listen to you. *(Turns away towards Master, left foot forward.)* Master Priest, Kokuumbo is drinking sake.

KOKUUN

(Turns towards Master, left foot forward.) Hakuumbo is eating octopus.

(On the dais behind a bamboo screen is heard a bell. NARUKAMI *rings bell twice. Both hear the bell, look at the priest, then at each other.)*

HAKUUN

That is the bell . . . .

BOTH

(Softly.) of our Master Priest.

(They look at each other. They leave the octopus and sake on the rocks and move to opposite sides of the steps. HAKUUN *kneels on the left of the step,* KOKUUN *kneels on the right of the step.)*

(Music starts.)

George Drew points out that "Japanese male characters sit back on their heels; an actor playing a woman has to learn to sit back between the heels, making his head level three or four inches lower than the male character opposite whom he's playing. Not a comfortable position."

さるほどに、鳴神上人。竜神竜女の飛行を封じ、国土の雨を閉じ籠る。巌伝いの山深き、壇上に行い済まし居たりける。

トこれにて伊予簾あがる。　（山台かくす）鳴神上人居る。

ト下座にて、

雲井を落とす滝の糸の岩に砕ける水音風音、渚浄感の床の上、威徳擁護のまなじりを垂れ、南無大聖不動明王　。

ト揚幕より雲の絶間、肩に薄衣をかけ、鉦を打ち出て、花道七三にて止まり、

絶間　南無大聖不動明王。南無大聖不動明王。

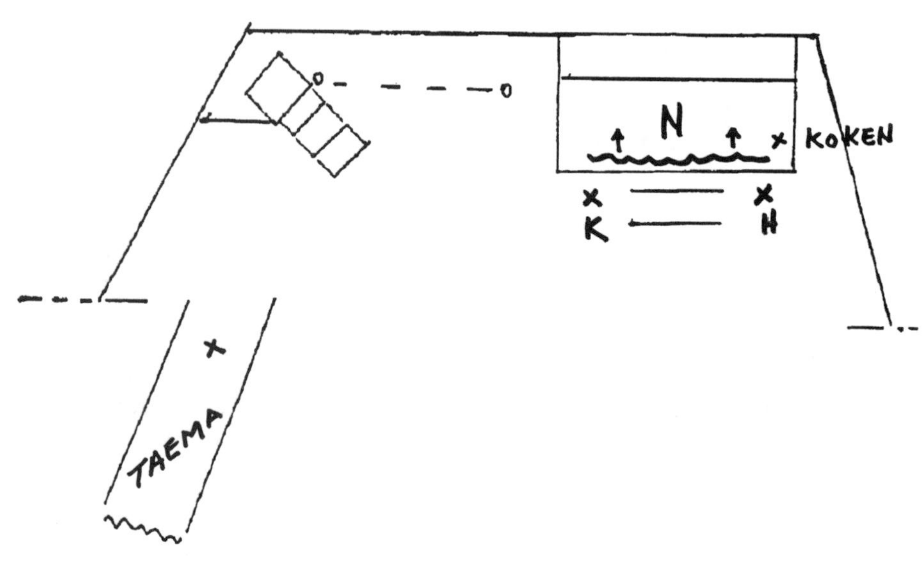

*(*HAKUUN *and* KOKUUN *sit on either side of steps. Left* KOKEN *enters; sits at altar.)*

CHORUS

For some time the Master Priest Narukami has shut in the Dragon God and thus has cut off the rain from the land. In the depth of the mountains among the massive rocks sits Narukami before the altar.

(Left KOKEN *rolls up bamboo blind revealing* NARUKAMI *on the platform. Left* KOKEN *exits.)*

The waterfall falls from the sky and against the rocks the sound of the water and the wind break. On the dais of virtue he is entreating Buddha for mercy in *(Rings bell.)* answering his prayers.

*(*Hanamichi *curtain opens.* TAEMA *rings bell 3 times.* HAKUUN *and* KOKUUN *fall asleep.* TAEMA, *striking the bell, enters on the* hanamichi *while striking the bell.)*

Ah, the great deity Fudo Myoo, the great Fudo Myoo.

ト立つ。この内白雲、黒雲眠る。

鳴神　一鳥啼かず山更に幽かなり。人跡稀なる深山に、はるか滝壷のもとに当たって、念仏の声の聞こゆるは、ハテ怪しやな。両僧、両僧。

両人　ハアイ。

鳴神　惰弱千万な、なぜ眠る。

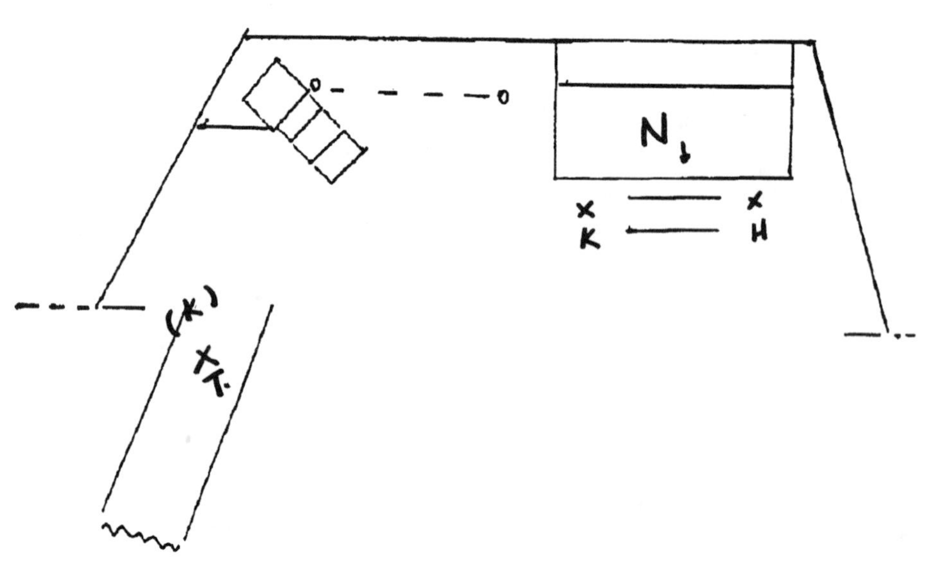

(Both Fudo Myoos are drawn out until TAEMA *reaches to shichisan, facing the audience.)*

TAEMA

(Chanting; sing-song.) Namu ami da Butsu . . . Namu ami da Butsu . . . *(Buddha, rest his soul in peace.)*

(Right KOKEN *enters up right, exits down to* shichisan. *He sets large aibiki behind* TAEMA. *She sits on aibiki.* KOKEN *kneels inconspicuously.)*

NARUKAMI

Indeed, how strange. In the depth of the mountains where not a bird is heard, where man rarely treads, I hear the voice of one chanting prayers far off in the distance beyond the basin of the waterfall Here, Hakuun and Kokuun. *(They do not answer.)* Do you not realize that I am calling both of you?

BOTH

Ai-i . . . *(Stifling yawns.)*

NARUKAMI

You indolent fellows. Why do you sleep?

白雲　イヤ勿体ない。私は眠りはいたしませぬ。あの坊主めが眠りました。

黒雲　コリヤコリヤコリヤ。その様な人に云い掛けをする。お師匠様、私は目を皿の様にして、見張って居りました。一郎が眠りました。

白雲　イヤ、おのれが眠った。

黒雲　おぬしが眠った。

白雲　おぬしとは。

黒雲　おのれとは。

ト両人腕まくりして、意気込む。

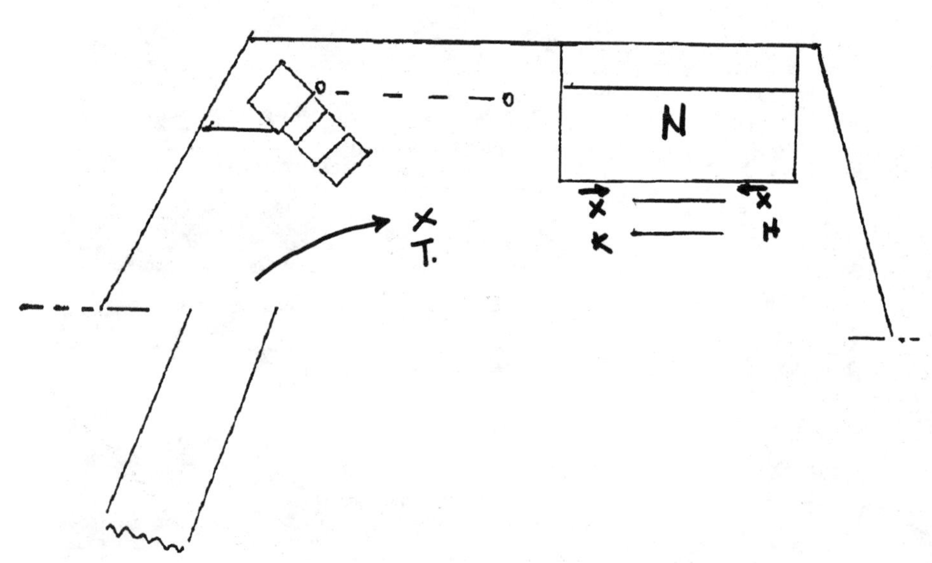

HAKUUN

Oh no, oh no, how impious that would be. I am not sleeping.

NARUKAMI

You certainly were *(Pause.)* fast asleep.

HAKUUN

Oh no, I did not fall asleep; it was *(Points to* KOKUUN.*)* that bonze over there who fell asleep.

KOKUUN

Here, here, don't accuse others. Master Priest, *(Bows to priest.)* I was standing guard with my eyes wide open. *(Makes circles of both thumbs and index fingers around eyes.)* It was my *(Points to* HAKUUN.*)* senior HAKUUN who was sleeping.

HAKUUN

It was you who were sleeping.

KOKUUN

What do you mean, it was I?

HAKUUN

"You," what do you mean by "you?"

Working with Baiko-sensei *has given me invaluable help in the areas of vocal and physical discipline, and in emphasizing the values of economy, pinpointing emotions and magnification of reality.*

The old art, Baiko says, teaches "humility and respect for etiquette*" and conveys traditional values, such as* giri *and* ninjo *(obligation and human empathy). Baiko's family can trace its roots in Kabuki for seven generations. He himself was adopted into a Kabuki family and trained from childhood for the stage as an* onnagata. *Now, about one of every ten roles he plays is that of a man.*

鳴神　コリャどうじゃ。それが沙門の行跡か。

両人　ハイ。

鳴神　よい、眠らぬが定ならば、今のを聞いたか。

両人　エ、。

鳴神　はるか滝壷のほとりにて、悲しき声に念仏を申すは、妖怪の類か。但しは幽霊か。

両人　エ、。

鳴神　両僧、滝壷の元へ行って、見届けて来い。

両人　エ、。

鳴神　行かぬか。

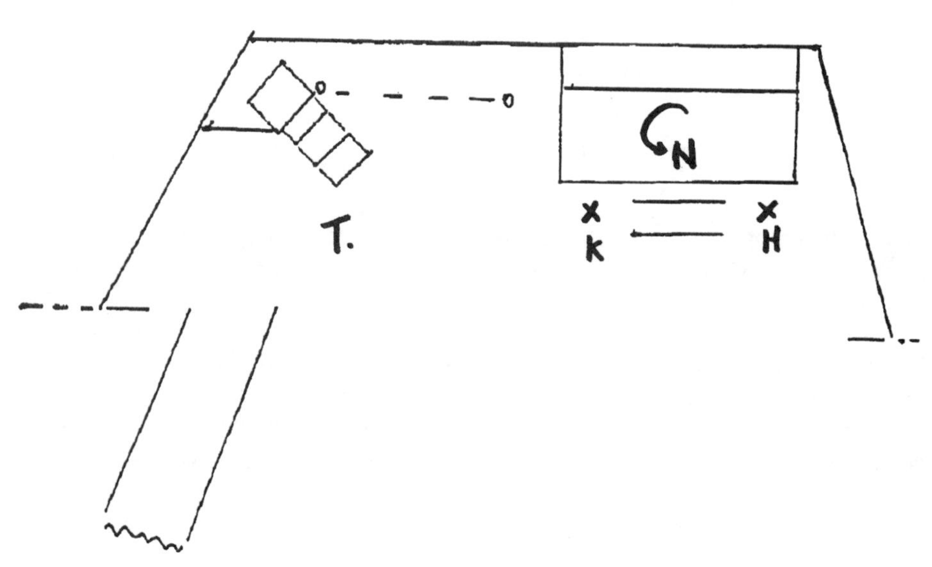

NARUKAMI

(Slowly.) Is that a Buddhist priest's way of behavior? If you contend that you were not asleep, did you hear what I heard?

BOTH

Eh-h?

NARUKAMI

Far off beyond the basin of the waterfall a sad voice chanting Buddhist prayers can be heard. *(He sits.)*

BOTH

Eh-h?

NARUKAMI

Both of you, go to the waterfall and investigate.

BOTH

Eh-h?

NARUKAMI

Go, I say.

The onnagata *should continue to have the feelings of an onnagata even when in the dressing room. When raking refreshments, too, he should turn away so that people cannot see him. To be along a tachiyaku playing the lover's part, and chew away at one's food without charm and then go straight out on the stage and play a love scene with the same man, will lead to failure on both sides, for the tachiyaku's heart will not in reality be ready to fall in love. [Excepted from: Charles J. Dunn and Bunzo Torigoe, editors and translators,* THE ACTORS ANALECTS*; New York: Columbia University Press, 1969, p. 280.]*

両人　ハーイ。

白雲　黒雲坊、師の坊の御意じゃ。見届けて来い。

黒雲　こなた見てござれ。こなたは一郎じゃないか。

白雲　それが何とした。

黒雲　正月の膳に坐る時は、その方が先へ坐るか、また俺が先へ坐るか。

白雲　そりゃ、俺が先へ坐るが、何とした。

黒雲　それじゃによって、そなたが先じゃ。

白雲　いやこつは、くらわすぞよ。

黒雲　くらわして見い。

両人　こいつ。

トまた両人腕まくりする。

鳴神　そりゃ、何じゃ。

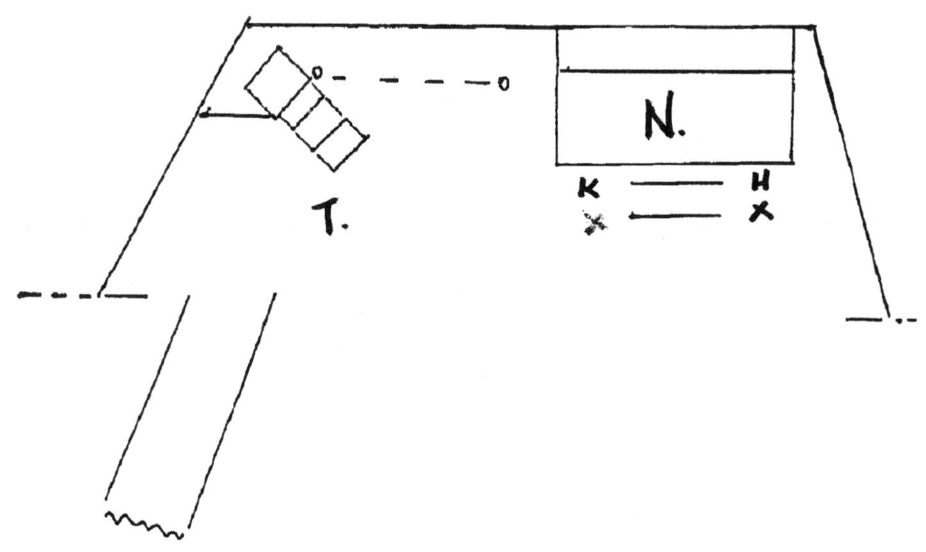

BOTH

Ai-i-i. *(They bow their heads.)*

HAKUUN

Kokuumbo, it is the will of our master. Go and see.

KOKUUN

You go and see.

HAKUUN

You go and see.

KOKUUN

You go and see.

BOTH

Confound you! *(Both raise their fists.)*

NARUKAMI

What is that? *(Both turn to* NARUKAMI.*)*

Even in the realistic, domestic plays, speaking is not that of daily life, but is an idealized elocution. Long monologues, in particular, have fascinating cadences half way between singing and conversation. This is especially evident when dialogue and monologues are delivered to the accompaniment of music. Too much inflection in the voice indicates a lower social status; a character such as Princess Taema *is limited to one tone of voice, compared to the vocal freedom and range allowed* Narukami, *the hero priest.*

白雲　セア、この様な蕪がありましたら、汁に致して、差し上げようと存じまして。

黒雲　私は又、この様なすくね芋がござりましたら、御ときの菜に致そうと存じまして。

鳴神　たわけめ。

両人　ハイ。

鳴神　争いを止めて、両僧共行って見て来い。

両人　畏りました。

ト両人おずおず行き、絶間を見て胆を潰す。

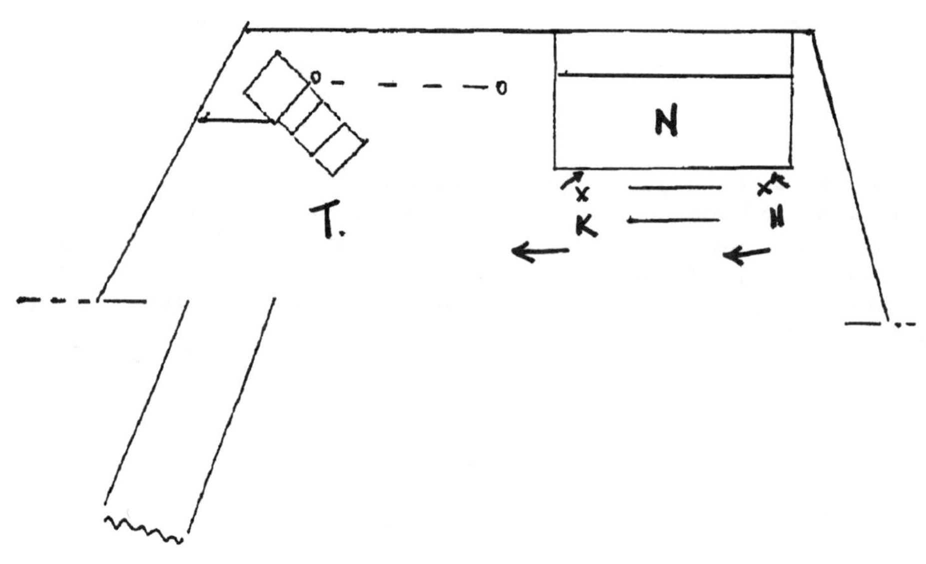

HAKUUN

(Holds fist a little above waist.) I was thinking that if there were a potato about this size, we could put it into the boiled rice for breakfast. *(Lowers fist.)*

KOKUUN

And I thought that if there were a turnip about this size, I could put it into your soup for you. *(Lowers fist and pantomimes offering soup.)*

NARUKAMI

Fools!

BOTH

Ai-i . . .

NARUKAMI

I said go.

BOTH

Ai-i . . . *(They bow, stand, then cross.) (Tsukegiwa.)*

Theatre of the Far East is a remarkable and catalytic experience for a Western audience.

白雲　ヤアー、みごとなものじゃ。

黒雲　無類大極、上々吉じゃ。

白雲　まず、あれは何であろう。

黒雲　天人じゃ。師の坊の行力で世界に水がないによって、天人が羽衣を洗濯にやって来たのじゃ。

白雲　イヤ、目違い目違い。あれは竜女じゃよ。師の坊の行力で竜が封じどめられたによって、一家一門に逢いに来たのじゃ。

黒雲　イヤ、天人じゃよ。

白雲　竜女じゃよ。

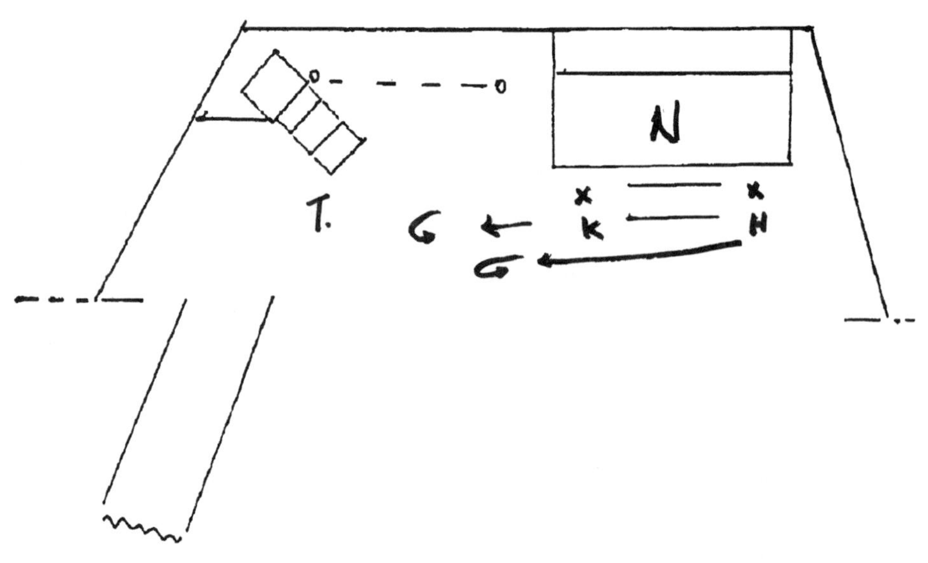

HAKUUN

Oh, *(Takes a step back.)* how exquisitely beautiful!

KOKUUN

This is most extraordinary! *(Drawn out.)*

HAKUUN

That is a celestial being. Since there is no water in the universe, the celestial has come to *(Makes washing motion.)* wash her feathered robe.

KOKUUN

No, you're wrong, you're wrong. That is the Dragon Goddess. The Dragon Goddess has come to see the Dragon God who has been trapped in the basin of the waterfall.

HAKUUN

No, without doubt, her beauty bespeaks that she is a celestial.

KOKUUN

(Arguing.) She is a Dragon Goddess. *(Nods head up and down.)*

黒雲　天人じゃよ。

白雲　竜女じゃよ。

両人　イヤ、こいつが。

トまた、両人こぶしを振り上げる。

鳴神　そりゃ、何じゃ。

両人　急急如律令。

鳴神　大だわけめ。

両人　ハイ。

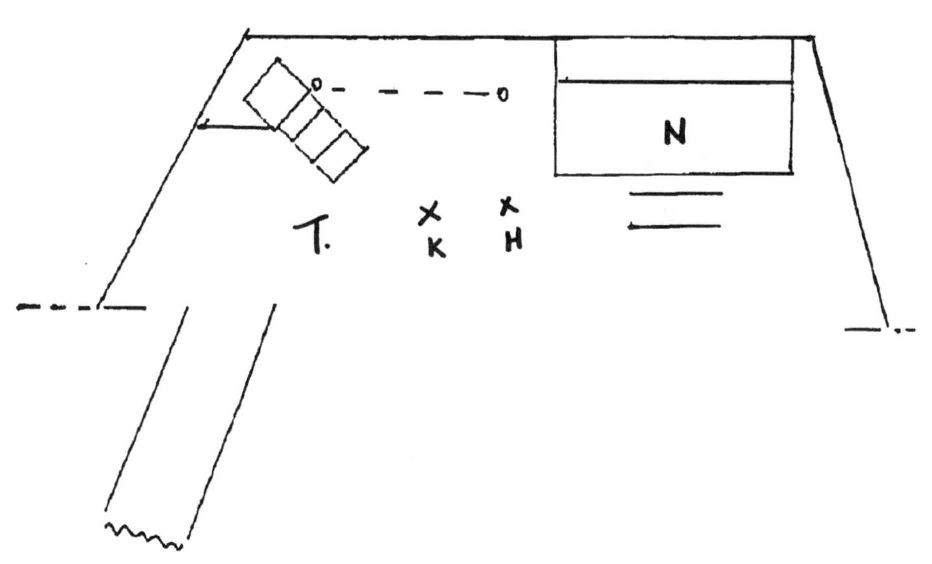

HAKUUN

She is a celestial! *(Nods head up and down.)*

BOTH

(Strongly.) Confound you! *(Both raise fists, upstage foot forward diagonally.)*

NARUKAMI

What is that?

*(*HAKUUN *and* KOKUUN *face forward in place, lower fists a bit.)*

BOTH

(They twirl fists back and forth; heads down. They pull foot back and swing fists in kimono.) Oh, praise great buddha. *(They bow their heads.)*

NARUKAMI

You fools!

BOTH

Hai-i. *(They bow.)*

Minor characters, like the ACOLYTES *have a colloquial dialogue which is in contrast to that of the leading characters. Since they are often played in Japanese comic characters, they have the freedom to improvise. They may even interject topical references (this was not true of our American productions).*

鳴神　よい、よい。俺が見届けよう。

ト立ち、下手柱に手をかけ、揚幕の方を見て、

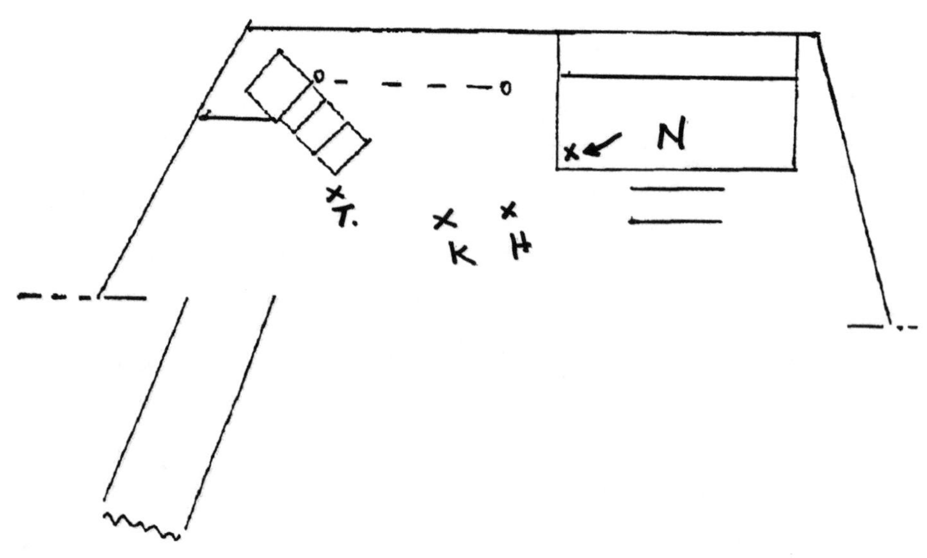

NARUKAMI

With you, nothing can be settled. *(Pause.) (To self.)* I shall have to see for myself. *(He stands.)*

*(*HAKUUN *and* KOKUUN *cross center and sit on knees.* NARUKAMI *crosses to right front pillar and calls out.)*

Here!

TAEMA

E-eh? *(Rising inflection.)*

BOTH

E-eh? *(Rising inflection.) (Imitating TAEMA stupidly.)*

NARUKAMI

Silence!

BOTH

Ai. *(Down inflection.) (They bow fast, simultaneously.)*

Danjuro as *Narukami* and Baiko as *Taema*

　　コレ、コレ、コレ。（ト呼ぶ）ハテ心得ぬ。飛禽猛獣だに通い難き、この山路を経て、さもやごとなき女性の、峨峨とそびえたる滝の前に立ったるは、アラいぶかしや。まずそなたは何者じゃ。

絶間　アノわしかえ。

両人　アノわしかえ。

鳴神　黙ろう。

両人　ハイ。

鳴神　なるほど、そなたの事じゃ。

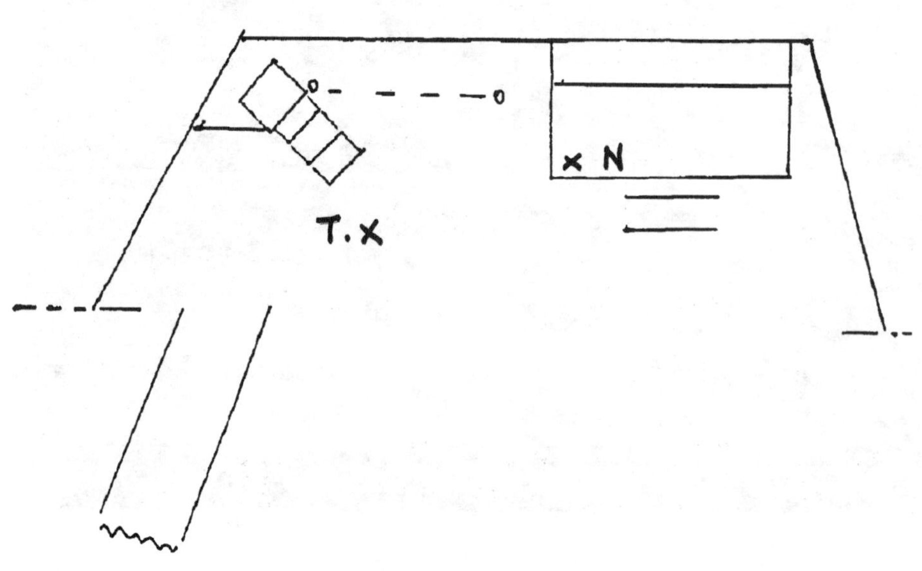

NARUKAMI

How suspicious that an exalted maiden should come through the mountain paths where even birds and animals dare not frequent. Tell me, what are you?

TAEMA

(At a distance.) Do you mean me?

BOTH

Do you mean me? *(Rising inflection.) (Imitating.)*

NARUKAMI

(Strongly.) Silence!

BOTH

Ai.

NARUKAMI

(At a distance.) (Light voice.) Yes, I mean you.

Natalie Ross states that "In the Kabuki, the voice is pitched to a sort of falsetto, traditionally tuned to a string of the samisen. The technique has to become second nature."

George Drew, actor and art director, says that "Kabuki was a novel experience for me, and as an American actor to be asked to perform as an *onnagata*, directed by Onoe Baiko VII, an *onnagata* designated by the Emperor as a National Treasure of Japan!" *The Japanese word* onnagata *means female style, not female impersonator. Even today upper class Japanese women and geishas go to performances of Kabuki to observe the* onnagata, *because the male actor playing a female role is playing what the Japanese call the essence of being feminine. Japanese women wish to emulate the feminine style of the* onnagata.

絶間　アイ、自らは、遥かこの御山の麓に住む者、恋しい夫に別れました女でごさりまする。

鳴神　なに夫に別れたか。

絶間　アイ。　（ト泣く）

鳴神　して生別れか、死別れか。

絶間　しかも、今日が七七日。

鳴神　四十九日か。

絶間　アイ。

鳴神　南無阿弥陀仏。

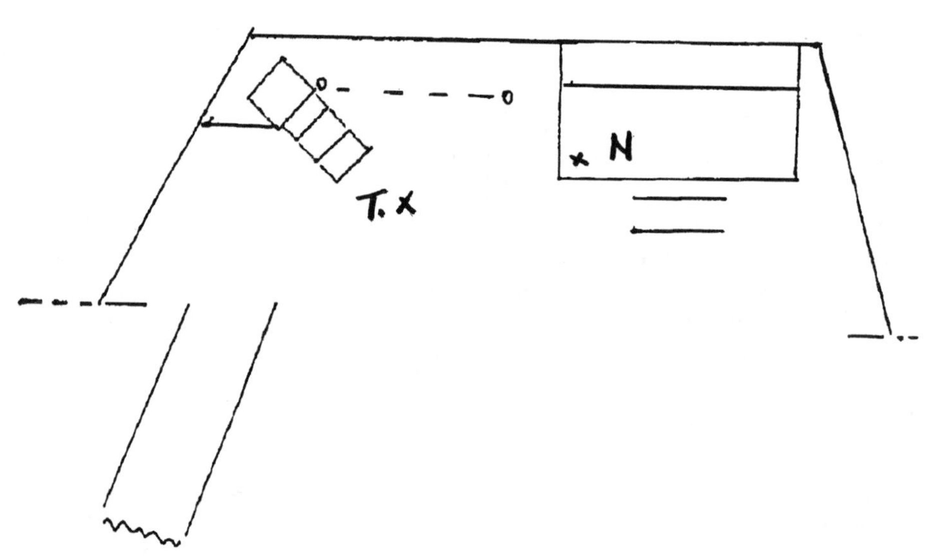

TAEMA

I live at the foot of these steep mountains and daily I pine for my beloved husband, from whom I have recently been parted.

NARUKAMI

Did you part from your husband in life or death?

TAEMA

Today is exactly the 49th day since his death.

NARUKAMI

The day for mass, isn't it?

TAEMA

Yes. Ai. *(Rising inflection.)*

NARUKAMI

(Closes his eyes, prayer beads around clasped hands, and prays to himself.) May Buddha's blessing rest upon his soul.

絶間　かたみこそ今は仇なれ、これなくば忘れる事もあらましものを、あらあらしきこの薄衣。浮世の垢を濯がんと存じますれど、如何なる事にやひでりして、井の水とても乾きまして、洗う水がござりませぬ。この御山の滝津瀬は、いかなるひでりにも水絶えぬ名水じゃと聞きました故、夫のかたみを洗わんものと、参りましてござりまする。ゆかしきは夫、なつかしきは妻、自らが心の内、御推量なされて下さりませ。

鳴神　さてさて憐れな物語り、それ程の語らいなら、添い連れていた頃は、いかい仲がよかったであろう。

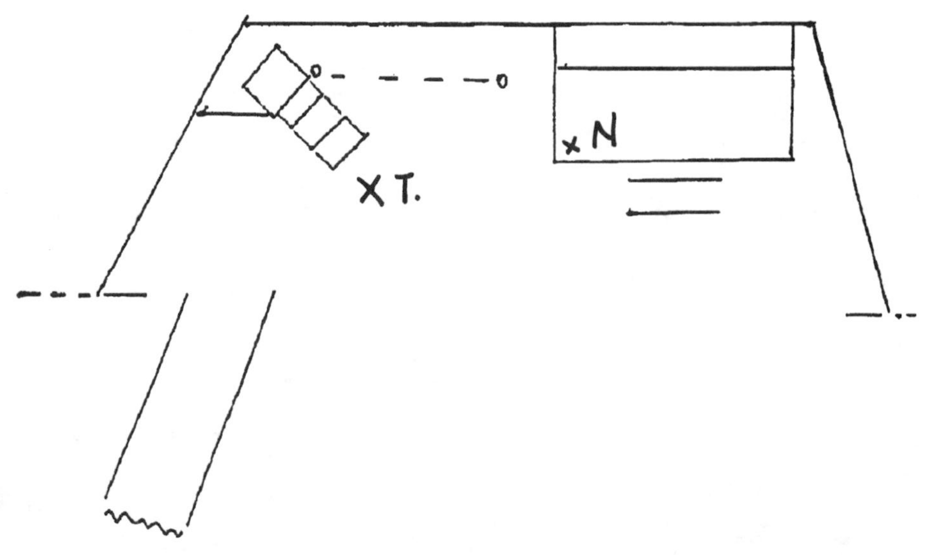

TAEMA

(Dainty manner.) This keepsake only tortures me. *(She has his robe. She touches garment with left hand.)* If I did not have this, perhaps I might be able to forget him. From his new, light robe *(Shows husband's robe which is on her shoulder.)* I wanted to wash away the filth of this mundane world, but for what reason I do not know, the drought has caused all wells to dry up and there is no water to be had. *(Pause.)* I have heard that at the waterfall in these mountain depths, the famed and precious waters never cease to run despite the drought. So I have dared to climb the hazardous mountain paths to wash the robe of my dear husband. Sweet and loving is a husband. *(Pause.) (To* NARUKAMI.*)* Please understand how I feel in my heart. *(Bows deeply.)*

NARUKAMI

Indeed, that is a pitiful tale. If you still think of him so dearly, you must have been passionately in love when you were together in life.

"Striving for perfection, from the moment you start to apply makeup, you become the woman you are to portray," *says Baiko.* "My predecessor as Baiko was 170 centimeters (5'3" tall). I am about 160 centimeters (5'3" tall). The heart that goes into the acting remains the same. If you are just presenting a form — with no feeling, no heart — you are just a doll. There is no impact."

絶間　そりゃもう仲のよい段かいなア。天にあらば比翼のとり。地にあらば連理の枝。思い出せば、面白い事でござんした。

鳴神　煩悩即菩提。婦人に対して、かく詞を文すも因縁。後世の回向、その話が聞きたいものじゃ。

絶間　さあお話申して、心の憂さを晴らしとうござりまする。何と、お話し申しましょうかえ。

鳴神　ウム、話しや、話しや。

絶間　サア、話しましょうが、そことここは、隔たって居りまする。どうぞ、お傍へ寄りお話し申しとうござります。

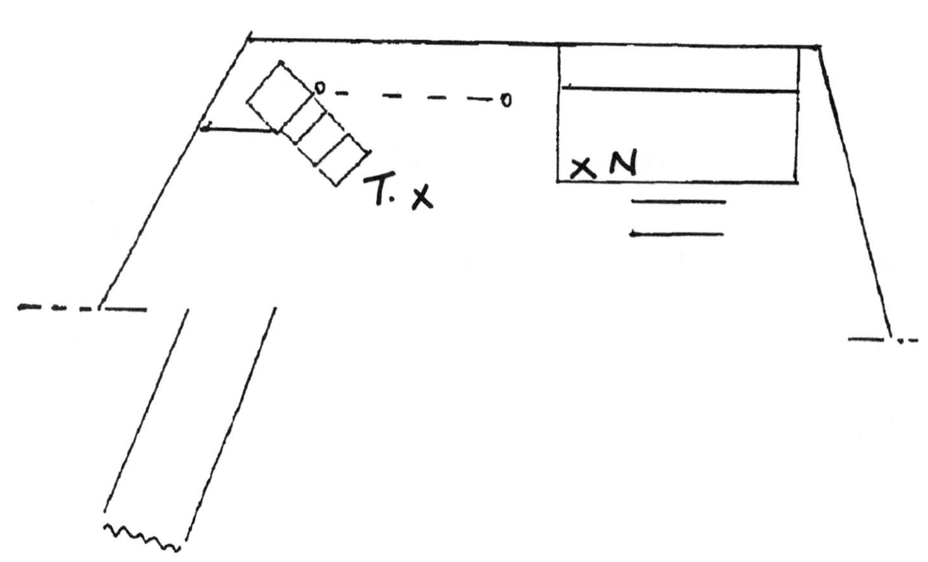

TAEMA

(Changes mood; becoming reminiscent.) Inadequate is the word passionate. In the sky we would be likened to the inseparable lover birds; on earth to the entwined branches. The more I think back on it, how heavenly was our life.

NARUKAMI

(Eager to hear her story. Prays to himself.) Worldly passions eventually lead to holy passions. That I should converse with a woman is probably some turn of fate. *(To her.)* To rest your husband's soul in peace in the next world, I should like to hear your story.

TAEMA

To divert my mind from sorrow, I wish to tell it to you. *(Pause.)* May I relate to you our past?

NARUKAMI

(Slowly.) That would be best. Do go ahead and begin.

TAEMA

I wish to tell you my story, but it's such a distance from here to there. I want to draw closer to you and tell you my tale, but I suppose I would not be allowed to go nearer your side.

Stephen Daley, in talking about what he learned from Kabuki, said. "Basically, the thing that I learned from Baiko was simplifying everything, gestures, speech patterns."

鳴神　大事ない。ここへおじゃ。ここへおじゃ。

絶間　そんあら、お傍へまいりましょう。

ト本舞台へ入り、ツカツカと傍へよる。両僧あわてて留める。

黒雲　コリャコリャコリャ、ならぬ、ならぬ。お師匠様の仰せ渡されで女人禁制。

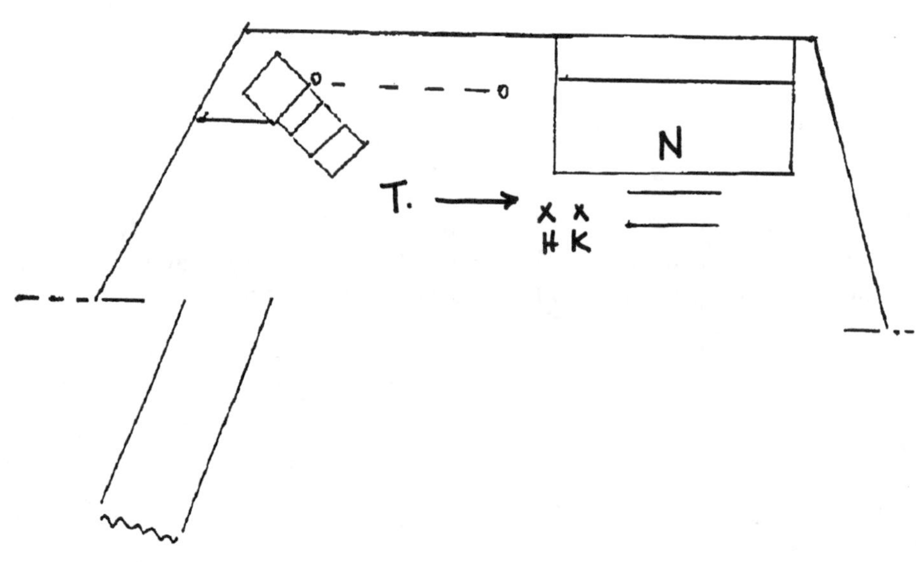

NARUKAMI

You need not hesitate. Come over here and tell me.

TAEMA

Then may I be permitted to draw nearer?

NARUKAMI

It's all right, it's all right.

TAEMA

Then I shall draw close to your side.

(Right KOKEN *strikes aibiki; Left* KOKEN *enters up left, crosses to altar, sets aibiki, exits up left.)*

*(*TAEMA *stands and goes on stage and is stopped at stage right by* HAKUUN *and* KOKUUN.*)*

*(*NARUKAMI *goes to center platform. His* KOKEN *puts aibiki under him.)*

BOTH

Here, here. You may not pass.

絶間　あれ、あの様に云うてでござんすわいなあ。

鳴神　あれ、あの様に云う筈じゃ。壇上近く女子は叶わぬ。両僧の膝元近く寄って、話せ、話せ。

絶間　アイ、アイ。そんならここでお話ししましょう。（薄衣外し、草履ぬぐ）お二人さんもマ、聞いて下さんせ。

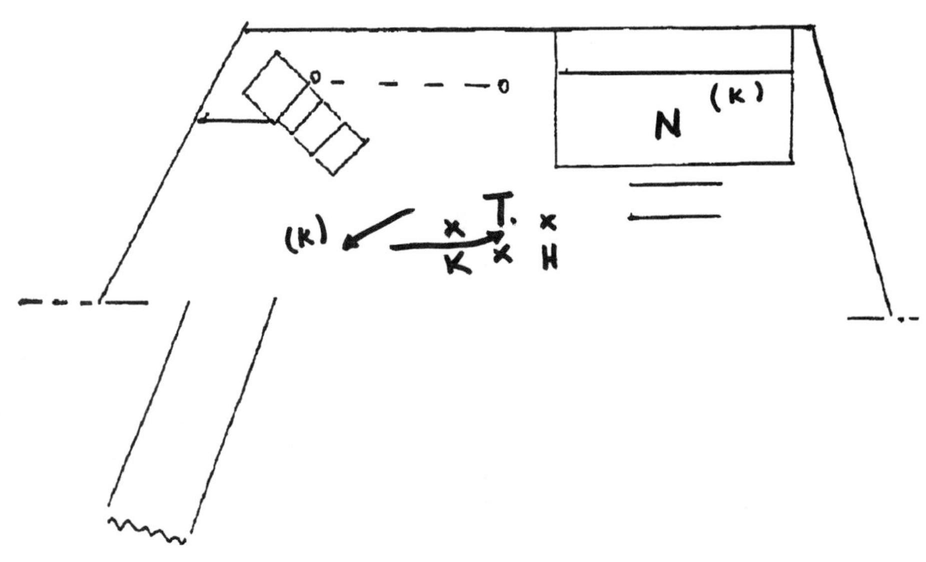

TAEMA

But the Master Priest has given me his permission.

HAKUUN

During the ascetic exercises admittance to women is forbidden.

KOKUUN

(Faster.) This is a restricted area, a restricted area!

TAEMA

(Raises up to see over ACOLYTES *arms.)* Listen to the way they are speaking, Master Priest.

NARUKAMI

It is only natural that they speak so. No women are allowed near the dais. Sit between the priests and relate your story.

(Right KOKEN *strikes bell entering up right. He crosses to* TAEMA *and is given bell, robe and slippers. He then exits up right.)*

TAEMA

Very well. Then I shall tell my story here. *(Pause.)* Both of you, *(Turns left hand.)* you too *(Turns right hand.)* must listen to my story. *(She sits between* HAKUUN *and* KOKUUN *center stage.)*

The position of the thumb is very significant: a female character's thumb should never show. The hand should look smaller than it really is, with the fingers closed together and curved and the thumb hidden.

鳴神　さらば聞こうか。

白雲　サアサア話した。

両人　話した。

　　　　ト千種の合方になり、

絶間　恥ずかしいことながら、その殿御に馴れ初めたはな、遠い事でもござんせぬ。去年の春の弥生半ば、清水へ花見に行ったと思わしゃんせや。したればな、

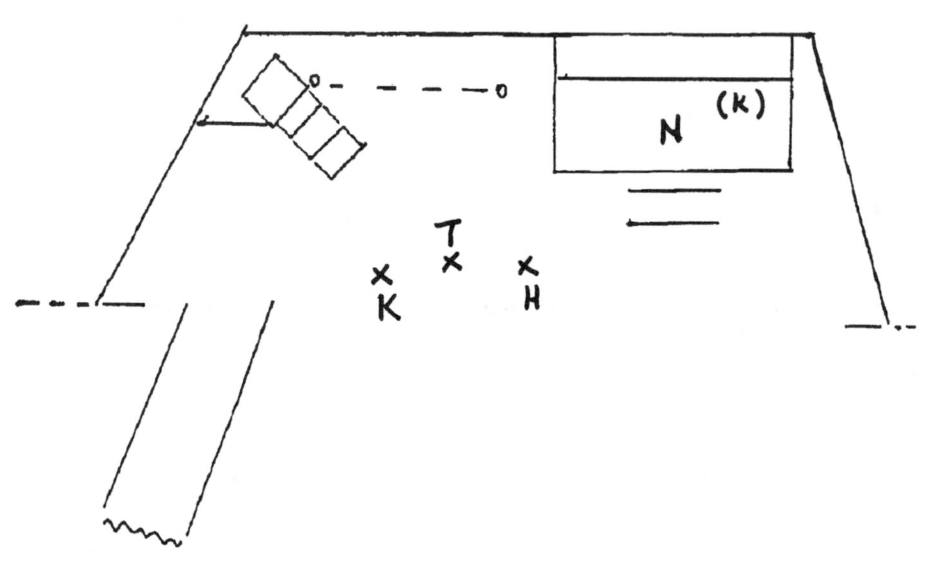

BOTH

Yes, yes. Go ahead. Go ahead.

TAEMA

Then *(Pause.)* I shall begin.

(Music starts.)

NARUKAMI

And I shall listen.

TAEMA

(Background music begins.)

It is not long ago since I became intimate with my lord. I went flower viewing at Kiyomizu *(Points to Kiyomizu.)* in the middle of March during the spring of last year. Mt. Otowa was covered with willowy cherry trees; it was truly a glorious spring personified. There were many private areas enclosed within curtains where the flower-viewing multitude assembled. Here you could hear the strings of the koto; *(Pantomimes plucking strings. Left hand presses strings, right hand plucks strings.)* there the tones of the shamisen *(Pantomimes with left hand holding neck of right hand and plucking it.)* and drums; *(left-hand fist to shoulder, right hand beats drum.)* everywhere people were singing *(Hand to cheek gesture.)* and dancing. *(Hands waving gesture.)*

幕の外に年の

頃は二十歳余りの殿御が、すんがりと立って、わしが幕の内を覗いていやしゃんした。その気高さ、可愛らしさというものは、どうも云われた事じゃござんせぬ。トントわしが方から、いとしゅうなったと思わしゃんせや。

白雲　あの、近付きでもないのに。

絶間　その可愛らしさというものは、ほんに ちりげ元から。

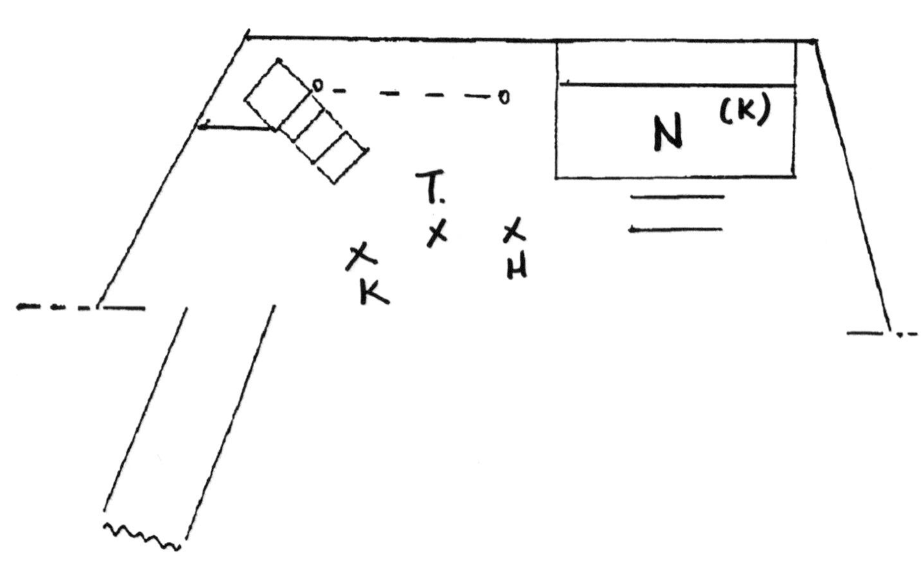

TAEMA *(Continued)*

The atmosphere was irresistible. *(Right hand to side of face.)* I, *(Right index finger up.)* too, received permission from my mother and father to go flower viewing. Outside our enclosure there was a slender, handsome *(Hands upward, palms toward body, fingertips lead hands down and twist and out.)* young gentleman about twenty years old, peering in at me. *(Leans forward.)* His noble bearing, his charm, his eyes, his lips . . . Oh, I cannot describe him in words. I fell deeply *(Right hand over heart.)* and completely *(Right hand down and bows.)* in love with him.

(The following five lines are delivered with overlapping excitement, and spoken a little faster.)

HAKUUN

Although you did not know him?

TAEMA

(Louder and excited.) Ai. So magnetic was his charm that from the nape of my neck . . .

For an onnagata, *playing a female character, the fingers are always to be together. The actor has to walk in a certain way, with the toes facing in, in a rather pigeon-toed way.*

Form dominates Kabuki. But to Baiko, heart is what counts — in Kabuki or any form of art.

黒雲　ぞっとしたか。

絶間　ぞっとしたの、段かいな。

白雲　がたがた震えたか。

絶間　震えたの段かいなあ。寒うなったり、熱うなったり。

黒雲　こりゃ、堪らぬわ。

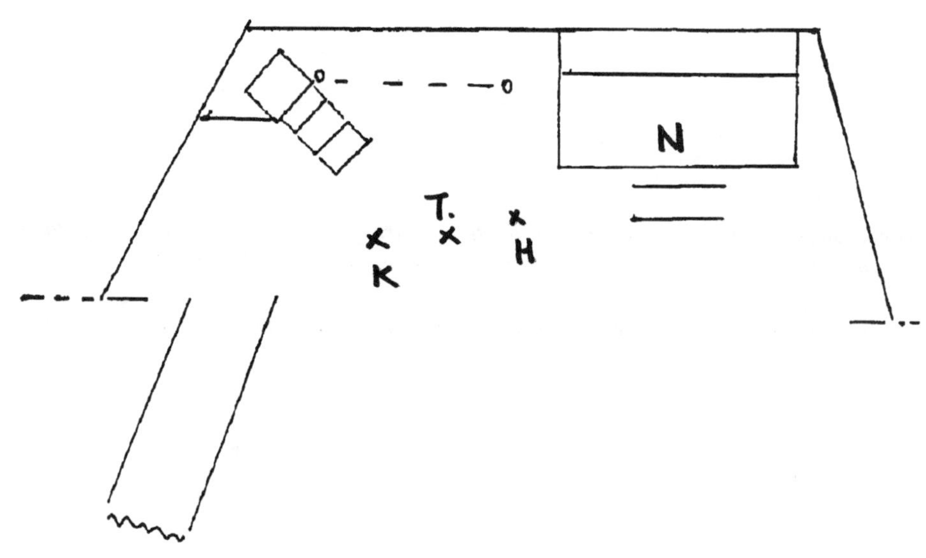

KOKUUN

Did you feel a chill creep over you? *(No pause.)*

TAEMA

Chill is not the word. *(No pause.)*

HAKUUN

Did you shake? *(He shakes.)*

TAEMA

Shake is not the word. Sometimes *(Hands crossed over chest.)* I would become cold; then *(Right hand takes left kimono sleeve and she fans herself.)* sometimes I would become hot. I was conquered by my lord's handsomeness.

HAKUUN

Fascinating!

KOKUUN

Irresistible!

The distilling of an emotion as in Kabuki. I learned by doing. I learned how to wed thought, action and speech; to make the action suit the word. Due to the tightness of form, I learned better how to be specific without any fear or imposition of rigidity. I became more deeply aware of the need for discipline and the use and development of sheer craft. Baiko taught me concentration, endurance, and control. Thanks to him I realized more strongly than ever, the technique of clarity of gesture and movement to illuminate meaning. —Steve Daley

絶間　したれば、先きの殿御もいたずらな。彼方からも、わしの顔を見るようで、見ぬようで。

白雲　うまいな、うまいな。

黒雲　水飴で、餅食うようであったかの。

絶間　そうしたれば、その殿御が懐から短冊を出して、矢立ての筆に墨を招いて送らしゃんした。

両人　能書か、能書か。

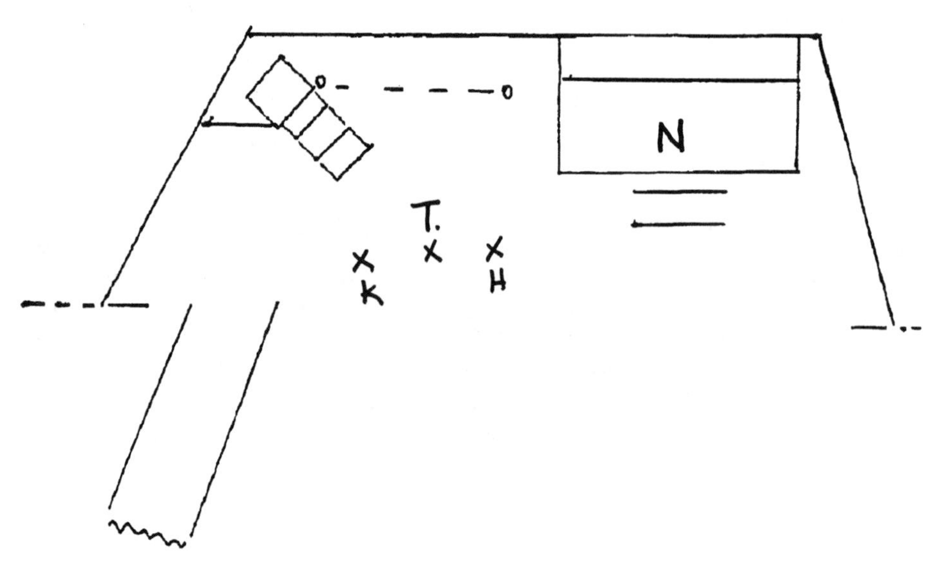

TAEMA

And the lord was flirtatious, too. He was staring at me steadfastly; yet pretended not to be looking at all.

HAKUUN

(Smiling.) (Laughter in voice.) Mmmm . . . How sweet, how honey sweet! *(Edges forward.)*

KOKUUN

(Smiling.) It's like eating rice cakes with dripping jelly.

TAEMA

Then the handsome lord took from the inner bosom of his kimono, a narrow strip of paper *(Takes fan from* kimono.*)*, uses like paper, holds it in left hand, pantomimes dipping brush in ink and pretends to write top to bottom.) and on it with his brush he readily wrote a poem and gave it to me. And his hand was so refined that words cannot describe its beauty.

BOTH

And was his writing elegant?

With the advent of realism, the word became central to acting, and gradually other theatrical elements of dance, poetry, and song were sloughed off. A poet has written that 'the art of allusion, or the love of theatre in arts, is at the root of the Japanese theatre, for it is an art of splendid posture, of dance, of acting that is not realistic.'

絶間　能書とも、能書とも。しかも面白い歌をかかしゃんしたわいの。

白雲　して、その。

両人　歌は。

絶間　見ずもあらず、見もせぬ人の恋しくば。

白雲　見ずもあらず。

黒雲　見もせぬ人の。

両人　恋しくば。

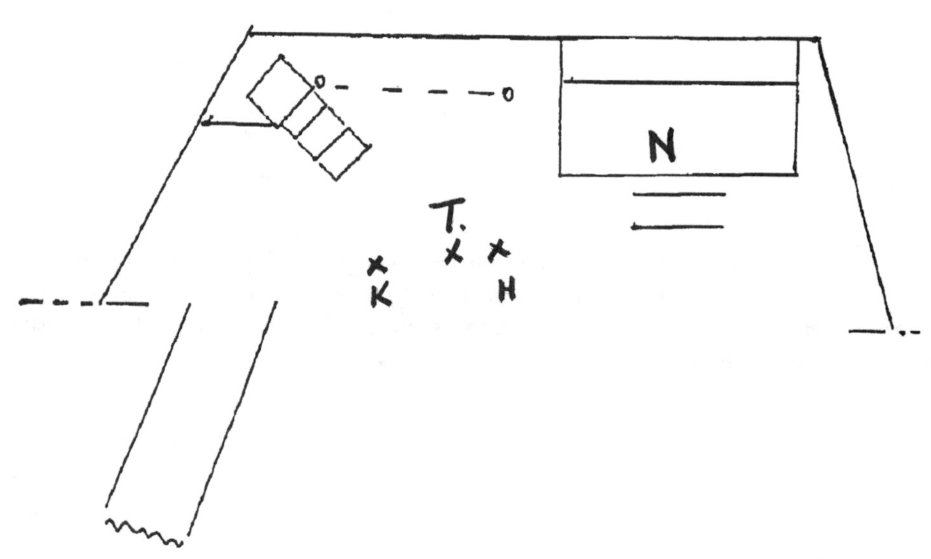

TAEMA

Extremely elegant; moreover, he had written a very entertaining old poem.

BOTH

And the poem said?

TAEMA

(Slowly. As if reading poem from fan, up and down.) "A lady whom I cannot say I have not seen and yet whom I have not positively seen has conquered my heart."

HAKUUN

"A lady whom I cannot say I have not seen."

KOKUUN

"And yet whom I have not positively seen."

BOTH

"Has conquered my heart."

Kabuki dance — or movement — is made rich with beautiful costumes, and dance is central to all traditional Japanese theatre. The language of Kabuki plays is old and hence removed — even for the Japanese.

絶間　ハテ、何んとやら云う、下の句でござんした。

白雲　エ、それを忘れるという事があるものか。

黒雲　板に書き付け、帯へでも括り付けていたがよい。

絶間　見ずもあらず見もせぬ人の恋しくば。

鳴神　あやなく今日や詠っめくらさん、という下の句ではなかったか。

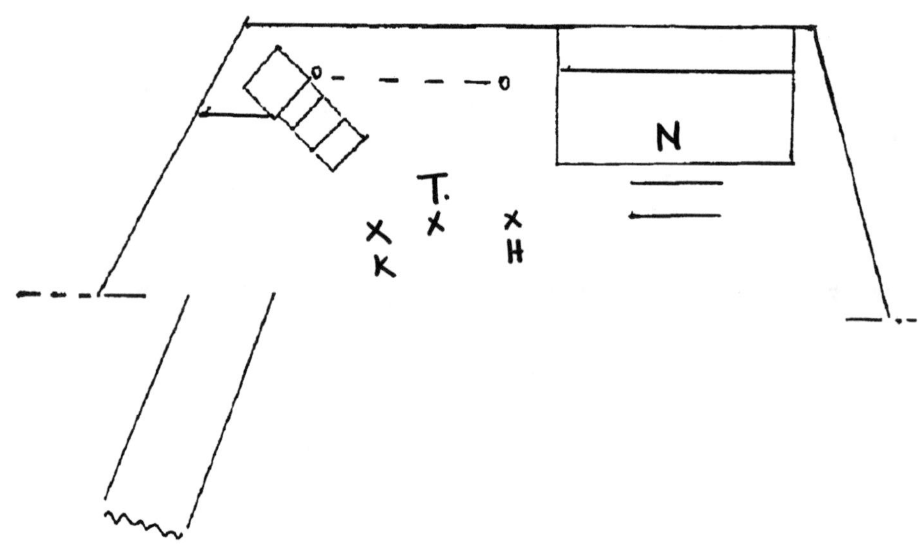

TAEMA

(Right hand to cheek behind ear, thinking; left hand parallel to floor, holding fan.) (Sighing.) Oh dear, what was the complementary line?

(Music Stops.)

HAKUUN

How could you forget such an important line?

KOKUUN

You should have written it on a tablet and tied it to your sash. *(Pantomimes it.)*

TAEMA

(Repeats poem.) "A lady whom I cannot say I have not seen and yet whom I have not positively seen has conquered my heart."

NARUKAMI

(To himself.) "And today I have idly passed the day futilely gazing." *(To her. Becoming interested in the story.)* Was that not the complementary line?

Kabuki is passionate, detailed, complex, ornate, extroverted. Kabuki tends to permit greater activity, greater mobility and greater participation on the part of actors and audience.

絶間　ほんに、そうでござんした。

鳴神　オ、シテシテどうじゃ。（経机にほおずえ）

絶間　とんと、それから面白うなったと思わしゃんせ。

白雲　その筈。

黒雲　その筈。

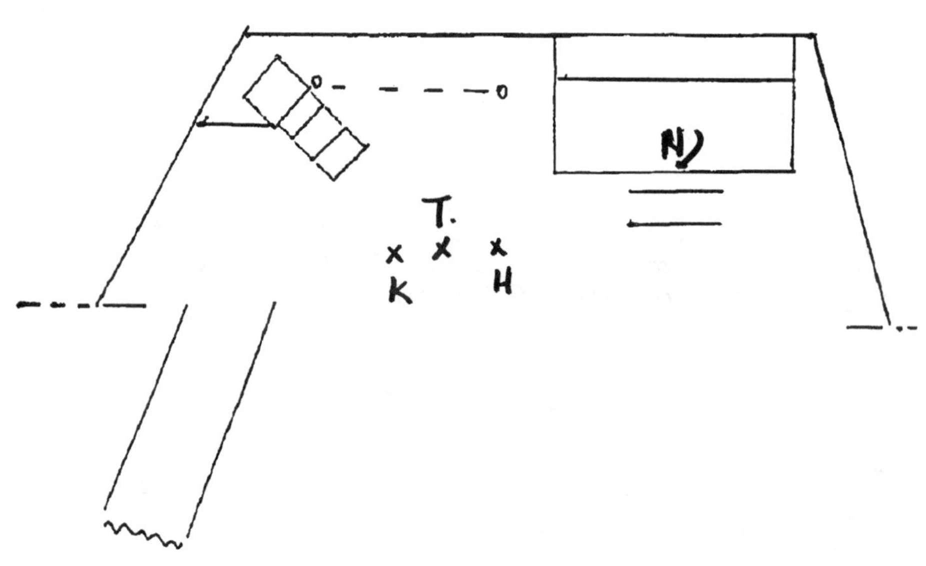

TAEMA

(Starts to build.) (Up on knees; her right hand slaps thigh with the feeling of 'Oh, yes!'; looks at NARUKAMI*; left hand holding fan. Draws out entire line.)*

Indeed, that is the very line!

NARUKAMI

*(*TAEMA *takes armrest, places it in front of himself and frames his face with his hands elongated.) (Speaking with rising and falling inflection.) (A little slower, mysterious.)* And then *(Pause. She places armrest securely in front of him.)* what happened?

(Music starts.)

TAEMA

(Places fan in obi.) (Faster, gaining his interest (keeping it lively).) After that, matters began to grow livelier.

*(*NARUKAMI *sneaks arms down, crossed on armrest.)*

BOTH

(Hands above kyosuku.*)* That is only natural; that is only natural.

George Gitto: *"One particular hand gesture, where, as* Narukami, *the priest, I used my hands to frame my face, had to be done at the end of the word and as the hands framed the face and the chin, my head had to snap into position* 'like a photograph taken with one click of the camera!' *All gestures, movements had to be very, very specific, to the syllable of a word of text."*

絶間　そこで、わしが局を呼んで、あなたのお名を聞いて。

両人　云うたかたか。

絶間　云わしゃんせぬわいなア。

両人　南無妙法連華経。

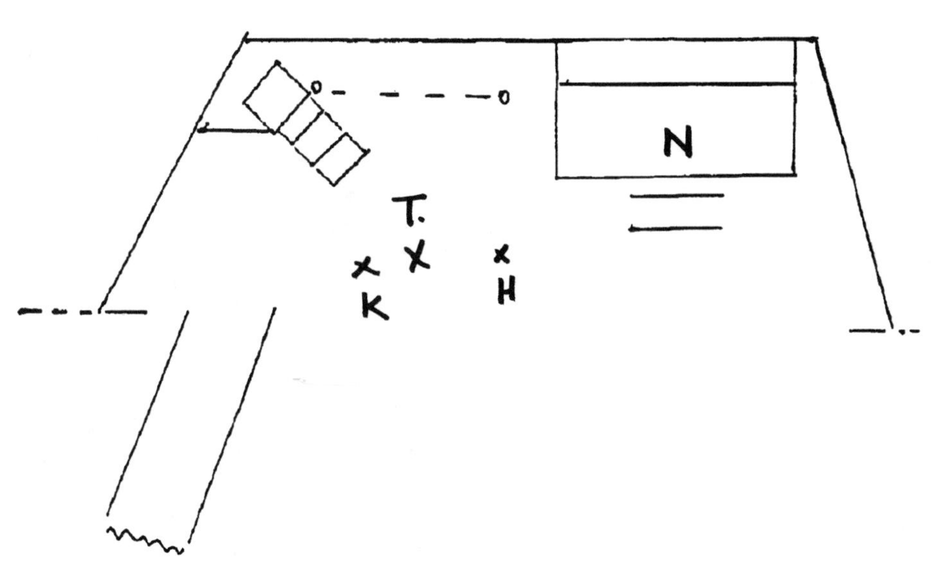

TAEMA

So I beckoned my lady-in-waiting, and had her ask him his name.

BOTH

And did he tell you?

TAEMA

(Disappointed.) No, he did not tell me his name.

BOTH

Oh glory to the Holy Sutra of the Lotus of the Supreme Law! *(*BOTH *make praying gesture.)*

TAEMA

Amazing is the benevolence of the Goddess of Mercy. *(Praying gesture.)* I prayed fervently for guidance and in my dream an oracle answered me.

BOTH

Very strange, very strange.

When a person comes out of the Noh playhouse, he is supposed to come out wiser. When he comes out of the Kabuki-za, he comes out entertained, refreshed, catharted. He has rid himself of something rather than having gotten something. He comes out as if he had been in a hypnotic trance, in a dream. It has been like a dream which permits us to sleep and awaken again refreshed, recuperated and ready to face a reality much less acceptable and satisfying than the Kabuki story.
—Dr. E. K. Schwartz

絶間　シタが、普門品の功徳ういついもので、その夜、皆を寝させておいて、わしたった一人、嵯峨野の奥まで行ったわいなア。

両人　きついわきついわ。

絶間　したればな、（扇しまい）大きな川があって。（両手ひろげ）

白雲　あるともあるとも。大堰川、桂川。

黒雲　名代の川じゃ。

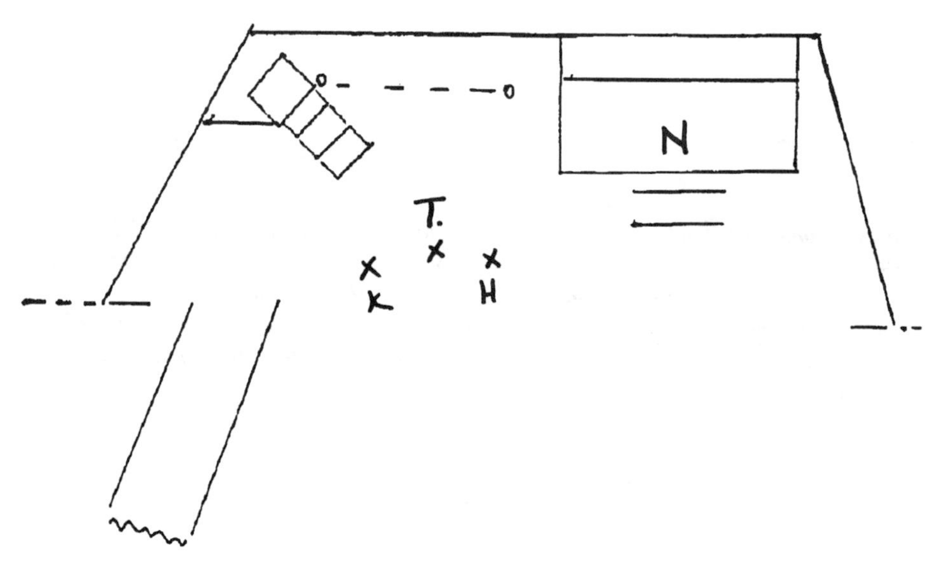

TAEMA

I was so happy, so thankful. That night after everyone had fallen asleep, all alone I ventured to the dwelling of my lord in the inner regions of Saga as directed by the oracle.

BOTH

(They edge toward TAEMA, *leaning toward her and the audience.) (Speaking fast.)* How brave, how brave!

TAEMA

And then . . . *(Pause.)* there was a large river. *(Hands together, then fluttering apart.)*

HAKUUN

Yes, there are the Oie and Katsura Rivers.

(Music stops.)

KOKUUN

They are famous rivers.

Natalie Ross points out that "The walking in a Japanese *kimono*, especially the kind worn by *Princess Taema*, was of many layers of kimono, and was very tricky. You use the ankle bone to push away the hem of the *kimono* to take a step. By doing that you're automatically pigeon-toed. The thinking is not to walk pigeon-toed, but the thinking is to walk as dictated for control of the costume, moving to get rid of the train."

絶間　サア、その川を渡ろうと思えば、船はなし、橋はなし。さらば胆を据えて、昼ならばよいものか、闇を便りの川渡り。女子の身の大胆な、裾をグッとからげてな。

両人　まくったかまくったか。

絶間　まくったの段かいな。とんとすそをからげて川の中へ入りゃんした。

両人　お、つめた。

絶間　向こうの方へぞんぶり。

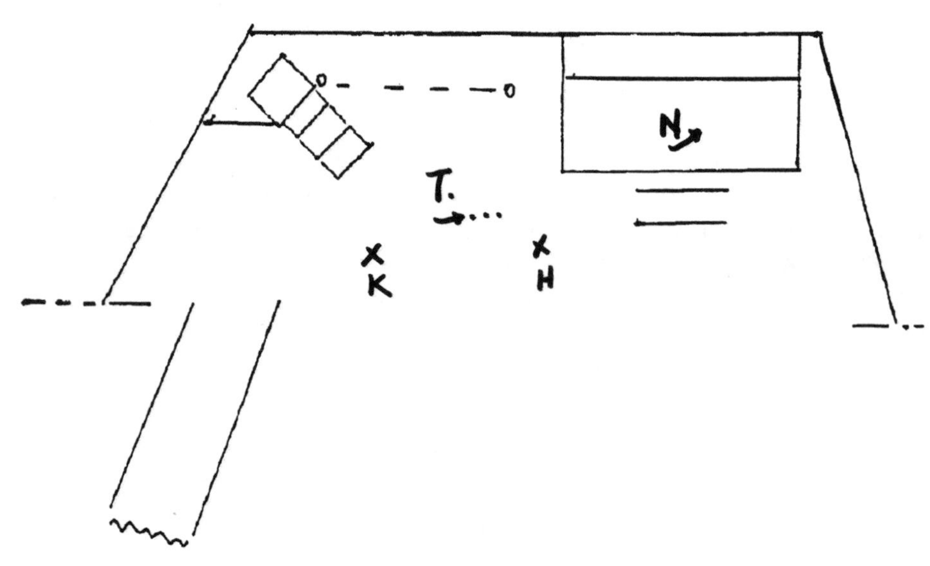

TAEMA

Even though I wanted to cross the river there was neither a boat nor a bridge. How I wished it were daytime, *(Stands in place.)* but there was only the pitch of darkness to rely upon. And, though a woman, I boldly pulled up the hem *(She pulls up her hem.* NARUKAMI *looks. He moves* kyusoku.*)* of my *kimono.*

(NARUKAMI *is amazed when she demonstrates. He puts his armrest aside.)*

BOTH

(Faster.) Did you roll it up? Did you roll it up? *(Chins up.)*

TAEMA

I certainly did. I lifted my hem up very high and stepped into the water. *(She steps 2 or 3 steps forward.)*

BOTH

Oh, it's icy cold. *(They stand.)*

TAEMA

Disregarding the cold, I headed for the other shore and . . . splash . . .

白雲　ぞんぶり。

絶間　ぞんぶり。

黒雲　ぞんぶり。

絶間　ぞんぶり。

両人　ぞんぶりぞんぶり。

絶間　ぞんぶりぞんぶり。

白雲　おう深いわ深いわ。

黒雲　これは、丈が足らぬは。

ト左手を顎の下に当て思い入れ。

この中三人して川を渡る可笑し味あり。

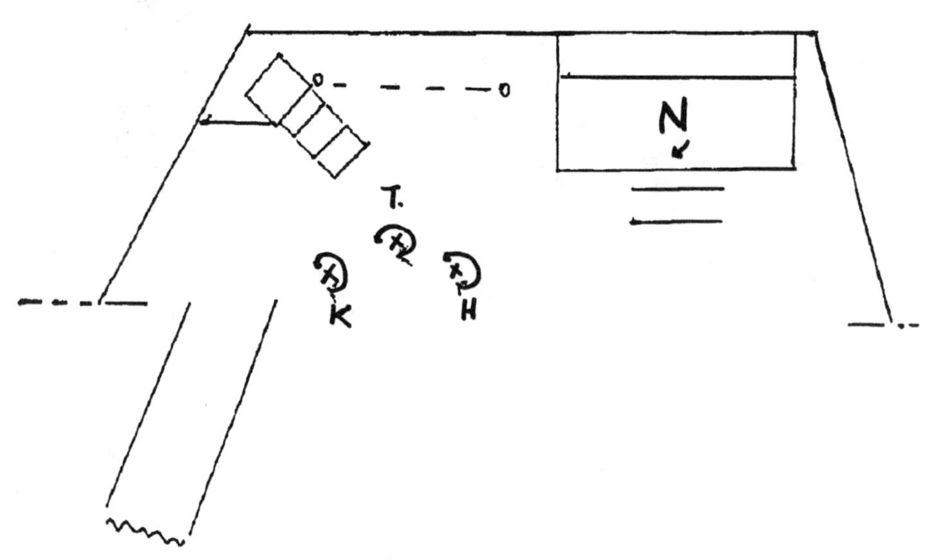

BOTH

Splash . . . .

TAEMA

Zomburi . . . . *(*TAEMA *and* PRIESTS *step right, step left, each making their own small circle.* PRIESTS *lift legs higher than she.)*

BOTH

Zomburi . . . .

(They all three walk around with hems lifted.)

ALL THREE

Zomburi . . . zomburi . . . zomburi. . . .

*(*Zomburi *is repeated until each has made his own complete circle.)*

HAKUUN

(Chin up.) Oh, it's deep; it's fathomless. *(Stepping, indicates water has reached his chin.)*

KOKUUN

It's getting out of our depth. *(Standing on toes.)*

Zomburi is pronounced zohm-boor-ee.

絶間　向こうの岸へ渡り着いたわいの。

白雲、黒雲　え、絞れ絞れ。

ト着物を絞る思い入れ。

絶間　濡れぬ先こそ露をも厭えと、小笹掻き分け萩踏みしだき、殿御の庵に着いたわいなア。

両人　着いたか着いたか。

絶間　柴折戸をズット押開けて中へ入るとナ、彼の殿御が、ヤレおじゃったかと云うて、わしが手を取ってすぐに床にはいらしゃんした。

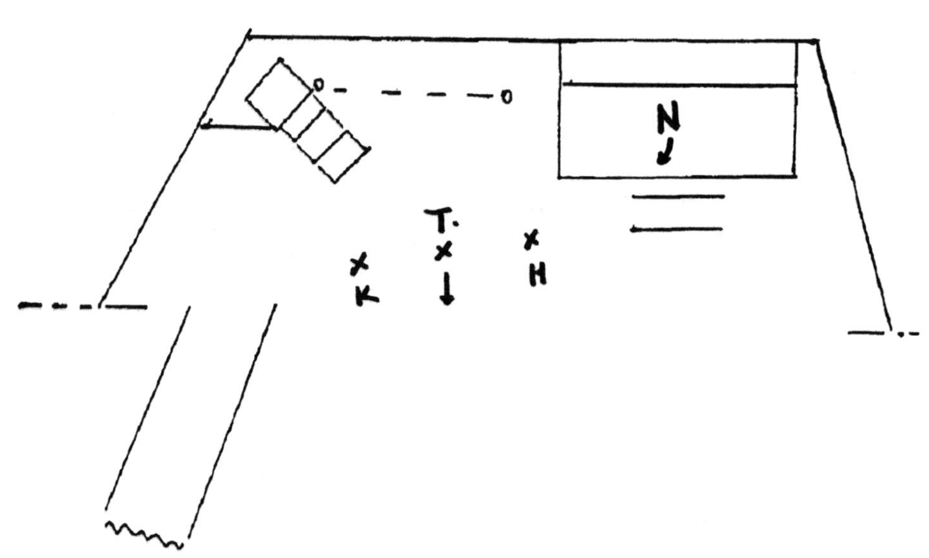

TAEMA

Finally I reached the other shore. *(Crosses left, pivots right.)*

(Music starts.)

BOTH

(Slower.) Wring it, wring it. *(They wring their hems, then sit.)*

TAEMA

My hem was dripping wet, but to me it no longer mattered. I pushed aside the bamboo Pantomimes pushing stems aside one by one, with right hand, then left hand.) grass and trod *(Hand to thighs.)* wildly on the reeds. To my lord's hermitage, *(Points to hermitage with right hand.)* I finally *(Twisting movement, left hand down.)* groped my way.

BOTH

Did you get there? Did you get there?

TAEMA

(Pantomimes pushing open a gate.) I pushed open the garden gate and went far inside. There my lord was waiting for me, *(Makes small circles with right hand, then puts hand inside kimono.)* and extending his hand *(Imitates his taking her hand, holds pose.)* to me he said, "Dear, did you come?" and pulled me in.

(NARUKAMI *edges forward.)*

"As a man playing a woman who is dancing, you must pull your shoulder blades together to lower the shoulders and the elbows," *Baiko observed.* "The most fearsome time for an onnagata is when you turn your back to the audience. If you lose control of your posture, you will quickly be seen as a man. From the front, you are wearing makeup and you can fool others easily." *Regularly rehearsing in the nude helps make feminine posture* "a part of you," *Baiko says.*

白雲　オ、こりゃとけるわ、とけるわ。

黒雲　そなたは、とけるか知らぬが、わしゃ木になった。

絶間　何かの積もる物語、香をきくやら酒を呑むやら、組んず転れつ、転れつ組んず。あんまり戯れがすぎて、つい口説になったわいな。

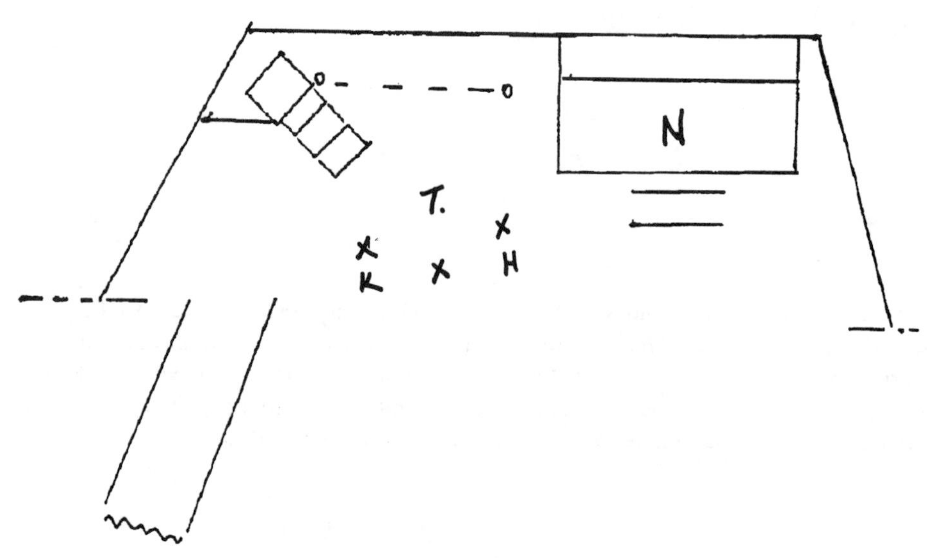

BOTH

I'm melting. I'm melting. *(Heads wobbling, quality of ice cream melting.)*

*(*TAEMA *sits.)*

TAEMA

(Lively tone.) We had many things to talk about. We enjoyed *(Hand cupped over palm, smelling incense.)* burning incense. We drank sake. *(Pantomimes drinking using both hands.)* We were so happy but our flirtations soon turned to lovers' quarrels.

(Music starts.)

HAKUUN

Oh, I can't resist this. *(Edges forward.)*

KOKUUN

When two become madly in love, they *(sometimes)* become discordant.

The form and content of the live theatre are always historical and culture-bound. The movement (process, plot) on the other hand, is more universal and less time-bound. The play may be experienced then from any or all points of view simultaneously.

エ、ずんとおかしゃんせ。おくまいが。エ、つねるぞえ、叩くぞや。叩かしゃんせ。叩いて見やと、殿御の頭をぴっしゃり。

ト両人の頭を叩く。両人痛がる。

黒雲　かんにんせいかんにんせい。

絶間　その云い上りが昂じて、わしゃもう去ぬる、（ト袖で表情）去のうとするわしが袖をじっと控えて。

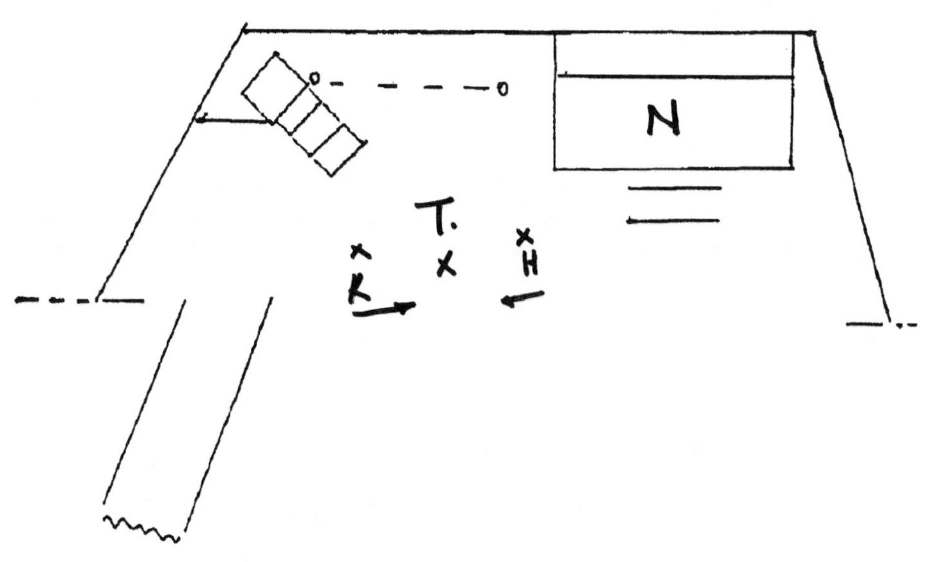

TAEMA

*(*KOKUUN *and* HAKUUN *edge closer during the following speech.)*

I said, "Oh, please stop it." "Of course, I'll stop," he said. "I'm going to pinch *(Pantomimes pinch.)* you; I'm going to *(Raises hand to strike.)* strike you," I continued. "Go ahead and strike me," he said. "I really will strike you," and I slapped his head.

(She slaps KOKUUN*'s head and stands on knees.)*

KOKUUN

(Slowly.) Please forgive me, please forgive me. *(*KOKUUN *bows with his hands over his head.* KOKUUN *and* HAKUUN *edge back.)*

TAEMA

"I'm bored; I'm going home," I said. "No, I won't let you go," he said. "No, I must go home." I quickly and smoothly stood and was about to leave when he pulled me back by the sleeve *(On knees gestures with left hand holding* kimono *extended left, right hand in left.)* and recited another old poem to me.

Natalie Ross remembers that "When the woman's kimono has long trailing sleeves, very often the character uses the sleeves, holding the edge of the sleeve, to hide the face; sometimes used as a half mask to peer coyly over the top. Use of the sleeves is part of the acting style . . ."

鳴神　オ、してして、どうじゃ。

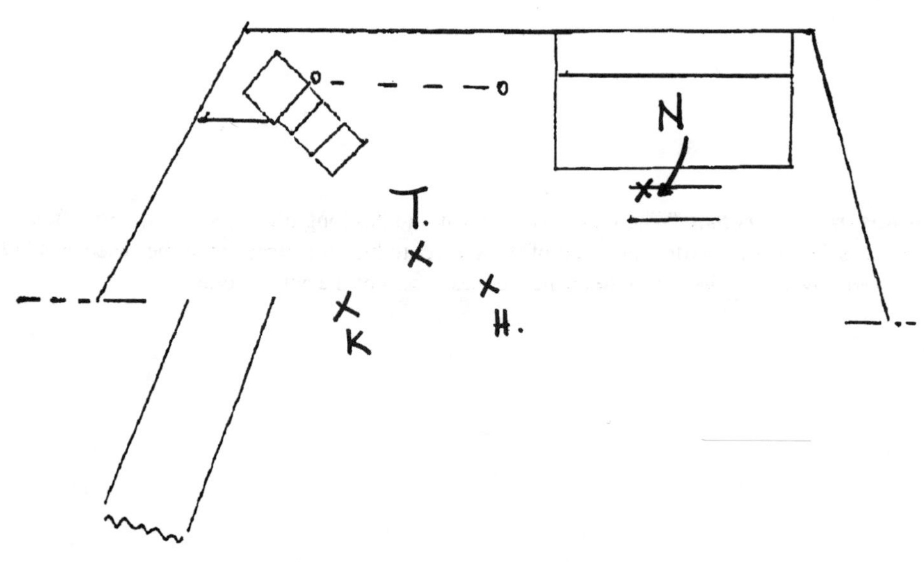

BOTH

And what was that poem?

(Music stops.)

TAEMA

"In this world where tomorrow's friends are unknown . . ." *(Right hand behind ear, thinking.)* Oh dear, I have forgotten the last line again.

NARUKAMI

"How I regret to part with my companion of today." Was that not the ending?

TAEMA

(Slaps right thigh with right hand.) Indeed, that was the very way in which it ended. *(Looks at* NARUKAMI.*)*

NARUKAMI

(Becoming excited. Right foot forward on second step; right hand on knee; left hand forearm.) And then what happened?

絶間　サア、なんぼ止めさしゃんしても、私しゃ去なにゃおかぬ。イヤ去なさぬ。イヤ去ぬる、引かれる袂を振り切って、つういと。

トこの時、壇上より鳴神滑り落ち、気を失う。

白雲　ヤア、こりゃお師匠様が、目を廻さっしゃれた。

両人　お師匠様お師匠様。

絶間　お上人様お上人様。

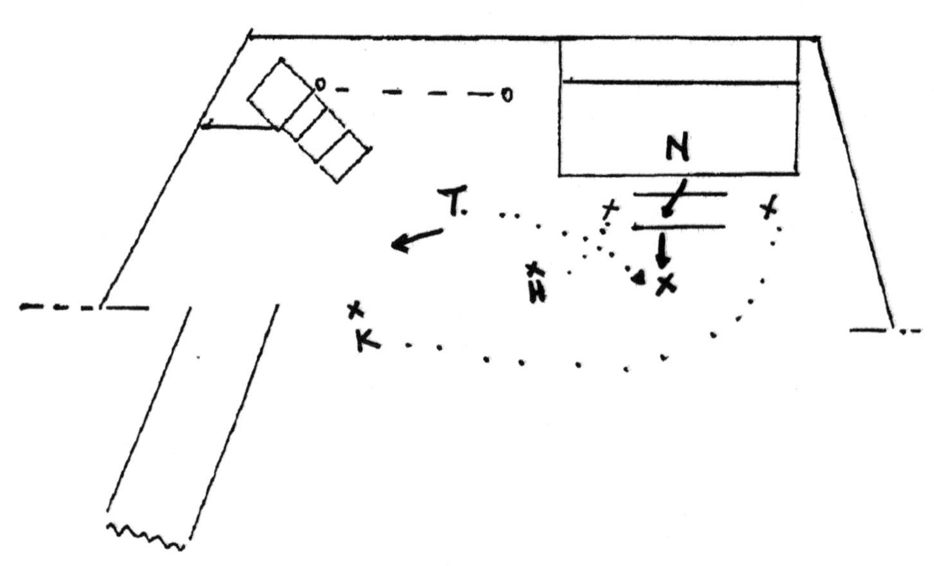

(Left KOKEN *enters; strikes aibiki; exits up left.)*

TAEMA

I said, "I'm going to leave," *(Stands.)* but he again firmly seized my sleeve and drew me back, saying, "I cannot let you go." Insisting that I must go, I freed myself *(Drops sleeve.)* from his hold and quickly *(Turns away from* NARUKAMI *to stage right.)* I ran away. *(She crosses right toward hanamichi as she spreads both arms from chest to open 'wing' position and kneels, arms in wing position. Feeling the part of her lover, as if pursuing her,* NARUKAMI *stands, crosses down center, falls down the steps —* tsuke *— and faints.)*

(Left KOKEN strikes pillow and kyosoku *from platform.)*

BOTH

Oh, our master has fainted. *(They cross to him and call out.)* Master Priest! Master Priest!

TAEMA

(Slowly, but hurried feeling.) Dear priest! Dear priest! *(She rubs his back.)*

ト二人ひき起こし呼び活ける。絶間、滝の水を手に掬う。

白雲　こりや、総身が。

両人　冷とうなったわ。

絶間　上人様上人様。

ト絶間ははじめ袂で、気付いて口に含み来て口移しに滝の水を飲まし、アト頬を胸に当てる。鳴神、気付く思い入れ。

鳴神　両僧。

白雲　嬉しや嬉しや。

両人　お気がついたわ。

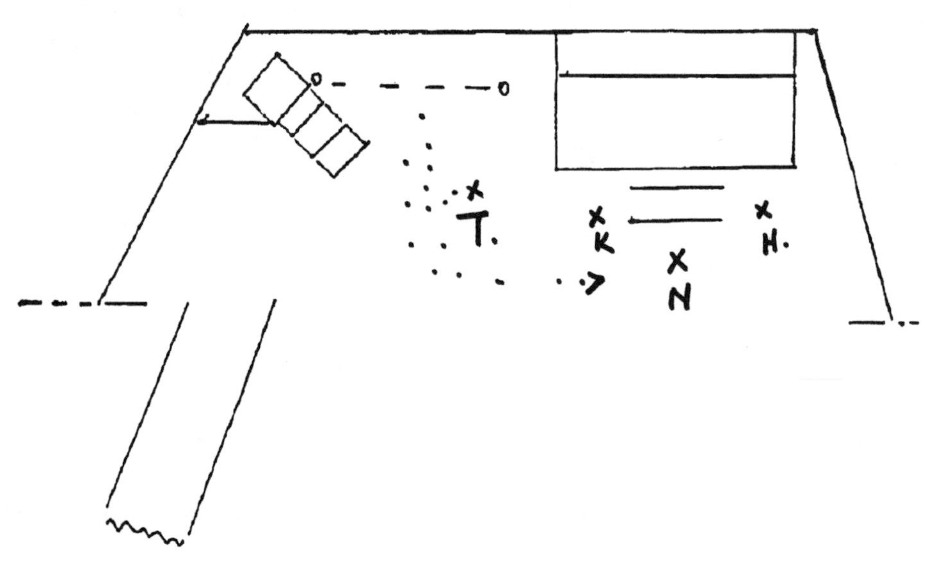

(HAKUUN *and* KOKUUN *withdraw and watch her.)*

(TAEMA *looks around, notices the waterfall and goes to it; makes a cup out of her sleeve, fills it with water and drinks; returns to* NARUKAMI, *lifts him by the shoulders. He pivots with left leg to sitting position. She gives him water from her mouth, shielding the exchange with her* kimono.*)*

(HAKUUN *and* KOKUUN, *embarrassed, they hide faces with left sleeve, then, crouching, watch her.)*

(TAEMA *sits* NARUKAMI *up.)*

TAEMA

Dear priest, dear priest, *(Strongly.)* dear priest! *(Simultaneously, as she speaks she rubs* NARUKAMI*'s chest up and down.* NARUKAMI*'s eyes open. She holds him, kneeling up right of him.)*

HAKUUN

How happy we are. *(Takes a breath.)*

BOTH

(More happily.) He has come to life again.

鳴神　沙門の身にあるまい事。婦人の話に聞きほれて、思わず壇上よりまろび落ち、今性根を失う中に、一滴の冷水口中に入ると思えば、気も爽やかになったわえ。

絶間　そりゃその筈でござんす。あの滝の水を私が口移しで上げたのじゃわいなア。

鳴神　ナニ、その水を飲ませてくれたはそなた。

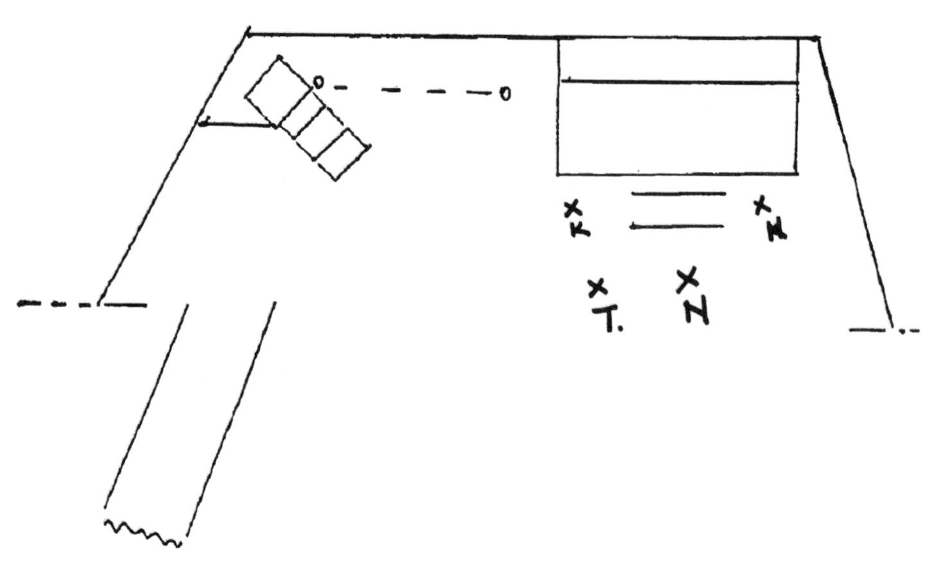

TAEMA

(She takes right sleeve from side to center; places arm behind NARUKAMI *on shoulder.)* Dear priest, have you awakened?

NARUKAMI

Priests!

BOTH

Hai.

NARUKAMI

Indeed, unbecoming to a Buddhist priest, I became enraptured by a woman's story and fell down from the dais. My reason left me, and suddenly I felt a cold drop of water in my mouth which made me feel refreshed.

*(*TSUKEUCHI *enters, sits down left.)*

TAEMA

That is only natural. The water from the *(Points to waterfall.)* waterfall was given to you directly from my mouth to yours.

NARUKAMI

Hmm? You mean to say that it was you who gave me the water?

George Gitto talks about playing the title role in NARUKAMI. *"Mr. Baiko had a precise idea of what we actors were supposed to do. I was fascinated. He was an actor directing us. I tried to emulate what he was bringing to me, an actor. That was very helpful."*

絶間　アイ。

絶間　又、胸をあたためてくれたも、そなた。

絶間　アイ。

鳴神　ウム。

ト絶間の顔をジッと見て、思入れありてその胸倉をとって突きのける。

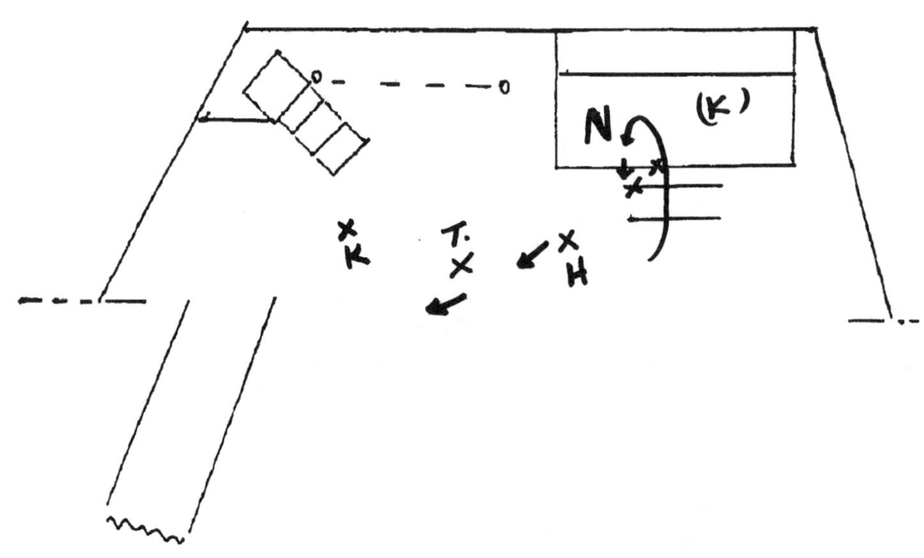

TAEMA

Ai-i.

NARUKAMI

And the one who caressed my chest, *(He caresses his chest.)* was you also?

TAEMA

Ai.

NARUKAMI

*(*NARUKAMI *glares at her.) (Strongly.)* Priests, *(Looks at* BOTH.*)* on your guard.

*(*NARUKAMI *shoves her, stand; he pushes* TAEMA *with right arm, then up; he climbs the steps of the dais and strikes a pose — right foot on second step, left foot on stage, hands meeting at center of prayer beads.)*

*(*HAKUUN *and* KOKUUN *pose with weight on up stage leg.* KOKUUN *crosses down right 3/4 arms out, feet spread.* HAKUUN *on left of* TAEMA *between* NARUKAMI *and* TAEMA. TAEMA *shields herself with left hand, palm toward audience, held high.)*

絶間　あれえ。

鳴神　両僧油断すな。

両人　ハッ。（トかまえる）

鳴神　ヤアいぶかしき女。昔天竺破羅那国に一人の導師あり、名付けて一角仙人という。或る時竜神と争いて、よし、国土に雨を降らせじと、巌窟に封じこめる。時の帝これをあざむかせ給い、かかる仙人が魂をとろかして通力を破って都に帰る。察するところ、その古き例をひき、おのれに手だてを教えしは、かの陰陽師博士安部の清行をおいて他になし。サア、正直正路の返答は、どど、どうじゃ。

絶間　勿体ないお上人様、思いがけもないお疑いを受けましてござります。何卒あなたのお弟子になりとう存じまして、ツイ申しました我が身の話、お疑い受けましては、所詮生きても詮ない事。あの滝壷へ身を沈め相果てるが申し訳、そうじゃ。

ト滝の方へゆく。

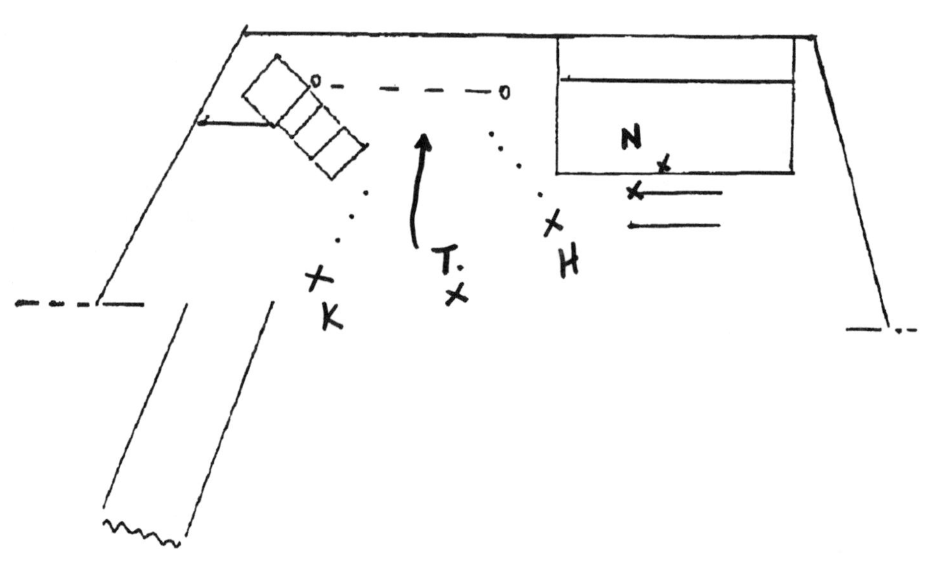

TAEMA

What are you doing?

(Music.)

NARUKAMI

(Slowly.) You conniving woman. *(Rapidly.)* Following the example of the Priest Ikkaku Sennin of India, who was ruined by a beauty, you have come to break my supernatural power. Now, confess. *(Faster.)* You are the daughter of what court noble in the Imperial Palace? If you do not confess, I'll tear you apart this very moment. *(Slowly.)* Woman, *(*NARUKAMI *turns back to audience facing* TAEMA, *left foot on step; right foot on stage.)* what is your *(Head jerked down toward* TAEMA.*)* answer?

TAEMA

(She kneels and bows throughout.) How impious that would be of me, dear Priest! Never would I degrade myself to such a being. In order to wash the keepsake of my beloved husband, I have with great difficulty climbed the mountain to this waterfall, though I am but a woman. Never did I suppose that I would be suspected by your highness, the priest. I have no choice; I shall throw myself into the basin of the waterfall and join my husband in death. To all *(Turns head left and right.)* of you I bid farewell. *(She bows, turns around and goes to waterfall. She kneels, prays, her back to audience. Priests look at her, on either side of* TAEMA, *hands slightly stretched out.)* Namu ami da Butsu.

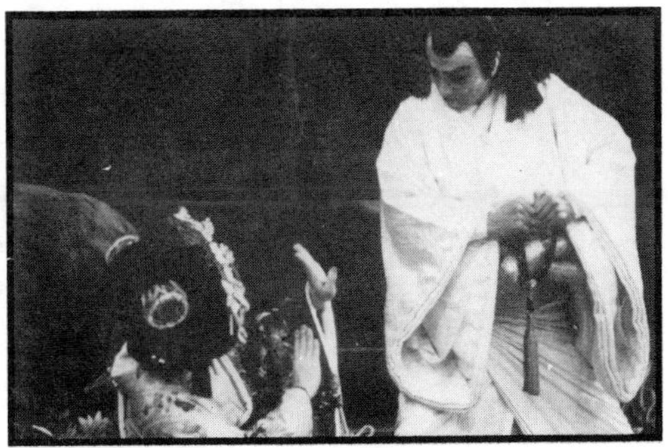

(As TAEMA *was doing upon her entrance to the stage, she once again calls upon the* Amida Buddha. *Throught calling upong* Amida Buddha, *the suppliant is saved.)*

鳴神　両僧止めい。

両人　マア、またっしゃれ。

ト両人とめる。

絶間　いえいえ放して、殺して下さりませ。

鳴神　ハテ気の短い。一旦咎めたれがこそ、そなたの本性が顔色に現われて、殊勝殊勝。死ぬるに及ばぬ、死んで菩提の為にはならぬぞ。

絶間　でも生きていて。

鳴神　尼になりゃ。比丘尼になりゃ。

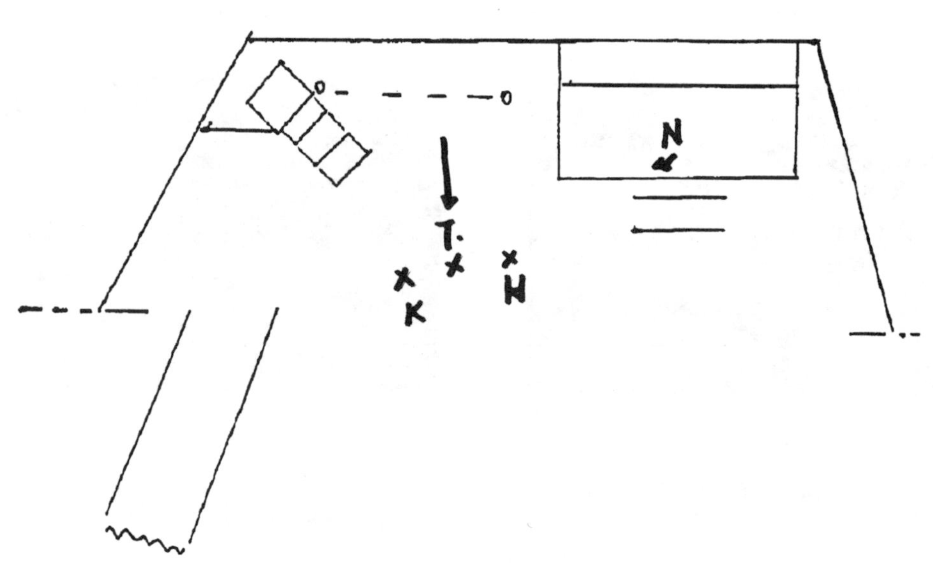

NARUKAMI

(Steps out on platform, left foot swings, right hand in "stop" gesture.)

Here, stop her.

BOTH

Hai. *(They bring her back to stage right, hold her arm. She kneels; they stand.)*

NARUKAMI

(As if teaching her.) My, how impetuous you are. I no longer doubt you. I did reproach you, but I can now see that your heart is true. You need not die a futile death. Death does not bring salvation.

TAEMA

Being thus suspected, how can I live any longer? *(She gets up and tries to go to waterfall to jump in again.* KOKUUN *and* HAKUUN *restrain her.)*

NARUKAMI

(Rosary in left hand.) Become a nun; become a priestess. (KOKUUN *and* HAKUUN *let go of her arms.)*

絶間　エ、。

鳴神　この鳴神が剃刀を当て、御仏の弟子にしょう。

絶間　すりゃ、この髪を剃って、あなたのお弟子になされて下さりまするか。

鳴神　おいのう。

絶間　ほんいかえ。

鳴神　鳴神に妄語両舌があろうか。

絶間　エ、有難うござりまする。

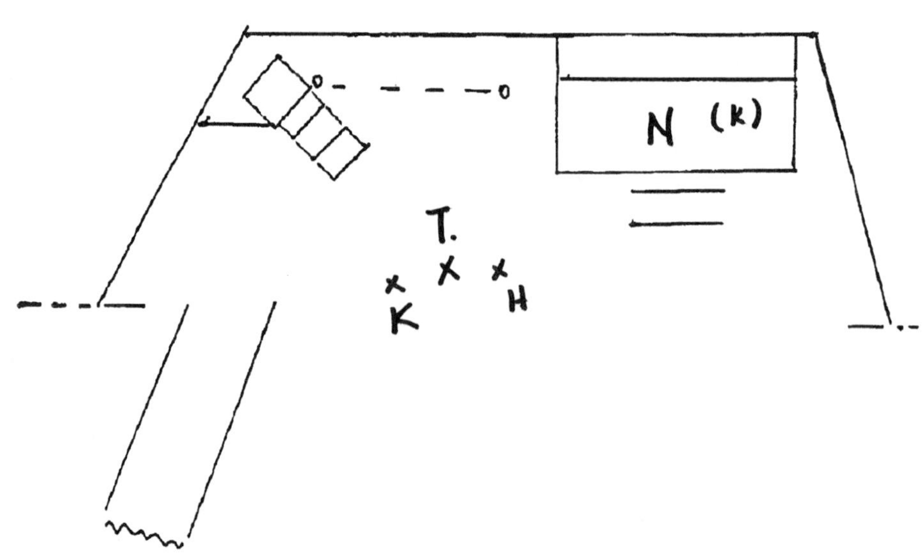

TAEMA

What? Then you will shave off my hair and make me your disciple?

NARUKAMI

Yes, indeed.

TAEMA

Do you really mean so?

NARUKAMI

Would I, Narukami, lie?

TAEMA

Oh, then I thank you very much. *(Bows low.)*

(Left KOKEN *brings out large* aibiki *for* NARUKAMI *and exits left after setting* aibiki.*)*

*(*KOKEN *brings out large stool and* NARUKAMI *sits immediately.)*

白雲　これで落ち着いた。

ト両僧離れて下手へ、

黒雲　わしも、またすくろびなと縫うて貰うには、まあよいが。

鳴神　両僧。両人をして、麓へ下って、剃刀と剃髪の具を購えて来い。（座っていう）

両人　エ、。

鳴神　行かぬか。

白雲　参ります参ります。もう日暮れじゃによって。

黒雲　いっそ、明日の事になされませぬか。

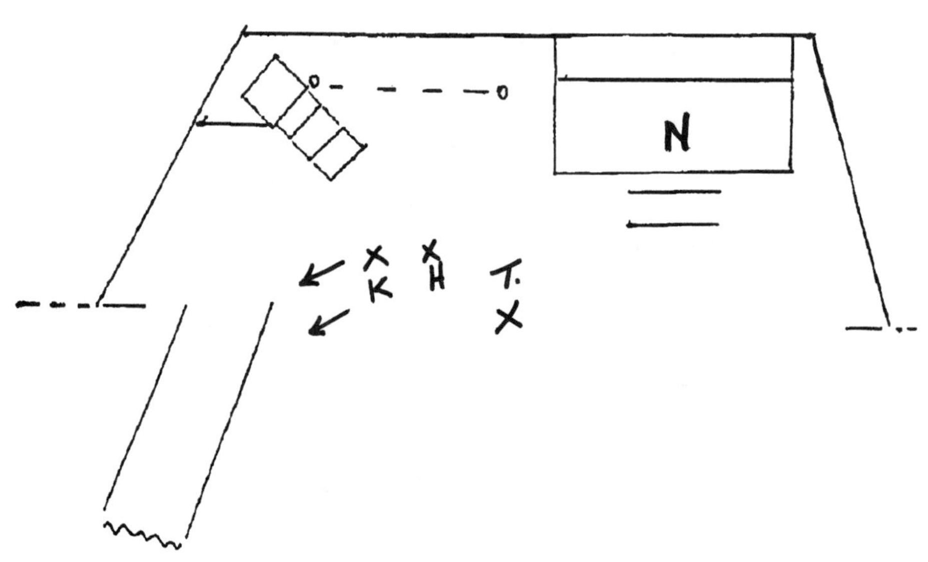

BOTH

Now we are finally relieved. *(Expressing relief with a sigh; hands rub their chests down. They kneel.)*

NARUKAMI

Both of you, go to the foot of the mountains and fetch the razor, the implements necessary for taking the tonsure, and the holy vestment. *(Throughout,* TAEMA *sits with left sleeve laid on left knee.)*

BOTH

(Skeptical, afraid of the dark.) (Strongly.) Do you mean now?

NARUKAMI

Do so immediately.

HAKUUN

But my dear master, the sun has gone down. *(Turns and looks at* NARUKAMI.*)*

KOKUUN

It's getting darker and darker.

鳴神　師匠の言葉を背くか。行こうと云うたら、早う失しょう。

両人　ハアイ。（ト両人立ち、舞台七三へ行きながら）

白雲　失せまする失せまする。失せは失せまするが、わし等が失せたその後は、お師匠様と。

黒雲　あの女中とたった二人。

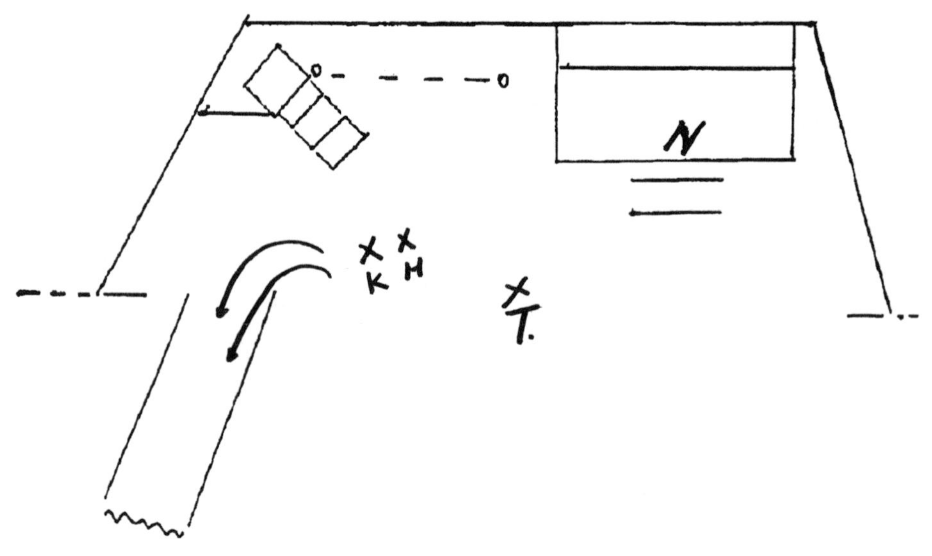

NARUKAMI

Whether night is closing in or whether it be break of day, do you mean to disobey your master?

HAKUUN

Oh no, to disobey . . .

BOTH

We have no intention.

NARUKAMI

Then be gone!

BOTH

Hai-i. *(They bow, then stand. They go upstage to* shichisan *on* hanamichi *and* KOKEN *helps them wear their slippers.)*

HAKUUN

Hey, Kokuumbo. He is sending us off to the foot *(Points down* hanamichi.*)* of the mountains.

KOKUUN

And later he *(Points to* NARUKAMI.*)* and the beautiful maiden *(Points to* TAEMA.*)* will be left all alone.

鳴神　ウム。

両人　見さいな。

鳴神　いや、こいつらは。

白雲　ナンボしからしゃりましても、お師匠様のアノどん亀で。（花道七三へと小走りに逃げながら）

黒雲　アノ女中をくんぐるべいとは。

白雲　お師匠様の。

鳴神　ウム。

両人　ずぼんぼえ。

ト両人ずぼんぼえの下座の唄にて七三にて振あり、花道へ入る。

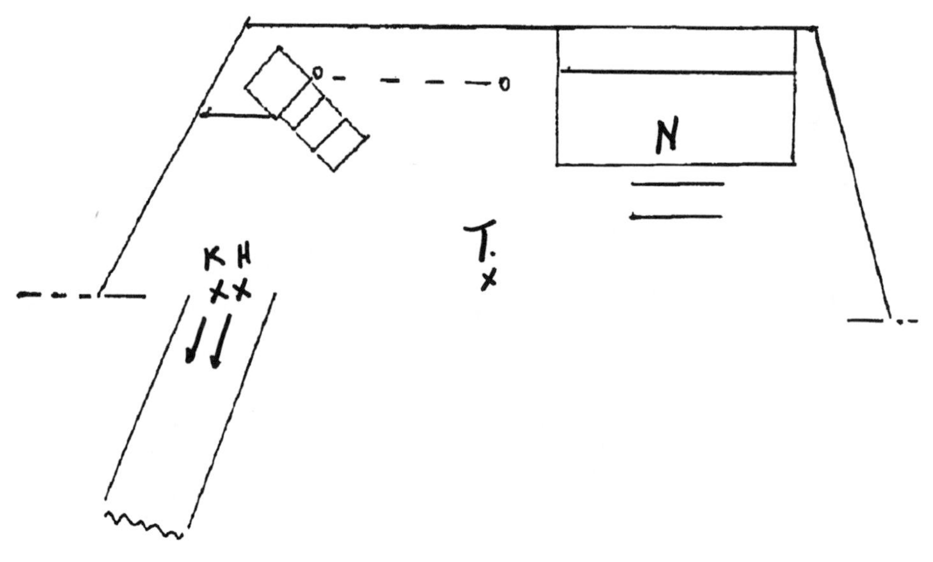

NARUKAMI

(Loudly.) What did you say?

BOTH

(Startled.) Oh, nothing. It was just a thought, just a lustful thought.

(Music starts.)

[At shichisan *on* hanamichi*:* HAKUUN *leads, followed by* KOKUUN. *When music and singin start,* KOKUUN, *with his left index finger pointed to stage, rhythmically points 3 times (at the same time* HAKUUN *raises and lowers his shoulders rhythmically 3 times).* KOKUUN *begins to go toward stage, from behind* HAKUUN *'pushes' him (circle each other) around himself. Now* HAKUUN *is nearer the stage. Spreads both arms out shoulder heigth to prevent* KOKUUN *from seeing* NARUKAMI *and* TAEMA. *Together they rhythmically, with light footsteps, step back 1,2,3 to the right — 1,2,3 to the left.* HAKUUN *starts to go toward stage (feeling), from behind* KOKUUN *turns him around behind himself and* KOKUUN *himself leans toward the stage.* HAKUUN *pulls him back with his left hand. Holding each other's hand they stop momentarily. Then (fanning)* HAKUUN *tapping his bald head with his right fingers and* KOKUUN *his bald head with his left hand rhythmically, lifting legs lightly they make their exit.]*
(Music stops after they exit.)

鳴神　阿呆な奴ばら、憎い奴ばらではある。

絶間　モシお師匠様え。

鳴神　もう師匠と云うか。俺は師匠なりそなたは弟子。追っ付け受戒じゃ程に、心を情浄に待ちましょうぞ。

絶間　そんなら、アノ剃刀が来ると、この髪を剃りまするかえ。

鳴神　オ、くりくり坊主にするわえ。

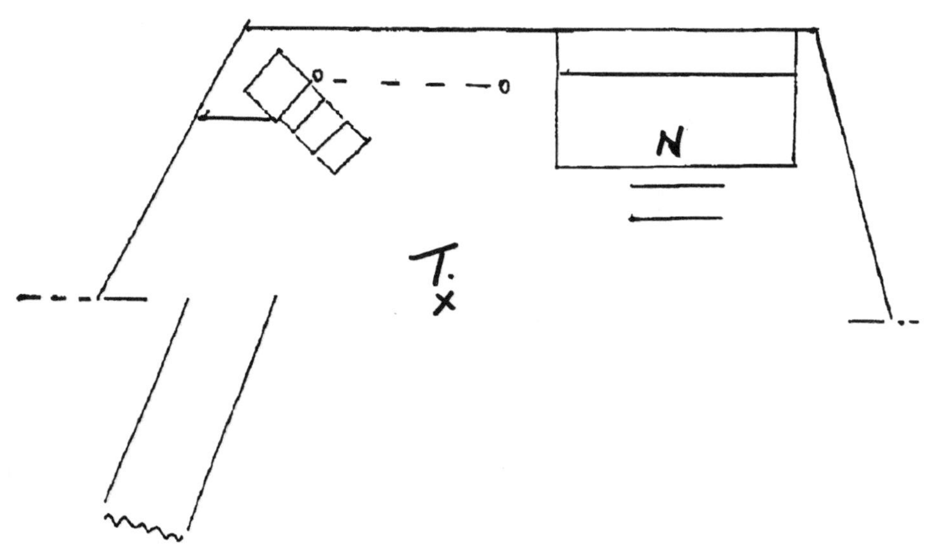

NARUKAMI

(Laughing.) They are certainly stupid fellows. *(Pause.)*

TAEMA

(TAEMA *looks left and right after* KOKUUN *and* HAKUUN, *sees that they're gone via the mountain path, then bows low on her palms on ground.)*

(Very sweetly.) My dear teacher.

NARUKAMI

(Teaching her.) That's right. I am your teacher and you are my pupil. Soon you shall be initiated and become a disciple of Buddha. You must keep your mind pure.

TAEMA

Then when the razor is brought, are you going to shave *(Right hand over right side of head.)* off my hair?

NARUKAMI

Yes, I'm going to make you a *(He circles his head with right hand.)* beautiful bald bonze. *(Hand on thigh.)*

Natalie Ross reminds us that "The female character's hand is to look smaller, at least from out front, more delicate, never showing the thumb, which is always tucked down into the palm of the hand. Gestures from out front are on a long line. The physical restrictions have to be made to look comfortable, automatic, and part of one before the actor even starts worrying about characterization and the lines."

ト絶間、泣く。

鳴神　なにを泣く。

絶間　一筋を千筋とめでし黒髪を、今剃って捨つると思えば。

鳴神　それが悲しゅうと泣くか。

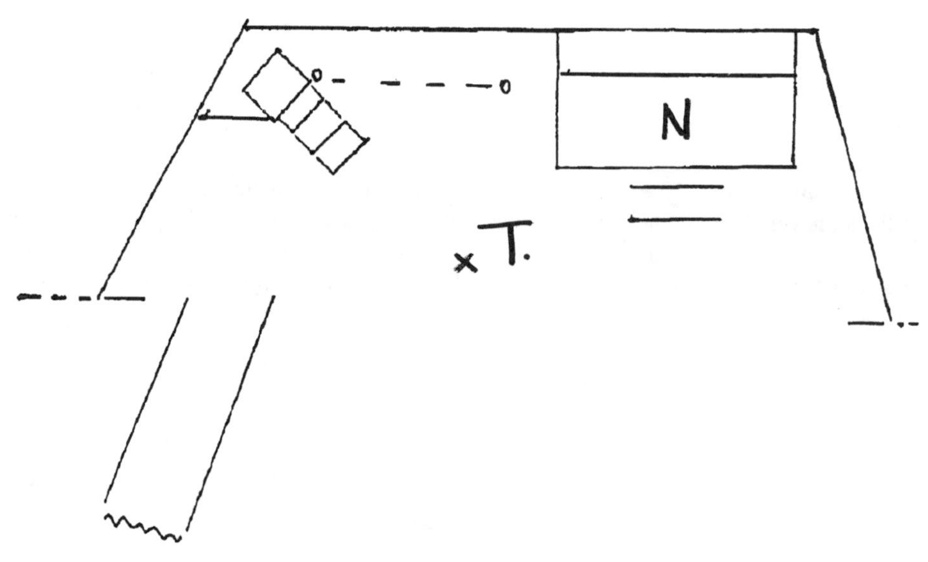

TAEMA

(Hand on ground. Left hand waving her head, head goes down on slant; left hand on floor, palm down. She cries.)

Ha-a-a-a.

NARUKAMI

Here, why are you crying?

TAEMA

To think that I should have to shave off these thousand strands of hair. *(Frames her head with right hand.)*

NARUKAMI

Does it disturb your heart? Is that why you are crying?

TAEMA

Ai-i. *(Bows down with palms down on floor.)*

NARUKAMI

A poem reads, "My parents have not caressed my raven hair. To be treated thus and cause me such despair." I well understand that you should be reluctant to part from your hair. *(Pause.)*

絶間　アイなア。（気をかえて）あいた、あいた。

トつかいが起きる思い入れ。

鳴神　なんとした、なんとした。

絶間　アイ、思い切っては居りまするが、アア悲しい事じゃと思いますれば、このつかいが。ア、痛痛痛。

鳴神　ハテ気の毒な。（ト下へ下りて）薬はなし、俺が背中を揉んでやろう。

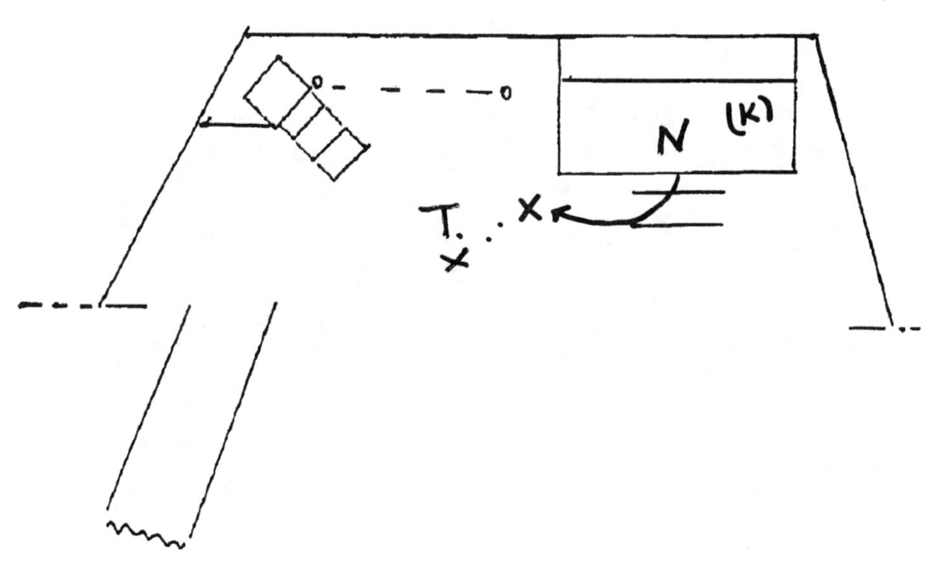

TAEMA

(TAEMA *sits up, scheming to get* NARUKAMI *to her. She circles her right breast with her hands. She feigns pain.)*

Oh, how painful, how painful.

NARUKAMI

(NARUKAMI *stands. Left* KOKEN *takes away aibiki and armrest, and exits up left.* NARUKAMI *approaches to center.)*

What is the matter? What is the matter? *(NARUKAMI comes down steps.)*

TAEMA

(TAEMA *physically wavers.)* The thought has upset me and my spasm grows more violent. Oh, it pains! Oh, it pains!

NARUKAMI

(NARUKAMI *comes closer to her.)* How pitiful, and yet there is no medicine to be had here. Here, let me massage you a little.

絶間　イエイエ、勿体ない。

鳴神　ハテ病の事じゃ。ナンノ遠慮があろうぞ。ドレドレ。（ト背をさする）

絶間　ア、いえ、いこうお腹が痛うござんする。

鳴神　鳩尾へ差し込んだのであろう。俺が手は苦手じゃ。この指が触ると積じゅは直り治まる。ソレ、よいか。ソレソレソレ。（ト懐中へ手を入れる。）

鳴神　そりゃ、虫がぐうと云うたわ。

絶間　いこう快うござりまする。

鳴神　ウム、それようか、それそれそれ。やあ　（ト離れる）

絶間　何とさんしたえ。

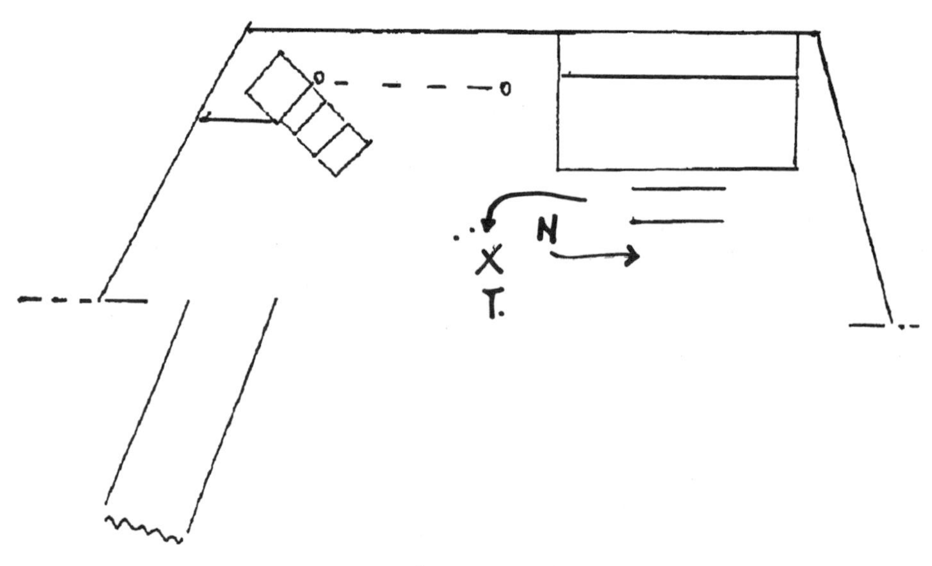

TAEMA

That would be more than I deserve. How could I ask a priest to . . . *(Left hand out as if to hold him off.)*

NARUKAMI

Lady, you are ill; you need not be modest. *(*NARUKAMI *goes behind her right side.)* Now, are you ready? *(*TAEMA *takes* NARUKAMI*'s right hand, guides massage up and down, short strokes. He rubs her left breast three times with his right hand. She wavers, right hand up, left hand holding* kimono *sleeve.)* There, *(He holds, then rubs again.)* it seems that the source of the illness has been suppressed.

TAEMA

It is pleasurably soothing.

NARUKAMI

(As NARUKAMI *is rubbing her breast, he suddenly pulls out his hand and looks surprised.)* Yòoh? *(He crosses to stage center looking at his right hand, held high. Then he crosses left center, looking very surprised, hands held high, then lowering his hand.)*

TAEMA

What is the matter?

鳴神　あじな者が手にさわった。

絶間　何がお手にさわりましたえ。

鳴神　生まれて始めて、女子の懐へ手を入れて見たれば、胸隔の間に何やらやわらかな、くくり枕のようなものが二つ下って、その先に小さな把っ手のようなものがあった。

絶間　お師匠様とした事が、ありゃ乳でござります る。

鳴神　ナニ、乳か。水子の折に育てられたは有難き母の乳の恩。その乳を忘るる様になったも、何と出家というものは、木の端の様なものじゃな。

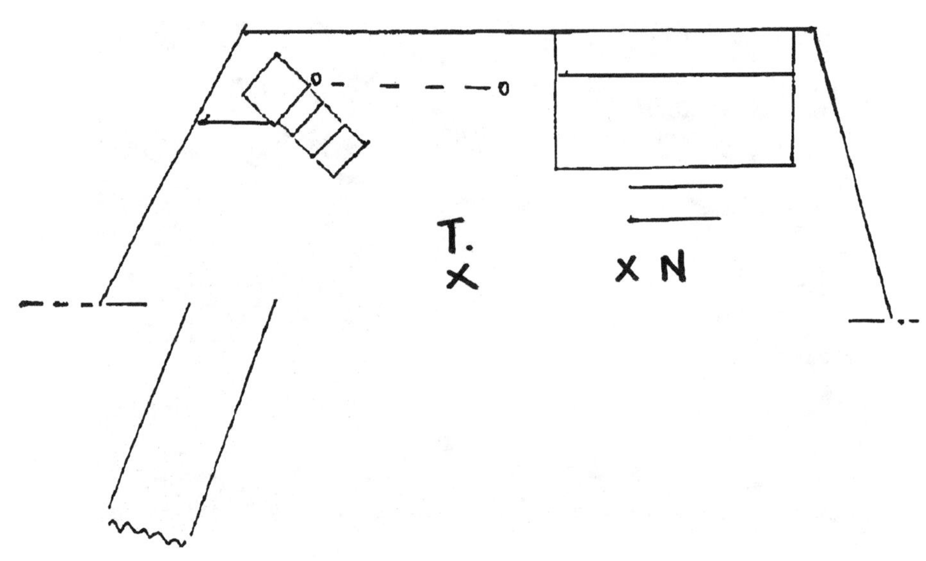

NARUKAMI

I touched something very extraordinary. *(Hand up, looks at it.)*

TAEMA

What did you touch?

NARUKAMI

It is the first time since my birth that I *(Lowers his hand.)* have put my hand into a woman's breast. On your breast I felt something very soft, like a pillow with a little tip.

(When NARUKAMI *is away from* TAEMA, *she is not sick; when he's close, she becomes sick.)*

TAEMA

(Very shyly.) Dear priest, how silly. That is . . . *(Pause.)* a nipple. *(She wavers low, covering her face with left* kimono *sleeve.)*

NARUKAMI

A *(More emphasis.)* nipple? How sinful of me. I have forgotten the gratitude *(Slight bow.)* I owe to my mother's *(*TSUKEUCHI *enters.)* nipple which reared me from a suckling. Truly, priests have no more human feelings than an offshoot from a tree. *(He hits his head with right hand.)*

絶間　御殊勝な事でござりまする。

鳴神　ドレドレ、ち脈をとってみよう。これが乳で、その下が鳩尾、かの病いの凝っている所じゃ。おお、さっきより、よっぽどくつろいだわえ、どうじゃどうじゃ。ナント、よい気味か。

絶間　お師匠様。

鳴神　拝む、拝む。上品の台に望みはない。下品下生の下へ救いとらせ給へ。

ト絶間振り切る思い入れ。

絶間　お師匠様、鳴神様。こりゃお前は。

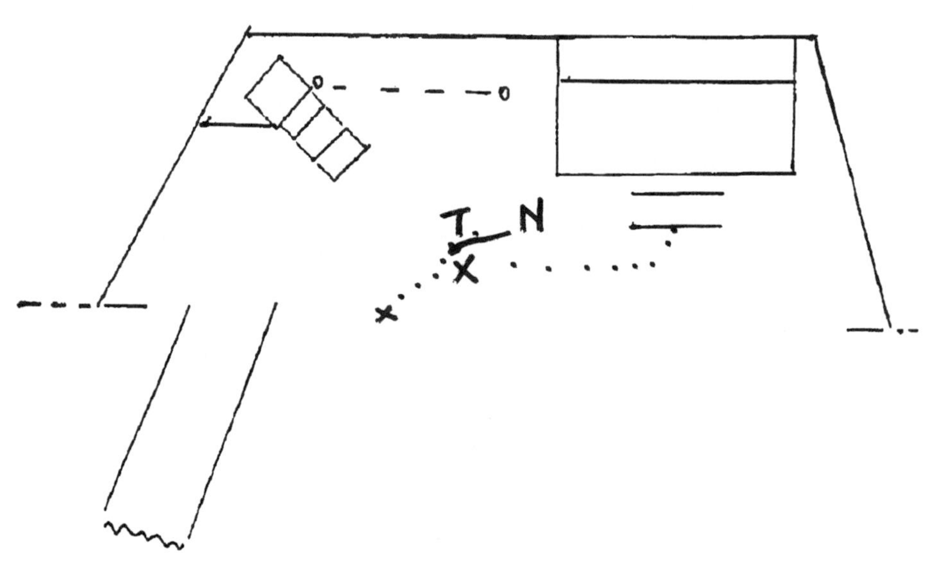

TAEMA

Your words are laudable.

NARUKAMI

(NARUKAMI *returns behind* TAEMA.) Come, let me massage you more. *(He starts massaging up and down, hand gradually descending as he speaks.* TAEMA*'s right sleeve shields his hand.)* Below the nipple is the center of breath, the center of health, where the pain originates; below the pit, there is Paradise . . . . *(Excited motion.)*

(TAEMA *bends, up together, she looks at him and he at her simultaneously. With both hands she pushes him awa y and crosses up left center to steps, back to stage. Steps right foot, floor level. Left foot steps first step. Pivots left foot. Right foot moves, 2 right hand circles, 1 left hand circle, bracing herself, leaning back slightly, sitting on step.* KIMARI, *crescent movement. Turn head sharply right)*

(KIMARITSUKE.)

(NARUKAMI *on floor stage right makes small head circle.)*

TAEMA

(Breathless, shaking, trembling.) My dear master, *(Pause.)* what are you doing? *(*TSUKEUCHI *exits.) (*NARUKAMI *goes stage right seated.)*

Annette Hunt, playing Princess Taema *under the direction of Baiko said,* "At first I was so uncomfortable. Every line of dialogue had been choreographed. Gestures had been handed down over years to generations of Kabuki actors. As *Princess Taema* in the Kabuki play I had to memorize gestures, as well as lines, words, putting them together. I just did each day of rehearsal what Baiko demonstrated. Suddenly, one day I got a key to that something inside, that mysterious something inside this character of *Princess Taema.* Through the kata, the movement and gestures, the physical, I grasped the mysterious inner life of the *Princess*. I found myself a key through the kata. Once I had the style, I could hang my whole performance on that."

鳴神　気が違うたという事か。

絶間　ご本性じゃござりますまい。

鳴神　破戒したという事か。

絶間　破戒の段ではないわいなう。御出家の身として。（入替って、ツケ廻し）

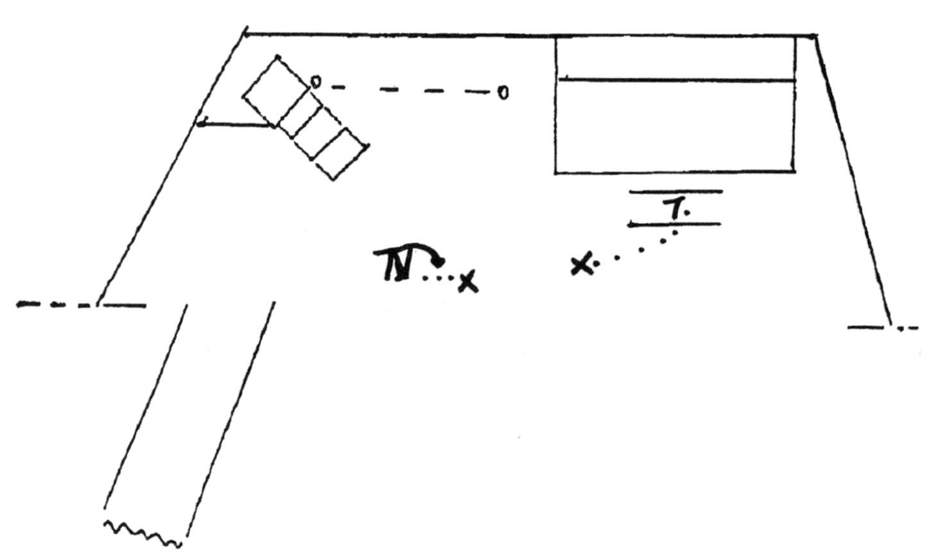

NARUKAMI

(Hands praying gesture.) I beg of you, I beg of you; the temptation is too great. *(Still sitting he leans front toward* TAEMA *who is sitting up stage.)*

TAEMA

(Slowly.) Dear Narukami, what has happened to you? *(Crosses to stage left center.)*

NARUKAMI

(Tormented.) Do you mean I have gone mad?

(He turns on right hand, left hand waves under right leg front and changes to left leg front. On his knees NARUKAMI *'walks' toward* TAEMA, *shifting his weight from right knee front, back to audience, then shifting weight to the left knee, body facing front.)*

TAEMA

You are not in your right mind. Listen please.

NARUKAMI

You accuse me of sinning against Buddha?

TAEMA

(She kneels on right knee.) The word sinning is mild. You, a priest. *(*TAEMA *sits, edges center. Extends right hand on floor, leaning forward, left hand holding right sleeve, pleading to* NARUKAMI.*)*

鳴神　堕落した、堕落した。生きながら地獄へ落ちた。落ちてもこけてもだんない、だんない。仏も元は凡夫にて、悉達太子のそのむかし、妻もあり子もあった。おうと云え云え。従わぬに於いては、我立ち処に一念の悪鬼となって、その美しい喉笛に食らいついて、共に奈落へ連れ行くが、女返事は、な、な、何と。

絶間　お上人様。

鳴神　ならぬか。

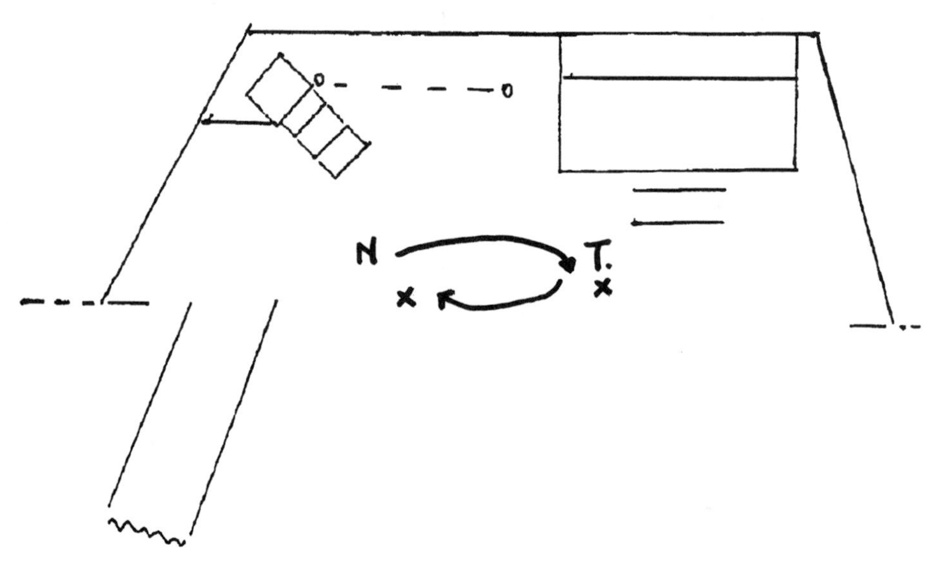

NARUKAMI

(Stands.) (To self.) I am corrupted. I am corrupted. *(To* TAEMA.*)* Answer yes! Answer yes! *(*NARUKAMI *holds rosary, right hand on top, left at bottom. From here on they circle each other slowly, reversing their positions.* TAEMA *sitting on floor with right hand over brow, left hand leaning on floor.)* I have fallen from grace. Do not deny me. Unless you submit, I shall become a fearful demon and bite into your beautiful throat and drag you with me to Hell. *(When positions are reversed,* TAEMA *shifts her weight,* NARUKAMI *bends toward her, hands on prayer beads,* TAEMA *in shrimp bend, hands up, left over brow, right over chin.)* Woman, *(*NARUKAMI *stamps right foot, and simultaneously bends toward* TAEMA*; hands clutching prayer beads.)* what is your answer?

TAEMA

(Submitting, goes near him, sits up stage.) Dear priest.

NARUKAMI

(He turns one step forward, back to audience.) (Intensely.) Is the answer "no?"

絶間　お前は。

鳴神　ならぬか。

絶間　なるわいな。

鳴神　やあ。

絶間　なんじゃ怖い顔して、その様な恋路があるものかいの。

鳴神　サアサア、どうじゃ。

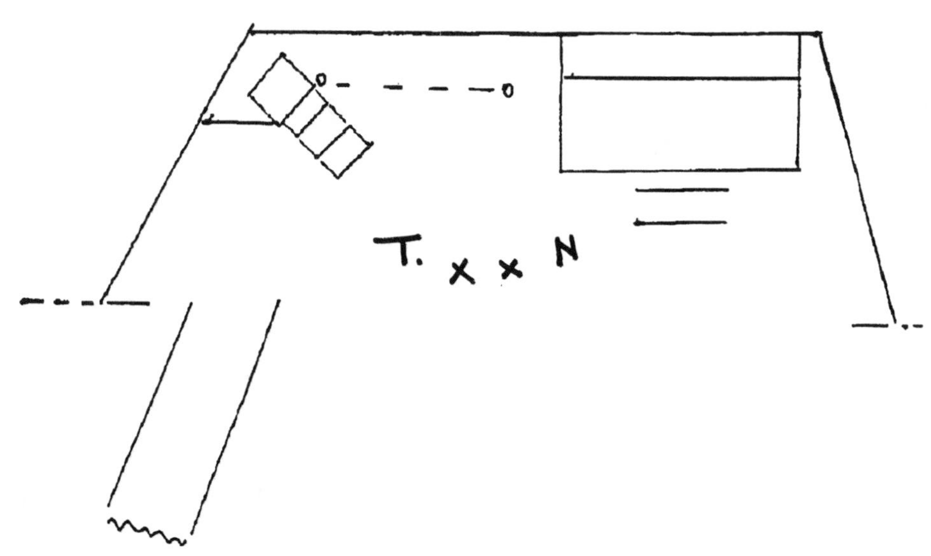

TAEMA

Oh, how could you? *(Pivots on seat, back down stage.)*

NARUKAMI

(Turns one step forward, facing audience.) (Intensely.) Is the answer "no?"

TAEMA

(Stands up, moves closer to NARUKAMI. *Pleads with outstretched hands, faces* NARUKAMI. *Edges forward, hands up on his thigh.) (Softly.)* Yes, I will submit.

NARUKAMI

(Shocked.) Oh?

TAEMA

(Teasing him.) My, what a ferocious look! *(She sits, left hand on left knee.)* Is that the way to make love?

NARUKAMI

*(Rapidly.) (*NARUKAMI *crosses to* TAEMA*'s left side, kneels, takes hold under left sleeve, makes her stand. She wraps sleeve and arm around his neck, kneels on right knee, facing forward, left hand clutching left sleeve.* NARUKAMI, *left foot on angle facing down left, right hand behind her.)* Then answer me. *(Left foot stamps.)* Again!

絶間　応じゃわいなア。

鳴神　往生極楽。サア蓮台へ。サアサアサア。

絶間　あれせわしない。そんなら、お前、ほんにわしと女夫になる気かえ。

鳴神　女夫が池へ、真逆様に落ちる法もあれ。

絶間　あれ待たしゃんせい。女夫になるはなりましょうが、わしゃ坊さんを良人に持つはいや。

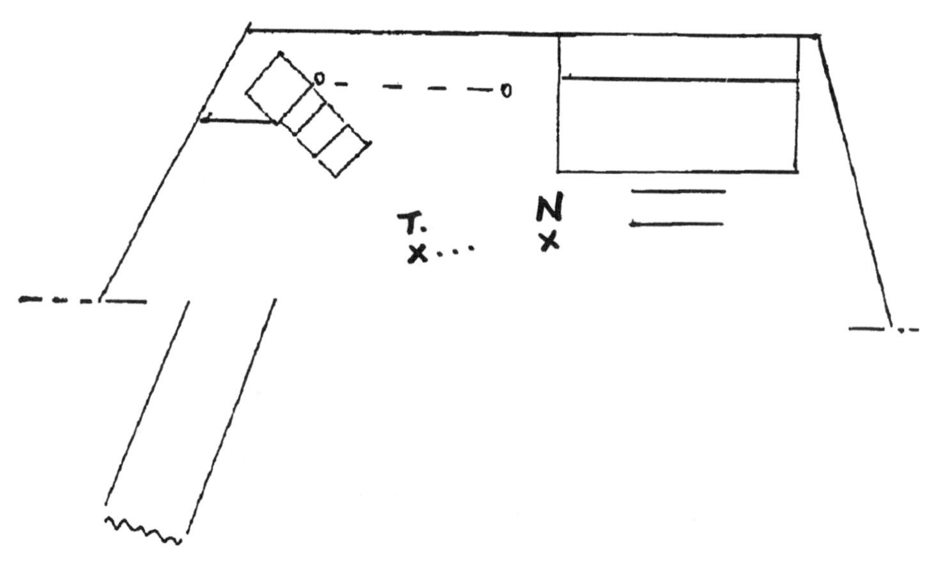

TAEMA

The answer is "yes." *(Looks at him.)*

NARUKAMI

Oh bliss, an easy and peaceful death. (He takes her hand, her left arm in his right hand, and pulls her left. Leads with left foot.) Now let's go to the land of the Lotus. *(Referring to her body.) (He begins to pull her over to the dais.)*

TAEMA

Be not so impatient. I have answered "yes" and you need not rush me so. *(Brushes his hand off. Withdraws hand and kneels.)* Dear Narukami, do you really wish to marry me?

NARUKAMI

Yes, we'll fall headlong into the hellish pond *(Facing front, hands rise framing head then descend forward, weight on right foot.)* of man and wife.

TAEMA

(As she sits.) Then I'll marry you; but I don't want to marry a priest. *(Shakes her head.)*

鳴神　坊主は脚気の薬じゃがな。

絶間　そんなら還俗さんすかえ。

鳴神　ただ今でも。

絶間　男にならしゃんすの。

鳴神　今様に髪結うて見しょう。

絶間　ほんにかえ。

鳴神　仏祖にかけて。

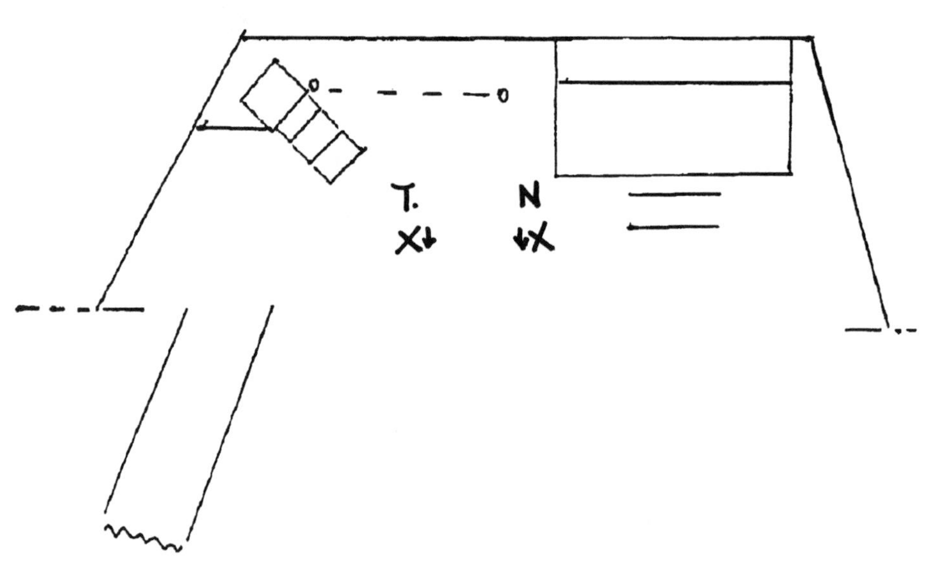

NARUKAMI

It is said that men with hairless legs are not afflicted with beriberi. A priest is only a prevention against beriberi.

TAEMA

Then will you renounce the priesthood?

NARUKAMI

Even now. *(Kneels.)*

TAEMA

Will you become a layman?

NARUKAMI

In today's fashion I'll dress my hair. *(He extends his arms sideways, downward, showing himself. Then he indicates hair style with his hands.)*

TAEMA

Do you promise?

NARUKAMI

I vow to the founder of Buddhism. *(Hands in prayer gesture .)*

絶間　エ、その誓文が抹香臭いわいな。それに殿御の名に鳴神上人とは。

鳴神　ウー、イヤイヤイヤ、名を変えるがや。

絶間　何んとえ。（数珠下へ置き）

鳴神　オ、　市川団十郎

絶間　よい女夫になりました。

鳴神　サアサア芝居を始めよう。

絶間　又せかんすわいの。したが、女夫じゃという盃事をしたいわいな。

NOTE: On this page the actor substitutes his own name.

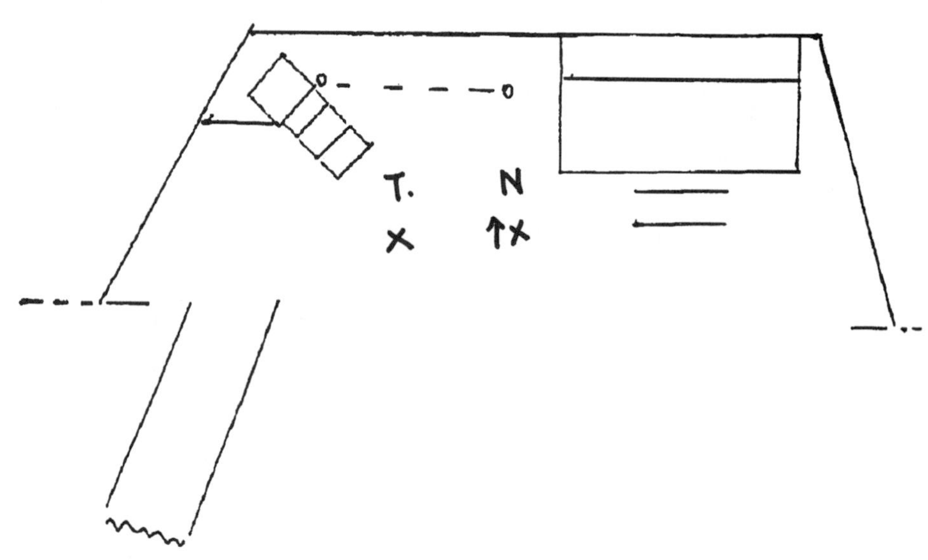

TAEMA

That oath reminds me of the temple. And your name is Priest Narukami.

NARUKAMI

I'll change my name.

TAEMA

To what?

NARUKAMI

Mm . . . *(Pauses, thinking, head to either side.)* I'll change my name to *(Loudly speaks the performer's own name).*

TAEMA

Now we are man and wife. *(Index fingers held up.)*

NARUKAMI

(Takes her hand and stands.) Now hurry, come with me. *(One step, begins to go toward dais.)*

TAEMA

Are you rushing me again? To prove that we are man and wife, I want to exchange nuptial cups.

鳴神　盃しょうしょう。酒もある。

絶間　エ、。

鳴神　盃もある。（ト、キンの合方、壇の脇から樽と大盃を持ち出る。）最前、あの坊主めらが、俺が目を抜きおって隠しておいたを、チロリと見て置いた。今用に立てるじゃ。

絶間　是はいかな事。合うたり叶うたり。サアサアお前始めなさんせ。

鳴神　イヤ、俗家で聞いた事がある。夫婦の盃は女子の方から呑んで、夫へ差すものじゃ、と云うぞ。

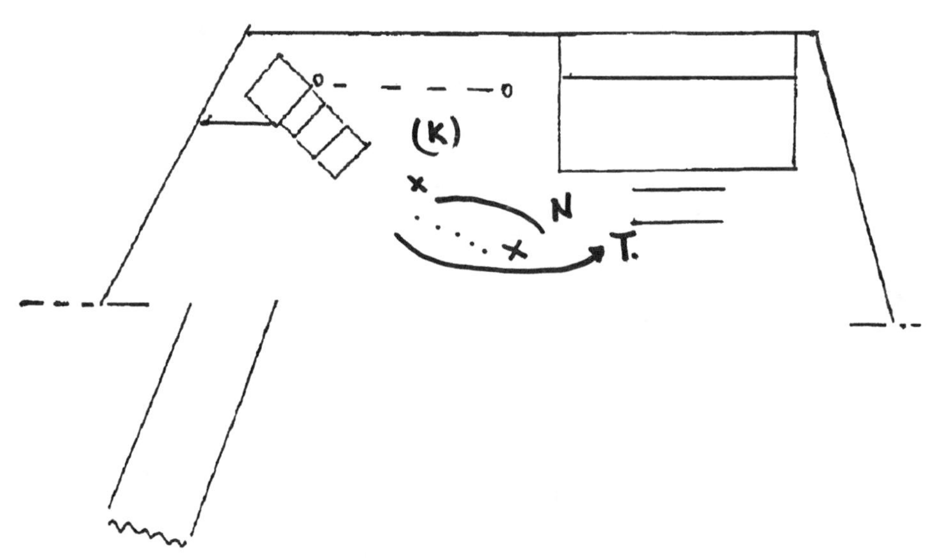

NARUKAMI

All right, we'll have our nuptial cups. *(He crosses behind* TAEMA, *she stands and moves a little to stage left, and he sits on her right.)* There's sake and a sake cup.

(Music starts.)

(Left KOKEN *in from up right, crosses to up center; kneels up center, back to audience.) (*NARUKAMI *turns, goes to* KOKEN *up center and gets cup. Left* KOKEN *gives* NARUKAMI *sake and cup. Jug in* NARUKAMI*'s right hand, cup in* NARUKAMI*'s left hand.)*

Are you surprised? I watched the stealthy movements of my acolytes, and I knew these were here. *(*NARUKAMI *crosses down right of* TAEMA, *kneels to right of* TAEMA. *He puts the jug down right, cup left.)*

TAEMA

How wonderful! They are just what we were wishing for. Here, you drink first.

NARUKAMI

In a secular home I heard somewhere that the woman should drink first and then she should pour for her husband.

When Princess Taema *is pouring sake for Priest* NARUKAMI, *there is a traditional kata or pattern of movement executed by* Taema. *Just to pour sake from the over-sized cup with the wrists is contrary to the totality of dance movement* kata*) of Kabuki: the kneeling onnagata enacting* Taema *starts the movement of pouring from the soles of the feet, the movement is carried through the torso to the wrists which tip the cup to pour. The maturing, talented* onnagata *may have achieved the traditional* kata *to perfection, but if it lacks* kimochi, *it is empty. The* kimochi, *the feeling true to character and action, must fill the vessel that is* kata. Taema*'s simple act of pouring* sake *involvesthe whole body, as does all acting in Kabuki. When we speak of* kata, *however, we do not speak of style alone.* Kata *includes handprops, costumes, stage settings, music and the script.*

絶間　ても、巧者な事じゃなア。

鳴神　まず飲め。（鳴神注ぐ）

絶間　エ、もう私ゃたんとはいけませぬ。せこれが二世までもの盃じゃぞえ。（ト注ぐ）

鳴神　オツト…………ト。

絶間　コリャどうじゃいな。

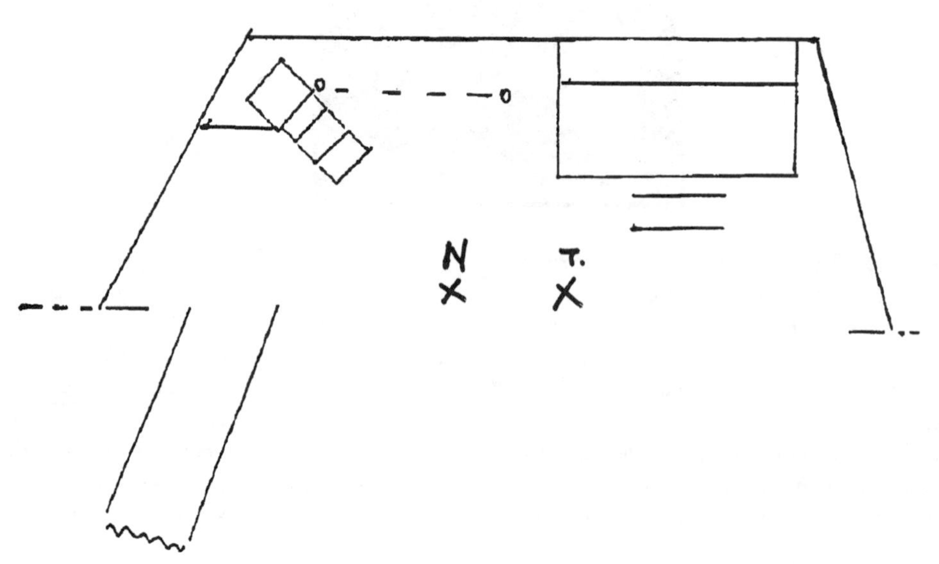

TAEMA

My, how clever you are. All right, then in celebration I shall drink first.

NARUKAMI

Let me pour for you. *(Gives her the cup;* NARUKAMI *picks up the sake jug and pours, throws cork up center stage.) (Right* KOKEN *strikes cork.)*

TAEMA

(She lifts cup, preventing him from pouring more.) I cannot drink much. *(She drinks.)* This is a cup uniting us in this world and in the next. *(She offers him the cup.)*

NARUKAMI

(Waves left hand refusing drink.) Oh no! A thousand pardons. *(*NARUKAMI *puts jug down.)*

TAEMA

What do you mean?

鳴神　酒一滴もならぬ。奈良漬さえ嫌いじゃ。

絶間　サア、今までは下戸で有ろうけれどナ、女房持たんすからは、オ、酒も上がったがようわいのう。

鳴神　でも呑めぬものを。

絶間　わしが呑ましゃんせと云うのに、呑ましゃんせぬか。

鳴神　呑もう。

絶間　エエ、おかしゃんせ。（盃置き下手を向く）

鳴神　あやまった。（盃取り）あやまったりと云うままに注ぎくされ。

トニ度ほど袖で覆い顔をしかめる。絶間＜サアサア＞と無理強いする。
ドロドロにて軸燃える。鳴神は科ある。

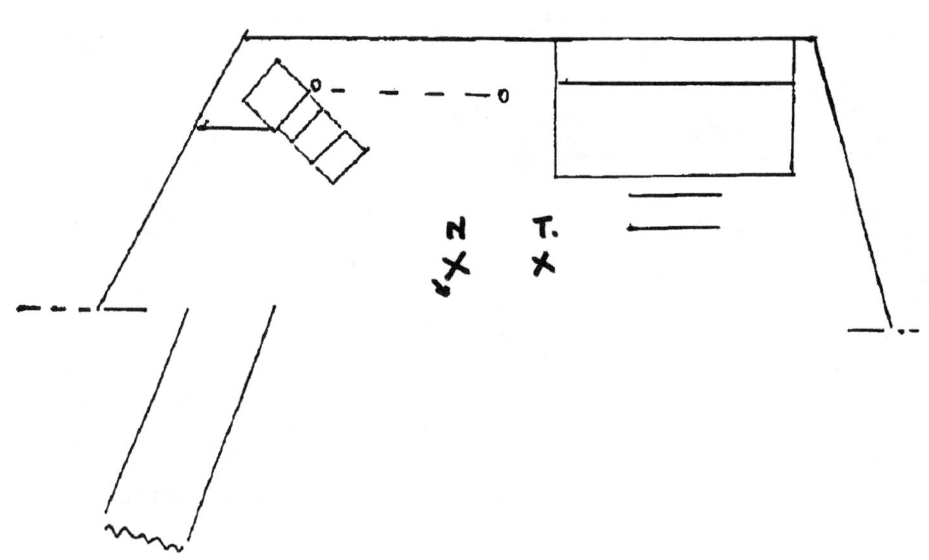

NARUKAMI

I can't drink a drop of sake; I even hate pickles. *(Waves left hand once.)*

TAEMA

You might have abstained until now, but now that you have taken a wife, it would be best for you to change your ways.

NARUKAMI

But I can't drink it.

TAEMA

(Stronger, demanding.) Are you not going to drink, even though I ask you to? *(Offers him the cup again.)*

NARUKAMI

(Waving stop gesture left hand.) Oh, I apologize, I apologize. And as I apologize *(Takes cup.)* you may pour all you wish.

*(*TAEMA *pours, puts jug down.) (*NARUKAMI *smells the sake, withdraws his head, he drinks.) (Drum roll until he shakes.) (*NARUKAMI *makes a distasteful expression after drinking. He shudders to left, smells the sake, withdraws, shudders to right. He stomps right foot forward to emphasize what he's about to do; he drinks and puts cup down, shakes, and makes awful sound because of taste, holds chest, and trembles.)*

絶間　何とさんしたえ。

鳴神　生れて初めて酒を呑んだれば、腹の中がひっくり返る様で、寒うなった。

絶間　（立って寄り）今の間に熱うなるぞえ。

鳴神　サアこの盃はそなたへ戻そう。

絶間　ハテ、祝言の盃に戻そうとは云わぬものじゃ。

鳴神　そんなら返そう。

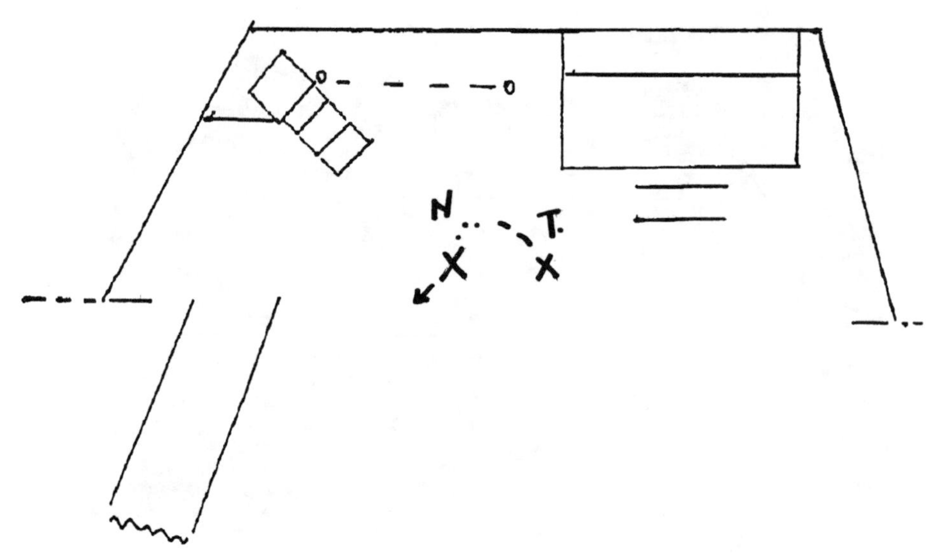

TAEMA

What's the matter?

NARUKAMI

It's the first time that I have ever drunk sake and my poor insides are churning. *(Shakes; hands up and down on his chest.)* Ah-h, I'm cold.

TAEMA

*(*TAEMA *goes behind* NARUKAMI, *puts right arm holding sleeve on his right shoulder, left hand holding sleeve on left shoulder.)* Soon you'll become hot.

NARUKAMI

Now I'll return it to you. *(Picks up cup and offers it.)*

TAEMA

*(*TAEMA *returns to her sitting position.)* It's bad luck to say the word "return" at a marriage ceremony; you would not want the bride to return home.

NARUKAMI

Then the cup goes back to you. *(Offers it again.)*

絶間　返そうとも云わぬものじゃ。

鳴神　そんなら、（ト盃を捧げ）オオ、納めさせられい。

（と注ぎかける）

絶間　そりゃ目出とう押さえようわいなア。

鳴神　イヤ、モウならぬならぬ。

絶間　わしが云う事聞かんせぬか。

鳴神　注ぎ給え。何と、なみなみ受けたであろう。

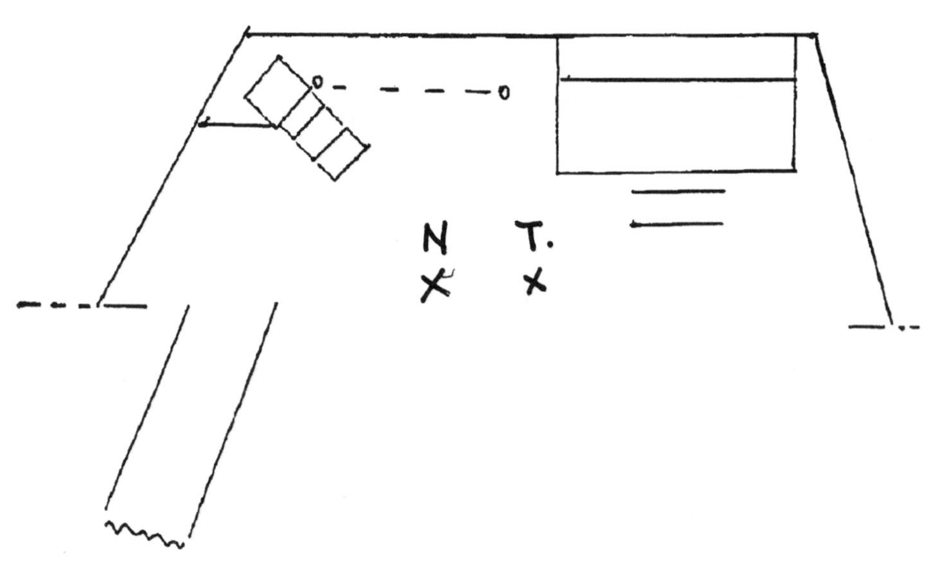

TAEMA

You are not supposed to say "go back" either.

NARUKAMI

Then finish the cup. *(Offers it again,* TAEMA *refuses.)*

TAEMA

(Takes the jug and offers him more.) With a toast to ourselves take another drink.

NARUKAMI

(Waves left hand.) Oh no, I can't stand a drop more.

TAEMA

(Pouting.) Are you not going to listen to me? *(Puts jug down, turns.)*

(Music stops.)

NARUKIMI

Go ahead, *(Pouring hand gesture, straight out, hand downward.)* pour! See, it's filled to the brim.

絶間　見事じゃわいの。アレ。

ト退く。

鳴神　何としたした。

絶間　ソレ、盃の中に蛇が居るわいな。

鳴神　いかい阿呆である。何もないものを。

絶間　でも、そこに居るわいの。

鳴神　（気ずき）ハア聞こえた。こりゃ蛇じゃない。あれは くちなわ だ。

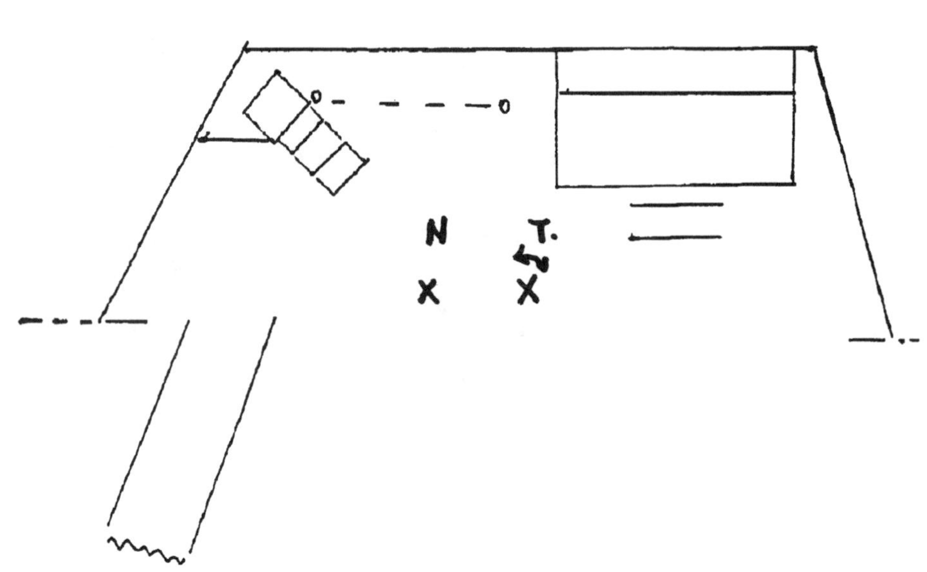

TAEMA

(She sits up and pours.) That is admirable! *(Puts jug down.) (She looks into cup and sees a reflection.) (Frightened.)* Are! (Ay-re.) *(She puts right hand in front of chest, left hand toward floor and sits, drapes right hand sleeve over her face, wavering, showing fear.)*

NARUKAMI

What's the matter? What are you afraid of?

TAEMA

(Stammering.) There's a *(Points with left index finger.)* snake in the cup. *(Still shaking right sleeve.)*

NARUKAMI

You're very foolish. *(Pause.) (He looks into cup.)* There is nothing.

TAEMA

Look, there is.

NARUKAMI

(Looks at cup, then at rope, then at cup again.) No, that's not a snake. That's the sacred rope. *(Stamps right foots, points to rope up right with right hand, looks at her.)*

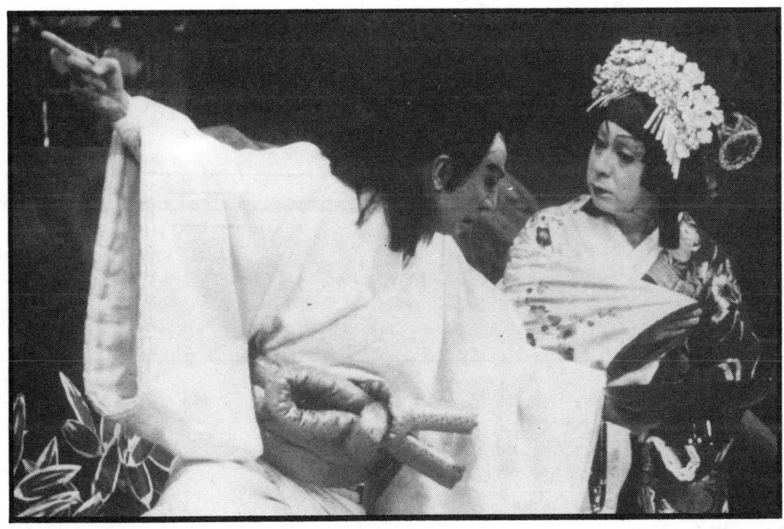

絶間　（見くらべて）ほんに〆じゃ。

鳴神　ハテ臆病な。

絶間　ありゃ、何の〆でござんすえ。

鳴神　アリャ、大事な〆で雨が降らぬじゃて。

絶間　どうしてえ。

鳴神　大事のこっちゃ、人には話すまいぞ。大内殿に恨みが有って、世界の竜神をあの岩屋に封じ込んで、その上密法の〆を引いたれば、今でも雨を降らそうと思えば、あの〆の真ん中を切るのじゃ。と、竜神が飛び去り大雨車軸。（両手上からさしかけ）ハ……大事の事じゃ。必ず人に云うまいぞ。

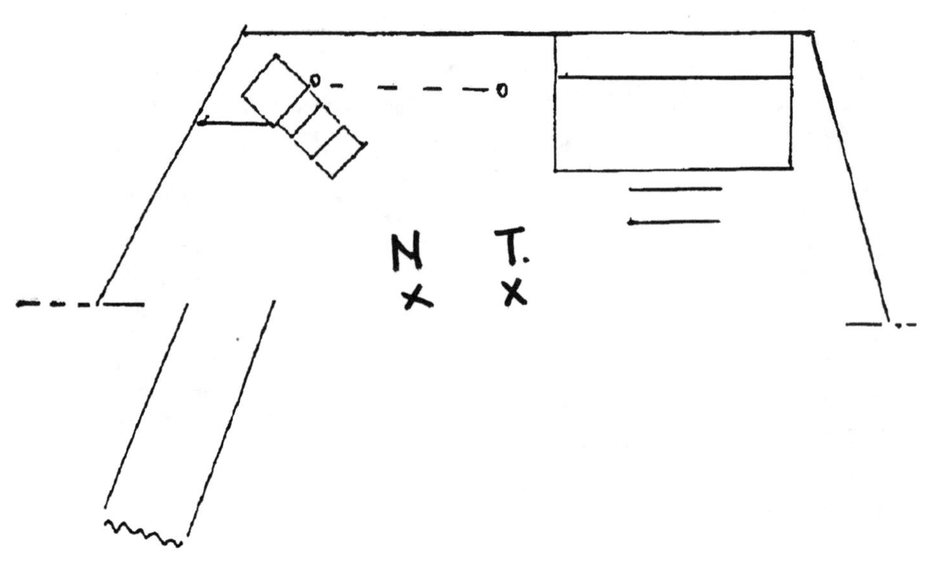

TAEMA

(She sits up, looks at cup, looks at sacred rope, sits.) Oh yes, it is a sacred rope.

NARUKAMI

(The sake is taking effect, NARUKAMI *talks like he's drunk.)*

That's a precious rope. *(Sits.)* It prevents the fall of rain. *(Drunker.) (Puts cup down.)*

TAEMA

(Interested.) Oh . . . tell me how.

NARUKAMI

(Drunkenly.) (Right knee up throughout.) This is a very important matter. Do *(Waves hand.)* not divulge the secret. I have a bitter grievance against the Imperial Court and have shut in the world's Dragon God *(Points with right arm.)* in that cavern. Furthermore, I have pulled across it the sacred rope *(Right arm draws line with hand.)* sanctified by esoteric prayers. To let the rain fall, all one has to do is to cut *(Arm downward, cutting rope gesture.)* the rope in the center. The Dragon God will escape *(Proudly, happily.)* and it will rain in torrents. *(Arm upward, points toward heaven.) (Leans toward* TAEMA, *waves left hand back and forth.)* This is a grave matter.

絶間　あの〆の真中を切りさえすれば、竜神は飛び交い雨が降るかえ。でも、あの、雨が……..、不思議な事の。サア呑まんせ。（ト酒を注ぐ事いろいろあり）

鳴神　（酒をうけながら）オット北山桜、こりゃこの狂言の名題じゃ。

絶間　祝うて三献。いやならおかんせ。

鳴神　いやとは云いも致しゃせぬのに。

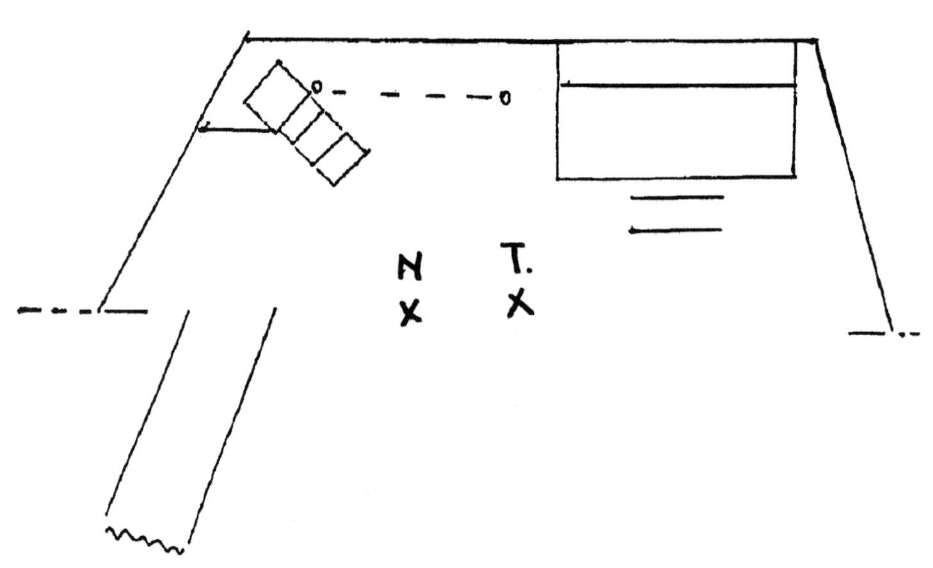

TAEMA

(She sits up on knees, looks at rope.) If that sacred rope is cut in the center the Dragon God will escape and rain will fall? *(She imitates his gestures with right hand.)* Indeed *(She sits, disguising her excitement.)* it is a very strange thing. Here, here, go ahead and drink more.

NARUKAMI

Yes, I shall drink more. *(He drinks, wobbles slightly as if falling to the right..)* Now I'll give you a drink. *(Offers* sake *cup to* TAEMA.*)*

TAEMA

Not yet, *(Picks up jug.)* the conventional rule is three cups. *(Puts jug down.)* If you're unwilling, do as you please. *(Turns and looks away.)*

NARUKAMI

(Left hand waves back and forth.) I didn't say I was not willing. *(Picks up cup.)*

TAEMA

Please drink more. *(While she pours.)*

絶間　　おうおう。よう呑まんした。それでこそいとしい坊さん。ナニ
坊さんじゃなかった。こちの殿御。モシ、是は成らぬ、起きさんせ。サア、こそぐるぞ
えぞえ。

辺りを見て思い入れ。下手にて手を支え、

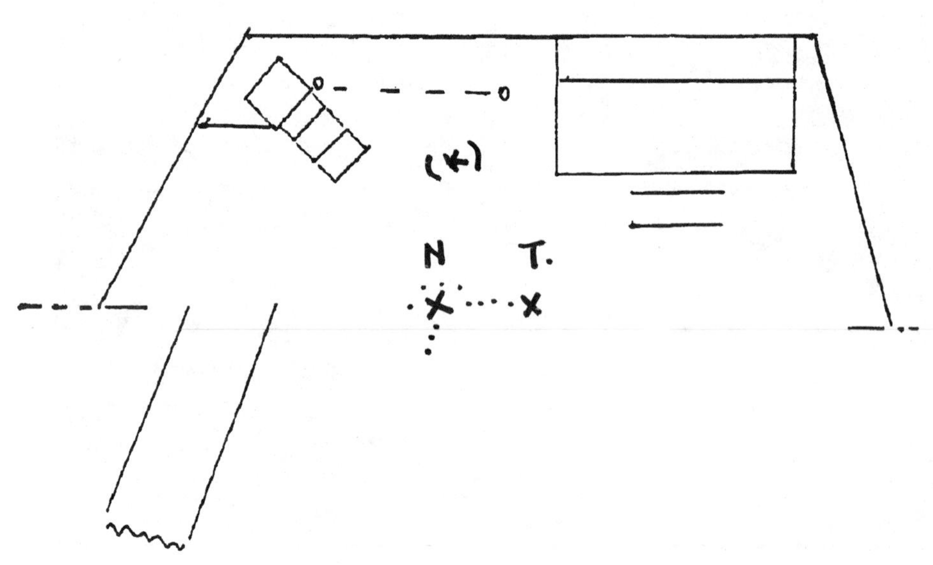

NARUKAMI

Oh, I can't drink any more. *(He drinks,* TAEMA *pours again.)* Oh, I can't drink any more. *(He puts cup aside, right.)* Oh, I can't drink any more. *(He collapses, falls on floor in front, head in front.)*

(Music stops on KOKEN *entrance. Left* KOKEN *takes cup, kneeling, waits stage center, back to audience.)*

TAEMA

Oh, wonderful, *(Left* KOKEN *takes jug, puts it under platform.)* you have drained the cup completely. Now I can consider you my darling husband. Here, wake up, wake up! *(Shakes him with both sleeves.. Massages his back.)* My, is there such a thing to fall asleep before the marriage ceremony. *(Goes around to the other side. Looks to see if he's really asleep.)* If you don't wake up, I'll tickle you. *(*TAEMA *crosses down right of* NARUKAMI. *She tickles him around arm pits with sleeves rubbing.)* Here, wake up, wake up! *(*NARUKAMI *nods his head, he's fallen asleep rapidly.) (*TAEMA *shows surprise and is now convinced he's really asleep.) (She goes stage right.)*

絶間　エ、勿体なや恐ろしや。お上人様お許しなされて下さりませ。自らが心より、お前を落としたのじゃござんせぬ。勿体なくも勅じょうを受けし身の役目。今酔いの中の教えの如く、あの〆を切らば、竜神竜女は海底へ飛び去り、五穀成就の雨は忽ち。

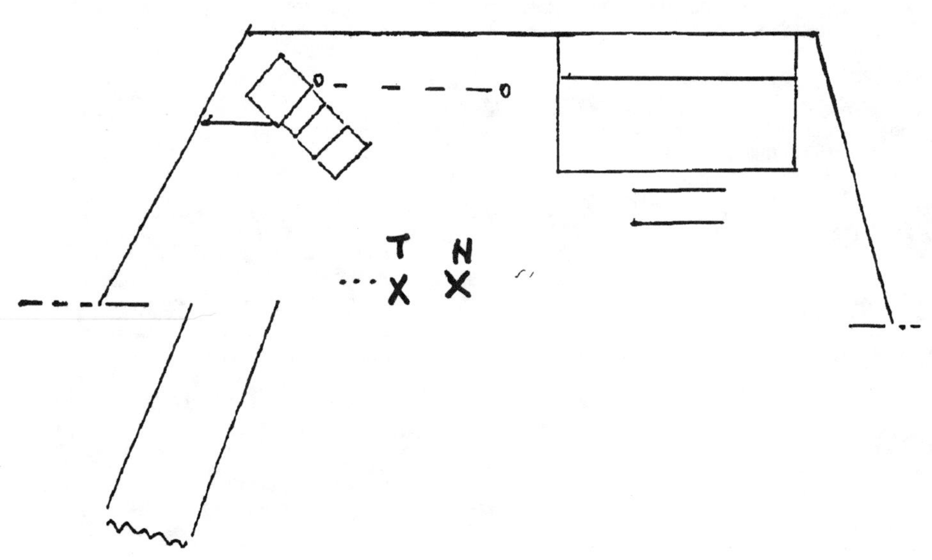

(Right KOKEN *enter, first time. The two* KOKENS *conceal* NARUKAMI *with a red cloth. While concealed,* NARUKAMI *changes wig and makeup.) (*TAEMA *goes to stage right.) (Changes manner, now speaks apologetically.)*

TAEMA *(Continued)*

It is most impious, most dreadful of me, dear Narukami, but please do forgive *(Bows.)* me. It was not my desire to ruin you. But it was the august Imperial order to demoralize you through seduction of lust and wine. I fear even myself *(Right hand to chest.)* to think that I have thrust you down into such a disgraceful state. As you informed me in your drunkenness, if I cut the center of that sacred rope, the Dragon God *(Left hand points upstage.)* will escape and jump into the bottom of the sea and there will be a torrential downpour to provide water necessary for the growth of crops. In the cavern of profound depth at which I now gaze, in it . . . . *(She rises on knees, turns right, hands holding right sleeve.) (Strongly.)* Oh yes! *(*TAEMA *goes through motions of tieing her obi. Simultaneously with her next line her hands hold right sleeves crossed and her head rolls looking toward waterfall.)* I shall perform my task.

(Music stops.) (Drum continues lightly on rock kimari.*)*

Annette Hunt, comparing the directing styles of Onoe Baiko VII and Yuri Zavadski, remembers that "When *Princess Taema* climbs up the rock to cut the rope to release the rain dragon, permitting rain to fall on the parched land, first I couldn't get the dance exactly as Baiko wanted it and with the requisite emotion expressed through the bodily movements. Baiko insisted I master the steps exactly. It was the essence of the scene. When, at rehearsal, I failed to project the inner emotion into the dance steps, Baiko made me climb the rock, release the dragon by cutting the rope realistically! Then, Baiko directed me to take the emotion of the realism and put it into the formalized dance steps. I realized, then, there's hardly any difference; absolutely no difference with Zavadski's 'method.' That day I suddenly saw that Baiko, really was no different as a director from Zavadski. The overt style of Kabuki, of course, is different. The essence of Kabuki theatre is different, but it seemed to me the acting was, underneath, the same. Truth is the same among artists anywhere; in this instance Baiko's method was the same as any other director's: to search for that truth within his actors."

ト注連縄をきっとにらみ、身ずくろひして滝壺より思い入れ。岩の上へ登る。この中震える思い入れ、さまざまあり、懐剣を取り、

絶間　南無諸天善神皆竜王雨を降らしてたび給え。南無帰命頂礼。

ト注連縄を切ると、仕掛にて女竜男竜天上す。大雷舞台先へ、雨降る。日覆より、紙張りの稲妻と、銀糸おろす。絶間花道へかけて入る。

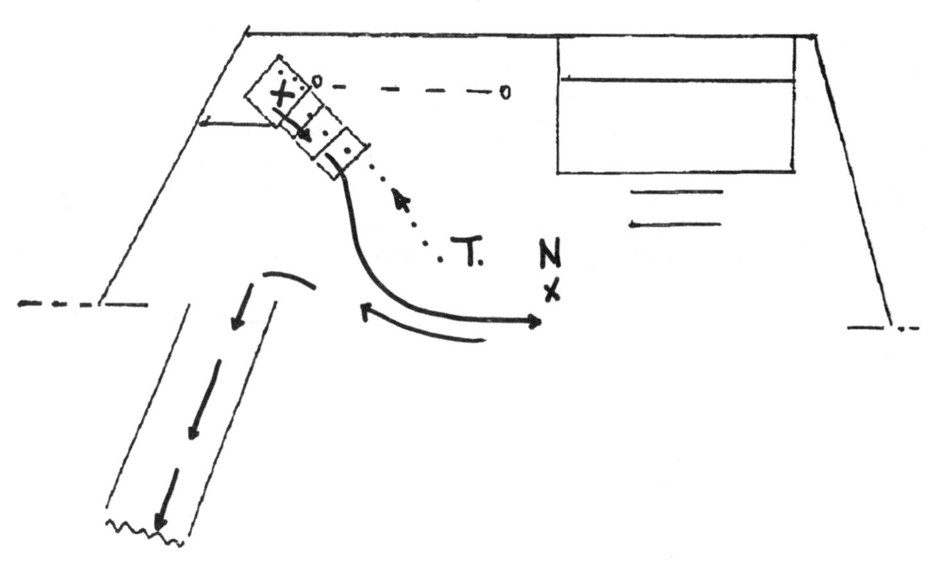

*(*TAEMA *looks down stage, crosses up right to mountain. She climbs the rock, struggles up vine on stage right. After she reaches top of mountain, she takes out her dagger from bag, back to audience, and turns forward, poses on rock, kneeling on right knee toward audience, right hand with dagger, left hand limp over chest.) (Music stops.)*

TAEMA *(Continued)*

(She prays with one hand, dagger in other hand.) Oh, great Buddha! Great deities! King of the sea dragons, I pray let it pour with rain. I implore you, great Buddha; I will promise to dedicate my life to you.

*(*KOKEN *pulls rope open.) (*TAEMA *rises, tries twice to cut rope but spray forces her back. Dagger is in her right hand. She looks at rope, cuts rope, drops dagger.) (*KOKEN *cuts rope on third attempt.) (Drum and cymbal loud.)*

*(*TAEMA *is forced down by waterfalls. (Water spray rains, she shields herself with sleeve and kneels.) (*Dragon God *goes up, rope falls, lightning drawn from stage right.) (*TAEMA *rushes down rock, crosses stage left. It rains. She shields herself from rain, crosses stage right, crosses stage left, arms folded on chest, and runs to* hanamichi. *She backs up with right foot, swings both sleeves to right; then back up with left foot, swings both sleeves to left, folds arms, rolls head. Arms folded. Three slow steps — right, left, right — focusing on escaping and exit.)*

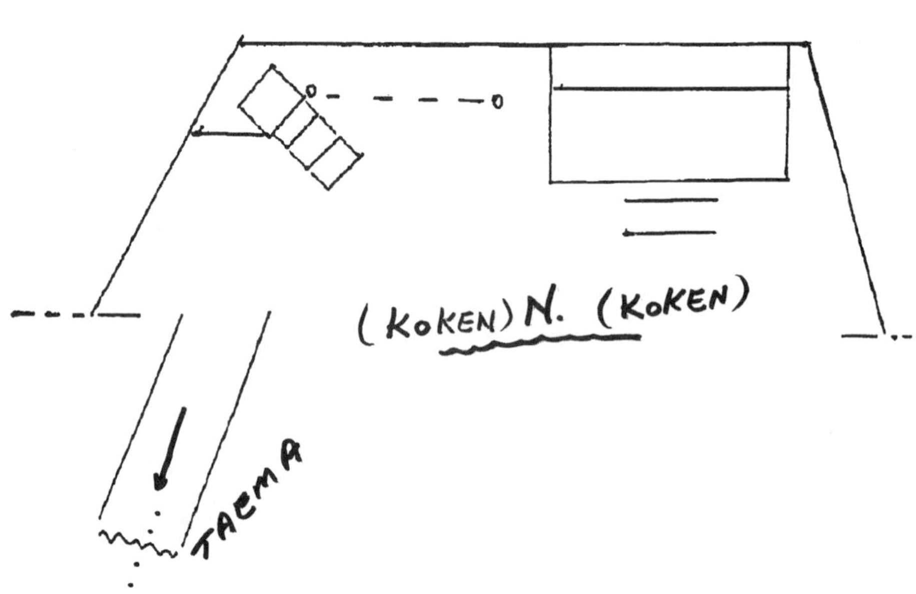
(KOKEN) N. (KOKEN)
TAEMA

(Music stops.) (Symbolic rain and lighting.)

(KIMARITSUKE*) (*TAEMA*'s left foot is forward, she pivots, faces stage, takes three short steps, crosses to* hanamichi *— accompanying* TSUKE.*)*

*(*NARUKAMI *and* KOKEN *are down center as* TAEMA *is about to exit.)*

(The two KOKEN with red cloth — held down stage of NARUKAMI *— change his wig; he adds to his make-up to heighten ferocious look.)*

(As TAEMA *exits,* NARUKAMI *returns to original position.)*

*(*KOKENS *exit up right and up left with cloth.)*

*(*KOKEN *reveal him, lying down center.)*

(Drum continues.) (Short pause between scenes.)

Annette Hunt remembers when her feelings about Kabuki changed. "It was no longer foreign, but one of the most exciting acting experiences I had ever had. The acting seemed so natural. Working with director Baiko who had choreographed every single thing for me, (gave) me its essence. Within that form there's a way, a very special way, by which I was able to act inside. It's very relaxing for an actress finally to have everything choreographed. It finally gave me great freedom."

Patricia Peardon talks about how taxing Kabuki is physically. "What we were required to do with our bodies; the directors were unrelenting. At the end of the first day, it seemed not so bad and the second day. By the third day I could hardly walk upstairs; I was so stiff. By the fourth day it wasn't so much a problem getting up the stairs, it was getting down the stairs. I never knew it could be painful to walk down a flight of stairs; it was awful. That went on for a good four or five days. Actors dropped out like flies. We had started with four full companies and by the end of the first two weeks there were barely two companies, male and female."

George Gitto marvelled that Baiko's "drawing on the eyebrows, making up the face and neck, and mouth seemed so easy: drawing the mouth with black underneath the red rouge, outlining the eyes. Baiko explained how everything had a meaning: wigs, costumes, designs on the costumes, makeup. Each of these are specific for a particular play; each costume is special."

白雲坊．黒雲坊．同宿大勢、法衣．　尻[illegible] からげ、花道より駆け出る。

皆皆　お師匠様いのういのう。

ト声声に呼び、鳴神を尋ねる。白雲坊鳴神を見付ける。

白雲　ヤアここじゃここじゃ。

ト大勢して抱き起こす。この内、鳴神真っ赤になり、酒に酔い他愛なき思い入れ。

白雲　ム、臭い臭い。

黒雲　酒蔵へ入ったようなお師匠様。

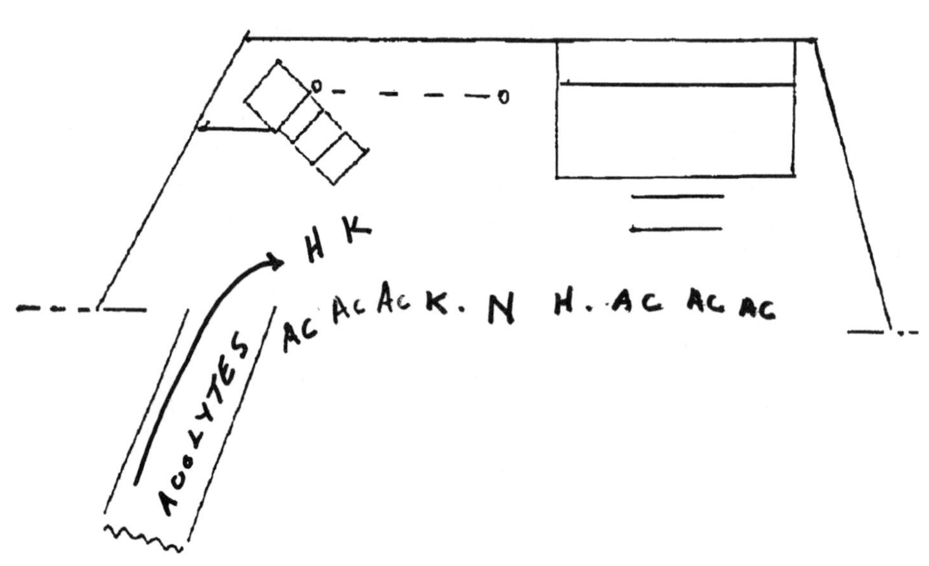

ALL

(Off stage.) Master Priest, Master Priest.

(HAKUUN *and* KOKUUN *lead the six* ACOLYTES *and enter from hanamichi, and keep looking around. Their sleeves shield themselves from rain. They separate into two groups: A: in line to center, left of* NARUKAMI, *B: in line to center, right of* NARUKAMI.*)*

ALL

(On stage.) Master Priest, Master Priest.

HAKUUN

Oh, here he is, here he is!

KOKUUN

Oh, it stinks, it stinks. *(ALL make waving off gesture with up stage arm.)*

HAKUUN

It smells like a wine cellar.

皆皆　お師匠様お師匠様。

ト鳴神、小小目を覚まし他愛なき体。

白雲　コレ、鳴神様。行法が破れましたわいの。

黒雲　見れば密法の〆も引っちぎれて竜神は天へ駆け落ち。

皆皆　しましたわいの。

白雲　じゃによって雨が。

皆皆　降りますわいの。

黒雲　雷が。

皆皆　鳴りますわいの。

ト大雷。

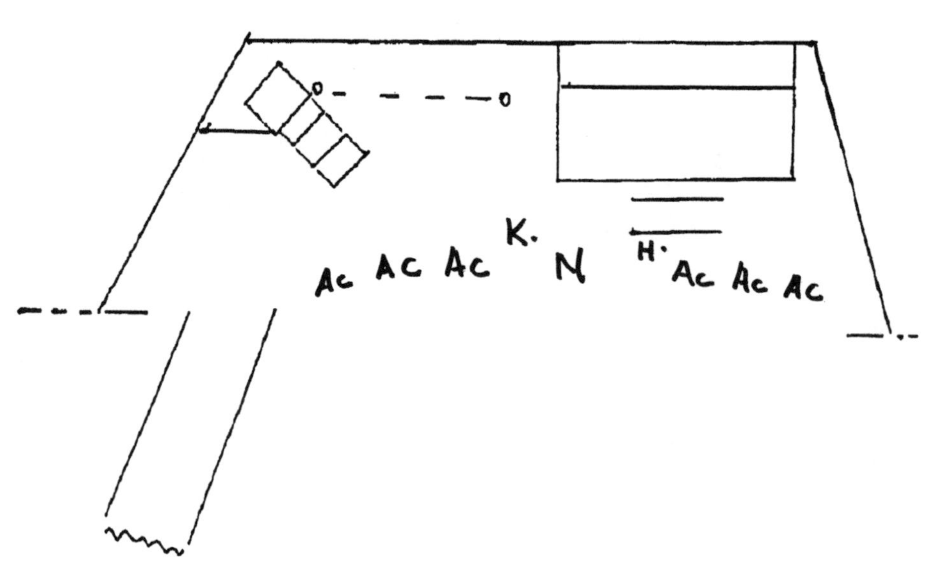

ALL

Master Priest, Master Priest! *(*HAKUUN, KOKUUN *and* ACOLYTES *have hands on bent knees — towards Narukami.)*

HAKUUN

Dear Narukami, your divine spell has been broken.

KOKUUN

The sacred rope has been cut and the Dragon God has escaped *(Hands up.)* to the heavens.

HAKUUN

And consequently rain . . . *(ACOLYTES look up.)*

ALL

(Shield themselves from rain as they did in beginning gesture.) Pours.

KOKUUN

(Warding off gesture.) Thunder . . .

ALL

(Hands over ears.) Roars.

　　　　トこの中大雷大雨、鳴神思い入れ。

鳴神　何だ、雨が降る。

皆皆　こぼれますわいの。

鳴神　なんだ、雷が鳴る。

皆皆　鳴りまするわいの。

　　　　ト雷が鳴る。

黒雲　アレ。

　　　　ト又大きく鳴る。鳴神思い入れあって、

鳴神　なぜ雨が降る、なぜ雷が鳴る。

白雲　コレ、師の坊、こなたは最前の女に、落とされさしゃったぞや。

黒雲　逃げて行った跡で聞いたれば。

同宿一　雲の絶間というて、大内第一の美女。

白雲　勅命によって、お前を落としに来たので。

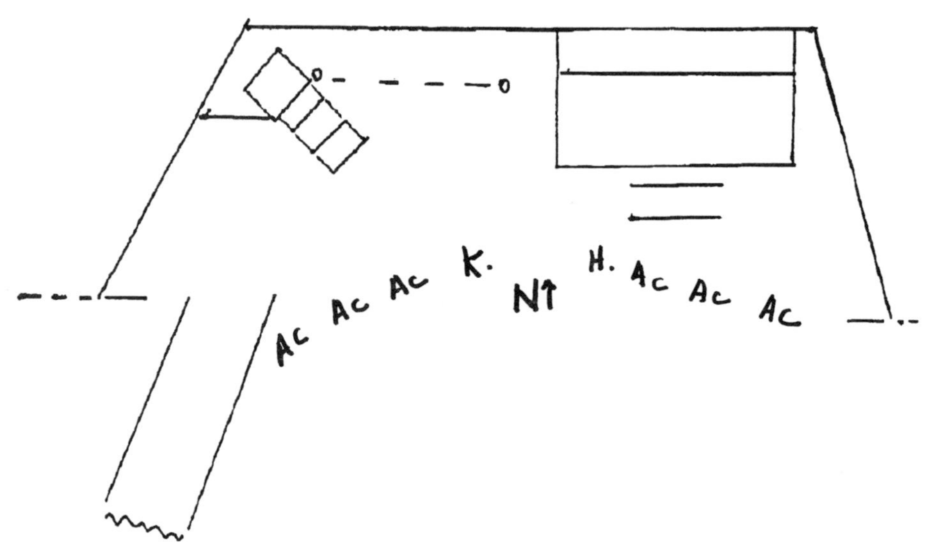

NARUKAMI

(Remains face down, still drunk.) (Groggily.) What, does it rain? (NARUKAMI, *groggily shaking body and head, rises to knees.)*

ALL

(Hands over heads.) It pours.

NARUKAMI

What, does it thunder?

ALL

It roars. *(Hands over ears, then to hands on bent knees leaning towards* NARUKAMI.*)*

NARUKAMI

(Palms on ground, head up.) Why does it rain? Why does it thunder?

HAKUUN

Dear master, you've been ruined by that lovely woman. Did you think that she was an ordinary woman? As she was fleeing, I asked her about herself.

KOKUUN

Her name is Kumo no Taema *(Rift of the Clouds)* and is the Imperial Palace's peerless court lady. By Imperial order she had come . . .

Kumo no Taema *is pronounced Koo-mo no Tie-ay-ma. No dipthong sound in vowels.*

皆皆　ござるわいの。

鳴神　扱は、我が行法を破らんがために、来たりしよな。ム、。

トこれより荒立ち。舞台中を飛び廻り捜す。皆皆跡について廻る。上手山台のカスミとり、浄瑠璃出語り。この中始終雷。

鳴神　あら無念や、口惜しやなア。

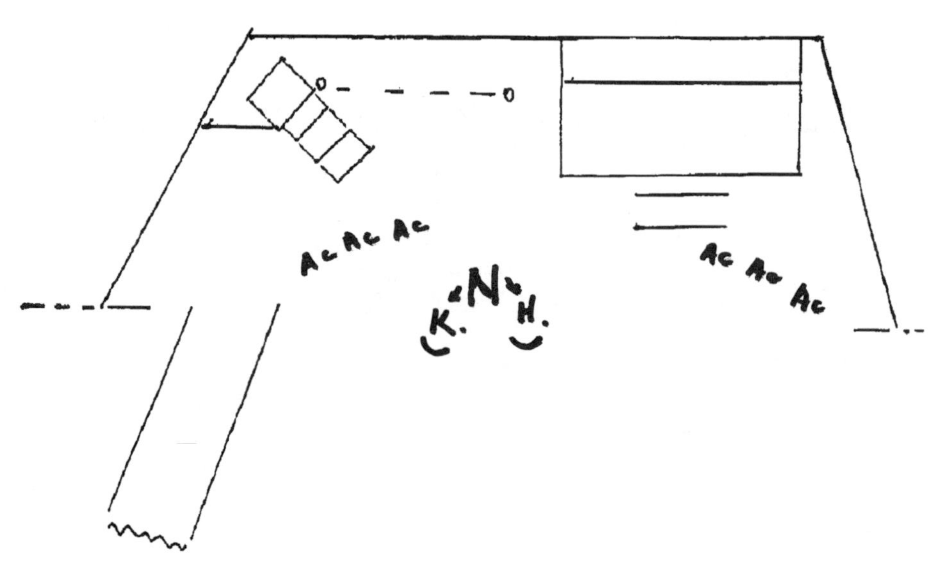

ALL

(Drum stops.) To cause your destruction.

NARUKAMI

(Growls.) Mm . . . .

(He rises, gradually becoming sober.)

*(*ACOLYTES *go upstage 2 or 3 steps, kneel on upstage knee, down stage arms extended in a stop gesture.)*

(Low, in anger.)

Then she came purposely to break my religious vows.

*(*NARUKAMI *stands, sober.)*

Oh, how humiliating! Oh, how mortifying!

*(*NARUKAMI *breaks prayer beads at this point.) (*HAKUUN *and* KOKUUN *try to grab* NARUKAMI. *They miss, he turns them, they kneel and* NARUKAMI *pretends to hold them. They hold their throats, kneeling on down stage knee, facing* NARUKAMI*; back to audience.)*

Baiko said, "If I can use a traditional form to portray an emotion, I do so. If the traditional form in a certain scene does not suit my style, I think it over and proceed to perform as I see fit, even if it means a change from the conventional manner."

寸善尺魔の障碍、仏罰を蒙り、かの密法の行破れしよなア。よし、我れ破戒の上からは、生きながら鳴る雷となって、彼の女を追っかけんに、何条難き事やあらん。

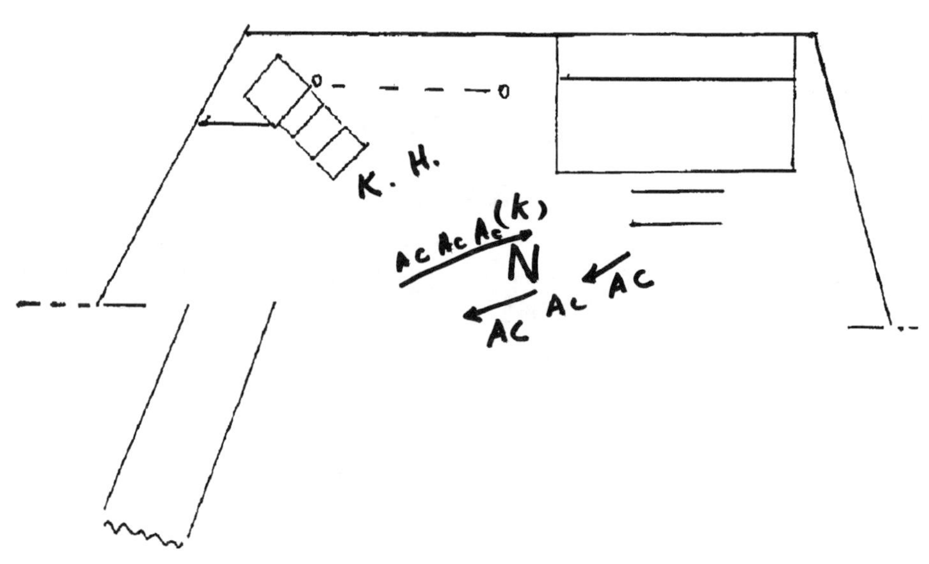

NARUKAMI *(Continued)*

Good is short-lived, evil prolongs. As long as I am to be punished by Buddha and my austerities have been violated, I shall become living thunder and pursue that woman.

*(*NARUKAMI *pushes* HAKUUN *and* KOKUUN *aside, one at a time. They sit, down stage leg under up stage bent leg; up stage hand in stop gesture.)*

How great is the challenge I face.

(Music starts.)

(Off stage: CHORUS, *tape.) (Simultaneously with speech,* NARUKAMI *takes two steps forward, discards* kimono *top. Left* KOKEN *tucks it in behind, then goes to up left platform.* HAKUUN *and* KOKUUN *go to up right center.* ACOLYTES *go to* NARUKAMI *in A and B side positions. He flips right group off, they fall back in line, return, he pushes them off. They go stage right and kneel. He pushes left group around down stage. They join up stage of other group. Two groups in double file kneeling on up stage knee.)*

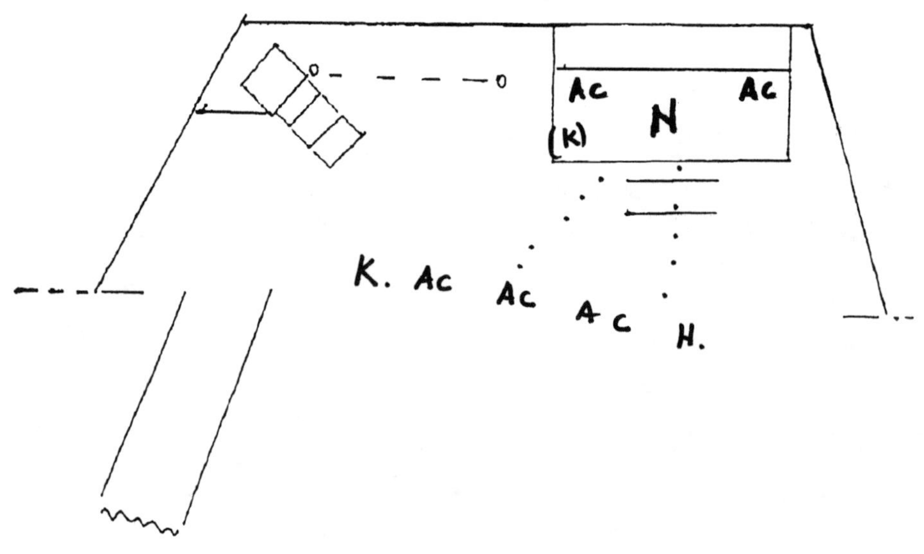
Ac
Ac
(K)
N
K. Ac
Ac
A c
H.

CHORUS *(Offstage; tape)*

With malicious spite Priest Narukami, The Thunder God,

(Music break.)

sails the clouds and rides the wind.

*(*NARUKAMI *takes two steps left.* HAKUUN *and* KOKUUN *go to him.* KOKUUN *to his right,* HAKUUN *to his left.* NARUKAMI *turns up stage.* HAKUUN *and* KOKUUN *grab his arms. He pushes them onto the dais.* HAKUUN *left,* KOKUUN *right, kneeling facing front.* NARUKAMI *goes to dais center of* HAKUUN *and* KOKUUN. *When he's reached it with his back to audience:*

ACOLYTES

Master Priest!

*(*NARUKAMI *looks at* ACOLYTES, *turns to them, grabs sutra books and, facing front, throws them at the* ACOLYTES.*)*

(TSUKE.) (Music stops.)

鳴神　東は奥州外外浜。

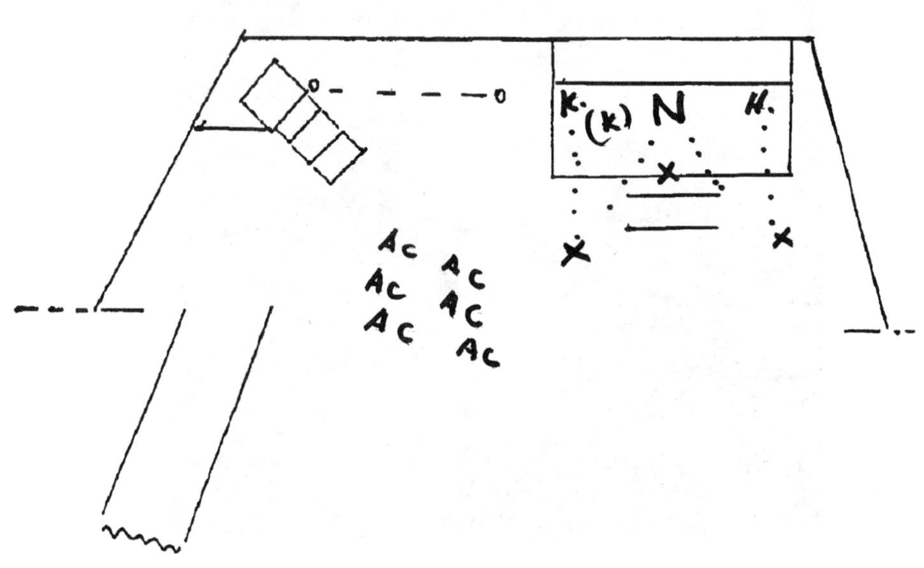

(Right KOKEN *removes books.)*

HAKUUN and KOKUUN

Yah!

*(*NARUKAMI *kneels,* HAKUUN *and* KOKUUN *stand, both take his hand, arms extended, and pull strings revealing new costum 'bukkaerie'. Left* KOKEN *adjusts costume if necessary.)*

*(*HAKUUN *and* KOKUUN *get sutra books, try to strike him. He grabs books, they jump off platform.* NARUKAMI *opens books, throwing them down.* HAKUUN *and* KOKUUN *grabs the other end.)*

(Fuji no mie: Mt. Fuji mie. NARUKAMI *right foot down on step, left foot on stage, rolls head to perform* 'fuji no mie.'*)*

(Left KOKEN *goes to prop rock stage center.)*

*(*HAKUUN *and* KOKUUN *cross up right, folding books, join* ACOLYTES, *give books to* ACOLYTES, *they pass books to Right* KOKEN.*)*

NARUKAMI

In the east there is the land of Oshu and Sotogahama.

Oshu *is pronounced Oo-shu.*

Sotogahama *is pronounced So-to-gah-ham-ah.*

西は鎮西鬼界島。

鳴神　南は熊野那智の滝。

北は越後の荒海まで。

鳴神　人間の通わぬ処。

千里も行け。

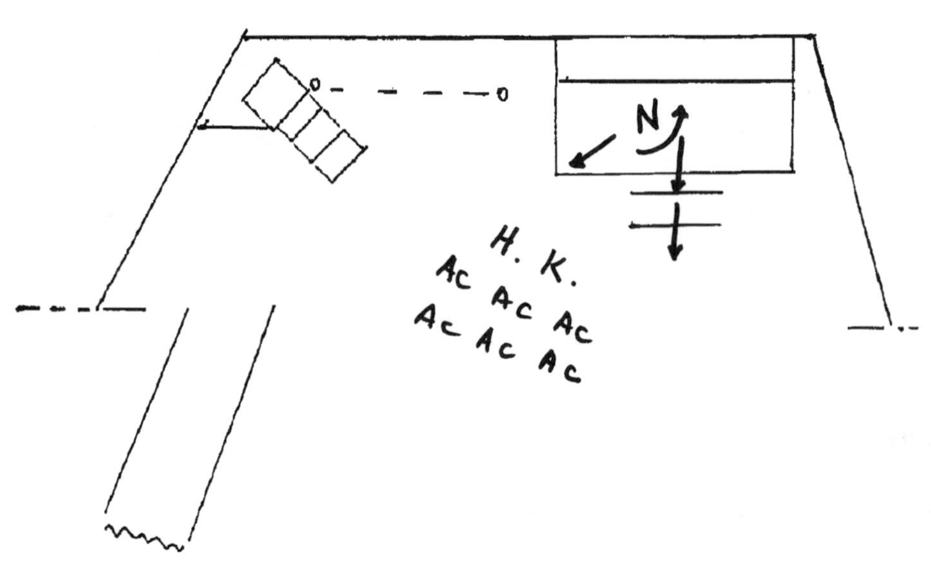

*(*NARUKAMI, *still in* 'mie' *position. Still on dais he crosses to down stage right pillar.)*

(MIETSUKE.)

CHORUS *(Tape.)*

In the west there is Chinzei and Kikai ga shima.

*(*NARUKAMI, *still on dais, goes to the right front pillar. He wraps his hands, one high, one lower, around the pillar, puts left leg on pillar and does* 'hashira maki no mie.*')*

(TSUKE: roll head.)

NARUKAMI

(Crosses left toward center of dais, facing down stage.)

In the south there is Kumano and the Nachi waterfall.

CHORUS *(Tape.)*

In the north are the rough waters of Echigo.

*(*NARUKAMI *pivots left, back to audience. He opens arms, right arm up, left arm down, left foot thrown out, right foot up stage, looks toward rear.)*

(Tape off.)

NARUKAMI

Where humans do not tread. *(He turns, crosses down center. He faces front, feet slightly apart.)*

CHORUS *(Tape.)*

A thousand miles I stride . . .

Baiko stresses that "*Though the world of Kabuki plays is far away from the present day, the actor should try to enter the heart of the character. From the public's viewpoint, we actors are practicing old things; therefore we are away from reality, but, being away from reality only happens on stage; once off stage we are just like other people."*

Kabuki acting may be considered to be a series of closeups, as in film, and during these closeups attention should be focused on the principal actor. It is important to be totally in control of the costume when a Kabuki actor momentarily freezes (mie) *in a dance.*

鳴神　万里も飛べ。

いで追っかけんと鳴る神は。

跡を慕うて。

ト大三重、大雷鳴、大雨、大どろどろにて、鳴神荒れに荒れ花道へ駆け入る。

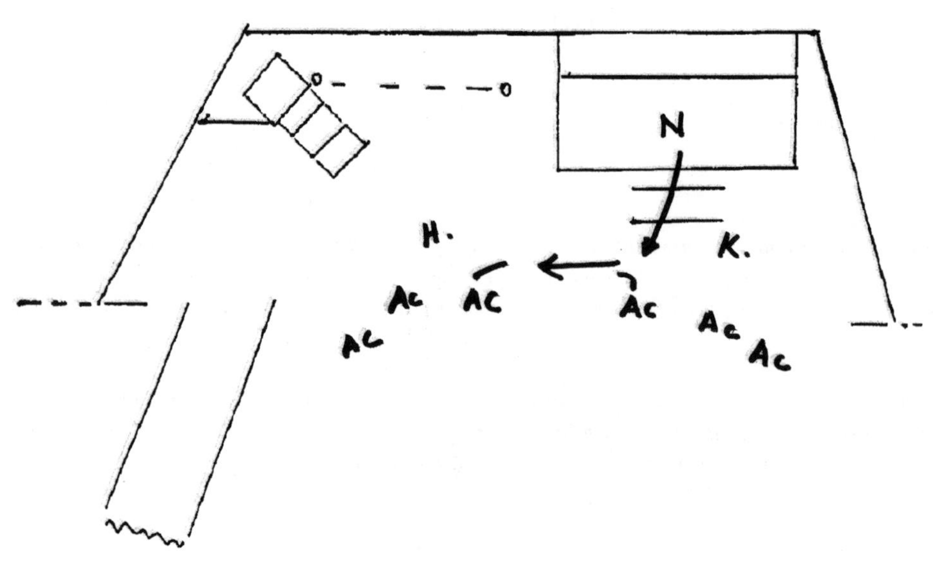

*(*NARUKAMI *pulls back right foot and right arm, in large movement, then brings feet together, right are pushed forward, he poses. Right hand around and forward, he pulls back, then leans forward.)*

NARUKAMI *(Tape off.)*

(MIESUKE.)

And speed over millions of miles more.

*(Simultaneous.) (*NARUKAMI'*s right hand claps left hand, left hand claps right hand, then he jumps from dais to stage, hands clasped.)*

(TSUKE.)

CHORUS *(Tape.)*
And go wherever she shall hide.

*(*NARUKAMI, *with bold gestures, cased* ACOLYTES *to fall to sitting position; then he moves in among the* ACOLYTES, *weaving between thm. Arriving at a central position, he causes two — each on his sides — to stand on the hands, feet in the air.)*

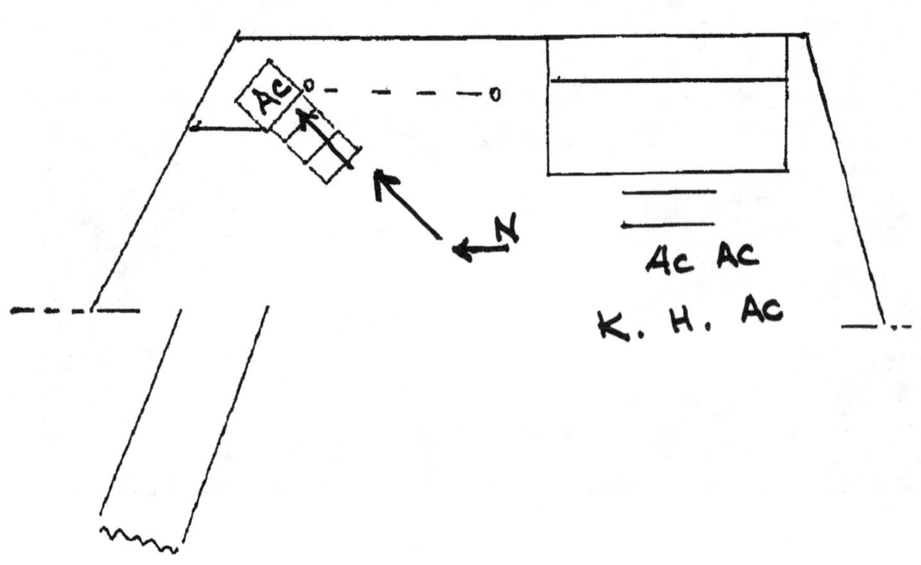
Ac
N
Ac Ac
K. H. Ac

*(*NARUKAMI *moves among the* ACOLYTES *— pushing aside. Some to the stage floor.)*

(He strikes to the platform with steps — by the falls — and he tosses off — in a somersault — an ACOLYTE *who has followed him. He completes a* mie.*)*

For the role of Narukami, *George Gitto ". . .r*ehearsed for six days a week. We had spent a lot of rehearsal time learning the technique, the *kata*, of Kabuki from Mr. Baiko. We spent many hours on movement alone. Baiko hinted gently, relying on the individual actor's creative ability. Beyond Kabuki movement and physical placement, he was satisfied to prod the actor a bit and then sit back and guide his development, interjecting only on the broader corrections. This, I think, is a much more satisfying way of working for the actor who is trying to '*spread*'."

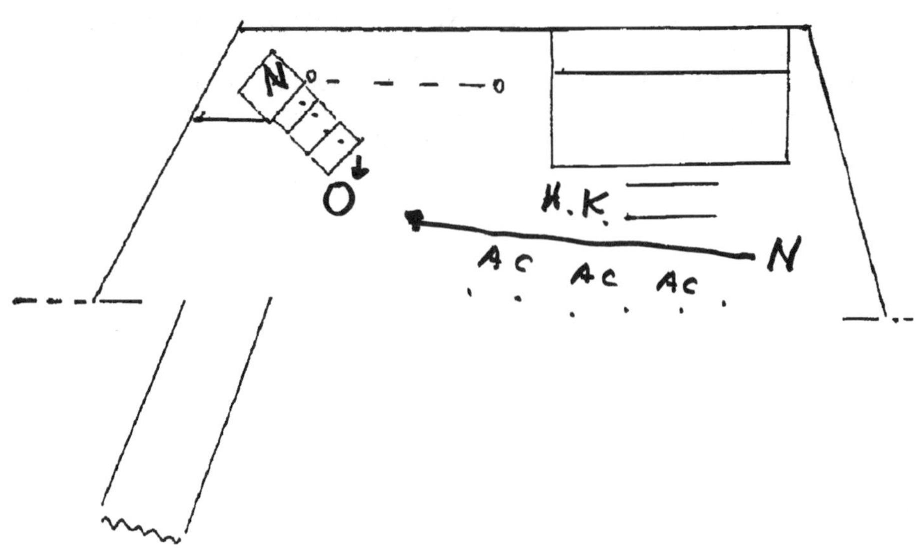
N
O
H.K
N
Ac
Ac
Ac

*(*NARUKAMI *moves among the* ACOLYTES, *grabs one, turns him around.The other* ACOLYTES *mask the substitution of a dummy* ACOLYTE *whom* NARUKAMI *tosses away in the air. Then, this is the choreographed rock-throwing* mie *[paper mache rock]. He crosses to stage right — among the ACOLYTES. The rock over his head, is held high. He crosses left. Then he hurls the rock at the lined up* ACOLYTES.*)*

Baiko reminds us that, "Truth is the same among artists anywhere; in this instance, I think, my method was the same as that of any other director: to search for truth within the actor. But, we worked from the outside in. The actor first learned from me the exterior movement, and then filled it in with meaning. I went, of necessity, onto immediate blocking. There was no time for deep probing of character. With my assistant, Miyoko Watanabe, I set the movements and line readings."

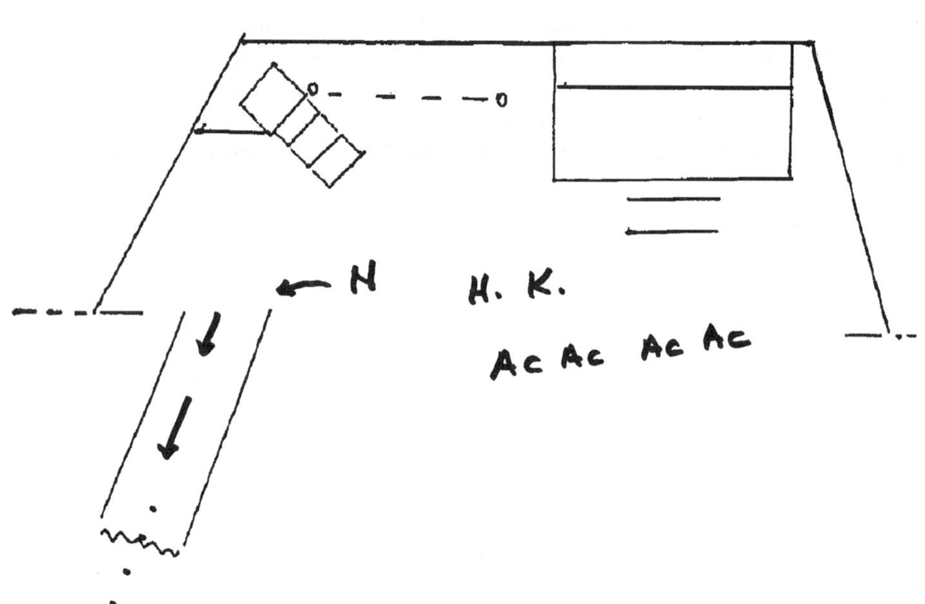
H
H. K.
Ac Ac Ac Ac

(At foot of mountain step, NARUKAMI *executes an elaborate* mie. *Then he strides — rappo style — an out via the* hanamichi.*)*

CURTAIN

(Hikimaku.)

Baiko continues: "They learned how to wed thought, action and speech; to make the action suit the word. Because of the tightness of form, they learned, I believe, how to be specific without fear or a feeling of rigidity. They became more deeply aware of the need for discipline and craftsmanship. Compassion and understanding are keynotes to good acting, and they only come with a greater "*look-see*" into lives other than our own. They told me that they learned concentration, endurance and control. I think they realize more strongly than ever, the technique of clarity of gesture and movement to illuminate meaning. With my assistant and interpreter, a bi-cultural American, I strove to give them help in the areas of vocal and physical discipline through emphasizing the values of economy, pin-pointing emotions, and magnification of reality."

KABUKI STAGE TERMS

Hanamichi	Runway
Shi-chi-san	Strongest spot on the runway
Agemaku	Curtain at end of runway
Kamite	Stage left
Shimote	Stage right
Ni-ju	Platform
Jeshiki maku	Act curtain
Tsuke	Wood block emphasis for MIE and sometimes entrances and exits
Tsuke Niwai	Area before entering hanamichi

KABUKI MOVEMENTS

Suwatte	Sit down
(Suwaru, the infinitive)	
Tatte	Stand
(Tatsu, the infinitive)	
Koshi Oru	Women's balance
Koshi o Waru	Men's balance in certain positions
Hidari	Left
Migi	Right
Ojiki	Bow
Mawatte	Go around
(Mawaru, the infinitive)	

SUPPLEMENTARY LIST OF STAGE TERMS

Mawari Butai	Turns table
Haikei	Scenery
Ichimonji	First border
Seri	Elevator on hanamichi
Geza	Sound
Kuro Misu	Musicians and sound
Kari	Hanamichi, second runway

PRINCESS TAEMA'S PROPS

Kane	Bell and hammer
Sensu	Fan
Kaiken	Dagger

PROP LIST

Preset

1. Check prayer books for rents
2. Sew brown break-away beads
3. Check dragon
4. Dust each prop, both set and personal
5. Helmet
6. Press Hakuun's and Kokuun's costumes
6. Tabis, make names are in them
5. Greet the world with a smile

Set Props

1. Sacred rope (rigged every night) and large paper chain
2. Prayer books (6)
3. Yellow rope on set rock
4. Rice bowls on altar
5. Little white confetti on alter (Paper and bathing cap)
6. Leaves for altar decoration
7. Brass bell on altar
8. Cross on tallest black box
9. Two white urns and frames on altar
10. Two candle holders on altar
11. Rock at foot of set rock, stage right
12. Dummy, up center in water (not real)
13. Brown mat on altar
14. Drum, off stage
15. Scroll (check for rents)

PERSONAL PROPS

1. Black enamel bell with stick	Miyoko
2. Japanese fan	Miyoko
3. Dagger	Miyoko
4. One big aibiki, stage right preset	Miyoko
5. Two musical sticks and one block	Idin
6. One tokko	Preset on rock (personal)
7. Large sake jug with cork	
8. Sake bowl	
9. Two pair glass beads, aqua tassels	Jack and Eric (personal)
10. Brown beads	Steve
11. Little aibiki	Steve (Ron)
12. Octopus	Jack
13. Small sake jug with cork	Eric
14. Red cloth	Eric
15. Makeup tray	Jim Johnson
Break-away beads	
Mirror	
Makeup	
Prayer Beads	Narukami
Kyosoku Armrest	Narukami
Shimenawa Sacred Rope	Temple Prop

BIBLIOGRAPHY

Gichner, Laurence *EROTIC ASPECTS OF JAPANESE CULTURE.* Washington, D.C.: Geichner, 1953.

Jones, Jr. Stanleigh H. *SUGAWARA AND THE SECRETS OF CALLIGRAPHY.* New York: Columbia University Press, 1985.

Keene, Donald *NO: THE CLASSICAL THEATRE OF JAPAN.* Palo Alto, Calif.: Kodansha International, 1966.

Keene, Donald *TWENTY PLAYS OF THE NO THEATRE,* New York: Columbia University Press, 1970.

Mitchell, John D. *THEATRE: THE SEARCH FOR STYLE.* Midland, Michigan: Northwood Institute Press, 1982 (p.232 — Noh; p. 104 — Kabuki).

Mitchell, John D. *ACTORS TALK: ABOUT STYLES OF ACTING.* Midland, Michigan: Northwood Institute Press, 1988.

Mitchell, John D.; Schwartz E. K. *A PSYCHOANALYTIC APPROACH TO KABUKI,* a study in personality and culture from Mitchell, John D.'s *THE DIRECTOR-ACTOR RELATIONSHIP.* New York: IASTA Press, 1992.

O'Neill's, P. O. *EARLY NO DRAMA.* London: Lund Humphries.

Royce, Jack *MURDER AT THE KABUKI,* Key West: Eaton Street Press, 1994.

Scott A. C. *THE KABUKI THEATRE OF JAPAN.* London: George Allen & Unwin, Inc., 1955.

Sakurai Chuichi, *KADENSHO.* Kyoto: Sumiya Shinobe, 1968.

Tames, Richard *ENCOUNTERS WITH JAPAN,* New York: St. Martins Press, 1991.

Ueda's,Makoto *THE OLD PINE TREE AND OTHER NOH PLAYS.* Lincoln, Neb.: University of Nebraska Press, 1962.

*JAPANESE NOH DRAMA,*Tokyo: Nippon Gakujutsu Shinkokai, 1955 and 1960; the first volume is available in reprint as *THE NOH DRAMA,* Rutland, Vt.: Tuttle, 1967.